EQUATOR

MIGUEL SOUSA TAVARES was born in Oporto. He gave up a career in law to pursue journalism, after which he moved to more literary writing. He is the author of several books of non-ficion *Equator* is his first novel, the product of a long period of maturation and historical research inspired by a complex chatper in Portuguese history.

A NOTE ON THE TRANSLATOR

PETER BUSH works in Barcelona as a freelance literary translator. He was awarded the Valle-Inclán Literary Translation Prize for his translation of Juan Goytisolo's *The Marx Family Saga*. Recent translations include *Queen Cocaine* by Nuria Amat, *The Havana Quartet* by Leonardo Padura and *The Enormity of the Tragedy* by Quim Monzó. Current projects include new translations of the renaissance novel, *La Celestina*, Goytisolo's *Juan the Landless* and Valle-Inclán's *Tirano Banderas*. He was Professor of Literary Translation at Middlesex University and at the University of East Anglia where he directed the British Centre for Literary Translation.

EQUATOR

Miguel Sousa Tavares

Translated from the Portuguese
by Peter Bush

BLOOMSBURY

First published in Great Britain 2008
This paperback edition published 2009

Copyright © 2003 by Miguel Sousa Tavares
by arrangement with Dr. Ray-Güde Mertin, Literarische
Agentur Bad Homburg, Germany
Translation copyright © 2008 by Peter Bush

The moral right of the author has been asserted

Bloomsbury Publishing Plc
36 Soho Square
London W1D 3QY

www.bloomsbury.com

Translation funded by the Direcção-Geral do Livro e das Bibliotecas/Portugal

A CIP catalogue record for this book is available from the British Library

ISBN 978 0 7475 9662 2

10 9 8 7 6 5 4 3 2 1

Typeset by Hewer Text Ltd, Edinburgh
Printed in Great Britain by Clays Ltd St Ives plc

For Cristina

Equator: the line dividing the earth into northern and southern hemispheres. A line symbolically marking the frontier between two worlds. Possibly a contraction of the expression in old Portuguese, '*é-cum-a-dor*', that is, 'it brings pain'.

1

Looking back on your life, you inevitably wonder how it might have turned out if you'd done things differently. Had Luís Bernardo Valença known what destiny held in store for him, he might not have caught the train to Vila Viçosa that rainy December morning in 1905 from Barreiro Station in Lisbon.

But Luís Bernardo now sat back in his first-class red velvet seat and nonchalantly watched the scenery rush by the window, observing how quickly the plains of holm oaks and sweet chestnuts, so redolent of the Alentejo, came to predominate and how the rainy sky he'd left behind in Lisbon was timidly clearing to allow the rays of a comforting winter sun to break through. He tried to devote the precious hours on the journey to reading *O Mundo*, his favourite daily newspaper, one that was vaguely monarchist, vigorously liberal and, as its name suggests, concerned with the state of the world and 'the elites that govern us'. That issue of *O Mundo* described the crisis facing the French government because of the escalating building costs of the Suez Canal that Engineer Lesseps was frantically excavating, creating a debt that would apparently last into the indefinite future. There was also news of the English Royal Family celebrating yet another birthday for King Edward VII, who was regaled with messages of congratulations from every king, raja, sheik, ruler and tribal chieftain from that vast empire on which, as *O Mundo* reminded its readers, the sun never set. As far as Portugal was concerned, there were yet more reports of a punitive expedition against the natives in the western hinterland of Angola, another episode in the mess in which the colony apparently liked to wallow. Also reported was a fresh skirmish in Parliament between the deputies of Hintze Ribeiro's Regenerationist Party and José Luciano de Castro's Progressives, as a result of the Palace 'civil list' – the part of the public purse set aside for the running of the Royal

Household, and which seemingly could never keep up with expenditure. Luís Bernardo put his newspaper on the empty seat next to him and decided to consider what had led him to board that train.

He was thirty-seven, single and as rakish as his circumstances and origins allowed. His romantic conquests included a few chorus girls of extremely ill repute, the odd sales assistant from Lisbon's Baixa, two or three virtuously married society women and a highly desirable German soprano engaged for a three-month season at the São Carlos, whose favours he was certainly not the only one to fancy. He was, however, a man who was also prone to bouts of melancholy. He graduated in law from Coimbra by the age of twenty-two but, to his now deceased father's great dismay, Luís Bernardo's projected career at the Bar amounted to a short interlude in a famous Coimbra law practice, which he soon fled, turning his back for ever on this vocation. He returned to his beloved Lisbon and pursued various occupations, until he inherited his father's position as senior partner in the Island Shipping Company: three vessels, some twelve thousand tons apiece, that transported freight and passengers between Madeira and the Canary Islands, the Azores Archipelago and Cabo Verde Islands. The company offices were lodged in a building at the end of the Rua do Alecrim and its thirty-five employees were scattered over the four floors of a vintage Marquis of Pombal building. Luís Bernardo was located in a large room with two windows overlooking the Tagus, which he watched like a lighthouse keeper, day after day, month after month, year after year. To begin with, he enjoyed the illusion that he controlled an Atlantic fleet, if not the fate of the world. As he received telegrams or radio bulletins from the three vessels, he updated their positions with the small flags he pinned on a huge map of the west coast of Europe and Africa that hung on the far wall of his office. The novelty of this daily plotting of the *Catalina*, *Catarina* and *Catavento* soon wore thin and, though he stopped pinning flags on the map, he did continue to appear diligently on the Rocha Conde de Óbidos jetty to see the company's ships arrive and depart. Out of a spirit of exploration or sense of duty he embarked only once in one of his vessels: he went to Mindelo and São Vicente, on a stormy,

2

uncomfortable voyage, only to reach a land he found desolate and entirely bereft of anything to interest a European of his time. They said it wasn't really Africa, but a slice of moon that had fallen into the sea. Nonetheless he wasn't moved to sail any further in search of the Africa about which he'd heard such exciting tales.

Thereafter he remained rooted in his office on the Rua do Alecrim and in his house in Santos, where he lived alone with an old housekeeper he had inherited with his parents' house and who proclaimed to all and sundry that 'the young gentleman should find himself a wife', plus a kitchen maid from Beira Baixa. He invariably lunched at his favourite club in Chiado, dined at the Braganza or the Gremio or quietly at home. He played cards with friends, met up with family at the São Carlos, or partied at the Turf or Jockey Club and was considered to be witty, intelligent company. He closely followed the state of the world in French and English magazines, being equally fluent in both languages, which was quite unusual in Lisbon at the time. The Colonial Question fascinated him. He read everything related to the Conference of Berlin and took part when overseas issues became the focus of passionate public debate, after the English Ultimatum when Portugal ceded territory linking Mozambique and Angola. Luís Bernardo published two articles in O Mundo that were widely quoted and discussed: his analysis was balanced and cool-headed. Bucking the patriotic, anti-monarchist frenzy that was fashionable and in stark contrast to King Dom Carlos's apparent aloofness, he defended a mercantile model of modern colonialism. His thesis centred on the effective exploration of things that Portugal might possibly achieve, through companies that were ready to engage with Africa, companies that were professionally managed and guided by a 'civilising spirit', and no longer 'determined by the designs of those who, being nonentities here, behave like potentates there'.

His articles were hotly debated both by 'Europeanists' and 'Africanists', and the reputation he gained as a result encouraged him to publish a short report, which brought together statistics related to imports over the last ten years from the African colonies. The purpose of this was to support his conclusion that this was trade in its early days for Europe, insufficient for the needs of Portugal and a considerable waste of the potential that could be

3

realised by the rational, intelligent exploitation of wealth overseas. 'It is not enough to tell the world that we have an empire,' he concluded, 'we must also explain why we deserve to possess and hold on to such a thing.' The ensuing debate was intense and violent. From the other side of the trenches, 'Africanist' Quintela Ribeiro, the owner of enormous landed estates in Moçamedes, riposted in *O Clarim*, asking, 'What real knowledge of Africa does Mr Valença have?' and inverting the turn of phrase against its creator, he concluded, 'It is not enough to tell the world, as does this Valença, that we own a head. We must also explain why we deserve to possess and hold on to such a thing.'

Quintela Ribeiro's *boutade* and the genuine public discussion generated by Luís Bernardo's statements opened many new doors for him. Lisbon's luminaries commented that it was a waste that a man of his age, intellect and knowledge should spend the best years of his life contemplating the Tagus from on high and wandering the city after amorous conquests.

All this had petered out some months ago. Much to his relief, Luís Bernardo was able to return to his tranquil life. He felt that the discomfort of being at the centre of a public polemic outstripped the eventual fame and admiration he had attracted. This, in any case, had only translated into an increased number of invitations to dinners where he was invariably forced to listen to stupid opinions on the Overseas Question, which always climaxed in the rhetorical question: 'And what is your view on this, Dr Valença?'

Momentarily drawn back to the present on his journey from Lisbon to Vila Viçosa, Luís Bernardo began to consider the strange summons he'd received from the King through the Count of Arnoso, the monarch's Private Secretary, to come to lunch on Thursday at the royal palace in Vila Viçosa. Bernardo de Pindela, the Count of Arnoso, a member of the famous 'Defeated by Life' group, which had so upset the country's intellectual life a few years earlier, unexpectedly honoured him with a visit to his company office to deliver the summons, and merely added, 'Forgive me, dear sir, but, as you will appreciate, I cannot reveal what His Majesty intends to say to you. I know it is an important matter and that His Majesty requested the meeting be kept a secret. However, you will appreciate that a trip to Vila Viçosa will help blow away the Lisbon smog and, moreover, I can guarantee you will eat extremely well.'

So here he was on his way to the Palace of the Dukes of Braganza, in the middle of that empty expanse known as the Alentejo, where every year His Majesty Dom Carlos dedicated the best part of autumn and winter to his favourite sport of hunting which, according to Republican wags in the capital, occasioned a diversion from the few moments he deigned to devote to matters of state. Luís Bernardo was almost the same age as the King, but, unlike the latter, he was slim, elegant and dressed with an apparently casual austerity that was the mark of a real gentleman. Dom Carlos de Braganza looked like a nonentity dolled up as a king; Luís Bernardo seemed a prince *à la mode*. Everything about him, his physique, the way he dressed, the way he walked, revealed his attitude to life: he cultivated his appearance, but didn't sacrifice comfort; he kept up with fashion, with what was happening in the wider world, but didn't abandon his own judgement; he was pained by the idea of going unnoticed, yet found that being a focus of attention cramped his style. His outstanding quality was his total lack of ambition: ironically, this was also his major weakness. Yet, when he analysed himself, with a modicum of impartiality, Luís Bernardo concluded, without being overbearingly vain, that he was several necks ahead of the social circles he moved in: better educated than those immediately below, more intelligent and cultured, and less vacuous than those above. Yet the years were slipping by and his youth with them. In love as in life, the women he found irresistible were always beyond reach; those he found available were always a disappointment. He was once betrothed to a very pretty young woman whose buxom charms had enchanted him. His eyes feasted on her, and his lusting hands and lips were soon roaming over her welcoming flesh. He was thus lured to the point of offering the girl an engagement ring, agreeing a date with his Aunt Guiomar, who stood in for his mother, and with his putative father-in-law, only to cavil finally at the girl's ignorance. She mistook Berlin for Vienna and reckoned France was still a monarchy. The terrifying prospect of endless years of inane conversation at the side of that preening creature and the boring Sunday lunches at his father-in-law's home proved too great a challenge, and he inelegantly and unapologetically beat a quick retreat. The girl's father shouted insults at him at the Gremio but he slipped out unnoticed, annoyed though relieved, thinking that it would all be forgotten in a fortnight and he'd still have a lifetime before him. That was the closest he ever came to being 'a respectably married man'.

He stretched out his cramped legs on the seat opposite, took a silver cigarette case from his coat pocket, extracted a long, slim Azores cigarette and a box of matches from his jacket, lit the cigarette and inhaled slowly and sensually. He was a free man: without partner, political party, debts or debtors, no millionaire but no bankrupt either, driven neither by a sense of futility nor a desire for excess. Whatever the King had to say, propose or order, he would always have the last word. How many men did he know who could boast as much?

Tonight, for example, he would dine as usual with friends at Lisbon's Hotel Central: a heterogeneous gathering of men between thirty and fifty, who met every Thursday to indulge in the fine cuisine prepared by the Central and debate world developments and problems of the realm. A ritual enacted by men cast in the likeness of Luís Bernardo: serious but not solemn, carefree but not frivolous.

This Thursday he had a very special reason to look forward anxiously to dinner and that was why he had decided to catch the five o'clock train, anticipating that the usual train delays might prevent him from reaching the Central in time. João Forjaz, a member of the Thursday dining club and a close friend from school days, was to bring him a message from his cousin Matilde. Luís Bernardo had met Matilde that summer in Ericeira, at a soirée in the house of friends they had in common. His thoughts flew back to that romantic moonlit night, when João had walked across the drawing room towards him with Matilde on his arm and Luís Bernardo had felt a *frisson* of immediate danger.

'Luís, meet my cousin Matilde, the lady I mentioned to you long ago. Matilde, this is Luís Bernardo Valença, the most sceptical mind of his generation.'

6

She smiled at her cousin and looked Luís Bernardo right in the eye. She was almost as tall as he was – and he was very tall – and her smile and manner were quite girlish. The right side of twenty-six, he thought. But she was already married and a mother, that much he did know. He also knew her husband was working in Lisbon and that she was holidaying here with her two sons. He leaned forward and kissed the hand she offered. He saw her hand was long and slender as he gave a slightly more prolonged kiss than good manners advised.

He looked up to find her still staring at him. And she smiled again.

'And what is a so-called sceptical mind? Is it the same as a weary spirit?'

João responded for him, right on cue.

'Luís weary? No, there are things Luís never wearies of, true or not, Luís?'

'I never weary of beholding beautiful women, for example.' That sounded less like a compliment than a declaration that battle was about to commence.

An embarrassing silence followed, which gave João Forjaz an excuse to depart the scene.

'Well, that's enough of introductions. You can explore the little matter of scepticism while I go and get you a drink. But, dear cousin, take care, I don't know whether this wandering sceptic is suitable company in the eyes of society. Anyway I'll be right back. I won't abandon you.'

She watched him walk away and, despite her self-assured manner, Luís Bernardo thought he saw anxiety darken her eyes as she asked, 'Are we courting danger?'

Luís Bernardo felt his declaration about beautiful women had been too forward, and had alarmed her.

He replied soothingly, 'Not at all, I don't see how. Obviously, you don't know me, but I can assure you my intention is not to cause harm.' His words rang true and immediately seemed to put her at her ease.

'I am so pleased you say that. But, as a matter of curiosity, why does my cousin think you might be company that is not to be highly recommended?'

7

' "In the eyes of society",' he said. 'And, as you know, the eyes of society are never innocent, even if what they can see is genuinely innocent. In our particular case, I expect the lack of propriety arises from the fact that you are married and I am a bachelor and that here we are together on a splendid night like this.'

'Oh, I see! Propriety is what he was referring to. Dear old propriety! What the world we inhabit regards as the real substance of things.'

Now it was Luís Bernardo's turn to look at her directly. His gaze disturbed her, and she suddenly appeared vulnerable, which he found both attractive and threatening.

When he spoke, he adopted the tone of absolute sincerity that had disarmed her earlier.

'Listen, Matilde, propriety and all that accompany it surely have a role to play in society and I don't intend changing the world or the rules that apparently guarantee people a quiet, if not happy life. I often wish there were fewer rules that led people to mistake appearance for life itself. But I think in the end we *do* have a choice, and I deem myself to be a free man. But I live among others and accept their rules, whether or not I agree with them. I will just add one thing: you are João's cousin and favourite lady, and he has always been my best friend. Naturally we speak about you and he always does so affectionately and enthusiastically. For that reason alone I was curious to get to know you, and now I have, I find you much more beautiful than he described. I've praised you but don't wish to embarrass you, and will now return you to João. It has been a great pleasure meeting you and it looks as if it must be a delightful evening out there.'

He bowed elegantly, and took a step forward, as if he expected her to turn away as well. But instead he detected an intense, slightly irritated, and unexpectedly firm tone.

'Wait! Why run away? Why must a man who proclaims he is free run away? Are you trying to protect me from myself?'

'Yes, I am, if you want to see it that way. Is there anything wrong in that?' He wanted to be equally firm, but it was Luís Bernardo who now felt insecure. Things were getting a little out of control.

'No, you are being *very* gentlemanly. I am very grateful. But I don't like being protected from non-existent danger. I apologise, but in this case and in this conversation I find your concern almost offensive.'

Good heavens, where is this leading? he wondered. He hesitated, not knowing what to say or do next. How ridiculous, I'm like a child frightened by an adult. Why doesn't João come to my rescue?

'Just tell me one thing, Luís Bernardo.' She broke the silence, resuming their game.

He replied almost fearfully, 'What?'

'Do you mind if I ask you a personal question?'

'Please feel . . .'

'Why have you never married?'

This goes from bad to worse, he thought.

'It's never seemed right. As far as I know, no law exists that obliges one to marry.'

'No, you are right. Nevertheless, it's strange. Now it's my turn to reveal a secret that, in any case, will be no great secret to you. Some of my friends have also mentioned you from time to time and in very mysterious terms. They describe you as handsome, intelligent and cultured, good company and wealthy. They say you're reputed to be a womaniser, so the mystery doesn't lie there. So what is the mystery behind your bachelor status?'

'There is no mystery. I have never fallen madly in love and so have never married. As simple as that.'

'It is strange all the same,' she insisted, as if he'd suddenly confounded her.

'What is so strange: that I have never fallen passionately in love or that I have never married?'

Luís Bernardo had regained the initiative and was now mocking.

She noted his change of tone and blushed, annoyed with herself and with him.

'No, what is strange is that you've never fallen in love with a woman . . . you could love passionately, and could marry.'

Her words came out in such a rush, and Luís Bernardo glimpsed such an intense look in her eyes he immediately

9

regretted what he'd said. But he had said it, and a silence descended upon them, as if they had tacitly agreed a truce.

When João finally appeared to break their mutual silence, Luís Bernardo took the opportunity to seek a breath of fresh air, bidding a polite farewell before slipping out into the night as the moonlight broke through the mist. The Ericeira sea seemed calm and at peace. Music wafted from a public dance far away and the chattering voices and laughter of a family who seemed happy enough drifted down from a window open on to the avenue. Luís Bernardo suddenly felt the need for instant bliss. He wanted to search out the party music, pick up a local girl and dance in her arms, press her hot, taut body against his, smell the cheap perfume in her hair and, driven by a sudden rush to the brain, whisper to her, 'Will you marry me?' He smiled at the very idea, thinking things would undoubtedly seem different in the morning, lit a cigarette in the dark and listened to his solitary footsteps making their way to his hotel.

He spent the next two weeks in Ericeira: mornings on the beach, lunches in fishermen's haunts on the seashore, where one ate the best fish in the world, cooked with utter simplicity. He passed his afternoons in the hotel drawing room or in the town's main square, reading the newspapers, dealing with his mail or talking to João Forjaz and a few friends. At night, if he had no invitations to dine out, he supped in his hotel, at eight-thirty sharp, with João for company or anyone else who had an empty diary. The hotel dining room had everything characterising the extremely tranquil social life of a summer hotel. Young married couples, whose children were entrusted to a governess with whom they dined elsewhere, whole families – grandparents, sons and daughters, sons and daughters-in-law and adolescent grand-children – occupying the two central tables, and solitary gentlemen, some in transit, some still on holiday like himself, and Queen Dona Amélia, who was also spending her summer there.

Luís Bernardo was fascinated by the imagination of the head chef who, day in, day out, never repeated a dish, but created menus with three soups, three entrées, three fish dishes, three meat dishes and three desserts. After dinner, he and the other gentlemen would transfer to the bar, and he would smoke his cigar while his fingers gently cradled a glass of French cognac. He sat and observed the others or played a game of dice or dominoes; the latter, however, was a game he heartily detested. At a given moment the bachelors disappeared into the night and only family men remained. The first group had a single destination: the casino, where they continued the same routine – cigars, cognac, gambling, conversation, only interrupted by the traditional summer balls, at the beginning and end of August. There was also a semi-clandestine, semi-official alternative, which nobody mentioned in public and about which everyone whispered in private: a visit to the establishments run by Dona Julia or Dona Imaculada. Gentlemen reckoned that Dona Julia's girls were more resourceful and Dona Imaculada's more reliable. Things usually started around midnight and carried on into the early hours. Married men, bachelors, respectable pillars of society, even fathers taking their barely shaving sons to be initiated nobly into the male condition. The nocturnal adventures of the gentlemen in Ericeira's summer society inevitably sparked off hushed conversations among the ladies the following morning in their beach huts.

'They say that last night there were two counts and a marquis at Dona Imaculada's! What is the world coming to, Blessed Lord?' Mimi Vilanova asked mellifluously from the exalted perch of her impeccable widow's weeds. She was a woman unanimously held to be the voice of virtue on Ericeira's beaches.

'They'll never catch my husband there. He spends his nights with me,' you might hear a married lady hurriedly explain.

And the ladies would go silent, scornfully shaking their heads.

But it never got to be more than gossip, because the 'girls' never opened their mouths, fully aware that secrecy was the soul of their trade, and the gentlemen, even those who never paid a call, always upheld the golden rule of male solidarity in the arena of extramarital affairs.

Luís Bernardo did make two forays in that direction accompanied by João and others. He went once to Dona Julia's and once to Dona Imaculada's, but unlike some he was always relaxed, for he had to give explanations to no one, not even to his own conscience. And, if he could satisfy the desires of his body without harming his spirit, he went to it as naturally as he would go to dine with friends.

But tedium had beset those summer days and was much more annoying than the cloudy mornings when children and bathers gathered on the sand far from the sea. The days were too long for continuous leisure. It was like a vice that gave no pleasure, a calm that seemed stupid and meaningless: he was enervated, in a permanent state of apathy. He promenaded by day, meandered by night, often wondering what he was doing there, feeling the days slip by, secretly, absurdly waiting for something to happen, though he had no real hope that it would.

In that fortnight, he saw Matilde only twice, or rather merely glimpsed her. The first time was at an after-dinner concert in a park. She was part of a group and he was with João and other friends. She kissed João effusively and only afterwards seemed to notice him.

'Oh, so you are still here? Still on holiday?'

He responded inanely, 'So it would seem,' and only wished she'd ask him for how long.

But Matilde went her way, disappearing with half a farewell smile into a crowd of ladies, children and gentlemen.

The second time he saw her was at a dance in the casino. He was on his way back from the bar after enduring the same conversations with the same people. He was idling in the shadow of the entrance to the ballroom, scanning the array of faces, when she suddenly appeared from nowhere. The sight took his breath away. She was wearing a yellow-and-white gown, the train of which she lifted over the floor, and her long black hair, lightened by the sun, was gathered under a diamond tiara. She seemed taller and more graceful than ever, dancing the slowest of waltzes in her husband's arms. She looked in Luís Bernardo's direction but still hadn't seen him. He watched her smile whenever her husband whispered in her ear. The moment she did finally meet his transfixed gaze, she seemed not to recognise him. Then she imperceptibly acknowledged him, without so much as a nod of the head. Her partner swerved suddenly and she disappeared from Luís Bernardo's field of vision into the middle of a room packed with happy swirling couples.

Luís Bernardo turned his back on the dance and the casino and went out to smoke a cigarette. He tried to analyse the turmoil he felt. He raged – a stupid rage without reason. It was envy, irrational envy quite beyond his control. From within, a voice was telling him: You'll never be happy like that. You'll never have a wife like that to call your own. We are all responsible for our own fate and you've sealed yours. You don't live on your own happiness, but on the happiness you manage to steal from others. He suddenly felt desolate. The dance had lost its charm. The holidays had become intolerable. He abandoned the ball-room just as it was bursting into life and rushed back to his hotel. He asked to be woken early, consulted the train timetable and retired to his room, removing only his coat before falling asleep exhausted on the bedcover, his window open to the sea.

Luís Bernardo woke early the next morning, before the other guests were up, to catch the ten-thirty in Mafra. He was making his way absent-mindedly down the stairs when without warning Matilde appeared on the stairs below him. She was wearing a pale-white, low-cut dress and seemed as agitated to see him as he was to see her.

They stood staring at each other.

Luís Bernardo broke the silence.

'Matilde! You up so early! I imagined you'd be asleep after last night's carousing!'

'And what happened to you last night, Luís? You disappeared . . .'

'You know, I really don't really like balls. I felt at a loss and left early.'

'At a loss? Why? What do you expect to do at a ball, if not dance?'

'I couldn't see anyone to dance with . . .'

'What a demanding fellow you are! Nobody at all?'

'I saw you and you seemed happy enough.'

'Yes, I was dancing with my husband . . .'

Luís Bernardo tried in vain to read some nuance in her tone that might be a signal, but he could detect nothing. It was as if she'd answered as naturally as possible. He sighed and brought himself back to reality. He could see a beautiful woman, apparently relaxed and happily married, from a world he did not inhabit, and where he did not belong.

'Fine, Matilde, all you have to do now is tell me why you're up so early.'

'I've come to say goodbye to an aunt of mine who's leaving for Lisbon on the ten-thirty train.'

'Well, I'll be travelling with her; I'm going to catch the same train.'

'You're going to Lisbon?'

'Yes, my holidays are over . . .' He hesitated and then added, 'Like last night's ball.'

Matilde said nothing. She looked him in the eye in a way he felt to be rather pitying.

He felt bereft and ridiculous. It was 8 a.m. on a shadowy hotel staircase and here he was gazing silently at a woman who'd captivated him on a terrace one moonlit night.

He held out a hand.

'Very well, it's time to say goodbye, I suppose.'

She took the hand he offered her. It was a simple handshake lasting as long as politeness advised. She didn't seem to rush or linger.

'Goodbye, Luís Bernardo. We'll meet again some day.'

'Enjoy the rest of your holidays.'

'Thank you.' She started to climb the stairs towards him.

Luís Bernardo instinctively moved aside to let her pass. They crossed without looking at each other; he felt a shiver run through his body as she passed him. He listened to her receding steps. Each step took her further away and he felt a lump in his throat. He'd now almost reached the point on the stairs from where he would no longer be able to see her or hear her footsteps.

He stopped, turned quickly round and, before he could stop himself, cried out softly, 'Matilde!'

'Yes?' She stopped. They had changed positions: she now looked down at him.

'Will I ever see you again?'

'See me? I don't know. Who can tell? The living are always likely to meet up again.'

'No, just living isn't enough. More important is the way you live. You don't find what presents itself, but what you actively seek out. Our destinies are like random leaves blowing in the

14

wind. We are human beings, and possess wills to determine the direction of our lives.'

'Tell me, Luís Bernardo, is it your will to see me again?'

'Yes, Matilde. My will is to see you again.'

'And why, if I may be so bold?'

'I really don't know. Perhaps to resume a conversation left unfinished one moonlit night.'

'One has so many unfinished conversations! Is the sensible thing to resume them or leave them for ever at the point they stopped?'

'Matilde, you ask many questions but are short on answers.'

'As if I have any, Luís!' She sighed deeply, a sound that seemed to come from so far away that he feared it would awake the slumbering hotel, and guests would poke their heads out from behind bedroom doors to find out why this woman had sighed so loudly.

Luís Bernardo was gifted with the ability to extricate himself from complicated situations, when things reached an impasse from which logic provided no exit. But quite unawares, as if his body functioned independently of his head, he found himself slowly climbing the stairs towards her, his eyes trained on hers. Matilde didn't waver: she watched him coming towards her, felt him reach her, place his hands on her shoulders, and lean forward to bring his lips down on hers. She closed her eyes and stood still, one hand gripping the banister, the other dangling by her side. She was expecting him to move quickly away from her mouth and body but he gently prolonged his kiss. Their dry mouths were now moist; she felt his tongue enter, slip around her mouth, meet hers and linger for what seemed an eternity. Finally, he did withdraw, kissing her very gently on the lips, and she heard him whisper, 'Goodbye, Matilde,' heard his descending footsteps until they echoed on the flagstones of the ground floor and disappeared.

Only then did she open her eyes and sit down slowly on the top step, staring into the void, a single thought in her head. She stayed like that for so long she couldn't have said whether she was there fifteen minutes or a whole hour.

★   ★   ★

Évora. Midday. The train stopped in the station, deep in the heart of the Alentejo. Almost twenty passengers alighted and ten or so got on. Hawkers of cold drinks and food – sheep's cheese, sausages, honey, fruit and medicinal herbs – paraded their wares up and down outside the carriages. A gypsy woman, with three ragamuffin children, stretched out a hand towards the windows, and passengers backed off uneasily. In the middle of the throng, an old woman dressed in black from head to toe had set up a stall selling small wooden boxes of dried fruit, while two men, leaning on their shepherd's crooks, looked on in silence, as if the spectacle of the Lisbon train were the most wonderful thing in the whole world.

Our Fatherland in all its splendour! thought Luís Bernardo. He stood by his carriage window, stretching his body, arms and legs, trying to cast off the lethargy that had gripped him after four indolent hours of travel. It was still over an hour to Vila Viçosa, on the branch line that had recently been opened – if gossip were to be believed, for the exclusive use of His Majesty Dom Carlos and family.

Luís Bernardo had read the newspapers he'd brought from Lisbon cover to cover, had dozed off for half an hour, and now couldn't think how to fill his time. He sat down and lit a cigarette, just as the train jerked and gathered speed leaving the white houses of Évora behind. His thoughts returned to Matilde and the three months that had slipped by since their goodbyes on the staircase in Ericeira's Hotel Grande. A whole autumn had already come between them.

Matilde lived in a large house belonging to her husband's family in Vila Franca de Xira, near Lisbon. But she might as well have lived in the provinces. A year could pass without a chance encounter: a meeting doesn't just happen. He wrote her a letter in the autumn that he entrusted to the discretion of her cousin João. João protested vehemently at the role of go-between Luís Bernardo was foisting upon him. He argued that his cousin was a married woman and that he had nothing but respect for her husband. He asked Luís Bernardo what he hoped to achieve from such a childish, dangerous game. Luís Bernardo had to work hard to persuade João to deliver the letter and, worst of all, felt the result wouldn't warrant the risks they were both taking.

It was a dull, deadpan, meaningless letter, and when he asked João how she'd reacted on receiving it, he shrugged his shoulders and replied, 'She didn't. She put it in her pocket, made no comment and didn't even ask what you've been up to.'

He would never forget the day he wrote the letter, November the 1st, the Day of the Dead, a Sunday and day of rest for his servants. He was alone at home, watching the rain pour down, with an acute sense of the futile passage of time. He imagined himself in that same house twenty years hence, the furniture covered in a fine film of dust that nothing would shift, looking at himself in the mirror and seeing his white hair and worry-induced wrinkles, with the wooden floorboards creaking in the passage-way, the silver-framed portrait of his parents summoning him from the depths of time, his desk waiting for Monday morning, and *Catalina, Catarina* and *Catavento* slowing down year after year.

He sat behind his desk with a sheaf of paper and started to write at length to Matilde. He surrendered himself heart and soul, declared everything, risked everything then finally apologised and declared that, if she didn't reply, he would never bother her again.

She replied at the end of that month. João delivered the letter to his office on the Rua do Alecrim.

'Here you are. It's a letter Matilde asked me to bring you. I'm sure this will all end badly and I'll never forgive myself for assuming the role of your carrier-pigeon.'

Luís Bernardo said nothing. He should have said something to reassure João, to defend Matilde and play down the importance that letter had for him, but he said nothing. Almost unable to restrain himself, he waited until João had left and then yielded to the pleasure of opening the letter unhurriedly, attentive to every detail, the thickness of the paper, the way it was folded, the perfume emanating from the paper.

Luís Bernardo,
    I reply to your second letter, not to your first. I reply to the kiss you gave me on the stairs, not to the word-games you tried to play on a poor pathetic woman, far removed from the wiles at which you seem to excel. I do not reply to your gifts as a seducer, but to the surprise that – this is my intuition! – I found

17

in your gaze. In a word, I'm replying not to any distress you may cause me, but to the goodness I think I glimpsed deep within you.

I have nothing to fear from this man, because he will do me no wrong. Isn't that so, Luís Bernardo, you will do me no wrong? I hope we may soon conclude the conversation interrupted that moonlit night in summer.

Yes, I know I ask too many questions, but if your response is yes, I will indicate, through João, how we might meet. Till then, I beg you to do nothing. And, when the time comes, if you intend harm, then do not come. I shall respect you even more and shall always cherish a loving memory of you.

M.

An indication he'd been waiting for had come the day before. He had bumped into João coming out of the Brasileira in Chiado, who'd told him, as if it were the most commonplace thing ever, 'I've a message from Matilde. I'll give it to you at the dinner at the Central tomorrow. You will be going, I suppose?'

So much all at once, he thought. That day promised so much: a king and a princess.

2

D OM CARLOS WAS woken at seven that morning in Vila Viçosa by his valet. He paid a quick visit to the bathroom, dressed in his rooms adjoining the Queen's and, as usual, required help from his servant to pull on and lace his tight-fitting calf-length boots – an operation that called for gymnastics the regal one hundred and ten kilos didn't encourage. Teixeira, the town chemist, appeared as usual to shave His Majesty with a sharp razor blade of Sheffield steel – a ritual he performed with consummate skill, giving the King visible pleasure.

Dressed, groomed and perfumed in eau de cologne, Dom Carlos strode ponderously through the antechamber linking the royal suite, chapel and dining room to the drawing rooms on the first floor. He went straight to the Green Room, so called because of the green damask lining the walls, where his hunting companions were waiting for him and warming themselves by the marble fireplace. The breakfast table was already set and his servants stood in a line waiting for the order to start serving.

Dom Carlos waved his hand and greeted them cheerily.

'A very good day to you, gentlemen! Let us make a start. The partridges await us!'

Apart from the King, twelve men sat at the breakfast table: the Marquis-Baron of Alvito, the Viscount of Asseca (Senior), the Count of Sabugosa, Manuel de Castro Guimarães, the Count of Jiménez and Molina, Dom Fernando de Serpa, Hugo O'Neil and Charters de Azevedo, Colonel José Lobo de Vasconcelos, duty officer, and Major Pinto Basto, aide-de-camp. Also in attendance were the Count of Arnoso, the King's Private Secretary, and the Count of Mafra, the Royal Family's physician, though the latter didn't accompany the King on shoots, as they preferred to devote their mornings to other activities. Only Prince Luís Filipe was missing. He never missed a hunt, but he had had to attend a ceremony at the School of War in Lisbon.

They served fresh juice made from Vila Viçosa oranges – generally agreed to be the best in the world – tea, buttered toast, cured sheep's cheese, peach compote, and scrambled eggs with ham. A few gentlemen lit their first cigars of the day to accompany the coffee, but there wasn't time to stay at table to savour the pleasure.

They all rushed downstairs to the ground floor and wrapped up against the icy, hoar-frosted December morning. Transport was ready and waiting for the hunting party in the big square in front of the main façade of the Palace of the Dukes of Braganza. There were three brakes for the hunters, two carriages for the secretaries, beaters and guns and ammunition. At the rear came the cart for the hunting dogs, who sniffed and pricked up their ears excitedly. Dom Carlos told Tomé, his personal bearer on every hunt, to bring the case with his Holland & Hollands, a present from Leopold, King of Belgium, and a pair of Purdeys, specially made to measure for his arm in London the previous year: depending on how things turned out, the King would decide to shoot with a Holland or a Purdey. Sometimes he even spent an entire morning shooting with one gun, but that was based more on his superstitions and manias as a hunter than on any kind of scientific knowledge.

That morning the King of Portugal's modest shooting party would embark on a partridge beat, in gently undulating terrain of holm and cork oaks some five kilometres from town, crossed by two streams half hidden by rock roses. They would engage in four 'strikes', or four beats, from two different places, following a system known as 'heads and tails': the partridges would first fly to a spot where the guns were waiting and then be driven back to the same place, from the opposite direction – in between the two beats: the shoot would thus only have to make a 180-degree turn. Afflicted by excess weight, the King had of late preferred beats to hunting 'on the hoof', when you had to walk for kilometres, up and down valleys, sinking in the mud, slipping on rocks, and trying to keep up with your dogs as they chased the fleeing prey.

The small army of poor, ill-shod beaters recruited in town for a handful of coins and a bird a-piece was waiting for the hunters in the first of the places agreed. As soon as the palace party proceeded to cast lots for the 'hides' for the beat – where they would go on each of the 'strikes' – and unload the guns and bags of cartridges, the dogs leapt down from their cart, the bearers gathered up the paraphernalia, and the beaters left to begin, two or three kilometres from the 'hides'.

The mist rising from the frosty fields only now began to disperse and it was still bitterly cold. Accompanied by Tomé, his bearer, and his two dogs – Djebe, a red-and-white mottled pointer and Divor, a grey Breton spaniel – Dom Carlos headed towards the 'hide' he'd drawn, a rudimentary shelter, made from criss-crossed branches of holm oak, which apparently concealed the gun from the partridges until they came within reasonable shooting range.

On each beat they rarely waited less than half an hour for partridges: sometimes one or two solitary partridges appeared, when the beaters' voices were barely audible, but most only surfaced at the end of the beat, when they had no choice but to fly in the direction of the camouflaged hunters. Meanwhile, Dom Carlos liked to sit on his portable canvas chair, with his dogs at his feet, and quietly enjoy the first cigarette of the day. His guns, already prepared by Tomé, were at the ready for the first whirr of the wings of a partridge in flight. He reflected on matters preoccupying him, like the telegram received the evening before from the Governor of Mozambique. He wanted, and believed he was right, full powers to govern the province, without having to bend to the moods and interference of the Minister for the Colonies and politicians in Lisbon. It was the same problem Mouzinho de Albuquerque had experienced years earlier, when, as the King's Commissioner, he finally resigned after he saw how he'd been betrayed by a decree which, though sealed by the King's signature, had been introduced against the King's will. It had deprived him of the power to decide urgent business at local level. He could not tolerate having first to satisfy the vanity of the politicians in the Royal Household. Dom Carlos admired Mouzinho's courage and military qualities, his patriotism and loyalty to his King. He sensed, from a distance, that Mouzinho was right in that dispute, but also knew hard-headedly that it would have been difficult to support him against the government without provoking a fresh political crisis that the times did not favour at all. 'Out of step with the government from love of his King; out of step with the King from love of his country.' And now, a dozen years on, history was repeating itself. Powerless, he continued to witness the vagaries of an overseas policy that was a pretext for a permanent public polemic instead of being a national issue, requiring general consensus. Dom Carlos sighed and uneasily swept such thoughts from his mind.

It was the first time the monarchy and Royal Household had been subject to such poisonous attacks. A day never went by without the Republican press raging against the King, the Queen, the princes and the institution of the monarchy. Dom Carlos opened the newspapers and saw himself under attack on all sides, caricatured, ridiculed, purely and simply insulted. Everything served as an excuse: if he got involved in politics, it was because he lusted after absolute power and then obstructed the governance of the land; if he remained deliberately aloof, it was because he was indifferent to the country and only interested in his Alentejo hunting parties and high-society life. The Republican Party expanded in tandem with popular discontent, the authority of the state was daily undermined, at the mercy of the first petty demagogue to appear, and the few friends he could trust had no political influence whatsoever or, if they did, soon lost it as a result of being friends of his. He was King of a realm where he felt alone and betrayed on all sides, and master of an empire that the great nations of Europe – the royal houses to whose families he belonged by blood – unashamedly coveted. England would take the first opportunity to grab the Empire and, with it, his throne. Mouzinho was right to denounce the manoeuvres of the English in Rhodesia and Zambia. But the idiots here never understood that the weaker their monarch, the more threatened their empire.

And it was no different when it came to São Tomé and Príncipe, where the production of coffee and cocoa so undercut English exports from Gabon and Nigeria. And, on the question of São Tomé, he remembered he had a lunch arranged that day with Valença, a man who came highly recommended. Initially, Dom Carlos had turned his nose up at the mere mention of the chap's name: he'd read the articles that he had written and didn't think he was serious or well acquainted with his subject. But the Royal Council had put his name forward insistently, emphasising the advantages of a new man, unsullied by politics and parties, who must surely be intelligent and eager for a higher profile.

The King was finally persuaded.

'All right. Summon him to Vila Viçosa and I will look him in the face and see if I can trust him. Bernardo, invite him to lunch here on a quiet day. And find out whether he hunts: that would be a good omen.'

But a cursory investigation by the Count of Arnoso revealed no evidence that Luís Bernardo Valença liked hunting: he was just invited to lunch. It is bound to be a boring affair, thought Dom Carlos. I don't know whether I will ever get to the real point of the meeting, or if I will have to keep prevaricating.

Two shots came from one of the hides on the left: the partridges had started to fly up; they always came from the far ends first because that was where the beaters got to first in their horseshoe movement. But most flew out in the centre. The voices of the beaters could be heard in the distance, sweeping the scrub to frighten the partridges that had gone to ground. The cry of a partridge went up on a hillock opposite, a bird that felt under attack, and Dom Carlos instinctively leapt to his feet and grabbed one of the Hollands primed by Tomé. He aimed his gun in that direction, from the hip: his right hand felt the cold of polished steel, while his left gently gripped the wooden butt. Suddenly, all thoughts vanished from his head and nothing was more important than that moment. He and his weapon were as one, attuned to every sign and sound from the scrub, adrenalin rising, heart beating faster, the whole morning dependent on the instant he guessed was ever more imminent. He stayed like that for minutes though nothing happened: the King, his bearer, dogs and gun, the silent hunter awaiting his prey.

The King looked right, from where the partridge's cry had just gone up, but the first bird came from the left, lured across, and now silently launching into flight twenty metres above the ground. Dom Carlos first saw it out of the corner of his eye – imagined rather than saw it, lifted his gun and took aim from his left shoulder. He swung the gun for a few brief seconds until the left barrel, following the partridge's line of flight, aimed almost a metre in front and then shot. Hit in full flight, the bird continued its journey, wings spread, gliding over a world that had suddenly closed down and then it plummeted to the ground, as if it had hit a wall. Dom Carlos didn't need to check if he'd killed or only wounded the bird: the way it had plunged head downwards was a sure sign the shot had been lethal. Tomé whistled his applause softly as he handed the King another rifle. That evening, as on so many others, he'd make sure he told of King Dom Carlos's prowess in the tavern on Vila Viçosa's main square.

Everything gathered pace as the beaters closed in on the spot where the hunters waited in their shelters. The partridges began to fly out – alone, in pairs, in groups of four and five. They flew forwards in every direction, some high up; others skimmed the ground and were the more difficult targets, because they got mixed up with the undergrowth and only came into sight at the last moment. A salvo of shots rang out: sometimes one partridge was hit by two or three guns; some miraculously escaped all fire, but most bid farewell to the heavens in a barrage of lead. The smell of gunpowder rose in the air and the rifles burned the hunters' hands. Standing his ground, looking ahead, even when handing a gun to Tomé to reload behind him and receiving a loaded one in return, Dom Carlos shot in a precise, deft manner worthy of a monarch. He finished the first drive with a dozen partridges and a hare, 'recovered' excitedly by Djebe and Divor.

By midday the shoot was over and a partridge-laden sheet was spread on the ground, where the bearers put the birds so that the hunters could contemplate them with their usual sense of pride. Dom Carlos had shot thirty-five partridges and two hares, using two cartridge belts of twenty-five shots. The King was euphoric, ruddy-cheeked from his high spirits as they walked back to their carriages. Nothing gave him more pleasure than a morning spent hunting with friends. He liked every detail, even when the day was winding down: the comments from his shooting party; the feats – each eagerly embroidered; the compliments he received from all sides; the conversations between beaters and bearers; the dogs leaping up excitedly; the collecting of partridges in burlap sacks; the gutting of hares on the spot to avoid unpleasant smells later in the kitchen; guns being slotted into their cases; the hunters handing over their cartridge belts and heavy coats and sitting in the shadow of a tree on the ground around a red check tablecloth, where a servant had laid out in advance bread, seasoned olives, fully cured sheep's cheese, sausage, ham, white wine and coffee.

A carriage drawn by a single horse was waiting for Luís Bernardo at the station in Vila Viçosa. A Palace employee, whose duty it was to welcome the King's visitors, introduced himself. He took his seat in the carriage next to Luís Bernardo, and ordered the coachman to drive off. It was Luís Bernardo's first visit to Vila Viçosa and he was stunned by the beauty of the town. The houses had whitewashed walls, were all one or two storeys high, and had façades with windowframes and doors of marble from the quarries on the outskirts of town, and wrought-iron balconies. There were fountains hewn from marble, and long pavements lined with orange trees heavy with fruit at that time of year. The sheer size of the main square in front of the Palace and surrounding gardens was striking. There was a sense of space and generosity, an obvious harmony between the architectural style and the peaceful manner in which the inhabitants seemed to let time flow by, conversing in huddles in shop entrances or walking sedately along pavements. Clearly, Vila Viçosa had been built for the outdoor and indoor life, to be enjoyed in the sun or by the fireside.

Luís Bernardo leaned back in the open carriage and watched the town pass slowly by, scrutinising each feature, astonished by the handsome lines of the buildings, gazing curiously at the people strolling along the pavements as he tried to imagine what their daily life was like. Enjoying an unexpected sense of well-being, undeterred by the cold December morning, he began to think he now understood why Dom Carlos seemed to prefer this place to his official Lisbon residence, to the rooms in the Palace of Necessities. They trotted down the drive to the Palace of the Dukes of Braganza and Luís Bernardo was astonished by his first sight of the royal terrace, the far side of which was occupied by a palace on four floors, perfect in its rectangular, geometrical lines. The front façade was all dark-pink marble, while an elegant whitewashed building at right angles to it, surrounded by cypress trees, housed the royal chambers.

Ten minutes after their arrival he was ushered into a small room on the first floor. He was contemplating the paintings on walls draped in yellow brocade, when he heard carriages bustling on the esplanade in front of the Palace, indicating that the shooting party had returned. He peered discreetly out of the window and recognised the King, who was alighting from the first carriage. Soon Luís Bernardo was joined by the Count of Arnoso, who asked politely after his journey and engaged him in trivial conversation while they waited on the King.

Minutes later, heralded by heavy footsteps over the tiled floor and his booming voice, Dom Carlos made his appearance. He was dressed in a subdued grey woollen suit, dark-green chamois waistcoat and matching tie. His slightly ruddy face, fair hair and deep-blue eyes revealed his Northern European blood. He spoke solemnly but his handshake was casual. To Luís Bernardo, the ensemble was impressive, all the more so because the King cut a stout figure and because he now stood before the man who was at the centre of all political conversation in Portugal, a man hated and venerated in equal measure throughout the land.

They did not sit down: after polite introductions and after the King had thanked him for making the effort to come to Vila Viçosa, Dom Carlos said, 'Well, sir, as you know, I have just been hunting and we hunters are ravenous. Besides, with or without the hunt, I have a reputation for fine food and, fortunately, this reputation is one I enjoy, unlike the others,' and Dom Carlos smiled broadly while an embarrassed Luís Bernardo didn't quite know how he should respond.

The whole nation knew King Dom Carlos did not hunt only partridges, hares, deer and wild boar, but also maids, the daughters of tenants, the wives of the town's gentry and girls from behind shop counters. In this, he and the King had tastes in common.

'Well,' his host went on, 'I hope your journey has given you an appetite because you shall soon see how well we eat in these parts. Come and let me introduce you to the rest of the company. If you don't mind, we will eat at our leisure, and then speak in private on the subject for which I had you summoned here.'

Lunch was an all-male affair. There was no evidence that Queen Amélia was also there in residence: he knew she spent her time with her ladies-in-waiting, friends and French cousins, who visited her in Lisbon or Sintra, and was known to complain that her husband the King had 'gone from the phase of separate rooms to that of separate palaces'.

The fourteen men present sat around a huge table that could easily have accommodated fifty. The King in centre position on one side signalled to Luís Bernardo to sit opposite him. Each place had a menu and everybody pretended to study it with interest. Don Carlos was known to attach great importance to these menus and sometimes even wrote them in his own hand, occasionally adding a drawing.

Once the hot tomato soup and white Vidigueira wine had been served, the hunters shook off their lethargy and began to converse animatedly. They discussed the morning's shoot, after they'd given the local gossip a run. It was rumoured that Father Bruno had made yet another parishioner pregnant. An altercation between a gypsy and a shopkeeper in the square had ended in a shooting that morning, though happily no one had been injured.

With the red wine, the conversation took a more serious turn and focused on the international situation. Someone mentioned the worrying news coming out of St Petersburg. Chaos seemed to be the order of the day leading to anarchist attacks. The *Potemkin*, the Imperial Navy's only remaining battleship, had turned its own canon on the power of the Tsar. The terms of the Russian capitulation to Japan were cause for general consternation and indignation. Japan had captured Port Arthur, the Island of Sakhalin, Korea and part of Manchuria. It was the first time an Asian power had defeated a Western power at sea and the scale of the defeat was such that Japan was now the main naval power in the whole Pacific. Russia had disappeared overnight from the theatre of operations, its two squadrons in the Pacific decimated; one had not joined battle, and the other had been pulverised in a single battle. Britain was gradually withdrawing from the Far East in order to confront what many saw as a growing threat from Germany and she remained faithful to the principle that was the cornerstone of Admiralty doctrine: British naval power should always be at least double the size of its closest enemy's. So all that remained to confront Japanese maritime power was the growing, theoretical opposition of the United States, where President Theodore Roosevelt strove in vain to ensure that the balance between Russia and Japan never inclined decisively one way or the other.

The conversation drifted to the situation in North Africa, where everything had apparently been stirred up by Kaiser Wilhelm II's visit to Morocco, his inflammatory speeches challenging the French protectorate and the establishing of the Entente Cordiale between Paris and London. The Kaiser worried everyone: it was obvious he wanted whatever he could get his hands on in Africa. But, even more worrying, was that he also seemed to want whatever grandiose piece of Europe he could snatch. In the tranquil Alentejo town of Vila Viçosa, the tone of the conversation turned serious whenever the Kaiser was mentioned: glasses of wine were slowly and anxiously raised to lips, and heads nodded in circumspect agreement. The Kaiser was an additional threat to a world that otherwise seemed locked in eternal peace.

Luís Bernardo limited himself to one or two uncontroversial statements, enough to show an intelligent interest and suggest he was far from claiming any special authority on the matter. But he felt at ease in that milieu: they were discussing the world's great powers and he was there, sitting opposite a king and joining in the conversation. He thought how the King seemed far removed from the ridiculous caricature of Republican propaganda: he was a man with an informed interest in events from Vila Viçosa to the Far East, and with definite opinions, though he didn't try to impose any intellectual subservience beyond the natural respect his person seemed to command.

A delicious Delaforce port wine from 1848 was served with excellent coffee. Dom Carlos hauled himself to his feet and the whole party followed him downstairs to a small room where two blazing fires, a cognac-laden table and a silver box of cigars awaited: they helped themselves. Another table displayed the latest newspapers that had come on the same train as Luís Bernardo. The small gathering broke up; some flopped on sofas and read the papers, others stood in front of the fire conversing, and others simply leaned back and smoked their cigars. Dom Carlos got up from the sofa where he'd been sitting and asked Luís Bernardo to accompany the Count of Arnoso and himself. They proceeded through several first-floor rooms that opened into each other, until they reached one of the back rooms with a window leading to a balcony overlooking the garden.

It was a small room, which served as the royal study. A long bureau piled high with reams of paper and newspapers occupied half the space. Four leather chairs were set in a semicircle in one corner and portraits in oils of the King and his Queen hung on the walls. There were several watercolours too, one depicting the yacht *Amélia*, all painted by Dom Carlos himself. Luís Bernardo sat opposite Dom Carlos and the Count of Arnoso, who listened silently to their conversation, interrupting only occasionally to clarify a detail in the King's remarks. From where he sat, Luís Bernardo could see the garden through the balcony window and hear the sound of running water from several fountains. Though the windows were closed, he smelled the scent from orange and lemon trees and, for the first time in his life, began to long for a bucolic life enshrined by the peace and order of a Mediterranean-style garden.

'To begin with, dear Valença,' Dom Carlos's booming voice interrupted his reverie, almost making him jump, 'I want to thank you for accepting my invitation. My only regret is that my son Luís Filipe cannot be here. He would like to have met you, and besides, he is particularly interested in the subject that brings us here.'

'I must thank Your Majesty for lunch and for the opportunity you gave me to see this magnificent palace and town.'

'You are most kind. The fact you like Vila Viçosa speaks in favour of your sensibility and good taste. I summoned you, not to entrust you with a mission, since nowadays there are people who think that serving one's king and serving one's country are two different matters, but to issue an invitation and, though you may not see it as such, as far as I am concerned it is to serve both king and country.' Dom Carlos paused and stared at Luís Bernardo.

Something had changed abruptly in both their demeanours. The King was talking to a subject. He cut to the quick.

'Luís Bernardo, I want you to accept the post of Governor of the Overseas Province of São Tomé and Príncipe. This post, or posting, whatever you prefer, begins in two months and will last a minimum of three years. At the end of this term you will only continue as Governor if I, and the government of the day, deem it necessary. You will receive the emolument that goes with the post, which I doubt is very great, but it will probably suffice. You will earn more than a minister in Lisbon, but less than an ambassador in Paris or London. You personally, and I do apologise for being so indelicate, won't be any the richer or poorer. And, before you tell me how alarmed you are by this appointment, I must add that I have not chosen you randomly. Several people, whose opinions I appreciate highly, talked of you as the right person for this task. I myself have had occasion to read your reports and articles on our overseas policy and I think that you argue convincingly for the ideas that we should be advancing. I am also sensitive to the fact that you are unsullied by politics or political parties, someone who speaks English (I shall explain in a moment how important this is), who is well informed on international matters and understands, through his own business activities, the economic basis of our colonies like São Tomé and Príncipe.'

Luís Bernardo didn't take advantage of Dom Carlos's latest pause to speak up. He thought it opportune to be quiet until he had thought through his own response. He felt the proposal absurd, but he had listened very carefully and hadn't missed how subtly the King had expressed his ideas about overseas policy. He had not said that he agreed with Luís Bernardo's ideas on the matter, but that they were the ideas 'that we should be advancing'. It was of a piece with his distinction between serving one's King and serving one's country.

Dom Carlos now changed his tone and stance. He stretched out his leg and began to contemplate the end of his cigar, as if he'd suddenly spotted something of more pressing importance. Before continuing, he gave a deep sigh of resignation, like someone yet again about to rehearse facts that were becoming tiresome.

'Before you reply, my dear fellow, and because I think you are a patriot who appreciates that the needs of the nation may drive a particular policy, let me give you the background to this invitation. As you know, there are those who think it is not economically viable for Portugal to maintain a colonial empire and that the best thing would be for us to sell off our colonies. The Kaiser and my cousin Edward have been whispering in our ears that it would be the best solution in terms of our finances and domestic problems. I, however, am not of the same mind: I am not persuaded that the reduction of the size of its problems increases the greatness of a nation. If I were to sell this palace I inherited from successive generations of the Dukes of Braganza, I would undoubtedly resolve one problem; but I am not sure this would make me feel happier or more fulfilled. There are also those who think that, in a constitutional monarchy, the King should not concern himself with or interfere in such matters: I would thus become the only inhabitant of Portugal indifferent to the state of the nation. I would be the King, not of what I inherited, but of what the Portuguese thought the country should become. This is an immense and profound issue, on which I will not pronounce now, except to say that, if I understood the situation in this light, abdication would be the most dignified solution. I regret that what should be crystal-clear is so blurred, and that the energies of so many Portuguese to whom Portugal owes so much have been sacrificed, as in the case of my dear friend Mouzinho, who died because he believed that by serving his King he was serving his country.'

Like everyone else, Luís Bernardo had been shocked by the unexplained suicide of Mouzinho de Albuquerque three years ago. Like everyone else, he knew Dom Carlos had boundless admiration for Mouzinho, which he'd expressed by appointing him as tutor to Prince Dom Luís Filipe: 'I couldn't put my son in the charge of anyone braver, anyone more loving of his King, anyone more loyal to his country.' But that love and loyalty had stood for nothing when, seven years before, the King had signed the decree the government presented to him that reduced in humiliating fashion the powers of Mouzinho, then the royal representative in Mozambique, and forced his resignation. Afterwards, it was generally agreed that the appointment of this Portuguese military hero to the less distinguished position of

31

the Prince's tutor was the reason for the tragic end to his career at the age of forty-six. Luís thus read the words of Dom Carlos, not as critical of others, but as expressing regret for his own actions, a regret from deep within his conscience.

Dom Carlos again broke the silence.

'And now, let's turn to São Tomé and Príncipe. As you know, my friend, São Tomé is the smallest of our colonies, and is only comparable with Timor. It has just two crops, lots of cocoa and a little coffee. But enough to allow it be self-sufficient and provide the state and farmers with a return that is far from negligible. But São Tomé's big problem is its lack of labour. All the plantation work is done by labour we import mostly from Angola, but also from Cabo Verde, and this works extremely well. The cocoa is of excellent quality; the coffee is very good and production levels are always high. The business functions so well that we represent a threat to the British companies competing against us on the cocoa market, which have their holdings in Nigeria, Gabon and the British West Indies. I suppose you are familiar with all this and that I'm not telling you anything new?'

'Yes, sir, I am aware of the figures and competition we represent in the eyes of the British.' Luís Bernardo now felt he was on familiar ground.

'You should know then that Soveral, our influential ambassador in London, has written to us of his growing alarm at the campaign English cocoa companies are unleashing against São Tomé and Príncipe. And I reveal no secrets of state if I also tell you that the Marquess of Soveral is a great friend of the British King, as I am too, and that it was because of that friendship that Edward sent me a personal message telling us to attend to the problem and do something to prevent the situation reaching the point where he would be forced by his government to act or to allow his government to act against us.'

'But what are the British complaining about?' asked Luís Bernardo.

'It began as a complaint lodged years ago by a British company called Cadbury, which produces cocoa in British West Africa, and also imports cocoa from São Tomé. Cadbury, which turns its cocoa into chocolate, complains that we compete unfairly with

British colonies, because we are employing slave labour from Angola on our São Tomé plantations.'

'And is it true?' asked Luís Bernardo.

'Well, apparently it depends on your point of view, on what one understands slave labour to be. In fact, we call them contract labourers but the problem is that every year an average of three thousand workers are contracted for the São Tomé and Príncipe plantations and the boats that take them return empty. In the eyes of the British, this is tantamount to slavery: if the workers are recruited in Angola and never return, it is because they are not free. It only remains for them to call us slave traders. The Minister for the Colonies explained to the Ambassador how the so-called "slaves" were paid, and were better treated and housed than workers on British plantations in Africa or the West Indies, and that, in terms of health, there was no better evidence than the fact that several plantations had their own well-equipped hospital, something quite unthinkable in the rest of Africa. But all to no avail: egged on by the Liverpool Traders' Association, the British press has attacked us quite mercilessly.'

At this point, Dom Carlos got up to fetch a newspaper from the top of his bureau. He handed it to Luís Bernardo, already open at a page where a large headline declared: 'Slavery Flourishing in Portugal's African Colonies'. He sat down and took up his thread.

'In London Soveral has explored all the usual avenues: he invited leading Fleet Street editors to dinner to see if he could at least curb the outcries. But was unsuccessful. In the end, we had to yield to British government pressure and welcome one Joseph Burtt, an envoy from the Traders' Association, to put the record straight. The man arrived at the beginning of the year and came so well prepared he had even taken the trouble to learn Portuguese. He stayed in Lisbon, and met a whole range of people: the Minister, representatives of plantation owners, journalists, everyone he wanted to see.'

'Yes, I remember hearing about that,' interjected Luís Bernardo, 'and what conclusions did Joseph Burtt reach?'

'The man is no fool: he drew no conclusions here. He sought permission to visit São Tomé and Príncipe and then Angola, in order to be in a position to present a properly documented report to his paymasters. The government, São Tomé plantation owners and I discussed this matter: we could not see a way to refuse him, without signalling that we were afraid of an on-the-spot inspection. If we had done so, it is certain the campaign in Britain would have reached a pitch of hysteria and the British government would finally have decided to bring to bear dramatic, unacceptable pressure that would have plunged the political scene here into turmoil.'

But that would be another *Ultimatum*! thought Luís Bernardo, not daring, however, to utter the dreaded word that so haunted the memory of His Majesty Dom Carlos.

'In short,' the King continued, 'we thought we had everything to lose and next to nothing to gain if we said no. No sooner had we given him authorisation than he embarked for São Tomé. He was there and in Príncipe until last month and is now in Angola. In the meantime he has sent a preliminary report to the Foreign Office in London based on what he saw in São Tomé. Soveral managed to intervene straight away and had a private audience with the Minister, who gave him the report to read. As soon as he had had sight of it, the Marquess told me it would be best if no one else did.'

'Obviously this is confidential and must not go beyond these walls,' interjected the Count of Arnoso, breaking his silence, 'but we received a letter from him a week ago where he writes that if the report were to be published as it stands, we would stand exposed to the whole world as the last slaving nation on the planet. And that would only be the moral side of the damage . . .'

'Fortunately,' resumed Dom Carlos, 'Portugal has the best ambassador one could wish for in London. Soveral managed to reach an agreement with the Minister, Lord Balfour: this preliminary report will be kept under wraps at the Foreign Office on the pretext that it lacks the part relating to Angola. So we have some time, time to try to erase the impressions gathered by Mr Burtt.'

'By appointing a new governor?'

'Not just by the appointment of a new governor; that would be too easy. We need to use this time to persuade the British that Mr Burtt's information is out of date. How do we do that? Well, that is why the new Governor we mentioned must possess the diplomatic qualities required by the situation and be a fluent English-speaker. The other side of the agreement negotiated by Soveral is that Portugal will accept the establishment in São Tomé and Príncipe of a resident British consul. We had no alternative but to agree that.'

'And Your Majesty expects the new Governor to persuade the British Consul that slavery no longer exists on the islands?'

'That is precisely what I expect *you* to do,' Dom Carlos replied emphatically, 'and I expect you to achieve three things: to persuade the plantation owners to accept all the measures the new Governor wishes to implement so the British Consul has no reason to confirm Mr Burtt's findings; secondly, to do this with utmost tact, so as not to invite insurrection on the islands or endanger their prosperity; thirdly, to keep the Englishman at a friendly distance, pay him due attention, the whole time making it perfectly clear that Portugal is in control there via its Governor who represents the country and its King.'

Dom Carlos relit his cigar that had gone out, stood up, went over to the window and looked out at the garden, as if he already had something else on his mind. He had apparently said all he wanted to say and was now waiting for a reply. Luís Bernardo still didn't know how to respond. It all seemed so unexpected, so remote from anything he might have imagined the reason for that meeting to be. But here he was sitting in a room in the ducal palace of Vila Viçosa, receiving a mandate from the King to go and govern two wretched, far-flung islands on the Equator.

'As Your Majesty will understand, I need time to consider your request and, before contemplating a reply, I will need more information concerning the extent of the prerogatives I am honoured you judge me capable of defending,' he began hesitantly.

'Time is what we have least of, dear fellow. I need your reply within the week. You must request here and now any other information of a political nature that you need. Then, naturally, you must also speak to the Minister and a series of individuals we think you should consult. As for everything else, the details of the journey, setting up there etc., Bernardo will see to all that.'

Bernardo de Pindela judged that that was his cue to intervene and give the King a helping hand.

'The situation has become all the more urgent because the day before yesterday we received a communication from the British Ambassador that they have already chosen the Consul they wish to appoint to São Tomé and that he is due to arrive at the beginning of June. It is now the end of the year and we believe that the new Governor must be established in São Tomé at least a month before the British Consul, in order to be fully abreast of the situation there. As we understand it, if you accept this posting, you will need at least two months to put your affairs in order here, and a fortnight for the journey. You must understand, Valença, why your reply is urgent. And this is discounting the possibility that, if it were to be in the negative, against His Majesty's wishes, we would have to find someone else to replace you in even more of a rush.'

Dom Carlos had sat down and was staring at him again.

'We really are in your hands, dear fellow. I hate to put things this way, but circumstances are such that events are beyond our control. You must realise, nonetheless, that I am only too conscious of the huge sacrifice I am asking you to make and the tremendous courage you will be showing if you accept. But you must also understand that I'm not demanding this for myself, but for our country. Now that I have met you, now that I have seen you face to face, I am totally persuaded you are the right man for this mission and I have been well advised. You cannot imagine the relief a positive response on your part will afford me.'

So that was that. He was well and truly trapped. How do you say no to a king? What words, what excuses, what irrefutable arguments could there be?

'I promise Your Majesty that I will reply within the week you have given me. I beg you to understand that at this time it is the most I can promise. There are things that are out of my hands: I have a life to see to and must endeavour to leave things minimally organised in my absence. And I have to agree to drop everything to depart to the world's end, to a land where nobody wants to live and where, as I perceive it, an almost unviable mission awaits me.'

'Why is it unviable?'

It was Luís Bernardo's turn to look the King in the eye. If he said it wasn't, it would be good for Dom Carlos to see the mandate was nigh on unacceptable. If he said it was, he would probably never again have occasion to speak to the King and it was best everything should be clear immediately.

Luís Bernardo responded after a suitably thoughtful pause.

'I think Your Majesty has made himself perfectly clear.'

'Then we are agreed. It only remains for us to await your reply, which I beg you to make as considered and generous as possible.' Dom Carlos got up, signalling that the conversation was at an end.

Luís Bernardo wanted to leave and be alone to meditate on his destiny.

But the King made one last gesture.

'I hope you will stay for supper and for the night. Nothing would afford me greater pleasure.'

'Thank you, Your Majesty, but, with your consent, I would like to catch the five o'clock train, as I have a dinner engagement in Lisbon this evening.'

The Count of Arnoso accompanied Luís Bernardo to the main door where a carriage awaited him.

Before saying goodbye, the Count put a hand on his shoulder and said, 'I will make His Majesty's words mine, but much more emphatically than his position allows him to: you are the right man for this task and many things that are important for our country depend on its adroit execution. I hope you understand the immensity of what is at stake: the day we lose our first colony will be the inevitable beginning of the end of our empire and, with it, the end of the monarchy, the kingdom, and perhaps the country. All that will remain is for Spain to come and swallow us up.'

The pressure was on Luís Bernardo to consider this invitation carefully. He got into the carriage and consulted the watch in his jacket pocket: it was nearly four-thirty. The sun was already beginning to dip on the horizon and the day that had been so full of light was now turning dark. Cold descended on the town and smoke from the various fires lit in the houses rose out of the chimneys. He imagined people sitting around big hearths, where sausages cooked and dinner pans steamed, exhausted men cradled children in their laps, prematurely aged women bent over the cooking; where dogs curled up enjoying the heat from the tiles, and old men dozed on wooden benches, waiting for dinner. He imagined miserable drunks slumped on bar counters, downing their last drinks before returning home.

The streets were almost deserted and just a few dark figures passed by, silhouetted against the whitewashed walls. The church bell struck a quarter to five and suddenly Luís Bernardo was overcome by a feeling of desolation, as if something inevitable hung in the air. Today he had started quite spontaneously to yearn after a provincial life where nothing happened, where time passed so slowly it would almost be possible to believe in eternity. But the train was waiting at the station to take him back to the sprawling city, the only world he knew, loved and understood.

In the train he closed his eyes and dozed off almost immediately. He dreamed he was in Africa, the hot sun beating down, palm trees and insects, the locals jabbering at the top of their voices and a rainbow of colours bursting out everywhere. And he was in the thick of the dust and the turmoil, watching over the site of the Palace of the Dukes of Braganza that King Dom Carlos had ordered be built in the tropics.

3

L UÍS BERNARDO TOOK a carriage from the station in Terreiro do Paço. He was already late for dinner, but hoped to arrive in time for coffee and *digestifs*. He only missed the weekly dinners at the Hotel Central when circumstances made it impossible to attend. It was not that they were exceptionally entertaining or instructive, but it was an opportunity to be relaxed among male friends and converse about any topic from women to politics via horse racing. They also occasionally did business, swapped books, recounted adventures from their travels, got up to date with gossip and procured favours or contacts. There were not many alternatives when it came to having a night out in Lisbon. Novelist Eça de Queiróz's cousin, Basilio, had already said that this was a city where 'one couldn't eat a partridge wing and drink a glass of champagne at midnight'. They had dubbed themselves the 'Survivors' in opposition to Eça's 'Defeated by Life' group, wanting to suggest, with less anguish and certainly less brilliance, that they were intent on squeezing as much juice as they could from fin-de-siècle Lisbon life. This was what Luís Bernardo liked about the heterogeneous dining club: they weren't moralisers; they hadn't pledged to save the Fatherland; they didn't believe in a perfect world or put themselves forward as a school of virtue or as exemplary citizens. They lived with what there was and on what there was. Perhaps nowhere else was the eternal monarchy versus republic rehearsed so peacefully. The dominant thesis of the 'Survivors' was that the solutions to the nation's problems didn't depend on the constitutional form the regime adopted: under a monarchy or a republic, the people would continue to be poverty-stricken and wretched and elections would always be decided by provincial political bosses. The apparatus of the state would continue to be manned according to personal acquaintance or political allegiance and never on personal merit, and the country –

39

. its vapid counts and marquis or hot-headed Republican demagogues – would inevitably continue in the grip of retrograde ideas and conservative forces for whom modernity was the devil incarnate. What Portugal lacked was a civic tradition, a desire for freedom, a wish to think and act individually: the unfortunate agricultural worker said and did what his employer ordered, the latter repeated what his political boss told him, and he in turn was a servile pawn of party grandees in Lisbon. However much the pinnacle of the pyramid moved, everything down to the bottom remained static. The disease was much more serious than an illness that could be cured by a simple constitutional *coup d'état*.

By the time Luís Bernardo arrived, the group had already been dining for a couple of hours and were now on their dessert, *crêpes Suzette*, a speciality of the Hotel Central. He sat in an empty place at one end of the table next to João Forjaz and opposite Dr Veríssimo – António Pedro de Athayde Veríssimo, an intriguing species of financier and intellectual, philanthropist and benign paterfamilias, militant agnostic and celebrated lover of Bertha de Sousa. She was all the rage on the Lisbon stage and blessed with attributes not to Bernardo's liking: short, chubby legs like tree-trunks, over-endowed buttocks, and a village girl's face all tarted up for the glitzy life of the stage. As a real gentleman who prided himself on being a man of the arts and literature, which he cultivated as if it were tantamount to membership of the priest-hood, Dr Veríssimo never mentioned the small matter of the privileged position he had gained with a woman whom half Lisbon's male population were desperate to know more intimately. There was a comparable interest in his business affairs: myths abounded about his infallible instinct for making investments that earned handsome returns. And, if he was a ruthless businessman, it was also common knowledge that Filipe Martins, for example, the youngest in the gathering, seated at the opposite end of the table, had only just finished medical studies in Coimbra, thanks to a student scholarship Dr Veríssimo paid over the years as a tribute to the young man's deceased father, with whom he had done business in the past.

'Well, do tell me, what did the man want from you?' asked João Forjaz, as soon as Luís Bernardo had sat down next to him.

He was referring of course to his friend's visit to Vila Viçosa, about which he was the only one with any prior knowledge.

'He merely wanted to suggest I change my life drastically. And go and bury myself alive, serving my country. But do *you* have any news for me?'

'Yes, I do, I do. Take it easy, I do.'

'Good or bad?'

'That depends on your point of view: I think it's bad; you'll think it's good. But let's leave that till later. I think we're not short of things to talk about.'

Some at the table were debating the charms of Lucília Simões, a young actress much in vogue, who'd just finished a three-month season to full houses at the Dona Amélia, in the ravishing role of Lorenza Feliciani Balsamo in *O Grande Cagliostro*. The conversation became more animated as they progressed from Lucília Simões to the daughter of a bankrupt nobleman who had recently been seen a lot at the São Carlos, *la Brasileira* languidly rolling her eyes as if carrying a sign on her head begging, 'Save my father!'

Luís Bernardo gradually disengaged from the gossip and guffaws. He felt himself floating adrift, half absent. His thoughts were of Matilde and what she might have said to João Forjaz, of King Dom Carlos and his palace in Vila Viçosa and the dream he had had on the train. But, although he had disengaged from the conversation, he felt mentally and physically comforted to be there among friends, listening to all that chit-chat, as if that day the only thing that made sense was the feeling that he was being swept along by people and events, and he was making no attempt to stem the tide.

When they transferred to the lounge for brandy and cigars, Luís Bernardo tried to catch João's eye, but before he could, Dr Veríssimo had grabbed his arm, pulled him to one side and asked if they could have a word in private. They sat down at the back of the bar, in worn leather armchairs that had sheltered generations of highly important private conversations.

'My dear friend,' the financier began, 'I'll spare you the preamble. When I'm talking business, I like to get straight to the point: would you consider the possible sale of your business?'

Luís Bernardo stared at him, as if he'd seen a ghost. I don't believe it! What day is today? What an extraordinary day when everyone wants to suggest I summarily give up my present life and livelihood?

'Do excuse me, Doctor: your question is so unexpected I'm not sure I heard you properly: you asked me whether I wanted to sell my company – lock, stock and barrel?'

'Yes: ships, premises, offices, employees, stocks, list of customers and agents. Your whole business.'

'And why should I want to?'

'Well, I can't say; there's no way I could know, is there? I'm just asking you if you would be prepared to sell. Some businessmen buy and sell, others stay in the saddle till the day they die. I don't know what your philosophy is, but as you know my business is buying and selling. The only things I hang on to are books, paintings and children. Everything else has its price: if the right offer is made, I sell; if I make the right offer, I am able to buy. Please don't be offended by my request; it's only a business proposition.'

'I'm not offended. Simply bewildered. I've owned this company for fifteen years, as you know. It's my life and I've never contemplated selling it. The idea is completely . . . how can I put it, unreal and absurd.'

'Of course, I understand you perfectly. I wasn't expecting you to give me a reply on the spot.'

'But tell me, Doctor: do you want to buy my company for your own use?'

'No, I'll be perfectly honest. My business, as I said, is buying and selling. It just so happens I have a foreign client I think will be interested in running a business of this kind in Lisbon and I intend to buy from you and sell on to him. With a margin of profit for myself, naturally.'

'And now, Doctor, should I ask whether you have any idea of the amount you are prepared to offer?'

'Yes, I do. I reckoned you would be in no state to table a figure and, as I prefer to get to the point, I did a brief analysis of your company, obtained information here and there about the state of your ships, for example, and did my sums. In my opinion, my dear Valença, your firm is worth some eighty thousand réis. I am prepared to offer you a hundred thousand.'

Luís Bernardo stayed silent, allowed what he'd just heard to sink in. It was evidently a generous offer. He himself had tried several times to estimate the value of his company and had never approached anything like eighty thousand réis. Seventy perhaps, seventy-five, but never as much as the eighty thousand quoted by Veríssimo who was prepared to offer twenty thousand above that. If he were selling, it would be a heaven-sent opportunity. But he wasn't selling. Unless . . .

'Doctor, as I said, the last thing I expected today was an offer of this nature. I will consider it seriously, out of respect for you. When do you want a reply by?'

'That entirely depends on you: two, three weeks, a month. Take as long as you need. What is paramount is that if we reach an agreement we must do good business. It must be a deal that will leave us as good friends as before.'

They returned to where the others were seated. João Forjaz was waiting there for Luís Bernardo.

'Where did you get to? It seems you're the mystery man today.'

'No, it's more like today my life has decided it wants no more routine predictability. It's making things happen!'

'What? Come on, out with it!'

'First, let me get myself a cognac. I really need one. I think it would be better if we went and talked elsewhere.'

They went out into the big lounge by the entrance to the hotel, now half empty, except for two French-speaking customers at reception who looked like they had just arrived from Rossio Station, on the Sud-Expresso from Paris. João Forjaz and Luís Bernardo sat down in a corner of the room, each holding a large glass of brandy. The latter lit a cigarette.

'First of all, tell me what the message is from Matilde.'

'No, first you tell me what happened in Vila Viçosa.'

'I'm sorry, but my self-interest is stronger and more legitimate than your curiosity . . .'

'More legitimate?'

'Come on, João, spare me the sermonising and give me Matilde's message.'

'All right, as you can't wait, I'll give you the bare facts and, I hope, conclude my mission as go-between. Matilde arrives in

43

Lisbon tomorrow, accompanied by her great friend and confidante, Marta Trebouce, also from Vila Franca. The excuse is that she is accompanying Marta who has business to resolve in Lisbon. They'll stay for two days at the Hotel Braganza. I made the reservations today: Matilde is booked into room 306 and Marta into 308, but, in fact, they'll swap rooms. Not even the devil will deceive them: if someone knocks on Marta's door looking for Matilde, Marta will say she is in the room next door and, as the rooms have a connecting door, she'll have time to warn Matilde someone wants to see her. If Matilde happens to have company, something I really hope will not happen' – João looked at Luís Bernardo cynically out of the corner of one eye – 'the company in question will have to hotfoot it to Marta's room, and leave the coast clear for Matilde.'

'My word, most ingenious! I'd never have thought of such a simple, foolproof plan.'

'And you think you know whose idea it was? Well, you're wrong. I didn't design this operation for you: it was all Matilde's idea.'

Luís Bernardo suppressed a whistle. The cool-headed way Matilde had planned things came as a surprise – one more on what was a day of endless surprises.

'Fine then, Luís, you've got your message and battle plan. If you want to go ahead, you need to go to the hotel tomorrow and book yourself in, for one or two nights, on the pretext that you've got building works at home or something similar. Your Lady of the Camellias will be expecting you from 10 p.m. onwards. But if you heed the advice of a really sincere friend, you won't go: write a letter saying you've had second thoughts for the noblest of reasons – you're rather good at this – and I'll make sure she receives it.'

'João, I'm grateful for all the help you've given and even this advice I know comes from a real friend. But I've got the whole of tomorrow to think this through and if I decide it's quite pointless, that it's madness that has already gone on for too long and could make Matilde unhappy or cause her problems, I won't go. I promise.'

They were silent for a moment.

44

Then Luís Bernardo raised his glass and chinked it against João's.

'Cheers. It *is* good to have friends like you.'

João had to force a smile. He remembered how a long time ago he had felt Luís Bernardo had let him down. Luís had said something he'd never forgotten: 'Don't expect me to be faithful to qualities I don't possess. What you can do is rely on the qualities I *do* possess because I will never go against them.' It was true. He would soon learn it was. For better or for worse.

'And what about Vila Viçosa, tell me what happened.'

'Well, what happened in Vila Viçosa was that I had an excellent lunch, followed by an hour's conversation alone with the King and his secretary, Bernardo Pindela. In a nutshell, His Majesty wants me to tell him, by the end of the week, whether I will agree to leave in two months to go and spend three years in São Tomé and Príncipe, where the post of Governor by royal appointment awaits me, and where he's charged me with the mission of convincing the British Consul who will take up residence there that, contrary to what the British press and merchants say, slave labour does not exist on São Tomé. At the same time I must convince the Portuguese settlers to put an end to slavery and allow their workers to become completely free men – free even to leave, but without that affecting the prosperity of the plantations.'

'Well, that's exactly your own thesis! The King has taken you at your word!'

'What thesis?'

'Well, the one you came out and defended in newspapers and drawing rooms, namely that our settlers were incapable of getting an economic return from the colonies without resorting to methods that history rendered obsolete long ago. Now you have an excellent opportunity to prove how right your theories are.'

'Don't make fun of me, João! Can't you see they expect me to achieve in months what should have been done years ago? And are you forgetting the level of personal sacrifice they want me to make? It means giving up everything, my home, country, friends and work in order to disappear to the world's end, where there's nobody to talk to and happiness amounts to avoiding sudden death by malaria, tsetse fly, smallpox or yellow fever.'

'There is no yellow fever on São Tomé.'

'Don't change the subject, João! I'd like to see you in my place!'

'In your place, I would go. Or rather, in your place, I'd feel morally obliged to.'

'You're a real friend.'

'Luís, I'm saying this as a real friend, and as proof I promise you that if you go I'll pay you at least one visit.'

'One visit! João, try to understand that it's about spending three years exiled on islands in the mid-Atlantic, eight thousand kilometres from Lisbon, where mail and newspapers arrive once or twice a month! Goodbye opera, theatre, dances, concerts, horse racing, strolls along the banks of the Tagus! Think jungle and sea, sea and jungle! With whom shall I converse, lunch, dine and, while we are about it, fall in love with?

'It's a mission on behalf of your country. And the majority of missions don't lead to embassies in Rome or Madrid.'

'But nor are they exile to the Equator!'

'Look, Luís, think it through. It's a post that will bring you prestige, give you the satisfaction of doing your patriotic duty, enable you to return with a reputation everyone will recognise and, for heaven's sake, you can challenge the dreadful monotony of our lives. Besides, Luís, there is nothing really to keep you here, apart from your friends: you're not married, don't have children, parents or fiancée, as far as I know; you've just your company – and surely you can arrange for someone to manage that in your absence. Once you're there, you can even negotiate better deals for your own vessels.'

'Well, as far as that goes, I can tell you I've just had an extraordinary offer from Veríssimo to buy the firm. The man has a hunch that this might be just the right moment.'

'He seriously wants to buy your company? What's he offering?'

'More than I'd ever dare ask.'

'Luís, this is an omen. It solves everything. The posting in São Tomé will give you prestige and an income you can save, because you won't have anything to spend it on. You can sell your company and make an excellent profit. Then you won't have to worry about it while you're away. You can deposit the money here in the Burnay or somewhere similar and when you return you will be a rich man. Simultaneously, the imbroglio with my cousin Matilde is also dealt with. Everything works out perfectly!'

'And what has your cousin Matilde got to do with all this?'

'Luís, just think for a minute: does it make any sense for you to get involved with her and create a scandal from which nobody will emerge unscathed, if you are contemplating the idea of abandoning the country in two months? Could you do that to her?'

'But who said I was contemplating exile? You're the one contemplating it on my behalf!'

'Of course you are, otherwise you would have said no to the King.'

'One doesn't say no to a king so easily: it's not like saying no to Veríssimo.'

'Of course not, but it is also true that, if you thought the idea was totally unacceptable, you wouldn't be so remiss as to wait a week to give a response you knew was going to be negative from the start.'

'Fine, João, all you have to do now is put me on a boat and dispatch me to the tropics! I believe what pleases you most in all this is the opportunity to get me away from Matilde.'

'No, that's not true, Luís. I think you should let Matilde be, whether you go or not. For other completely different reasons and as a friend, I think that you should go.'

'If you don't mind, João, that's a matter between Matilde and myself. What my honour tells me is that, if tomorrow or afterwards I go to see her and still haven't made up my mind about São Tomé, I'll let her know in advance what is happening.'

'Well, that's as good as it will get today. Come on, let's go and join the others and tomorrow we'll talk more calmly.'

The following morning, Luís Bernardo reached the offices of the Island Shipping Company at about ten. He asked to see Captain Valdemar Ascêncio, who had sailed between Lisbon and São Tomé before working for Island Shipping. Then he told his secretary to pass on the day's business to his chief clerk, and asked for the company's recent accounts and the reports from the Ministry for the Colonies with the yearly breakdown of freight transported to and from São Tomé, including the lists of passengers and their provenance. He ordered his secretary, who was astonished he had not yet opened the newspapers on his desk, the perusing of which was his first ritual of the morning, to ensure he received no interruptions apart from the visit from Ascêncio. He began to jot down on a sheet of paper all the people he knew who were linked in some way with São Tomé and Príncipe.

Captain Ascêncio appeared around midday, shaking off the deep sleep of a sailor on dry land. Experience in the trade had taught Luís never to judge the competence of a naval officer by how he acted on land.

Otherwise, he'd have sent Captain Ascêncio packing as soon as he saw him set foot through the door. Physically repelled by the man's appearance, he dispensed with polite introductions and got straight to the point, asking him what in his opinion a person from Lisbon should take if he were going to spend a long period on São Tomé, explaining it was a question he'd been asked by a friend considering the possibility of spending a while on the islands.

'Everything,' the Captain of the *Catalina* replied quite spontaneously.

'Everything? No, that can't be: isn't there anything on Sao Tomé – isn't there food?'

'Yes, there is food, Mr Valença. That's the only thing the island isn't short of. There's lots of good fish, fruit you can pick from the trees, hens, pigs, *matabala*, that's a kind of potato, though not so tasty, and manioc flour. There's no rice, no garden vegetables.'

'And what about everything else?'

'There is nothing else.'

'Nothing? What don't they have then?'

'Well, we're talking about a gentleman, aren't we? A gentleman like Mr Valença, who wants to go and live there, right?'

'Yes, a gentleman.'

'Well, sir, there's nothing for a gentleman. There's no ink or writing paper, no razor blades, no towels or bed linen, no cutlery or crockery, no clothes or shoes, no tackle for horses, no candles, hardly any wine or alcohol, except for the horrible firewater they distil there, no musical instruments, no iron cooking pots or irons. Nothing at all, sir.'

'Is there no tobacco?'

'They occasionally get some from the Azores or West Africa.'

In a foul mood he dismissed Ascêncio and, with no great enthusiasm or inspiration, began to write a list of everything someone, other than himself, should take to São Tomé, if that person agreed one day to go and live there for three years.

He then turned to the day's newspapers, starting with *O Século*. He'd always considered it a good newspaper, one that was well informed, well reported, well written, with good sources of information and serious analysis. Recently, however, *O Século* had been clearly sliding into the Republican camp, though not with the demagogic tones of *A Luta* or *A Vanguarda*, or the insults they directed daily at the Royal Family and the institution of monarchy. But *O Século* increasingly bent with the wind, and the prevailing wind was Republican, particularly after the Republicans had started to defend the poor and exploited, in the wake of the big workers' strike of 1903 in Oporto, which the government had tried to repress by sending in the National Guard and the cruiser *Dona Amélia* against the textile workers. Nevertheless, Luís Bernardo was a passive monarchist – more from family tradition than personal persuasion – and considered some arguments the Republicans invoked to be quite sound. The country had been plunged into deep crisis from 1890 – the date of the British Ultimatum – and it was political, economic, cultural and social. When slavery was ended in Brazil, emigrants stopped sending income that had balanced the foreign trade deficit. Everything the country needed to modernise itself had to be imported, and the only real exports were cork and canned fish. Products like port wine or São Tomé coffee were a small contribution to the huge current trade imbalance. Every year the budget showed a shortfall of five to six million réis, which only increased a floating debt of some eighty million. More than three-quarters of the population of five and a half million lived in the countryside but, entirely dependent on a pitiful, poverty-stricken peasantry, the crops produced were nowhere enough to stave off hunger. Eighty per cent of the population was illiterate; ninety per cent had no healthcare and lived prey to illness and epidemics, just like in the Middle Ages. Portugal was the most backward country in Europe, and its population the poorest, most miserable and most uneducated. The elite could only generate perennial student revolts in Coimbra against examinations, or the opera season at the São Carlos that lasted three months in winter. A dilettante, retrograde aristocracy reckoned that, beyond the São Carlos, the world came down to horse races organised by the Turf Club, nights spent in the Parada in Cascais, and summers in houses in Ericeira or mansions in Sintra. They were only marginally worried by *nouveaux riches*, intellectuals and Republicans whose influence they knew didn't reach beyond the meagre physical territory of half a dozen Lisbon cafés. The people believed as ever in the designs of Providence, fatalistic sermons from the Holy Church of Rome and in divine will that decreed their infinite wretchedness and the extravagance and useless inherited wealth of the country's lords and first-born.

But Luís Bernardo was equally dismayed by the inflammatory rhetoric of the Republicans. The country's sickly state did not stem, he believed, from the monarchy as an institution or from the figure of Dom Carlos. The sickness came from the rotation system of government controlled by two political parties who alternated in power in São Bento and all offices of state, serving themselves and their own rather than serving the country. The sickness stemmed from electoral chicanery, from elections fixed in advance by the two parties, from the lack of any sense of duty or loyalty to the state. As a matter of fact, the opposition was led by Hintze Ribeiro, of the Regenerationist Party, and the government by the Progressive Party of José Luciano de Castro, who, though paralytic and officially retired from public life, continued to stack the decks and create and curtail governments and policy. The King just let them get on with it, as a constitutional monarch properly should. As a result, he would be accused of being indifferent to the state of the nation and the state of the Portuguese; but if he decided to mess with concrete issues of government, to put an end to the parties' monopoly of power and call on the best of his entourage to govern, the press and political rabble would fall on him with cries of 'tyrant' and 'usurper'. Nobody was more in a position to influence Portuguese foreign policy positively than Dom Carlos, as attested by the visits he received from Edward VII of Great Britain and Alfonso XIII of

Spain and, in the current year, Kaiser Wilhelm II and the French President. But inevitably all the King's diplomatic initiatives floundered against government invective and mistrust and insults from the press. And it was exactly the same in relation to the colonies, the existence of which really came to the country's notice with the Ultimatum, for which Dom Carlos got the blame. He was suspected of not sharing the same patriotic spirit that inflamed the hearts of the Portuguese, when 'perfidious Albion' did not agree to cede a few square miles of Africa so the territory of Angola could be linked to Mozambique, and thus extend from coast to coast the African Empire, which no Portuguese knew or inhabited, and where the authority of Lisbon had never imposed itself and would not do so for decades. Luís Bernardo sensed from his Vila Viçosa conversation with Dom Carlos that the King shared his views on the matter: there was no point in proclaiming an empire that nobody nurtured, managed or civilised. Every year the public chest lost three million réis to the economy of the colonies and still the politicians longed for 'a pink-coloured map'.

The plantation owners in Africa demanded and were granted import duties on foreign goods that competed with their exports from Africa: ordinary people lost out, because they had to buy at a higher price what could have been cheaper if competition hadn't been blocked; the state lost out, because it earned less from one area than it exempted in another. African plantation owners were the only ones to benefit. Henrique Mendonça, a big landowner from São Tomé, recently house-warmed his sumptuous palace on the highest hill in Lisbon, where his extravagant parties were the talk of the town. He visibly waxed rich on colonial trade, whereas, year after year, the country bankrupted itself on its colonies: what kind of imperial policy was that? When Joaquim Augusto Mouzinho was Governor of Mozambique, Dom Carlos tried to make the state and public interest predominate. But, for a year and a half, in the midst of military campaigns, Mouzinho had to confront the private interests of big companies in Lisbon who, with the complicity of government, did their best to undermine his actions and sabotage his efforts. And, without Dom Carlos's approval, rather with his silent agreement, Mouzinho finally resigned.

Luís Bernardo had recorded all this in the two articles that had caused such a stir, and later developed his case with supporting facts and figures in a pamphlet on the economy of the colonies. His livelihood depended on the colonies – not as a producer but as a shipper – and he was in no doubt that Portugal was wasting the potential its coveted African empire offered. At very different levels, Mozambique and São Tomé were immensely rich agriculturally. With the resources now being discovered, Angola sat on infinite hidden wealth in minerals and raw materials as well as agricultural produce. But it all had to be found, exploited and organised.

Luís Bernardo put the newspaper down and sighed deeply. It was clear that changes on a grand scale were called for, both in the country and his own life. Politics had never attracted him. He liked to say that one should do something really important or else do nothing at all. He preferred to go with the flow, taste the good and pleasant things, and skilfully sidestep obligations or anything limiting his freedom. He hated faith and fanaticism, in religion and politics, in social life and at work. He thought nothing was really important enough to warrant upsetting his routines and making him exchange the comforts of life for the discomfort of ambition.

And now there was the São Tomé challenge. '*Par délicatesse*', he hadn't immediately told the King he had got the wrong man for such a mission. But he didn't intend ruining his life '*par délicatesse*', like Rimbaud. He would pretend to consider the King's invitation and devote the next few days to finding the best formula to rid himself of a commitment he felt strongly he could well do without. After gathering the necessary information he would write to His Majesty and decline his invitation, adding that he remained at the King's disposition for any other patriotic task His Majesty might consider he could carry out. Life could then resume its normal course.

Matilde looked at the clock for the tenth time: it was five past ten and, outside her bedroom door, not a sound from the third-floor corridor in the Hotel Braganza.

Perhaps he won't come, she wondered ingenuously, the nagging doubt creating a tremor of horror and humiliation.

Yet she was unsure whether she wanted Luís Bernardo to come or not. If he didn't, she would emerge unscathed, with her life unblemished and her peaceful, predictable future undisturbed. She had children, a husband, and an orderly, agreeable life in their large house in Vila Franca. There everything was in place. There was no pain, no secret, no fear she couldn't share, neither was there this terror, this choking feeling now in her chest. If he didn't come, it would merely have been a brief moment of midsummer's night madness. There wouldn't be this hotel room, this premeditated betrayal, this shadowy, shuttered rendezvous, as if she were hiding from herself and from a world that was all ears outside the window. She wouldn't have to suffer the nightmare she could already imagine, presenting one face to day and another to night, one face to others and another to herself. In the morning, she could leave smiling to the world, intact, faithful, the same as ever.

But if he didn't come . . . if he didn't come, she would stay there the entire night as if she had been abandoned, like second-hand goods; as if their arrangement had been a mistake, a misunderstanding. She'd feel like the betrayer betrayed, rejected by the very object of her own betrayal. The next morning, he'd probably leave a note in reception – using some last-minute unforeseen circumstance as an excuse or, even worse, saying he'd concluded it would be best for both of them not to take it any further. Yes, she could go into the street and hold her head up high: nothing in the end had happened. And yet it was as if everything *had* happened! She'd exposed herself and he had fled; she was on the point of surrender and he had declined the opportunity. That night, at home, she'd look her husband in the face and feel deeply ashamed and humiliated: I can't even tell myself I betrayed you. It was worse: I was all set to betray you and was rejected. I deceived you, within myself, and was myself deceived. And she'd meet his usual elegance, the civilised routines of his passion, his gentlemanly rituals in bed, and feel unimaginably defiled within herself.

Ten-twenty. Footsteps in the corridor, fingers tapping on someone else's door. She heard voices and the loud laughter of people who weren't hiding, were expecting to meet and were unafraid and not acting like criminals. Now she had only one option: leave immediately, go and get Marta from next door, pack their cases quickly, settle their bills and flee. But flee where, at that time of night? Calm down, Matilde. Keep calm! She sat on her bed and looked at herself in the mirror: she was beautiful and desirable; no man in his right mind would scorn such a woman. And suddenly she felt lucid: she'd leave the following day, collect the note, but not open it. She'd place it next to a letter *she* would write to *him* and which she'd get João to deliver. She'd say that she regretted all that had happened and had decided to leave the hotel in a hurry, before the time agreed for their rendezvous. In the late morning, she'd get someone to retrieve her case from the hotel, and would get Luís Bernardo's letter, which she'd send back unopened, though she imagined it would be a letter where he'd seem at a loss after he'd turned up for an assignation that *she* hadn't honoured. She'd thus turn the situation on its head and, if she ever bumped into Luís Bernardo again, would have no need to feel embarrassed. It didn't solve everything, but it solved what was crucial. And – she suddenly thought – what if he did come? If she saw him, she'd act as if she were merely meeting a friend, someone she wanted to get to know better or whatever, though circumstances meant they had to resort to peculiar subterfuges. She'd take the opportunity to explain, it would be easy enough, how the Ericeira kiss had been only a panic reaction to the unexpected, then would add matter-of-factly: 'I don't mean it wasn't nice, but let it be a thing of the past.'

This time she heard steps differently, coming to the top of the stairs and walking down the corridor outside, hushed yet hurried, as if someone wanted to reach his destination unnoticed. Her heart began to pound even before she heard the steps stop in front of her door and then the short pause before a gentle knock on the wood. She stayed on her bed, petrified, staring at the door. Another knock and she knew she should open her door before some other door opened on the corridor. She released the bolt, turned the handle and took two steps backwards, opening the door without really seeing Luís Bernardo come in. She closed and instinctively bolted the door, leaned back, and regarded him lingeringly. There was no denying he was handsome and urbane. He wore a dark-black suit, white high-collared shirt and a neatly knotted damask-green tie with a small mother-of-pearl pin between his collar and jacket. His dark hair was ruffled, lightly pressed down, as befits the hair of men who use their fingers as combs. His elegant moustache made his mouth seem bigger and his liquid brown eyes smiled roguishly at her. Despite her plans of the moment before, she was unable to repress a smile, thinking: Matilde, this is the last man in the world a woman should trust.

He offered his hand, and she gave him hers, naturally. They stared at each other silently, hands clasped, not knowing how to make the next move. He pulled her towards him and she, avoiding his mouth and face, leaned gently on his shoulder.

'Matilde . . .'

'Don't say anything, Luís. Don't say anything now.'

'But there is something I have to tell you, Matilde.'

'I have things to say too, but I just want to savour this moment.'

He pressed against her and she could feel how well their bodies fitted. Her bosom melted into him; she was about to let herself go. She closed her eyes and let him push as he pressed her head back and in the darkness she let him enter her mouth and stay there.

Luís Bernardo led her slowly towards the bed, where he gently sat her on the edge, knelt at her feet and only then broke off the endless kiss. He touched her breasts, neither roughly nor timidly, more in wonderment, as he undid with one hand the bow on her blouse, then slowly began to unbutton it. Matilde kept her eyes closed, preferring not to see her breasts, where his hands wandered uninhibitedly, his tongue licking her moist, warm nipples. She was naked, exposed. She could resist no more, put her hand on his neck, felt his fine hair between her fingers, and pulled him against her, yielding herself to him.

'Oh my God!'

'Matilde' – he raised his hands – 'there is something I must tell you and must do so now: it's very likely I will have to leave.'

'Now?' She opened her eyes at last.

'No, not right now. I may have to leave Portugal in two months' time and be away for three years.'

'But where are you going, Luís? And why?'

'I can't go into every detail, Matilde. It's a confidential matter. All I can say is that I have to go to São Tomé and Príncipe on a mission of state. I can say no more, but I promised myself and João that I would tell you before anything irrevocable happened between us.'

'Anything irrevocable? Can anything be reversed at this point?'

He gazed at her silently. He didn't know what to say. He hadn't planned for things to happen this way.

'Irrevocable, Luís?' She gripped his face with both hands, as if wanting to force him to look her straight in the eye. 'Irrevocable? Here I am, hidden away in a hotel room with a rake, half-naked, swooning in his arms, as passionate as anyone could be, and you think this can be reversed? How? Should we interrupt the scene until you know whether you will leave Portugal or not and, if not, do we then resume at the point of interruption?'

'Of course not, my love! I only wanted to say I will do whatever you want, only what you want.'

'Well then, Luís, do it, Luís. Do everything I want, everything we both want. From now on, at least as far as I am concerned, there is no going back.'

Luís Bernardo was the second man in her life. She'd been married for eight years, had never known another man and had never thought she would. Luís Bernardo was the second man to kiss her, to undress her and explore her whole body. The second man to see her naked, whose body she'd touched, first with embarrassment, then possessively, as if she wanted to adore him for ever.

Lying back in bed, she found herself staring vacantly at the flowers on the wallpaper, the colour of the shutters, the design of the dressing-table, where the familiar objects of her toilette suddenly reminded her she was there, though it seemed impossible she was surrendering her naked body, moaning pleasurably, instinctively opening her legs so a man who wasn't hers could enter her. She felt in a state of abandon, in freefall down a bottomless well; she was the well and that man touched her depths; everything was wet and liquid; everything led to her burning skin, to her nails painfully sinking into his sides, to her fingers gripping his hair, to her sighing, as if he could save her; 'Luís Bernardo! Luís Bernardo!'

4

THE MONOTONOUS HUM from the *Zaire*'s engines, aided by the equally monotonous seascape he watched pass by from his canvas deckchair on the poop deck kept him in a half-conscious stupor. He spent the sunny days on the voyage from Lisbon at the ship's stern, contemplating the foam froth under the propeller, which faced towards Lisbon, while he was a prisoner of destiny travelling further and further away, kilometre after kilometre in the opposite direction.

To fend off bouts of melancholy he buried himself in the large portfolio of books and documents on São Tomé and Príncipe he had received from the Ministry for the Colonies. He thus whiled away the interminable idle hours between meals – high points, when he dined at the Captain's table with twenty or so crew and passengers. They were all that remained of the known world he was abandoning. His Excellency the Minister had insisted on personally handing over the portfolio they'd prepared for him, adding for good measure his learned counsel and a reminder of what constituted 'government overseas policy': a hotchpotch of a few logical, yet quite useless ideas, alongside others that were out of this world and wholly impractical. He knew that was so, and so did the Minister. The King, at least, attempted a long-term view; the Ministry, on the other hand, reduced it to a note published in the following day's papers to the effect that he had received the new Governor appointed to São Tomé and Príncipe, 'whom he had advised on the key issues of policy pursued hitherto and to be pursued in the future by the government in its overseas territories; particularly in São Tomé and Príncipe, the overall development of which in recent years was a perfect illustration of the correctness of the political strategies implemented so far'. His Excellency was sure Luís Bernardo would do very well and did not doubt his enthusiasm or the success his mission would meet on São Tomé.

His Excellency wished him good luck and accompanied him to the top of the staircase in the Ministry, which he saw himself walk down as if he were somebody else and expelled in all but name from Lisbon and his usual life.

At least the endless voyage was now almost over; late tomorrow morning they would anchor off the coast of São Tomé. Ever since they'd left Benguela, he had noticed the air start to turn gradually heavier, the fresh Atlantic breezes giving way to an expanse of humidity that settled on the water as they approached the Equator and the ship advanced through mists beyond which an unknown world awaited. He thought how sixteenth-century Portuguese sailors must have been terrified when the coast of Africa vanished and they sailed across an empty ocean on their way to the haze-shrouded lands of Adamastor.

He had departed Lisbon at break of day, on a March morning, after stowing his luggage aboard the previous evening: a suitcase full of medicine selected by his dining friend, Dr Filipe Martins, two cases packed with books in a ratio of one a week for a hundred and fifty weeks, a gramophone and some of his favourite records – Beethoven, Mozart, Verdi and Puccini – a trunk full of tropical clothes, his own crockery and silver services, two dozen cases of wine and one of cognac, eight boxes of cigars bought in Havaneza in Chiado, a three-year supply of writing paper, pens and ink, his favourite walking sticks and bureau and chair from home. These things would be all he had to remind him of what he was renouncing.

His decision to go had not been sudden or impulsive. On the contrary, it had been gradual, imperceptible, as if deep down, from the very beginning, from that afternoon in Vila Viçosa, his destiny had eluded his grasp and his will was no longer his to control. He sensed he'd been caught in an ambush, everyone set on rushing him to his impending fate: there were the King's words, backed by the Count of Arnoso; João's arguments making him feel ashamed to say no to the King: the offer to buy the Island Shipping Company, which fell so extraordinarily and simultaneously from the sky. He felt hemmed in, harried, increasingly prey to a set of circumstances from which there was no honourable escape. A challenge had been issued to his spirit of adventure and discovery, his sense of patriotic duty and service to a noble cause, the integrity of his ideas and character and, above all, as João would say, to his need to give a sense of legitimacy, via a grandiose, unexpected, altruistic gesture, to a life that had until then been dedicated to idle self-indulgence. That was how they had set his trap.

But Matilde also weighed heavily in the making of the decision, and that was the least noble side of the situation. To his own conscience, Luís Bernardo would coldly admit São Tomé gave him a dignified excuse to flee from Matilde. Because he *had* decided to flee from her and that was the only decent way to do so. Like all seducers, he was attracted by the chase, the irresistible temptation of an impossible goal, the brush with danger on every front, the combined thrill of scandal and desire, the final triumph of seduction, the booty of conquest at his feet – clothes scattered over the floor, a naked married woman, another man's wife, surrendering in his arms, moaning with pleasure and terror at the discovery of the unexplored frontiers of her own sexuality.

The following night he had returned to the Hotel Braganza to see Matilde once more. They took the same precautions, followed the same strategy, embraced each other with the same passion; Matilde surrendered herself even more freely and passionately, now rid of her initial fears, and he loved her lingeringly hour after hour, refining their pleasures throughout the night. But in his heart, Luís Bernardo knew it was probably their last night. While he caressed, kissed, stripped and possessed her, he was bidding her a furtive but definitive farewell. He hadn't deceived himself, and had given her the choice the previous evening when he'd told her it might be a brief adventure without future or further consequence. For that reason, he tarried languidly by her side until daybreak when they could hear the first cries of the street hawkers outside, offering fresh milk and vegetables or the morning newspapers, and the racket from the trams transporting early-risers to yet another day of toil.

They had talked through the night: she about her children, about life in Vila Franca, about her husband and the respect and friendship she felt for him. He had listened in silence, lying by her side, running his right hand down her naked body, as if sculpting her or wanting to etch her for ever on his senses and memory. I must remember tonight when I am in São Tomé, he'd thought, hoping the night would extend beyond the day outside and drain his passion to the point of exhaustion.

But cold common sense prevailed and killed it. It couldn't continue for all manner of reasons: how often could they meet alone like this? How often until they were found out and scandal broke? Her husband would put her out on the street and, at the very least, he Luís Bernardo would be expected to take her in with her children. Is that what he wanted, a life tied to a woman rejected by her family and society? They would be a couple nobody invited or visited; he would suffer the hatred of another man's children in his own house, the gossip of neighbours and his club – that is, if his club did not delicately ask him to resign his membership.

Thus he reasoned, but he couldn't simply abandon her. That would be to use, then discard her. Matilde didn't deserve such treatment; João would never forgive him and would hold him in contempt for ever. Though Luís Bernardo knew he'd chosen the best, the most sensible course of action, he felt so sullied that even the memory of those two nights of passionate love could not clean the filth from his wounds.

The only option was to flee. But it must be a dignified flight, better still, romantically haloed with an aura of heroic sacrifice. São Tomé was a heaven-sent pretext: suddenly everything worked in his favour to preserve the image and memory of the man she would for ever cherish. He would leave against his will, cursing his fate, plucked from the arms of his lover to serve King and country so that the world could not say there was still slavery in Portugal; and he would be the man to end that indignity, if indeed there was any truth to the slander. He was like a soldier going off to war and relishing his last nights of love. João was quite right when he said he had a way with writing letters on such occasions, and João readily agreed to deliver to Matilde Luís Bernardo's farewell letter:

Matilde,
    What I mentioned has come to pass and I will soon leave for somewhere very far from you and everything I love. I can now

60

reveal what it is all about, given that tomorrow it will be published in the newspapers. His Majesty the King has appointed me Governor of São Tomé and Príncipe, on a mission to put an end to the remnants of slavery that may still persist there and do whatever is necessary to convince Britain, public opinion there and throughout the world, that Portugal is a civilised nation, where such practices can find no place. The nature of the mission, its pre-eminence and importance at several levels for our country, the way in which the King appealed to my sense of duty and to the coherence I feel obliged to keep regarding ideas and positions I have often forwarded in public, left me no margin to deliver what would have been a dishonourable snub.

As a result, I have had to accept the summary dispersal of everything that constituted my life till now. I am abandoning house, family and friends. I am abandoning all comforts and pleasures, social habits and cultural activity, without which I cannot imagine what day-to-day life will be like. I am abandoning my own work, my business, and hastily selling my company in order to settle on an island in the middle of the ocean at the world's end. Convicts would prefer the gallows to being transported there and blacks only sail there under duress, according to the British. But I complain about none of this: there are circumstances in which destiny overrides our own desires; there are higher purposes that individuals must put before all else. I must serve my country as best I can in its hour of need, and be worthy of he who deemed me worthy of this task and it is undoubtedly one of those occasions when one's own choice and freedom do not exist.

I do lament and feel despair about meeting you at long last, only then to lose you straight away. About being yours as no man was or ever will be, and then departing. About knowing this well of love, access to which I'd always been denied, and then to have only this, two nights as short and intense as the days now before me will be long and empty. Don't be upset if I say that all things considered it would have been better if I'd never met you, had never lost myself in your gaze, in your gestures, in your voice, in your mind, in your body; had never carried from here the burden in my soul that travels with my luggage, the burden in my memory that will pursue me night and day on the Equator; had never experienced what will now make me wonder to my dying day what life at your side might have been like.

I beg you to memorise, then tear up this letter, together with the others I wrote you. I ask you to do so sincerely. So your life can continue, so you can be happy with those you love and those who love you and do not waste your youth struggling against the inevitable. It was ever written thus and we could have done nothing differently. I beg you also, when you think of it, to pray for me – to be spared danger, fevers and other very real threats – but also to be spared this chronic illness of living for ever without you and this horror of never being happy again.

Matilde, I promise you will never hear from me what these days, months and years of exile now awaiting me are like. You will never hear what I have suffered without you, how I have wept, how I have despaired. Out of respect for you, I will preserve this unbridgeable distance between us. It is pointless to deceive ourselves, pointless for me to deceive you: there is no return from São Tomé. Pray for me and, for all that perhaps you love me, be happy.

Yours for ever,

Luís Bernardo

It all happened very quickly and time rushed by in frantic activity, as it could only for someone who had two months to say goodbye to everyone and make all his preparations for the new life awaiting him. He asked to be received by the Count of Arnoso, and informed him of his acceptance of the King's invitation. Two days later, his appointment was published in the newspapers, accompanied by a short biography and, in some cases, as in the *Jornal das Colónias*, by a comment on his appointment that was neither for nor against: it said he lacked experience on the ground though his views on the administration of the overseas territories were well known and that, if applied locally with necessary care and forethought, they could prove beneficial to the well-being of the colony and the interests of Portugal.

He had audiences at various ministries, including the War Ministry, because the jurisdiction of the Province of São Tomé and Príncipe also encompassed the Garrison of São João Baptista de Ajudá in Dahomey. He frittered away endless hours at lunches, dinners and working parties with landowners from São Tomé and former administrators of plantations. With doctors, judges and priests who had lived on São Tomé and his two predecessors in the post. By the end, there was so much information, so much advice that he was exhausted before he'd even set out.

He devoted the rest of the two months to sorting out his private affairs including the complicated sale of the Island Shipping Company and its holdings. He achieved an excellent deal, but when the time officially came to hand over his company, where he had spent most of the last fifteen years, he felt terribly distressed. He thanked those who had been his closest, most loyal colleagues and made a point of saying goodbye individually to all his workers. What his life would be like when he returned was a great unknown; all he did know, for the moment, was that he was rich and that afterwards he would be both rich and free. Meanwhile, his life as he knew it was on hold. Given he had no choice but to leave, the best way was to shut every door behind him.

The most painful part was bidding farewell to his friends. He disappeared night after night to private parties, to dinners that lasted into the early hours, to recitals at the São Carlos where the season was in full swing. He twice saw the night out at the brothel of Dona Maria dos Prazeres, whose establishment and girls were the most visited by gentlemen of his social standing. An idle, no doubt deliberate, word from friends led Dona Maria dos Prazeres to address him as 'His Honour the Governor'. He didn't know whether to laugh, feel embarrassed or annoyed by such japes: 'Does His Honour the Governor desire to choose his girl or will he accept my recommendation from the novelties on offer?'

His Honour the Governor didn't know whether he would rather savour the novelties one by one as if he were saying goodbye to women for ever or just converse with Dona Maria dos Prazeres, and indulge the gloom the estimable lady later

63

described to his friends: 'His Honour the Governor feels very sorry for himself! It's all because of an affair. If a man snubs my girls, it's because he's broken-hearted.'

On his last weekend he decided to visit Bussaco, one of his favourite places in Portugal. 'I want to take Bussaco into my eyes and soul!' he declared, so tragically, that João Forjaz, Filipe Martins and Mateus Resende, his closest friends, immediately agreed to accompany him. They had planned an outing to Coimbra, but nobody could shift him from the hotel, where he spent two mornings and an afternoon obsessively contemplating the countryside and pondering such philosophical considerations as: Add a woman and a good book and all one needs to be happy is here! Conversely, and in confirmation of his thesis, he proceeded through the hotel menu like a starving convict, devouring every scrap and always insisting on a grand finale of roast lamb. To his friends' great joy, he invoked his new status as a rich man with nothing to spend his money on as an excuse for paying for the drinks for the whole weekend, indifferent to the prices attached to the best wines from the famous cellars of Bussaco. He ate, drank and smoked as if the salvation of his soul depended on it and his friends had to carry him back in a state unbefitting a governor by royal appointment.

It all came to an end one sunny March morning that recalled the unique light of the city in springtime. Lisbon was so beautiful on the morning he boarded the *Zaire* and said goodbye to those who had gathered in his hour of need: half a dozen of the usual friends, the two women who looked after his home and who were entrusted with it in his absence, and the Director General at the Ministry for the Colonies (the Minister busy preparing for a debate in Parliament that afternoon). The King sent a messenger to the jetty with a brief note thanking him for his 'patriotic gesture' and wishing him the greatest good fortune in fulfilling the mission he had entrusted to him.

And that was that: the Fatherland, his world, started slowly to fade into the background as the *Zaire* slipped away from the Doca da Fundicão and steered to avoid the Bugio Sands. Lisbon was soon an insignificant dot on the horizon. Leaning over the side, looking without really seeing, he caressed the wooden balustrade as if he were caressing his past disappearing over the horizon. A cold blast from the open sea suddenly made him shiver and retreat to his cabin, where he was greeted by a complete selection of the morning newspapers. The Lisbon dailies, bringing news of a world of which he was longer a part.

5

AFTER STOPS AT Mindelo, where he had been before, and Sal, on the Cabo Verde archipelago, Luanda loomed on the horizon like a genuine metropolis. A dozen towering steamers were anchored out in the bay or by the jetties, and the port was bustling, teeming with men loading and unloading, doing deals, meeting and bidding farewell. It was difficult to imagine their colonial army fighting against tribes whose weapons were bows and spears, in a vast territory the boundaries of which the Portuguese had only begun to establish some twenty years earlier when the Conference of Berlin adopted the principle that effective possession of territory prevailed over the right that came from discovery. Angola was ten times bigger than Portugal, a hundred times bigger than São Tomé and Príncipe. Its effective colonisation, as with Mozambique, seemed a task beyond the physical, human and financial possibilities of a country as small as Portugal. For years, Britain and Germany had secretly connived to get their respective hands on a slice of the Portuguese Empire, the excuse being the country's desperate situation that they proposed to help by giving loans against the mortgaging of the two colonies. As opinions were divided, Dom Carlos managed to impose his will and the poisoned chalice was rejected and he took advantage instead of the outbreak of the Boer War and the English need to use the port of Beira in Mozambique to disembark to negotiate the Treaty of Windsor. Suddenly, a Britain that had scoffed at Portuguese pretensions to a 'pink-coloured map' and conspired with Germany to summarily liqui-date Lisbon's Empire, now recognised Portugal as its 'oldest ally' and solemnly committed itself to use the Royal Navy, if neces-sary, to help Portugal defend her overseas possessions.

But the British were in Angola in force. Livingstone travelled through Luanda on his way back to London, after one of his journeys in search of the source of the Nile. The Royal Geographical Society, which financed his voyages, was careful to omit his meeting in the depths of Angola with Serpa Pinto, the Portuguese explorer, asserting, on the contrary, that he met no other European in the boundless Angolan jungle. In Luanda there was a resident British minister, a consul, maritime agents, a military attaché and two itinerant agents, whose unofficial function was to oversee the effective prohibition of the slave trade.

In the hullabaloo of their arrival on the jetty, Luís Bernardo heard English being spoken and turned round just in time to see two elegant ladies moving off in the company of a gentleman wearing a white pith helmet and giving orders to the men carrying their hand baggage in a tone that revealed his familiarity with the locality.

Luís was met on the quayside by the secretary to the Governor, who rapidly saw to all the arrangements for his luggage. His Excellency the Governor could not come in person, as he would have wished, as he had to see to urgent business, but he was expecting him at his residence, where he was obviously a welcome guest for the two brief days of his stay. They drove in an open car (one of the very few cars) through the din on the main streets and the haze of dust that hung like a curtain over the city. They soon began to leave the centre behind, the animals, all manner of vehicle and hundreds of shops and stalls: tailors', butchers', barbers', bicycle repairers', dressmakers', quack doctors', grocers', and chemists' promising an instant cure for diarrhoea and 'other tummy upsets'. Luís Bernardo was half groggy, still feeling the ground move under him as if still on deck, and now at the mercy of the heat and humidity. They proceeded down the long, half-empty avenues of the European quarter, its pavements lined with trees. The secretary to the Governor took advantage of the respite to give him two telegrams that had arrived from Lisbon.

The first was from Matilde and was totally unexpected. He had never received a reply to his farewell letter to her, or any other message from her via João. He read the telegram twice, not really knowing what to think. On the one hand, it seemed strange to him now so far away; on the other, it was reassuring to receive it here, where everything felt alien and hostile. It was like an outstretched hand, a kiss, a bond from across the sea. She had written it nine days ago, the day of his departure: 'I learned from João that you had set sail. It was the best way to find out. I pray God protects you. Matilde.' A ridiculous tear came to his eye, triggered by the dust, nostalgia for the Lisbon light and the uncertainty of what awaited him. It was not because he was remembering Matilde's face, hair or body, or her voice sighing, 'Oh, my love!' as she held him tight.

The second telegram was official, on headed notepaper from the Ministry, and was signed by its Secretary General:

I am honoured to inform Your Excellency that on the 19th of this month I took responsibility for this ministry that is now designated for the Navy and the Colonies, General Ayres d'Ornellas e Vasconcelos STOP I inform you more-over the British Minister has instructed us that Mr David Jameson has been appointed British Consul to São Tomé and Príncipe, a member of the Indian Civil Service, former Governor in the British Province of Assam STOP He will take up post in the first week of June, ship and definitive date to be notified STOP Request prepare suitable permanent residence and political framework according to instructions sent STOP New minister sends best wishes for success in mission entrusted Your Exc.

Oh, Lisbon, the tentacles of Lisbon and its tireless political activity! Fancy that, he thought, I leave Lisbon with one minister and, before I take up my post, the Minister has already changed! At least nobody could say the new one wasn't right for the job: Ayres d'Ornellas was one of Mouzinho's generals in his Mozambique campaign and was well-acquainted with the problems of the Overseas Territories. Who knows, with him as Minister perhaps Luís Bernardo would never have been sent to govern São Tomé – just a matter of ten days, a mere ten days . . .?

The Governor of Angola was also nervous about the appoint-ment of the new Minister, but unlike Luís Bernardo was more concerned about keeping himself in post.

'You know we have a new Minister?' he asked, not even giving him time to sit down, let alone a proper welcome. 'These constant changes at the Ministry always bring confusion and paralysis. Until the new Minister familiarises himself with the issues, we will receive no advice, and won't know what he wants. Though, mark me, I am not referring to the person of General Ayres, whom I respect highly. I think it would have been difficult to make a better choice. But think of the time, dear fellow, one wastes on such things, the uncertainty, precisely when what one needs here is certainty, a principled policy and not one subject to the whims of Lisbon politicians. We govern thinking of the years ahead and they only think of the next few months. You, for example, my dear fellow, do you think the instructions you bring from the previous Minister still apply?'

Luís Bernardo stared at him, as if he had just been asked the most extraordinary question. He found the man's appearance distinctly unpleasant – short, balding, beady brown eyes, and a sweat-stained face and chest. His manner was that of a little dictator continually suggesting his own superior knowledge of the context and his keen insights based on experience. He fitted exactly the profile of the colonial civil servant Luís Bernardo had lambasted in his own writing. Could he be aware of that?

He decided to reply straightforwardly to the man's irritating question.

'Well, I suppose you must know that I was chosen directly by His Majesty the King and first received my instructions from him. And that they have been confirmed moreover by the new Minister, in a telegram your secretary has just given me.'

'Well, of course, that is greatly reassuring. You know, what people are saying is that you are the man the King chose to stand up to the Englishman being sent to São Tomé. You speak fluent English, I believe?'

Luís Bernardo detected a change of tone. The Governor of Angola had stopped treating him as a colleague and was now looking down on him, as if he were saying, 'I'm the professional at this game, you're a mere interpreter. I govern a continent in Africa, you're going to govern two cocoa warehouses in the mid-Atlantic.

Luís Bernardo nodded, yes, he did speak English.

'My dear chap, it is sometimes as well to pretend one does not speak English that well. One should not converse too much with such people. Either they shout or one pretends not to hear them. At any rate, it is good they understand we are the ones still in command of our colonies. I'm sure you must agree with me . . .'

'Of course, that's self-evident,' Luís Bernardo quickly concurred.

'But you know it is not as self-evident as you might think. These fellows come here to invoke treaties and agreements they signed with us and reckon they have the right to stick their noses in everywhere.'

'The Treaty of 1842 . . .' Luís Bernardo referred to the treaty signed with England, as a result of which the English were authorised to inspect Portuguese vessels coming from Africa when they suspected the transporting of slaves.

'That and other things. They want to stick their noses everywhere. We've got the English on all sides in Luanda, and outside Luanda they have informers reporting on everything happening in the province. But what would happen if we decided to inspect British vessels taking blacks from Accra to their colonies in the Caribbean!'

'Nobody suspects they are slaves . . .'

'Really? And why not? My dear chap, you've only just arrived and, forgive me for saying this, but I've lived in Africa for several years and know this much: a black who leaves here for São Tomé knows as much about where he is headed as one leaving the Gold Coast for Jamaica. There is absolutely no difference.'

'How many left here for São Tomé last year?'

Luís Bernardo asked the question, and then wished he hadn't. The other man looked at him askance, as if he didn't trust him.

'I am sure you know the number: four thousand or so. They were all registered and had work-permits issued in São Tomé.'

'Work contracts with a finishing date?'

'What contracts? That depends on you in São Tomé and that's why you have a commissioner whose job it is to see to that. I don't get involved in these matters and would like you to be clear on this point: the Angolan government does not contract anyone to go

70

anywhere, likewise with the government of São Tomé and the government of the realm. I merely check which citizens of the Portuguese territory of Angola want to work or embark or spend holidays in the Portuguese territory of São Tomé and Príncipe and, as there is free movement between Portuguese territories, I leave the matter there, for I cannot countermand a business agreement freely entered into by individuals and private companies.'

'But Your Excellency just said they didn't have the slightest idea about where they were going . . .'

'Please, I beg you, my friend, stop addressing me as Your Excellency and listen: it isn't my problem; it's yours. I am just telling you how things are and hope it comes as no surprise. Now if you think São Tomé can continue to exploit its cocoa planta- tions and enjoy the profits that ensue without importing blacks from our jungle who are not the faintest use here, that is your business. You must speak to the plantation owners and they will inform me if they do not wish me to send any more. You know the instructions you bring from Lisbon and the King. In relation to São Tomé, I will do what is asked of me. If it is for the good of the country, as has been the case so far, to satisfy São Tomé's labour needs, I do what I can and I don't infringe any laws. If you think it is different now, I repeat, you only have to tell me.'

'No, of course not!' Luís Bernardo felt he should beat a tactical retreat. 'It is obvious that São Tomé will need to import labour for many years to come and, even if that isn't the case, it is about doing things properly. Because, as you well know, this conflict with the British, the accusation made by Liverpool and Birming- ham merchants that we export slave labour from Angola to São Tomé, is damaging us in the British press and with British public opinion and, if it continues, we risk seeing a boycott imposed on our cocoa exports to the British market and then to the American market and that would be a tragedy for São Tomé. It would be the end of the colony.'

The Governor of Angola looked straight at him: it was a shifty, devious look.

'Hmm . . .'

He got up and went over to the open balcony window and stood and looked at his garden for a few moments, a tiny man contemplating the continent of Africa. Then he swung round on his heels and glared at Luís Bernardo. He leaned back on the balcony, hands clasped over his belly, a tropical Napoleon sizing up the enemy.

'The English! The arrogant, hypocritical English! So civilised, so concerned, who can't tell a black from a yellow man! Tell me, Valença, when did an Englishman ever fuck a black woman? No! But we do, like anything. Do you know how we settle and occupy this huge land that is Angola? Not through the army, which shoots, and then clears off. Not through the families of settlers – where is the lunatic who would take his wife and children into the thick of the jungle, where there is no sign of civilisation? No, that is not how *we* do it! Do you know how *we* settle this place?'

'No, do tell me.'

'With poor wretches from the Minho and the Alentejo, with a motley crew from Trás-os-Montes who land here without a place to drop dead and we the government offer them title deeds. We offer title deeds to poor devils who can't even read, who don't even know where the property is. But the land belongs to them, people who've never owned a cent in their lives! And the hapless fellows set out, God knows how, and ask where the Nova Esperança farm is in the Uíge District or Paraíso farm in Northern Quanza. And if, by some miracle, they arrive safely and take possession of what's impenetrable jungle, if they manage to survive and plant potatoes or sell trinkets to the blacks, how do they get a family? Well, their family is the black women they buy from the local village chief, a sack of beans for a woman, a pig for two. A priest, marriage, registered children? Good God! It's about survival and the poor beggars feel very happy if they've one, two or three black women to call their own because they know they'll never get out of that hole. We the government are very pleased we've got destitute peasants to go and live in the jungle. All we ask is that they teach their mulatto offspring to speak Portuguese! That is how *we* are populating the interior of Angola. Everything else is fine for treaties and conversations in diplomatic drawing rooms. But I would like to see an Englishman, in his white flannels from Savile Row, living on a shitty Nova Esper-

72

ança farm, turning to his black wife and asking, "Oh, would you care for a gin and tonic, my dear?" – you see, I can also get by in English.' The Governor of Angola shut up and looked smugly down at his guest.

He had been eloquent, devastatingly eloquent. Luís Bernardo was silenced and embarrassed, even quite upset. My God, what am I doing here, what's all this got to do with me, this little Napoleon of the tropics, these peasants with their black concubines in the jungle, this humidity and foul heat, the savagery one senses everywhere and in everybody, whether white, black or English?

'Do you know, my dear fellow?' The Governor started up again, confident of his victory, relishing the impact his speech was having on Luís Bernardo. 'Do you know who best dealt with the British, who really took them seriously? It was my illustrious predecessor in this post, General Calheiros e Menezes. You have heard of him, I trust?'

Luís Bernardo nodded. General Calheiros e Menezes was a mythical figure for the São Tomé plantation owners; their correspondence was in the portfolio he'd been given by the Ministry in Lisbon. In 1862 twenty years after signing the treaty with Britain, British inspectors in Angola went to the Governor and complained that Portuguese ships were dedicated to trading in and transporting slaves from the Angolan jungle to the plantations of São Tomé and Príncipe in flagrant violation of the 1842 Treaty. Calheiros e Menezes wrote in reply, rehearsing the usual arguments: that the would-be slaves were all free men or freed men; that they were paid and could return when they wished, although it was quite clear they preferred to stay in São Tomé rather than return to the savage state in which they used to live in Angola. They all had proper papers and a passport, and legally speaking they were simply workers migrating from one part of the territory of Portugal to another. While he was about it, the General asked the British why they didn't inspect the French vessels that were quite openly and freely transporting slaves from Guinea to the Caribbean. The British counter-attacked, recalling they had not signed a treaty with France, but had done so with Portugal and, backed by that treaty, were demanding the transportation of Angolans to the islands of São Tomé and Príncipe be halted. Calheiros e Menezes stuck firmly to his guns and returned the letter they had sent to him with a note to the effect that in the future any 'information' he received from them he'd investigate through the offices of the British Consul. In the meantime, to satisfy the persistent demands from the island plantation owners, who had seen their population of black labourers decimated by a smallpox epidemic years before, the General speeded up the dispatch of workers, whether slaves or not, to São Tomé. Anticipating the complaints of the British to Lisbon, he explained to the Minister: 'So that Your Excellency can appreciate the sacrifices the urgent need for labour imposes on São Tomé landowners, I must point out that, as they cannot take on blacks as slaves or freed men, they are engaging at onerous cost free men, and even buying slaves to whom they give their freedom, transporting them as free men, with the risk that once in São Tomé they will forget the freedom they were given in Angola and only work for those offering the best pay. Such measures deserve all the help we can give.'

As a result of pressure from the British, Calheiros e Menezes was removed from his post after seventeen months as Governor of Angola and the 'transfers' were cut back, first to four blacks per ship, and then to none. This led the then Minister for the Colonies to send workers to São Tomé from other Portuguese colonies: from Mozambique and even from faraway Macao, in the Sea of China! When sufficient time had passed to cool off the British, everything returned to normal and Angola resumed its role as the main exporter of labour to São Tomé.

Nothing had changed in almost forty-five years. The facts remained the same as did the justifications that were invoked. A lawyer by training, Luís Bernardo recognised the sophisticated legal architecture erected to buttress arguments invoked almost half a century ago by the Portuguese: what right did a foreign nation have to interfere with the movement of Portuguese citizens, who changed their place of residence and work within Portuguese territory? If Portuguese from Minho happened to migrate to the Algarve (as some had in earlier times) what right did Britain have to point the finger? Now, Portugal was the Minho

74

and the Algarve as well as Angola, Mozambique, Macao and São Tomé. And how could the blacks be thought of as slaves when they had been saved from slavery by São Tomé landowners who paid the asking price to the people who had kept them as slaves in the depths of the Angolan jungle, where the rule of law barely penetrated, and then took them to work in São Tomé and provided them with food, lodging, medical care and pay? But could a slave who became a free man in exchange for immediate transportation to work far from his land and family, with no sense that that was what he really wanted, be judged to be free?

There were too many questions with too many fuzzy answers. There were moments when it all seemed a legal sleight of hand and word games rather than clarity. But exhaustion, torpor and intellectual indolence seemed to take its toll as he neared his destination, and what had seemed crystal-clear in Lisbon when conversing with friends in cafés, commenting on the news in the papers and listening to the opinions of others was no longer so. Luís Bernardo was and would always be a man with rigid convictions when it came to important matters. He was against slavery and in favour of colonising carried out via modern, civilised methods – for that alone could guarantee, in the twentieth century, the right of possession that was predicated on discovery or conquest. He believed, as the American Constitution stated, that all men were born free and equal, and that only intelligence, talent and effort – along with luck – could make any legitimate difference. But, he wondered, was Britain really worried about slavery or was she simply protecting her own business interests in her colonies? Did the British, French or Dutch treat their blacks better than the Portuguese, or was it mere hypocrisy behind which the strongest imposed its rule?

He still had a few days to reflect on these matters as the *Zaire* went down the coast of Angola, anchored for half a day in Benguela and sailed along Moçâmedes, before turning westwards on the final strait to its destination. The long, monotonous hours he spent watching the Angolan coast pass by gave him some idea of how vast and different that land was from São Tomé. Angola was one million two hundred and forty-six thousand seven hundred square kilometres,

São Tomé eight hundred and thirty-four square kilometres, and Príncipe one hundred and twenty-seven square kilometres. Just forty-five thousand blacks lived on the two islands on the Equator, almost all imported from Angola, and almost fifteen hundred whites – around thirteen hundred on São Tomé and no more than two hundred on Príncipe. Luís Bernardo reckoned five hundred of the whites worked managing or administering the plantations, another two hundred in public administration, the police and the armed forces, and some thirty were traders, priests, or in other occupations; the remainder were women and children. In comparison, Angola had half a million inhabitants in the coastal districts of Luanda, Lobito, Benguela and Moçâmedes and a number that was difficult to calculate in its huge, largely unexplored interior – another two million perhaps.

While Angola had several sources of wealth, Sao Tomé was dependent on two products, coffee and cocoa – of which it produced thirty thousand tons annually, as opposed to Accra, which produced eighteen thousand tons and the Cameroons, three thousand, only just behind Bahia which produced thirty-three thousand tons annually, though the quality was much inferior to the São Tomé harvest. Angola was all potential, its wealth yet to be explored and realised; São Tomé had discovered its vein and was rich and self-sufficient as a result of that single resource – cocoa.

Beyond this, there was almost nothing on the island of São Tomé. There was not a single car and, subsequently, not a metre of road. The best way to transport cocoa from the plantations to the city was by the coastal cutters that some plantations owned. There was only public lighting in the capital and its centre: oil-lamps working on oil imported from Russia. There was no livestock farming or fishing fleet even at a basic level. There was a telegraph service, which operated only from post offices, and fifty-two telephones. These were for exclusively internal use and thirty-four belonged to the administration – perhaps so civil servants could phone to say they were on their way home for lunch. There was no factory or industry worthy of the name, beyond the drying and packaging of cocoa. There was no theatre, cinema, concert hall or town band. Luís Bernardo, who had read the complete list of imports to the islands over the last twenty years, knew that a single piano existed on the island, imported the previous year by the husband of some nostalgic lady.

But what really distressed him was not this lack of distraction, but that he was required to live three years on this small island, adrift in the vastness of the ocean, surrounded by virgin jungle, where everything would be frustratingly similar every day. He could see why until forty years ago São Tomé was the penal colony Portugal favoured for the worst criminals from the realm.

6

T HE *ZAIRE* CAST anchor in the Bay of Ana Chaves, opposite
the city, about five hundred metres from the quayside that
protected the seafront avenue from the Atlantic waves. The city of
São Tomé had neither harbour nor mooring jetty: freight and
passengers were transported to land in ordinary rowing boats,
which in rough sea made that short crossing riskier than the
journey across the ocean.

Like all the passengers and crew, Luís Bernardo leaned on the
rail and contemplated the city and human commotion next to the
jetty. The *Zaire* had greeted land with three strident whistle-blasts
that must have been audible over the entire island, the traditional
way to signal 'Governor aboard'. The response came from land:
three whistle-blasts from the Garrison and a salvo of seventeen
shots from the Fortress of Saint Sebastian. It suddenly seemed as if
the whole city were converging on the jetty.

Luís Bernardo, the 41st Governor of São Tomé and Príncipe
and São João Baptista de Ajudá observed the spectacle with uneasy
fascination. He got his luggage ready and entrusted it to his servant
on board, and now prepared to disembark with the pomp and
ceremony the occasion demanded. He could see almost the
whole city, to his left the Government Palace, the most visible,
imposing building, looking down on a great spacious square. Palm
trees on the main avenue opposite swayed in the wind and more
than anything else reminded Luís Bernardo he was in Africa, even
though on the high seas at the Equator. But, in the background,
the tiled roofs reminded him he was in Portuguese territory and,
though he was apprehensive, the sight made Luís Bernardo feel
strangely at home. He was intoxicated by the suffocating smell of
chlorophyll coming from land, enervated by the dank humidity in
the air, and distressed by the din from the crowd waiting for him
on the jetty. He looked at his watch: it was half past twelve. An

hour behind Lisbon, he thought, before striving to put aside such thoughts. He sighed deeply, looked all around, to the mountains shrouded in damp mist, and looked back, whispering enthusiastically, 'I'm going to enjoy this! I'm going to love this!'

The flower-bedecked boat to carry him ashore moored next to the *Zaire* and everybody on board waited for him to make the first move. He stepped decisively towards the ship's gangway, where the Captain was waiting for him.

'My mission finishes here. Now it is your turn.'

'You're not coming ashore?'

'No, we shall stay here only a couple of hours and I know this place well. I will use the time to sort out my paperwork.'

'Goodbye, Captain. I thank you for looking after me so well.'

'It was my pleasure, sir. I wish you luck – you're going to need it.'

He bid him farewell with a firm handshake and went down to the gig from the *Zaire* with as much dignity and aplomb as he could muster.

As soon as he was on dry land, a small-built fellow walked towards him, wearing a black suit, waistcoat, tie and white shirt, the collar of which was drenched in sweat. He looked in his early forties and introduced himself as Agostinho de Jesus Júnior, Secretary General to the Governor. Fourteen years on São Tomé, 'And Your Excellency is the fourth Governor I am honoured to serve'. He exuded sweat, respect, languor and adaptability. He was clearly one of those Portuguese who'd come to Africa driven by dreams and ambition and who had stayed on, their ambitions tamed and their dreams transformed into a fleeting recognition of the impossible distance separating them from the Fatherland. The Agostinhos of this world never returned from Africa.

The Secretary General took Luís Bernardo and introduced him to the other whites who were lined up according to their position in the hierarchy of the island's pillars of society. They were the Deputy Governor on the island of Príncipe, a young man in his thirties, who seemed nervous and pleasant enough, by the name of António Vieira; Monsignor José Atalaia followed by the Bishop of Luanda, a man with sweaty hands and a sly look who was at that moment sopping wet under his white soutane; Jerónimo Carvalho da Silva, Mayor of São Tomé, an appointee of the Minister for the Colonies, bald as a coot, eager and ready 'for whatever Your Excellency requires'; Artillery Major Benjamim das Neves, Commander of the Garrison on São Tomé and Príncipe; Captain José Valadas Duarte, second in command, and Captain José Arouca, head of the National Guard; the Crown Commissioner for São Tomé and Príncipe, official representative of black contract labour on the plantations and man of influence, Germano André Valente, thin as a rake, aloof, greeting him with half a dozen well-chosen words of welcome. Luís Bernardo looked straight at him but he remained deadpan, preferring to look at anything but the new Governor. Then came the Commissioner for Public Health, a rather sickly youth in his early twenties, clearly a trainee sent from Lisbon; the Judge, Dr Anselmo de Sousa Teixera, on the other hand a robust fifty-year-old; the Public Prosecutor, Dr João Patrício, yellow-skinned, his face unpleasantly pitted by smallpox, and the two lawyers on the island – the aged Dr Segismundo Bruto da Silva, who also acted as notary and keeper of the Civil and Property Register and who looked like a man for all seasons; and the extraordinary attorney for litigants who went by the impossible name of Dr Lancelote da Torre e do Lago, clad in a garish lettuce-green suit, lilac tie and dark-red straw hat. After officialdom came the representatives of civil society: the President of the Traders' Association of São Tomé and owner of Faria the Chemist's, the best-known commercial establishment of the city, island and colony, Mr António Maria Faria; two or three heavyweight merchants; two doctors, a public works and hydraulic engineer; two priests and, finally, a dozen administrators of the island's most important plantations, whose names he didn't catch, let alone retain.

'Welcome, Governor, sir', 'Delighted to meet you', 'Congratulations, Governor, sir', 'May you be really happy on São Tomé' – everyone greeted him with a polite formula, some genuinely, others curiously, others suspiciously. But he thanked them all equally and tried to concentrate on the impossible task of remembering all their names, respective faces and posts.

These introductions lasted a good half-hour in the full midday heat. A military band then struck up the national anthem and a military contingent marched by, comprising two battalions of eighty men, one made up of men from the metropolis and another of indigenous recruits, led by ensigns and under marching orders from two Portuguese sergeants. Sweat was now streaming down his head, neck and chest. His shirt stuck to his skin and his cream alpaca Savile Row suit had lost the discreet elegance and intended allure. He was exhausted, made drowsy by the intoxicating smell of greenery that made the atmosphere even heavier and more humid. He didn't know whether he could continue and was even afraid he might faint on the jetty, in the middle of that symbolically important event.

'If Your Excellency would like to follow me . . .' The Secretary General indicated with his hand where he should now walk.

And Luís Bernardo began to walk along the pontoon, holding himself as erectly as he could, nodding and smiling left and right, not really knowing where he was headed. He felt unhappy and ridiculous in the organised confusion, maddening heat and steaming humidity. At the end of the pontoon was a waiting carriage driven by two small horses, with a flunkey seated in front, wearing ridiculous grey livery. He flopped on to his seat, with an ill-disguised sense of relief, and asked his faithful shadow, always trailing a pace behind, 'What now?'

'If Your Excellency thinks fit, we shall ride to the Palace, where His Honour the Governor can rest after his journey until he wishes to receive me in his office.'

'Let us be going then.'

And they departed, flanked by a small crowd, who peered at him as if he were a strange animal in their neck of the woods. Luís Bernardo made a move that visibly shocked Mr Agostinho de Jesus Júnior and went against all the traditions of protocol. He got up, took off his jacket, placed it on his seat, loosened his collar and undid the knot to his tie. After that, he sat down again and smiled at all around who stared at him from the roadside unblinking, as if his every gesture should be recorded for posterity.

He leaned back in his seat and, suddenly much relieved, also smiled at Agostinho, at his side.

'Keep repeating the names of the streets, my man, so I get used to them . . .'

They went along Avenida Marginal, where the Customs House stood out, and then right into the Rua Conde de Valle Flor, which seemed to be the liveliest in the city. They continued down Matheus Sampaio, on the corner of which Agostinho pointed out the Elite Brewery, 'the most visited in the city', as if there were many alternatives, he thought to himself. Alberto Garrido on the Rua do Comércio was just beginning to resume its usual activity, now that many of its customers were returning from the jetties where they'd gone to welcome the new Governor.

They came out on to the Praça General Calheiros with its delightful bandstand, followed by the street of the same name and two of the city's main landmarks, the Casa Vista Alegre and Faria the Chemist's. The road came to an end in front of the ugliest of cathedrals, which dominated the horizon. Then came a new square, with two buildings opposite each other: the Town Hall, a square, brown, rather graceless structure and the building that housed the court and post office, a beautiful cream-painted colonial building with faded blue Venetian windows, open on the first floor, and a tile-covered porch that cast a shadow over the entrance and ground floor.

They then turned down a long avenue flanked on the right by the municipal marketplace, which was almost deserted at that time of day, and began to move away from the centre and houses and people became a rare sight. The horses broke into trot down the avenue and, without his Secretary General needing to announce the fact, Luís Bernardo saw his destination, the end of his journey: the Government Palace on his right, at a point where the avenue swung leftwards, creating a kind of bend in the road facing the sea. It was a rather forlorn square with patches of garden, and on the right the Palace, in the middle the bandstand, on the left the sea, beyond a stone wall that snaked along the coast.

The avenue disappeared round the bend, apparently following the line of the sea away from the city that by this stage had almost vanished. Luís Bernardo looked on, still unsure what to think: his new residence was a sturdy, strangely designed building, a broken line that did not neatly fit the main façade. It was on two floors and painted almost the same shade of brown as the Town Hall, but brighter and slightly ochre, and the corners and big pointed windows were finished in white. Railings ran round a heavily planted garden and a sentry box denoted an opening in the middle of the railings, which acted as the main point of entry. It was through this point that Luís Bernardo now entered in order to assume his mandate.

Another welcome committee – the Palace servants – was lined up by the door. Dressed in white cotton, gilt buttons gleaming, a tall, broad-shouldered black man walked towards him; he must have been nearly sixty and his almost white hair was beginning to thin.

Once again Agostinho made the introductions.

'This is Sebastião, the head servant, who will be a sort of officer under Your Excellency's orders. Sebastião started here as a young boy, as a porter, and has been here . . . how long is it now, Sebastião?'

'Thirty-two years, Mr Agostinho.'

'So how old are you?' asked Luís Bernardo.

'I am forty-one, Governor, sir.'

He looked twenty years older, but Luís Bernardo appreciated his open, winning smile, and noted two rows of dazzlingly white teeth, and bright, friendly eyes that communicated an immediate feeling of warmth.

Luís Bernardo also smiled broadly and held out his hand.

'Very pleased to meet you, Sebastião. I am sure we will get on well.' There was a moment of hesitation as Luís Bernardo stood with one hand hanging in the void.

Sebastião looked askance at the Secretary General, whose momentary embarrassment did not escape the newcomer's notice. Then he quickly came to a decision and shook Luís Bernardo's hand, mumbling a 'Very pleased to meet you, Governor, sir' and the formality of that greeting soon vanished in the smile from his lips and eyes. He immediately introduced his small contingent of servants: Mamoun, the cook, and Sinhá, his wife and helper; Doroteia, the maid for his rooms and 'outside', responsible for the Governor's wardrobe, a young black beauty with a body like a palm tree and a timid gaze; Tobias, the coachman and stable boy, who had driven them in the carriage from the jetty; and Vicente, Sebastião's godson, who worked as a porter and jack of all trades. Luís Bernardo greeted them all with a nod and a few polite words, to which they responded by bowing their heads and staring at the ground.

The Secretary General then explained that the Governor's rooms were on the top floor, except for the room for audiences or balls on the ground floor, which one entered by a side door. The Government Secretariat was downstairs where his own desk would be and where Agostinho de Jesus and a dozen civil servants worked every day. As soon as His Excellency the Governor honoured him with a visit to the ground-floor installations and welcomed him in his office, he would introduce the civil servants employed at the Government Secretariat. But, for now, he presumed His Excellency wanted to rest awhile, have a bath and something to eat. He would leave His Excellency to his devices until His Excellency summoned him, even if it were outside working hours, since he lived very close by. Luís Bernardo agreed with alacrity and stood by the door and watched him slowly leave.

The servants had all gone back inside with the exception of Sebastião, who waited for him by the door. Luís Bernardo remained outside for a moment, looking at the empty square and listening to the sound of the distant city. It continued to smell intensely of jungle, but the humidity had dropped considerably and blue sky was now appearing through the haze. There was even a light salty breeze coming from the sea and that made everything seem suddenly extraordinarily calm. And, for the first time in ages, the anguish that filled him whenever he thought of São Tomé and Príncipe gave way to a sudden, incomprehensible joy that surprised him like a piece of good news. He turned and walked inside, saying, 'Come on then, Sebastião, show me round the house!'

Great quantities of the finest island woods had been used in the house – *cambala, jaca, cipó* and *ocá* – in the entrance, the upper floor, the panelled doors and French windows, the balconies and even the flooring. The uniform tone was dark brown, worn and softened by decades of wax polish, and he noticed how it did not squeak underfoot but sounded solid like antique hardwood. The house spread out in three directions from the lobby: to the left, bedrooms; opposite, seawards, the main reception room; and to the right, the kitchen and servants' quarters. The main room acted as a reception area, with furniture that was predictably adequate for the needs of the Governor of Portugal's smallest overseas possession. The colour of the upholstery on the two maple armchairs and sofas had faded from old rose to merely old; the huge mirror in a carved frame occupying half of a side wall now merely reflected attenuated shadows in between stains from years of damp, and the chandelier in the ceiling seemed straight from an auction of a middle-class Lisbon family's furniture. Generally speaking, nothing matched and the only saving grace was the sea beyond the two enormous open windows that reached down to the ground. To the side, there was a small, much more appealing little room, and that was where Luís told Sebastião to put the table and gramophone he'd brought from Lisbon.

In the opposite direction, next to the reception room, was the official banqueting room, which, unlike the reception room, was rather simple and attractive: a long wooden table was the single piece of furniture, with a seating capacity for thirty, framed on one side by the same balcony windows over the sea and, on the other side, by a mural, representing a dinner on a plantation with its Casa Grande, slave huts and white overseer ordering blacks around, and a forest of cocoa trees as the backdrop. A rectangular wooden structure bearing a stitched cloth, like a lateen sail, hung over the table: levered by a servant on each side of the table, it worked as a huge fan to keep guests cool during the meal, which, Luís Bernardo later remarked, was an essential attribute in the house of every plantation manager and an indispensable symbol of social status. Between the dining room and kitchen there was a pantry with cupboards full of china from floor to ceiling, namely, the two services that were the property of the Palace, and a single window over a small veranda, also pointing seawards. Luís Bernardo ordered a table for four people to be put there and told Sebastião it was there and not in the huge dining room that he would eat all his meals, breakfast included.

He also proceeded to make changes to the bedrooms. There were three, the biggest of which was huge, with sea views, a double bed made of *pausanto* wood and two Indo-Portuguese pieces of furniture he loathed. He scorned the master bedroom and decided to move into two small bedrooms at the back overlooking the Palace garden, from where the cries of strange birds would serve him well as a natural early morning alarm clock. Adjacent was a fine bathroom with a zinc bath. But it had no running water, and a makeshift shower that worked with water from a fifty-litre tank he himself had to activate by yanking on a steel chain. It was Doroteia's job to fill the tank or bath with cold or warm water, according to his orders.

After these arrangements were complete, Luís Bernardo sat down for a moment's rest in the lobby opposite the reception rooms that faced away from the sun. He accepted Sebastião's offer of pineapple juice, lit a cigarette, and contemplated the bay, with its scant movement of boats, half of which now loaded up the *Zaire*, that was already preparing to raise anchor. He fought off his drowsiness, finding the strength to visit the kitchen and exchange a few words with Mamoun and Sinhá on the subject of his culinary preferences. He learned how the Governor's Palace had its own land outside the city, which supplied fresh fruit and vegetables every day. It also had a farm for breeding its own pigs, chickens, turkeys and ducks, and fish from the market was fresh, abundant and cheap. There was excellent coffee from the island; everything else came regularly from Angola: rice, flour, sugar and, when ordered, beef. In that respect, even for a gourmet used to eating as well as he was, prospects seemed more than adequate. Nevertheless, upsetting the general expectations in the kitchen for a grand welcome, he ordered them to bring only scrambled eggs and bread, very strong coffee and a big glass of water, to be served on the veranda. Fifteen minutes later, when he had taken a cold shower and put on clean clothes, he sat down on the veranda to be served for the first time by Sebastião, who was very confident in his own role, and visibly saddened by the lunch's lack of substance, in terms of food and formality.

He stood there quietly and attentively watching Luís Bernardo as he ate.

86

'Sebastião . . .'

'Yes, Governor, sir?'

'The first thing I have to say is that I do not want you to call me "Governor, sir" – it sounds as if you are talking to a monument, not to a person.'

'Yes, Boss.'

'No, Sebastião, "Boss" won't do either. How about if you address me as "Doctor"?'

'Yes, Doctor.'

'Good, let's agree something else while we're about it: when I am eating, you will only come when I call you. I can't eat with a statue peering down at me.'

'Yes, Doctor.'

'And, now, Sebastião, I feel like some conversation. So pull up a chair and sit down, because I don't like talking to someone who is standing up.'

'I should sit down, Boss?'

'Doctor. Yes, sit down there, come on!'

Sebastião reluctantly pulled up a chair and sat down a respectful distance away from Luís Bernardo's table, after he'd glanced round to make sure nobody was looking. He was evidently making an effort to understand and adjust to his new master.

'Tell me: what is your full name?'

'Sebastião Luís de Mascarenhas e Menezes.'

Luís Bernardo whistled softly, and stifled a desire to laugh out loud: his tropical butler, bereft on two bereft islands on the west coast of Africa, profoundly black by the grace of God and his daily sun, bore two of the most ancient and noble surnames of Portuguese stock. The Mascarenhas and the Menezes had not trod the wilds of Africa, where very few civilised people had gone, but the mythical plains of Goa and the Portuguese Province in India, where nobles of the Empire served from the sixteenth century. They had embarked with Vasco da Gama, fought with Alfonso de Albuquerque and Dom Francisco de Almeida, had been warriors and Jesuits, governors and viceroys and, of late, lawyers and builders. In each generation a Mascarenhas and a Menezes set sail, some stayed for ten or more years, others never returned and were buried in the cemeteries of Pangim, Diu or

Lautolim, where nowadays their gravestones were engraved in English: 'To the memory of our beloved . . .' Perhaps Sebastião was a grandson or great-great-great grandson of a Mascarenhas or a Menezes, whose ship had been wrecked somewhere off the African coast or the islands adrift on the Equator, on their way to India. Or had just inherited, as was sometimes the case with former slaves in Africa, the names of the planters who owned their ancestors. Or else he might be the descendant of a freed man – the first generation of inhabitants of the islands in the sixteenth century, the children of the first settlers who came from the metropolis and the first blacks who came from the continent, a local mulatto 'aristocracy', in fact, the first masters of the islands, though the latter may have started off life as the property of captains who received these distant, inhospitable possessions on the Equator as gifts from the Kings of Portugal, on the single condition that they settled, peopled and cultivated those lands. Luís Bernardo who at half past one had begun to look favourably on Sebastião, now viewed him even quite respectfully.

'Well, Sebastião, yours is an illustrious name . . .'

'That's so, Boss.'

'Doctor.'

'Sorry, Doctor. It is a name I inherited from my parents who came from Cabo Verde. But they told me it came from Goa.'

'Undoubtedly. Now tell me something else: are you married?'

'No, Doctor, I used to be but I'm a widower now. And have been for fifteen years.'

'And do you have any children?'

'Two, Doctor. One works on the Boa Entrada plantation, where he has a good responsible job in charge of the warehouse. The other's a girl – she's married and lives on Príncipe and I've not seen her for two years.'

'And you never remarried?'

'No, a wife is expensive and I'm happy here, I don't need a wife.'

'And is Mr Agostinho the Secretary General married?'

'Yes, he's married to a . . . lady from these parts.'

To a black woman, thought Luís Bernardo.

'But her father was Portuguese . . .' Sebastião hastened to add.

A mulatto, concluded Luís Bernardo.

'And does that make any difference here with the Portuguese?'

'Among whites, Doctor? Shouldn't it make a difference? White is white, and black is black, but a mulatto here doesn't kiss a hand or offer a hand to be kissed. It is best they stay put at home, you understand, Doctor?'

Luís Bernardo had eaten his eggs and drunk his coffee. He stretched out in his chair, and then got up with difficulty. He felt completely indolent, wanted to sway with the wind, follow orders, but certainly not give them.

'Tell me, Sebastião, when do people dine here?'

'Whenever the Boss wants. But it is usual to have dinner at around seven-thirty, after the rain.'

'After the rain? But does the rain always come at a particular time?'

'When it's not the dry season, it pours and always after sunset. Then, at around seven-thirty, it stops.'

'Very good: so dinner at seven-thirty. Here.'

'Not here, Doctor, Boss.'

'No Boss, Doctor. Why not?'

'Because of the mosquitoes. Sorry, Doctor.'

Luís Bernardo fought off his lethargy and told Vicente to inform Mr Agostinho de Jesus that in an hour's time he would go down to the ground floor to find out about the Government Secretariat. He then spent that hour unpacking and arranging his things, helped by Sebastião and Doroteia. While she was hanging his suits up in the wardrobes and bending down to arrange his shoes in his bedroom wardrobe, Luís Bernardo couldn't refrain from sizing her up from time to time, with the eyes of an interested connoisseur. She moved like the stem of a flower over water, her light, dancing gestures exposing parts of her dark-brown body and gleaming skin. The folds and openings of her yellow, floral cotton dress allowed the occasional glimpse of a firm, sweaty thigh, or the start of a breast that rose and trembled to the rhythm of her fiery breathing. When her gaze met his, Luís Bernardo caught a glint of wild innocence in the whites of her eyes and felt his heart leap and he had to look away: the hunter hunted.

He remembered his last conversations with João in Lisbon, when he had complained of the sexual abstinence he anticipated in voluntary exile on São Tomé, he a man so accustomed to the pleasures of women. And João replied, half seriously, half jokingly, 'You, I bet! At the end of a month, I promise you black women will seem mulatto, after two they'll seem dark-skinned white women and, after three, when you're in dire need, you'll think they're blue-eyed blondes!' Now, here he was, after three hours, greedily eying his chambermaid, whom nature had favoured with the body of a Greek goddess painted black.

He rushed out of his room annoyed with himself and cursing, 'Come on, Luís, you're the Governor here, not some passing visitor!'

Agostinho de Jesus Júnior had already known and served under three governors on São Tomé and Príncipe and São João Baptista de Ajudá. The first was a colonel, who owed his appointment to a political 'leg-up' and who thought he could disguise his monstrous stupidity by reciting formulas and performing ceremonies as incongruous as his own person. The second was a poor devil, an alcoholic widower who had nowhere to go on this earth and who, unlike the first, was at least honest enough never to take himself seriously. With him Agostinho learned how to govern from the wings, skilfully pulling the strings of petty intrigue in a petty palace – a fondness for which became second nature. But the third Governor was the epitome of a complete fool who fortunately went to die in Lisbon before the end of his mandate. After fourteen years of colonial service, two almost fatal attacks of malaria, a mulatto wife who was now fat and uninteresting and two late, toffee-coloured children, Agostinho de Jesus Júnior only craved to serve a governor who was normal and adaptable in a peaceful, untroubled mandate, and to wait for the years to go by until he could retire. Perhaps he had savings and energy enough to return to the Fatherland and buy a plot of land in the Minho: a small granite house, with a warm hearth for the winter and a patch of potatoes, where his fat wife could amuse herself while he spent his days playing dominoes in the village bar with his contemporaries, yielding from time to time, rather tetchily, to demands he should recount his African adventures – yet again. Oh, if only he could sleep without mosquitoes, without waking up soaked in sweat, could feel the cold again, a dry wind and four seasons in a year! And could forget this accursed place by the name of Africa and the years wasted looking out to sea and counting the coins for his return home. He knew the lives of many like himself who never wanted to return, who had penetrated the hinterland of Angola and Mozambique, opened up clearings in the middle of the jungle and sown seed in the new fields, enlisted in the army or public works, shacked up with black women and spread children all over, going native to such an extent that they forgot where they had come from or why they had come. But he was not of that ilk: he had hated that land from the moment he first stepped on it and there hadn't been a single day in the eternity of those fourteen years when he didn't look out to sea before getting into bed, wondering whether destiny would allow him the good fortune to return one day to where he had come from.

Agostinho was now feeling ill at ease, not knowing what to think or expect of his new governor. He seemed too young for the post and people on the island were saying he'd never been to Africa and had an 'intellectual's' ideas concerning the Overseas Territories. The way he'd taken his jacket off as he proceeded through the city and had greeted his butler with a handshake boded ill. Either he's a good-natured fellow or a bastard disguised as a good-natured fellow. Either hypothesis meant problems in the pipeline.

He received his summons to be in the Secretariat at five and arrived early to ensure, once again, that everything was spotless and in order for the new Governor. He had nothing to fear for everything was as it should be, yet he felt uneasy, preoccupied by something he couldn't rationally pin down.

He guided Luís Bernardo through the Secretariat's rooms and introduced him to its staff: a white man with a shrivelled face and feverish eyes, and ten São Tomeans, the most humble version of the most humble Portuguese civil servant, for whom to possess and wield an erasing rubber or stamp was to perform a service of the utmost responsibility on behalf of the Fatherland. Afterwards, they retired to the Governor's office and Agostinho de Jesus delivered a detailed inventory of the state of the colony's administration: the movement of personnel, enforcement of the budget, service orders in operation and to be implemented. There was also the state of repair of the patrimony and replacement of equipment, tax collection, public works programmes, relations and correspondence with the Ministry in Lisbon and Town Hall on the island, with the government representative on the Island of Príncipe, the administrator of the district of Benguela, in Angola, and with Angola's Governor General.

After an hour, Agostinho de Jesus seemed more enthusiastic and engrossed than ever, while Luís Bernardo drifted between drowsiness and nervousness expanding to explosion point.

He waited for him to pause, then stemmed the flow.

'Very good, Mr Agostinho, that's enough of that! Give me the dossiers to take away with me and I will study them when I've had a sleep. Now, let's get to the real point.'

'The real point?'

'That's right, politics here. You know, Agostinho, I am quite sure government administration, staff, finances, and taxes couldn't be in better hands than yours. And that will continue to be the case. You will manage day-to-day business, filling me in on the detail, and occasionally, let us say, every three months, we will sit down and you will bring me up to date with the situation. But you must understand I did not come here to see to all that, to look over the accounts from supplies, to see whether third desk should be promoted to second or a new horse should be bought to replace the old mare: if that were the case, I would have stayed at home, where that kind of problem was always beyond me. I want you to inform me on issues that concern my mission here: the political situation in the colony, the context in which people live and the real problems that exist. Do you understand me?'

No, clearly, the Secretary General did not, or preferred not, to understand what the Governor wanted. His mouth gradually opened, in what seemed genuine dismay, and he scratched the back of his head, unsure how to pick up the thread.

'The political situation, the context, Governor?'

'Yes, Mr Agostinho, that's right: the political situation and context. How would you describe them?'

'Well, Governor, everybody is busy working here with no time or inclination to bother about politics.'

'Everybody, who – the Portuguese?'

'Yes, of course, the Portuguese.'

'But, what about the blacks?'

'The blacks?' Agostinho de Jesus Júnior was taken aback or was the world's best actor.

'Yes, the blacks, Mr Agostinho. Are they happy with their conditions of work on the plantations? Do they intend to return to Angola when their contracts run out? Do you have any idea how many want to go back or how they will do so?' Luís Bernardo spoke as calmly as he could, trying to decipher whether the man was plain stupid or acting stupid.

'You know, Governor, it would be best for you to speak to the Crown Commissioner on this question. As you know, such matters are his concern. I live in the city and am responsible for the Secretariat, which does not get involved in such matters. Fortunately, if I may say so.'

'Yes, I will of course speak to the Commissioner as soon as I can. But I wanted you to tell me what people are talking about in the city and the colony. How they see the instructions from the government of the realm in this matter, what the feeling is like among the blacks, what they expect from my mission, and so on. That is what I mean by political context.'

Agostinho de Jesus said nothing, and just shook his head. He glared and his silent glare was defiant. Luís Bernardo now saw that he was not so stupid. He had just issued a silent challenge, knowing full well that silence was equivalent to a declaration of principle: Don't count on me, whatever you are trying to do. At least everything was now out in the open: and from the very first day.

Luís Bernardo got up from his desk and walked over to the window. He carelessly lit his cigarette and took three of four puffs until he began to sense the other man's discomfort was excessive.

He swung round and smiled.

'Very good, let's change the subject: what does a new governor do here when he takes up his post? I would like to give a dinner for twenty or thirty people – the Commissioner, the Mayor,

Monsignor, the Judge and main plantation owners or administrators. Is that the done thing?'

'Yes, it is the done thing, but first the Governor must give an official reception to introduce himself, with or without a ball.'

'A ball?' The idea of an official ball on São Tomé with plump girls drenched in sweat waltzing, and of himself opening the ball (inviting who to a dance, Monsignor?) was too much for his self-restraint and he burst into loud uncontrollable laughter that horrified the Secretary General.

'Is the ball usually given here in the Palace, Mr Agostinho?'

The other man nodded, perplexed, while Luís Bernardo now wiped away the tears of laughter.

'But are there women who know how to dance? And a band? And scores? What do people dance here?'

'People dance the same, I imagine, as they dance in the metropolis. The band is from the Garrison and plays modern music. And the *women*' – at this point Agostinho inflected his voice, suggesting how offensive the word 'women' was – 'are the colony's most respectable ladies. The wives of men in authority, of plantation administrators and their suitably aged daughters.'

Luís Bernardo turned to face away from Agostinho, because he was beginning to feel uncomfortable and was afraid he might dissolve into laughter once more.

He spoke over his shoulder in the firmest tone he could find.

'Very good, Mr Agostinho, we shall have a ball then. It's Tuesday; do you think we could fix it for next Saturday and have invitations ready to send out tomorrow?'

'I am sure we could.' Agostinho was master of the situation once again, 'We have the invitation cards printed and only have to write them and three or four staff can distribute them tomorrow. With your permission, I will prepare the guest list and will then present it to Your Excellency for approval.'

'Excellent, excellent. And how many people are we talking about, Mr Agostinho?'

'A hundred and thirty-six, Governor.'

'A hundred and thirty-six. You won't miss out anyone, will you, Mr Agostinho? I would hate inadvertently to insult some-one.'

'Of course not: the list is already there, and is the same one we used for the farewell ceremony for Your Excellency's predecessor.'

'Marvellous. And now I would like you to draw up a list of up to thirty people for the dinner I spoke to you about and which I want to give a few days afterwards.'

'Very good, Governor.'

'Good, that's all for today, you may go home. We should reconvene in the morning.'

'With the Governor's permission, I still have matters to deal with here. I beg to take my leave. Goodnight.' He withdrew very quietly, slightly bent, like a comma, pulling the door gently behind him.

Luís Bernardo stared silently at the door. He picked up the dossiers and went out, ostentatiously leaving his office door open. He went into the garden and breathed in the scent from the flowers. He heard the *Zaire* whistle in the bay to announce it was about to return to Benguela, Luanda and Lisbon. It sounded like the farewell of a friend, a sign that his solitude was now complete. The sun had disappeared and night had fallen. A dense swathe of grey cloud descended on the gardens and now silenced the bird song he'd heard all day long in the background. Thunder resounded on the distant mountain and the steam-laden atmosphere seemed ready to explode. He stopped in the middle of the garden to contemplate the scene, but soon felt mosquitoes attacking his neck, face, arms and hands. He turned to go back into the house but, before he could reach the door, a giant lid lifted in the sky above his head, and suddenly it was as if a dyke had burst. Large drops of rain, like grapes, cascaded down, eliminating all other noise and the last flickering of sun dying on the horizon. Puddles formed on the ground, transforming into small lakes and rivulets running in every direction. Grey night now took over a garden that smelled of waterlogged earth and marooned greenery, as if the deluge had interrupted all life. Luís was bewildered: he'd never seen rain like that, had never realised that rain, as well as being an element of nature, could crush nature itself. He extracted his watch from the pocket of his linen jacket: it was six-twenty. Drenched to his soul he went back in.

Sebastião was waiting for him in the entrance, holding an oil-lamp with which he lit the way to his bedroom. Luís Bernardo was in a dark mood and demanded to have a hot bath immediately, which Sebastião hurried to supply. He stripped off his soaking clothes. He was a fool, a complete idiot. He'd tried to confide in someone who manifestly didn't merit or want that. He'd attempted to establish an absurd complicity with someone who was a mere subordinate, hierarchically and spiritually, one who'd never commit to him or to what he wanted to do. I couldn't have made a worst start! he thought. He'd been prepared for deceit and trickery, and was ready to guard against wrong moves he might make, the most predictable being trying to share the loneliness imposed by his role. And immediately, on his first day, with the first, most unlikely interlocutor, he'd fallen into the infantile trap of seeking out an accomplice and ally in someone to whom he represented everything that was most hateful and despicable. He wasn't a *gravana*, a 'loose leaf' – as people on the island described visitors who just came for the dry season, when everything was more tolerable, starting with the climate. Nevertheless, in the eyes of someone like Agostinho de Jesus Júnior, who'd given fourteen years of long-suffering, silent service to that uninhabitable exile, he represented the most undesirable evil to befall the island: a politician coming from Lisbon, hoping to reform and change things, to attack outmoded ideas. Agostinho – Luís Bernardo knew and felt this and consequently couldn't forgive himself – had seen several people like himself come and go. Saw them come, saw them adjust, or give up and leave. Whereas he, Agostinho, stayed for ever, waiting for the next incumbent to arrive, and unlike these men he would never have a land to return to.

The tepid bath succeeded somewhat in soothing Luís Bernardo. From now on he would keep his own counsel. He took a solemn decision to keep alert and never open up to anyone else. He emerged from his bath in a different frame of mind and, to Sebastião's delight, devoured his dinner with real pleasure and appetite. There was red mullet with plantain fried in palm oil, and grilled chicken, served with slices of *matabala*, that served as fried potato on the island. For dessert, oven-roasted papaya and freshly ground coffee, the taste and aroma of which was unrivalled, he soon concluded.

When the rain stopped, leaving a cool freshness in the air, he sat on the veranda to the room facing the bay, lit up a cigar and told Sebastião to serve him cognac in a brandy glass selected from the Palace's collection of glasses. He leaned back on a padded wicker armchair, stretched his legs to rest on the balustrade, listened out for the muffled sounds from the city centre, and relaxed.

At ten o'clock, when the house was shadowy and silent, he sat down at his desk to write his first letter from exile. To João.

São Tomé and Príncipe, 22 March 1906, 10 p.m.
Dearest João,

Today I came, saw little and conquered nothing – quite the contrary. I don't know if I will be the one to conquer the islands or it will be they who conquer me. I know I have a strange feeling that an eternity has passed since I left Lisbon, from the moment I disembarked here in São Tomé.

I have been given the customary honours, been introduced to the right people, taken possession of what falls within my competence, and been installed – myself, my scant belongings and the sorrows that afflict me – in the house pompously dubbed 'the Palace'. I have just dined, smoked a cigar and drunk a cognac on the veranda, contemplating the sea and the tropical night, so different to the ones we know. I really wish you could be with me now, experiencing all that seems so different, so intense, so primitive and so dangerous. I find it hard to believe that the King knew what he was doing when he chose me; I cannot see the logic behind his choice (and now after I've accepted his challenge and am here, I can admit as much to you quite sincerely). If anything makes sense in all of this confusion, it is that I must stay loyal to what I am and to what I think, and not transform myself into someone you, and I myself, would no longer recognise.

But today, on my first night, I don't want to write to you about that. I just wanted to relate the first impressions of a Portuguese innocent abroad, who goes straight from Chiado to a village in the middle of the jungle, adrift somewhere in the mid–Atlantic on the Equator: he feels oppressed by the rain, melted by heat and humidity, eaten alive by mosquitoes and lives in fear and terror. João, I feel an immense, boundless solitude.

By the time you receive this letter, another eternity will have passed and all I feel will have intensified or been transformed – for better or worse. But, because I have nobody to talk to and wanted to relate to you my first feelings on disembarking at this latitude, I send you these brief lines, where you will note that nothing irrevocable has happened, that I am neither over-whelmed nor devastated. I look, I listen, I smell: as if I'd just come into the world. Wherever you are now, João, wish me happiness tomorrow.

Your most remote friend,
Luís Bernardo

7

O N THE FRIDAY afternoon before the ball, the city of São Tomé was buzzing with anecdotes and gossip about the new Governor. In his first days in charge, the new Governor had not yet visited the plantations, and to the great consternation of his Secretary General, didn't spend very much time in the Secretariat at the Palace. Instead he preferred to walk around the city, go into shops, greet shopkeepers and chat to their customers. He would suddenly appear in the morning market and buy wicker baskets and a decorated turtle shell, interrupt the conversations of old people in the park or go to the quayside to see fishermen unloading their catch early in the morning. People even recounted – though by now many of the stories seemed figments of the imagination – that he would stop to play games with black children in the street, and end up spinning tops with them. He *did* break the rules of protocol by visiting, after giving notice only the previous evening or a few hours in advance, the Mayor, the Judge, the Crown Commissioner and the health inspector in their respective offices and Monsignor José Atalaia at the cathedral. He met Major Benjamim das Neves, the island's military commander, in the street, and, as if it was the most natural thing, invited him to lunch at the Palace. But the most amazing piece of gossip was that, on these visits and promenades in the city, the Governor, accompanied by Vicente, the Palace porter, twice found time to go to the beach. He had been sighted once on the Beach of Seven Waves and once on the Beach of Shells, his bathing-suit straps pulled down to his waist, swimming, diving or lying on the beach to sun himself. Unlike the resident settlers on São Tomé, who rarely went to the beach or sunbathed, and whose skin as a result was yellowish, within a few days Luís Bernardo looked like a sunburnt Indian, his hair and face tanned by the salt of the sea. It was no surprise that Dr Luís Bernardo

Valença quickly managed to ruffle the placid atmosphere and become the hub of conversation on the island. Nobody really knew what the blacks thought about his behaviour, or if they even thought about it at all, but the whites couldn't talk about anything else and couldn't decide whether to be upset, sceptical or suspicious.

The Governor's nocturnal activities were yet another subject for discussion. Every night, after dinner, one could glimpse his silhouette on the Palace's main terrace, where two candles flickered and the end of his cigar glowed in the dark as music from his gramophone records – unique specimens on the island – wafted beyond the gardens. Whites found an excuse to walk past the Palace and see with their own eyes and hear with their own ears if the stories being told had any truth to them. But on the second night, it had been reported that the duty guard tried in vain to shoo off some blacks who had sat down outside the garden railings and listened in religious silence to the strange sad music the Governor's gramophone spread through the night. In white bars and black dives people chattered particularly about one piece of music, a heartbreaking lament that people attributed to Luís Bernardo himself.

When a half-embarrassed Sebastião informed him of the rumours circulating in the city he dispelled the conjectures, explaining it was merely music known as opera. And, as he was short of people to speak to about music, he explained to Sebastião that what so impressed the listeners was an aria called 'Era la notte' from an opera by the name of *Otelo*, sung by the Neapolitan Enrico Caruso and composed by Giuseppe Verdi, a man who also fought for the independence and freedom of Italy. Sebastião listened very intently and by Friday night the city knew the real story behind the music, which broke the hearts of all who heard it: it was 'opera', music one could only hear at night from that machine and sung by a friend of the Governor, who was also Governor of Italy. It was, Sebastião elucidated, as if they both spoke on the telephone.

Apart from all this, Saturday's 'presentation ball' ensured that the men were increasingly curious and the ladies uncontrollably anxious. The invitations did not mention dress, and that only deepened the general anxiety. And the fact that the invitations came from a still-youthful governor, a handsome bachelor, who bathed half-naked on the beach and listened at night to music from a gramophone, on a terrace open to the street, particularly fed the anxiety in the minds of the ladies. Two questions buzzed in every head: What will *he* wear? and, How does he expect *us* to dress? The dressmakers on the island hadn't the capacity to respond to last-minute requests and Mr Faustino's emporium of cloths and patterns took almost as much money in three days as it had in the previous three months.

Carriages and brakes were carefully cleaned, brushed and polished. Plantation owners pulled out their most ceremonial suits, smelling of naphthalene, from the bottom of trunks, army officers ordered their buttons, épaulettes and medals to be polished till they blinded, and the civil authorities almost halted services to the public so that their heads and their respective wives could cope with the state of emergency. In the end, the colony was unanimous they hadn't had such a society event for more than five years and that in the circumstances it assumed even greater importance, particularly in the political arena. People merely regretted the Governor had given only four days' notice of the ball, thus causing consternation in all quarters.

The ball to be given by Governor Valença was already a success, even for the hypercritical or the most prone to complain. It was set to start at eight o'clock, the precise moment when the rain stopped and allowed the little bowls of wax lining the ground to flicker in all their glory, as they pointed the way from the entrance through the garden to the ballroom. Inside, beautifully elaborate flower arrangements adorned tables set with place-names, and marked off the dance floor and stage where the band from the Barracks played tunes carefully selected by the Governor himself, who needed all his powers of diplomacy to root out any score that sounded like a military march or cavalry charge. A host of servants, rigorously uniformed in white and individually contracted by Sebastião, plied guests with an endless supply of drinks of every kind and canapés that kept them happy until it was time to sit down for dinner.

Luís Bernardo – and this would be the talk of São Tomé and Príncipe for years to come – welcomed his guests at the entrance to the ballroom wearing an exquisite black dinner jacket, a white dress shirt, a white silk handkerchief in his pocket and a tastefully sky-blue cummerbund. Simply startling! 'What a dandy!' the men commented later. 'So elegant, simply dazzling,' the ladies whispered to each other. Even Agostinho de Jesus Júnior was impressed and made a point of always keeping two steps behind Luís Bernardo, who, tall, relaxed and smiling, wooed his guests at the door one by one with phrases such as 'I am so delighted you were able to come!' The Chiado, Gremio, or Jockey Club, even a touch of Paris, seemed to have momentarily been transplanted to the Equator that night, in the person of the new Governor sent by King Dom Carlos.

The Count of Souza Faro, the only aristocrat resident on the islands and administrator of the Água Izé plantation, one of the biggest on São Tomé, was himself agreeably surprised and, as he came in, felt compelled to address Luís Bernardo in a tone of social complicity he rarely had occasion to use in that backwater.

'My dear chap, I do hope you have instructed the band to spare us those frightful marches they inherited from the Napoleonic campaigns!'

Luís Bernardo had studied the matter of dinner places as punctiliously as a military strategist and seated at his table Monsignor Atalaia, the Count of Souza Faro, old Dr Segismundo Bruto da Silva and his very proper wife, Colonel João Baptista and *his* equally proper and silent wife, the administrator of the Boa Entrada plantation, the second biggest and most productive on the island, and the widow Dona Maria Augusta da Trindade, owner and resident administrator of the Nova Esperança plantation, a woman of some thirty plus years, endowed with attributes abundantly in evidence thanks to the low sweep of her bright-green dress's neckline – though slanderous city gossip had yet to pin on her anything more tangible than unconfirmed intentions or unsatisfied desires. Besides, from that perspective, she was the latest in a long line of combative women very much in control of themselves and their love lives that the colony cherished as legends – from the remote Ana Chaves, a king's concubine and farmer, who was exiled to São Tomé and gave her name to its bay and one of its mountains, to the more recent Maria

Correia, who married the Brazilian José Ferrera Gomes, introducer of coffee to São Tomé, and to whom, according to the legend, she was never unfaithful in his lifetime, let alone after his death.

As for the effervescent Dona Maria Augusta da Trindade, at whom Luís Bernardo occasionally directed his most gallant smile, people said she managed her plantation with a man's determination and much more competently than most. Luís Bernardo strove not to look at her neckline, and registered that her face and figure were far from unpleasant. Quite the contrary, there was a spark of youth in her eyes and manner, a restless, untamed spirit that after five nights in São Tomé he found as natural as the humidity drenching everyone from the neck down.

He made a real effort to focus on the conversation round the table. They were talking about the Viscount of Malanza, Jacinto de Souza e Almeida, who died less than two years ago and who was perhaps the most celebrated, most intelligent person the island had ever known. Obviously Luís Bernardo had heard of the Viscount and was familiar with the story of his renowned family, perhaps the most illustrious lineage on São Tomé and Príncipe, and to which the island was most indebted. The Souza e Almeidas were not white, but mulatto, and were not from the islands or Portugal, but from Brazil. When the greatest, richest of the colonies in the Portuguese Empire gained its independence in 1822, Manuel de Vera Cruz e Almeida, a native of Bahia, was one of the many Portuguese who came to settle on the Island of Príncipe that was then only a wild, half-populated rock.

His elder son, João Maria Souza e Almeida, was a mere six-year-old when he disembarked with his parents on Príncipe, and seventeen when his father died. By that time he was already responsible for the Public Purse on São Tomé and soon went to Benguela in Angola, where he began to buy and cultivate land with remarkable persistence and success. He quickly became one of the major landowners in the district, where he held every public post until he became Governor, and where, apart from his competence and capacity to work that everyone recognised, he was famous for never accepting bribes. At the age of twenty-three, he fought in the military expedition against the Dembos, who were ravaging the frontiers of the province: he armed his troops, supplied their food and commanded his men so heroically that he was awarded the Tower and the Sword, the highest Portuguese military decoration, given only for the bravest of deeds on the field of battle. But what really distinguished his life were the scientific foundations he gave to the cultivation of cocoa on São Tomé and Príncipe, to which he devoted a detailed tome that remained the bible of all local growers. He also introduced and taught the cultivation of coffee, tobacco and cotton, to the point of importing and offering seed to local farmers. But, unlike many 'empire-builders' who turned into cruel, angry characters by the desire to pioneer the new, João Maria was a pleasant, approachable man always ready to serve and help others and the public sphere. King Dom Luiz was quite right to ennoble him and make him Baron of Água Izé, Peer of the Realm, Gentleman of the Royal Household Cavalry and member of the Royal Council: he was the first man of blue blood and black skin in the Portuguese aristocracy. He died in 1869, after amalgamating all his properties on São Tomé into the Água Izé plantation, and establishing a system of 'dependencies' that from then on became the model for making all the main estates on the island more efficient.

He left as heir his son Jacinto, who was born on the Papagaio plantation on Príncipe. He was summoned back from Lisbon where he was studying to help administer their lands. When his father died, Jacinto, the future Viscount of Malanza, was twenty-four and had inherited his father's passion for colonial agriculture. He entrusted the management of Água Izé to his brother, loaded up samples of wood and seeds from plants native to the islands and went on a long research trip to various European countries, where he had the samples analysed and collected useful information and data on other crops that could be introduced to São Tomé. On his return, he threw himself into the cyclopean labour of clearing, ploughing and planting the virgin territory he'd inherited; it was in the far south-west of the island, an area known as Terrenos de São Miguel. It was the most inhospitable of terrains, where the jungle imposed its laws, in a torrid, unhealthy climate, without access by road or track, or even a point where it was easy to disembark from the sea. But he founded two new plantations there, São Miguel and Porto Alegre – the latter crossed by the strait of Malanza – introduced coffee cultivation in exemplary conditions and set up an experimental area to nurture all manner of tropical plants. He successfully survived the terrible turmoil that followed on the declaration of the freedom of slaves in 1875, and immediately afterwards the ravage and human waste caused by a smallpox epidemic that swept the island like wildfire.

In 1901, following his father's precedent with the late Baron of Água Izé, Dom Carlos conferred on Jacinto the title of Viscount of Malanza – the site of his achievements on behalf of São Tomé. Until his death, three years later, the Viscount dedicated himself as energetically as ever to farming and the scientific study of tropical flora and agriculture. He died without realising his dream of seeing a School of Colonial Agriculture created on the island. Água Izé, the plantation that gave prestige to his family and ennobled his father, then passed into the hands of the Príncipe Company and the National Overseas Bank, now managed by the Count of Souza Faro, who was seated at Luís Bernardo's table. Jacinto had, in Luís Bernardo's eyes, been a man like his father, who stood for progress against stagnation, for the belief that science, training and technical advance were the alternative to the forced labour of blacks on the plantations. It was a pity he was gone.

Luís Bernardo noted, however, that the comments on the Viscount's life were not as glowing as one might have expected. It was true nobody present referred to him without a few appreciative remarks. But there was a lack of warmth and enthusiasm, and no regret in the appreciations. As if the Viscount's disappearance essentially inspired a sense of relief rather than praise. Or perhaps he was imagining things. Perhaps.

The two-course dinner, in the meantime, came to an end. Desserts and coffee were served and it was time for port and speeches, or rather for his speech, a moment he had planned to precision. He leapt to his feet, tapped his knife three times against the side of his glass. He waited for silence and began to speak. In a nutshell, he said it was an honour and privilege to be able to serve Portugal by serving São Tomé and Príncipe. That everything he had read or learned about these islands had convinced him that it was the land there that had brought the best out of the colonising genius of the Portuguese who, starting from zero, against all the odds, had extracted from the most adverse jungle conditions a fertile, cultivated, prosperous land, a source of wealth for its farmers and the state and a cause for national pride. He was conscious of his responsibility to keep São Tomé on the path of progress in times when new realities were being asserted and, with them, new difficulties, new challenges, but also new expectations. He had come prepared for challenges, believed wholeheartedly in the expectations, and was ready to share in the difficulties, and wherever he could, to seek and willingly accept the help of those who offered it.

'This,' he concluded, 'is a land of men of goodwill and I only aspire to be one more among you.'

The room burst spontaneously into applause and, to do justice to his reputation as eccentric, the new Governor then summoned Sebastião and the cooks, and called for an ovation for them, 'Because this is a land of work and their work went into the making of this dinner'. And, to smiles and asides, he orchestrated a second, if less spontaneous, round of applause.

As he finished his speech, Luís Bernardo signalled to the band to strike up a slow waltz, as previously agreed. He got up and, fulfilling everyone's expectation, went to the other side of the table and offered his hand to Maria Augusta da Trindade.

'Will you give me the honour of starting the ball?'

This was also something Luís Bernardo had rehearsed. He knew the fact that he, a single man, had approached the only single woman in the whole room would perhaps encourage even more gossip on the island. But who else could he invite to be his partner, without offending other susceptibilities? It was just that he could never have predicted Dona Maria Augusta would be such a glamorous, desirable woman. And hadn't foreseen she would blush the moment she got up to partner him and take his outstretched hand.

The ball couldn't have got off to a better start. Luís Bernardo was probably the least prepared of men for the governorship of a couple of cocoa islands, but in that São Tomé ballroom no man could rival his elegance and style as a dancer, perfected over twenty years in the ballrooms of Lisbon. In his arms, swept along by his lithe twisting body, the somewhat portly Maria Augusta felt herself glide, as if skating on ice rather than defying a temperature of thirty-five degrees with ninety per cent humidity, though the windows were open to welcome in a cool breeze. An unchanging half-smile masked the emotions she felt, and she beamed at all the onlookers, though not at him. She couldn't hide her feelings when her bosom lightly brushed against him and heaved to the rhythm of her panting breath. As he looked down, it was a beautiful sight for a man who hadn't been within ten metres of a woman for nigh on a month. But he was on his best behaviour: he took just one look and waltzed only once with her. He then invited on to the floor two respectably mature ladies no man would otherwise have had any reason to disturb.

After three waltzes, Luís Bernardo disappeared from the dance floor for the rest of the night. He dedicated himself diligently and diplomatically to performing his role as the perfect host, constantly circulating, asking his guests if everything was to their liking, keeping a discreet eye on the service provided by his servants and the band's repertoire, filling a gentleman's glass or retrieving a fan a lady had dropped. At about one in the morning, he positioned himself by the door and began to bid farewell to his guests individually. At half past two – dawn in those latitudes – the last couples and last gentlemen retired rather the worse for wear and he could finally take off his jacket, unbutton his shirt, order a last cognac from Sebastião and withdraw to his terrace overlooking the bay. It had been a success.

After fulfilling his first public duty – introducing himself, the Governor of the colony – Luís Bernardo was now eager to get down to serious business. He wanted to visit the plantations immediately, to get to know the interior of the island and engage with the task that had brought him there. But he also knew there were the rituals to abide by: hospitality was the most important tradition on the São Tomé plantations, but, given that it was the small matter of the Governor's first visit, there was a minimal protocol to respect. That implied that there had to be a formal invitation, even if it was at his request. He was equally annoyed that he had to agree to his Secretary General's suggestion that he defer to the following Saturday the dinner offered to the administrators of the main plantations, since Sunday was the only day when plantations weren't working. It would be quite wrong to invite to supper people who would come from afar, on horseback or by carriage, and would then have to return during the night and be up and about at four-thirty the following morning. He'd have to wait another week, though at least he took advantage of the ball to issue invitations to the people on his carefully prepared list.

There were dozens of plantations on São Tomé and he wouldn't invite all the administrators – there was little point in that. The owners of the small plantations were descendants of former *forros*, the original settlers or exiles who had stayed on the island and were their own administrators and a political irrelevance; they had to accept without consultation what the big owners did and decided. Many of the main plantations belonged to companies and their owners, by definition, were absentee: some came for a few months each year, others put in a fleeting appearance in the *gravana* season, others never visited and had no intention of ever doing so – they were big shareholders in agricultural companies based in São Tomé or Príncipe and just read annual reports, participated in the General Assembly in Lisbon and turned up for meetings when summoned by the Minister. But it was the absentee owners who *de facto* decided on policy in São Tomé and they did so on the basis of the reports and information sent from the island by their resident managers and administrators. Luís Bernardo wanted to dine with the latter; he could only achieve his mission through them.

His plan was first to pay a visit to all the plantations on São Tomé and then go to Príncipe. It was no easy task: though small, the island had only a few dozen open roads along which one could drive a carriage. Most of the plantations had to be visited on horseback or by sea in the cutters that carried freight along the island's coast. Coast-cutting was in fact the most practical way to get from the city to the plantations, since the latter had usually been established on the coast from where they penetrated the jungle, as far as clearing and planting would allow: the interior of the island was virgin jungle, just as the Portuguese had found it in the fifteenth century, with two volcanic peaks rising up like needles, the highest being the Pico de São Tomé, two thousand one hundred and forty-two metres high, its summit rarely visible, eternally shrouded by clouds and mists. The dense central area, which made up most of São Tomé, was the realm of the *óbó*, an impenetrable, closed labyrinth of enormous trees: *jacas, ocás, cipós, micondós, marupioes* and mangoes. Creepers lived beneath them, coiling round, desperately climbing to the tree tops in a strenuous effort to reach the light far from the perpetual liquid mantle hanging down: *a lemba-lemba, a corda d'agua, a corda-pimenta* and climbing liana. The horrendous black cobra lived in the undergrowth, or clung to branches, ready to drop on anyone walking unsuspectingly beneath, its bite a rapid, devastating kiss of death. Old people related how the only man to escape death from the black cobra's bite was a black fugitive from the Monte Café plantation, who now lived one-armed in Angolares. When he felt the cobra's teeth enter his arm he reacted like lightning with two telling swipes of his machete: the first cut his enemy's throat, the second severed his own arm at the shoulder, and he survived. Because the *óbó* is the territory of shadows where blacks from plantations take refuge, driven there by a moment of madness, a crime committed in the heart of the plantation, or lunatic desire for freedom. It welcomed them in its deathly embrace, offering a sombre, elusive freedom. No one else in his right mind ventured more than a few steps into that opaque, submerged universe.

Luís Bernardo's only acquaintance with the *óbó* came from a conversation with Sebastião, when he happened to confess he wished to explore the jungle.

A genuine terror filled Sebastião's eyes and his voice trembled.

'Doctor, look to your soul, do not do such a thing! The *óbó* is a place of shadows, a territory of cobras, thunderclaps, lightning and darkness. Lunatics galore have tried to survive there but none have returned: people say they turned into cobras.'

Consequently, Luís Bernardo had to travel along the coast, round the *óbó*, to the right and left of the city of São Tomé to visit the first plantations he'd selected. These were the biggest: Rio do

Ouro, Boa Entrada, Água Izé, Monte Café, Diogo Vaz, Ponta-Figo and Porto Alegre, the plantation founded by the Viscount of Malanza in the far south-west, on the Equator, opposite the Ilhéu das Rolas. São Miguel and Santa Margarida were among the largest, and the most important of those with saints' names: São Nicolau, Santo António, Santa Catarina and Santa Adelaide. Besides, Luís Bernardo was fascinated by the fantastic imaginary names given to the plantations. Some of the large estates had names that evoked other landscapes, and some were unexpected: Vila Real, Colónia Açoriana, Novo Brasil, Nova Olinda, Novo Ceilão and Bombaim. Even more extraordinary were the names of states of the soul: Amparo, Perseverança, Esperança, Caridade, Ilusão, Saudade, Milagrosa, Generosa, Fraternidade, Aliança and Eternidade. Who knows, perhaps some poet with nothing better to do in those parts had been contracted to conjure up plantation names to match the dreams of their founders. Perhaps Costa Alegre, the poet Luís Bernardo now read at night before going to sleep, São Tomé's favourite son, black as the night, whose life was curtailed by a passion stirred by a white woman, and who was driven to write painful verse like:

> If slaves are bought,
> White woman from afar,
> A free man, I am your slave
> Bought by your gaze.

Or:

> A shadow, heart of my body,
> pursues your body in the street:
> Near or far, like a shadow,
> My soul follows yours.

Late one afternoon, Luís Bernardo was riding back to the city, accompanied by Vicente as usual who served as his guide and as his interpreter with blacks who spoke Portuguese badly, or simply as someone to talk to in idle moments. But Vicente soon learned there were times when his master liked to converse and others when he didn't, when he preferred to be silently engrossed in his own thoughts. This was one such moment. Luís Bernardo rode a few metres in front, looking distractedly at the landscape parading by in time to the rhythm of his horse. They were returning from a visit to Nossa Senhora das Neves, the most distant of island settlements. He was taking advantage of that week to make a long-awaited start on his visits to plantations, a task facilitated by their closeness to the city, with the exception of Nossa Senhora das Neves. Apart from the latter and the capital city, the clumps of humans on São Tomé amounted to four tiny villages: Trindade, Madalena, Santo Amaro and Guadalupe, all situated inland to the west of the city, though within a radius of thirty kilometres. They were sad places, without prominent public buildings, and with a few white inhabitants who sold goods to the wretched blacks.

As they rode by one of several huts alongside the track – simple wooden constructions covered with palms or sun-baked mud – Luís Bernardo's attention was caught by something Vicente hadn't noticed. The Governor reined in his horse and contemplated the scene: two naked children were bathing in a stream the rainwater had steered by the side of the cabin. Smoke rose up from inside through a hole in the precarious roof and mingled with the smells from the forest. The children's mother, a woman of indeterminate age, peeped out; she wore a garish yellow dress that reached down to her feet. Luís Bernardo greeted her with a 'Good evening!' and she replied with an incomprehensible monosyllable. Vicente quickly spoke to her in patois, saying something that made her look at Luís Bernardo and lower her head rather fearfully, respectfully. She repeated her unintelligible response. Luís Bernardo didn't seem to know what he wanted to do and just kept staring at her, at her children, who'd now stopped their water-games and just stood there.

He made up his mind and told Vicente to explain he'd like to visit her house. Vicente's eyes bulged, but he insisted.

'Tell her!'

When she heard this, the woman began to jabber nervously at Vicente, pointing inside the house and at the road in the direction of the city.

'Doctor, she says . . .'

'I know what she's saying. Tell her I want to visit her house and I will give her réis as a present.'

He dismounted, gave the reins to Vicente, and lifted his hand to his jacket pocket to extract a handful of coins for the woman. She looked at the coins, seemed to hesitate, then gripped them tightly and moved from the entrance so he could go in.

The heat and stench inside the hut were stifling: an unpleasant smell of burnt flour, jungle and filth enveloped in a cloud of smoke rising from the ground, where a fire flickered under an earthenware pot. The air was almost unbreathable. Initially, as he had come in from the light outside, he could see nothing. Then as his eyes got used to the smoke-filled half-dark, he could make out a number of kitchen utensils, work tools and horseshoes scattered over the ground or on a home-made wooden table, large mud bricks and mattresses on the floor. He felt the sweat soaking his hair and streaming down his chest and sides; his legs suddenly weakened and he struggled to choke down the vomit rising in his throat. He thought he must be feverish, in a flash imagined it was all over, that he was poisoned by malaria. Then he gathered all his energy and rushed angrily into the light and fresh air outside that were like real blessings. They all stared at him silently. He stood as firm as he could, then mounted the horse Vicente was steadying by the reins. Flustered, he lifted two fingers to his hat, said goodbye to the woman and broke into a trot.

A hundred metres on he slowed down and waited for Vicente.

'Do you know these people, Vicente?'

'Yes, Boss.'

'Where's the husband? On a plantation?'

'No, Boss. He's in the city; he works at the post office.'

Luís Bernardo went quiet again. He was meditating on what Vicente had just said: the man responsible for that hovel wasn't an ordinary plantation labourer; he was a post-office employee. It was the house and family of a civil servant who worked for the São Tomé Public Administration. The poverty and sadness of the scene had shocked him. No white would survive such degrading conditions. The Governor had just seen with his own eyes what no official speech in Lisbon ever mentioned. He had almost vomited when he discovered the secret side to 'the mission of progress and development Portugal is committed to in São Tomé and Príncipe'. Yes, it was true, there was a counter-argument. On the night of the ball, in the conversation around the table, someone had remarked, 'Give a black a white's stone-brick house, bathroom and all, and he'll wreck it in a flash.' It was also true nobody starved on the islands, as was clear from the healthy-looking bodies he saw by roadsides and in settlements. There was no hunger because nature didn't allow it: the breadfruit the Baron of Água Izé introduced to the islands grew of its own accord and every year gave a profusion of fruit that was just as much bread. All other fruit was within hand's reach to be plucked from the trees, beginning with seven magnificent varieties of bananas, of which Luís Bernardo preferred the golden-banana and banana-apple that, as its name suggested, tasted of banana and apple. Fish was so abundant that his own eyes saw men fishing on the beach by the city jetty throw out a keep net from the sand and pull it in teeming with fish and prawns, without even getting their feet wet. Supply was such that the natives scorned lobsters, declaring they were jinxed, and, in São João dos Angolares in the south, on nights with a full moon, schools of giant squid crawled on the beach and the women could simply collect them live in their wooden buckets. Half-wild pigs roamed the beaches or suddenly ran out of the jungle and belonged to no one. And for eager hunters, São Tomé was a paradise of doves, thrushes and other edible birds. Besides, there was manioc, there and throughout Africa, the favourite staple food of blacks. In São Tomé nobody could starve to death. So given they didn't suffer from the droughts afflicting other parts of Africa, and didn't have to wander in search of food, why did São Tomé blacks live in such wretched conditions? Because of their own laziness and natures, as whites explained, or because of the latter's lack of sensitivity, as few dared to say?

In the meantime, he too was soon in excellent physical shape and unimaginable good health. The brief fainting fit he'd experienced on his visit to the hut was an isolated incident. It is true he continued to suffer horribly from the climate, though he was gradually adapting and now only soaked two shirts a day. The nights were the worst when, under the obligatory mosquito net, the heat turned even more oppressive. But, like all Europeans in Africa, he soon learned to sleep little, going to bed well past midnight, after the ritual music and cognac on the terrace had brought his day to a close. He woke up around 5 a.m., as soon as the morning light shone through the windows and he heard the first parrot squawk in the garden, the whistles of 'San Niclá' and the strange sound of the *ossóbó*, which when it sang like a choir augured rain. When it did rain, invariably at the end of the afternoon, it was his favourite moment of the day, signalling the end of work, a cool drink on the terrace and the cold shower preceding dinner. The rain silenced all other noise, drowned the stifling heat and created a smell of wet earth that momentarily burst the giant bubble of chlorophyll where their island lives were trapped. It was as if the heavens suddenly burst, unable any more to contain what they held inside: like pleasure kept on hold to the last moment in a woman's body. The whole island was liberated from the stifling agony of hours exuding sweat, and days of unbridled violence.

In the city, shop doors and shutters closed, the recorder shut up the courthouse, the health representative, the Mayor and all other functionaries went home or lingered in the Elite Brewery, and listened to the rain fall as they chatted. The priest left the sacristy and celebrated six o'clock mass in the Sé to a congregation of devout women he invariably greeted with these words: '*Introibo ad altere Dei . . .*' To which they responded: '*Ad Deum qui laetificat juventutem meam*' – but, in truth, the youth invoked was mortified sadness, buried for ever in a merciless exile, pacified for a few moments only by the rain. Soaked to the skin, the blacks from the city, post office or shop employees, now returned along dirt tracks to straw-thatched homes on the edge of the jungle, where a pot boiled on the fire and a heavy stench no white could stand greeted them. But far off, further up, on the plantations, labourers had long since returned to their huts in the compound, had cooked and eaten, and their farewell chants now merged with the sound of the rain outside.

On his Palace terrace, holding a gin and tonic, chasing away the mosquitoes with a straw fan, the new Governor of São Tomé and

Príncipe peered though the rain, apparently able to see what no one else could see.

'Governor, this is what we would like to know: what exactly are the instructions you bring with you from Lisbon?'

Colonel Mário Maltez leaned back in his chair, lit his cigar and stared over the table at Luís Bernardo. It was an intimidating glare and the Colonel was an intimidating man: in his mid-fifties, tall, stout, red-faced, veins bulging, a head of white hair, huge hairy hands and unpleasantly chubby fingers. He had lived in Mozambique, fought in the campaigns led by Mouzinho, and it was said he had fought in the famous battle of Chaimite, as a result of which the princeling Gungunhana, the leader of the insurrection, was captured. He served in Mozambique under Ayres d'Ornellas, one of Mouzinho's generals and now the Minister for the Navy and Colonies, and that undoubtedly gave him a political weight Luís Bernardo couldn't afford to ignore. Moreover, he was still the resident administrator of Rio do Ouro, the island's biggest plantation, in terms of land and number of workers – an army of two thousand and thirty souls. The fact he had been the one 'to open hostilities' as soon as coffee and brandies were served, pushing the conversation towards the subject that had gathered them all there, showed he was the planters' natural leader.

Before replying, Luís Bernardo pulled a candlestick towards him and also lit a cigar, to mark a deliberate pause. It had been an excellent supper: fillet of sole stuffed with prawns, leg of pork roasted with pineapple and rice in the oven, banana ice cream and coffee. A white Colares wine and a Bairrada red, the Governor's own special reserve, and an 1832 Quinta do Noval from the Palace cellar. His first puff on his cigar, a Hoyo de Monterrey, felt richly sumptuous: it was moist but not wet, perfectly lit and drew easily.

He stared at its glowing end and replied, without looking up, 'Well, Colonel, as I am sure you know, my instructions and appointment come from His Majesty the King, and were later confirmed by his previous minister.'

'And you have had these instructions confirmed by the new Minister?'

The Colonel was cunning, but Luís Bernardo was no fool. Now he looked him in the face.

'Given that my instructions came directly from the King, the change of minister should make no difference. Nonetheless I can tell you I received news of the change of minister when I was in Luanda, through a telegram from his Secretary General, telling me – I suppose on orders from the new Minister – to proceed according to the instructions I was given in Lisbon.'

'Very well, what then are these instructions that seem so cloaked in mystery?' interjected the Count of Souza Faro, as if wanting to make it clear he was no makeweight.

'There is no mystery at all, Count. What is at stake is the creation of conditions to ensure that São Tomé and Príncipe continues to be a prosperous colony for everybody and, at the same time, to rebuff with facts the accusations that, as you must know, are being made about us by influential voices in England, in relation to the indigenous labour force.'

'And do His Majesty the King and his ministers think these accusations are at all well founded?' asked Colonel Maltez, assuming the leader's mantle once more.

'What they think or do not think is not at issue. What matters is what the English Consul will think when he arrives here within the month. What *he* sees, concludes and writes in his reports to England is what matters.'

'Matters to who?' bellowed the administrator of the Monte Café plantation, a short man with a deadpan face, from the opposite end of the table.

Luís Bernardo turned in his chair to look at the newcomer to the conversation. He was one of fifteen plantation administrators he had carefully selected to invite to dinner, together with people in authority who, directly or indirectly, were implicated in life on the plantations: the Crown Commissioner, the government representative on Príncipe, the District Judge and representative of the Commissioner for Justice. He was pleased to see the conversation broadening, even if the tone better suited an interrogation than a conversation.

'It is possible that with time, effort and the necessary investment São Tomé will relatively easily find an export market to replace the British Isles. For the moment, however, as you know, a temporary suspension of purchases or a boycott by this cocoa market would bring chaos, in some cases bankruptcy, to the estates Your Excellencies manage. This is what is at stake, if by any chance we do not manage to convince the English their accusations are unfounded.'

'In other words?' riposted the Colonel.

'In other words . . .' Luís Bernardo paused almost theatrically to glance round the whole table. 'If we do not manage to convince them that slave labour does not exist on São Tomé and Príncipe.'

During the whole meal, the Crown Commissioner, Germano André Valente, had refrained from looking at Luís Bernardo and had stayed silent. When introduced to him the day he arrived, Luís Bernardo had registered his shifty look and lukewarm greeting. At the official reception he'd perhaps deliberately stayed away from the Governor and now seemed to want to remain as invisible as possible. Even if he wanted, Luís Bernardo could not avoid him: Germano Valente's official function was to monitor and report on work conditions on the plantations, the legality of contracts, supervise the importing and repatriation of workers, and represent simultaneously the interests of the labourers and their bosses. He reported and communicated directly to the Lisbon government, which could imply a clash of interests with the Governor himself – though until now the Governor and Crown Commissioner had never diverged publicly in their estimation of what happened on the plantations.

However, in the silence following the Governor's last words, when everyone seemed to gaze absent-mindedly at the cigar smoke curling above the table, Germano Valente finally took up the baton.

'What does Your Excellency consider slave labour to be?'

Luís Bernardo was displeased by the tone of this remark, and replied bluntly, 'What I – the community of nations and international treaties – consider to be slave labour the honourable Crown Commissioner will find described in what I have published on this matter, publications he is most certainly familiar with.' From the corner of his eye, he was pleased to see his adversary turn even redder and stiffen in reaction to his riposte. He continued. 'Slave labour across the world – including, consequently, for the Portuguese government – means a worker is forced to work against his free will.'

'Come now, we have no slave labour here on São Tomé,' piped up the Count of Souza Faro once again and Luís Bernardo began to appreciate how easily he seemed to intervene to deflate the situation.

'Labourers on our plantations, unlike what happens in some English or French colonies' – Colonel Maltez leaned his elbows on the table to underline his intervention – 'are not shipped over by force, are paid the minimum wage stipulated by law and, as *you* must know, have proper work hours, rest on Sunday, medical welfare, lodgings and rooms supplied by the plantation. Does Your Honour consider this constitutes slave labour?'

'Let us be quite clear.' Luís Bernardo spoke softly, as if he'd not noticed the latent tension. 'I am not here to accuse you of anything. I am merely passing on accusations made by others who *are* in a position to damage your interests. I will repeat that you do not have to convince me but Mr David Jameson, who will be the next British Consul on São Tomé and Príncipe.'

Souza Faro got up from the table and began to walk across the room, which was another elegant way to defuse the atmosphere. He spoke as he walked and Luís Bernardo thought he might perhaps prove to be an ally.

'It will be difficult to persuade the Englishman, if we can't first persuade you . . .'

'What does it require to persuade you, Governor?' This time one of the administrators who had been silent so far spoke up.

'As must be obvious, I have to see the situation on the ground before I can form an opinion: until I do that I can have no opinion. But if, with the authorisation I request here and now from you, I begin to visit all the plantations on São Tomé and Príncipe from tomorrow, all without exception, big or small, rich or poor – I think I might be in a position in two months' time to answer that question seriously.'

'You mean what I have just told you is of no value?' Colonel Maltez was not going to go away.

'No, I don't wish to imply that at all. I mean I wouldn't be acting seriously in my eyes or on your behalf, gentlemen, and particularly on behalf of the person who appointed me, if I did not draw my own conclusions, one way or another, and base them solely on what I have heard or been told. I noted what the Colonel said as information that will certainly be of use, though it is incomplete.'

'Incomplete in what sense?'

'For example: the honourable Colonel says the labourers on the plantations are shipped here of their own free will, are paid according to the law, fed, lodged and treated –'

'Exactly.'

'But you didn't say whether they are also free to leave when they wish.'

'To leave?'

'Yes, to leave, to leave whenever, to leave to go to another plantation or go back to their own land.'

'Yes, they are free to leave,' rasped Germano Valente the Crown Commissioner.

Luís Bernardo now addressed him directly.

'So why do they *never* leave? Why do two or three thousand land here every year and only a dozen or two return to Angola?'

'Because they don't want to!' Colonel Maltez's tone verged on a perfectly modulated declaration of war. He also got up, to signal that dinner or at least that political exchange was at an end.

'Good, if you are right, there will be no problems whatsoever. Dear gentlemen, I would like to thank you all for coming and, with your permission, will give you as you leave a schedule of plantation visits I intend to make and which cannot be changed, unless you have exceptional circumstances or *force majeure*. I do apologise for the speed at which I am trying to do everything but, for reasons you must certainly understand, I'd prefer this to be sorted out before the British Consul arrives.'

That night, after they'd all left and he'd had his half-hour to meditate on his terrace, he sat down at his desk and wrote a short note to João.

Dear friend,

Today I gave a dinner for the administrators of the main plantations and that sinister figure, the Crown Commissioner. War is about to break out and it is highly unlikely I will succeed in escaping unharmed. How I wish you could be here today to advise!

Your friend,
Luís Bernardo

8

A BELL BEGAN to chime in his dream. At first, it seemed to come from deep down, from a distant horizon, then it sounded clearer and louder until he was forced to wake up. He saw no light penetrating the gaps in the shutters, and realised it was still night-time and, when he tried to turn over to get more sleep, he found his pillow and hair were soaked in sweat.

It must be summer. It must be the church bell ringing mass, and he's lying in a bunk on the upper deck of his friend Antonio Amador's yacht. They're sailing to the Algarve. It's the summer holidays, and outside the transparent sea of the Alvor Estuary awaits him, where he'll soon dive and properly wake himself up. But he'll sleep on for a few minutes more. Everything is quiet and in order and nothing bodes ill.

But the bell began to ring again and its rhythm was no welcoming peal; it tolled threateningly. He thought he heard voices outside and a feeble light entered the window. He groped in the darkness and found a few matches on his bedside table. He lit one and looked at the hands of the watch he'd left within reach on the table: 4.30 a.m.; now he really did wake up.

He pulled the mosquito net aside, got up and went to open his shutters. The sky was still a mass of stars and only a glimmer of light rose behind the mountain, where morning was ushering the night away. The bell finally went silent and dark shadows rushed across the open yard, signalling that the reveille had been heard on the Porto Alegre plantation. Luís Bernardo breathed in the soft, vanilla scent of night and the perfume spreading from the 'mad rose', that fickle equatorial flower, which is white in the morning, pink at midday and red at dusk, the red of the sun sinking into the sea. Night rapidly gave way not to the brightness of dawn but to a white mist eddying above the ground like liquid cotton. In the background he could make out the outline of barrack huts and a growing throng of black shapes, blurred by the haze, looming larger by the minute. Suddenly, a sad, lilting song rose up from one of the huts, a voice singing in Angolan dialect, a canticle to chill the bones, and soon chorused by myriad voices. The chant swelled and filled the huts, crossed the open yard and reached the Casa Grande, where Luís Bernardo was watching early morning rise from a window. It was a song of sadness for a day that began swathed in mist, for a sun they had left behind, for a sea of no return they imagined but would never see, for a night that buried all their dreams. Yet it wasn't a song: it was a chanted lament for a lost world that barely survived in their memories of happier days. They wept for their other Africa, for open plains, for grass dried in the sun, for animals running free, for the bush where lions stalk zebras and leopards silently pursue antelope, for rivers navigated in frail canoes between sleeping alligators and hippopotami, for nights on the savannah, listening to cries from the jungle, fears allayed by a fire burning among stones. Africa with an endless horizon, and not that fifty-by-thirty-kilometre prison camp, dense, always drenched suffocation, narrow jungle paths, and the eternally foul stench of cocoa, and that bell, which rang inexorably at 4.30 a.m., 6 p.m. and 9 p.m., imprisoning their time, unerringly to the second, as if God had marked them at birth with a cycle no happiness or tragedy, no joy or grief could ever break. And there, at the window over the open yard of the Porto Alegre plantation, founded by the Baron of Águas Izé with titanic effort in a place where no man would choose to live, Luís Bernardo made the most unexpected discovery: that he had heard the song before. He had heard it in another language, though it sounded exactly the same: at the Paris Opéra, four years ago, at a performance of Verdi's *Nabucco*. It was 'Va, pensiero', the chorus of the Hebrew slaves.

Half an hour later, the Governor of São Tomé, accompanied by the plantation administrator, presided over the headcount. Some seven hundred blacks, divided into groups of ten, barefoot and summarily dressed, all wearing a metal badge round their necks with the name of the plantation and their contract number, saluted like gladiators, raised their arms with the inevitable knife – a short all-purpose blade for clearing undergrowth, cutting a path through the jungle or beheading a black cobra, if it was caught in time. After the overseer and his two helpers finished the count, the administrator gave the nod to the overseer to shout. 'Off you go!' and the entire host of black shadows left in silence, disappearing almost immediately into the dense undergrowth.

Five minutes later, the whole plantation was awake: servants shouting, the cries of women who'd been spared plantation work, the noise of the Decauville-line engines leaving to load up cocoa, the din of saws and anvils in workshops, of woodcutters' axes in the bush. As the forest awoke, flocks of birds began to sing everywhere and fly to other perches. At eight o'clock, work was stopped for half an hour, for the *mata-bicho* or 'kill the swine', the first meal of the day. Then at around eleven-thirty, lunch was, distributed at the place of work and an hour later (or perhaps later, according to the overseer's mood and the results of the last harvest), work was resumed until six-thirty, invariably to sunset. It was neither a lot nor a little; it was the maximum nature would allow – from dawn to dusk.

At midday, when the plantation bell had rung three times for lunch at the Casa Grande, Luís Bernardo had already sweated three litres on visits to nearby buildings. He had seen various workshops – the carpenters', blacksmiths' and tinsmiths' – been to the overseer's house, to barrack huts, four metres by four with windows on each wall to take advantage of the slightest breeze to cool the air. He had entered a crèche, where some forty children and a woman seemed busy doing nothing in particular, and visited the plantation hospital, a long building, preceded by a kind of 'operating theatre', where wooden cupboards stored solemn lines of labelled bottles, with a low table set with strange iron surgical instruments, sinisterly shaped, as medical instruments tend to be, and then a huge ward, with windows and some fifty cream-coloured iron beds on either side. A resident doctor, exuding self-satisfied complacency he made no attempt to disguise, accompanied him on a visit that had clearly been well prepared. Most beds had freshly washed sheets; there were three black nurses in newly ironed uniforms, a floor still wet from its morning wash, recently whitewashed walls and no groaning patients in bed. Everything was perfect, except for the odour of formaldehyde and death. Neglect, terminal silence and resignation impregnated the air and senses, and could shelter no kind of deception. No place in the world had ever made him feel such desperate loneliness. Luís Bernardo listened quietly to all the explanations the doctor and administrator gave and asked no questions as he walked at their speed through the wards, trying not to stare into the eyes of patients curled up in bed like captured animals.

Before lunch, he went to see the extensive flagstoned yards where the wooden trays for sun-drying cocoa were set out, which the women immediately took indoors at the first sign of rain. Before that the cocoa transported by the Decauville line trucks – a recent innovation on the main plantations – was shelled by women and children, in an operation that they called the *quebra*.

Defying the administrator's visible antagonism, Luís Bernardo demanded to see with his own eyes the food being served to the labourers.

'It is a necessary part of my task,' he stated emphatically and the administrator had no choice but to agree.

That day – as he would soon verify – and almost every day on every plantation, the workers lunched on a bowl of boiled rice and a litre of water served in tin mugs.

They – the administrator, overseer and doctor – lunched in the Casa Grande on *feijão* with fried pork and a banana–vanilla dessert followed by coffee, and a brandy that he refused. It was a moment of respite on a sweaty morning allowing Luís Bernardo to change his sopping-wet white cotton shirt.

After lunch they moved to the veranda that ran the whole length of the house and from where they could see the whole estate, its white stone buildings and Portuguese roof tiles, a simple, uncluttered architectural style that reminded Luís Bernardo of villages in the interior of Portugal. He felt comfortable on the veranda and almost on the point of surrendering to sleep, from exhaustion and the heat coming from the open yard only now subdued by the shadow from the canopy.

It was the Porto Alegre administrator's insistence he take a siesta that finally brought him back to the call of duty. He asked them to harness a horse and left for the plantations, once again dripping with sweat as he penetrated deep down the tracks between the cocoa trees and along broader paths lined by palm trees.

The labourers worked like an army of ants in the middle of the plantation, sometimes melding into the trees themselves. They cleaned, cut, opened clearings, picked and gathered the cocoa others collected in baskets and carried on their backs to the Decauville railway that seemed like a toy train. He didn't see any whips or cudgels or the other things he'd heard about in the hands of the deputy overseers or 'bush chiefs'. It all seemed quite normal and in order, like a banal factory assembly line, the only difference being that it was open-air, oppressively hot and intolerably humid. That's how they built the Pyramids, and constructed empires, he thought.

After two hours, he left the horse in the care of one of his helpers and returned to the centre of the plantation on the Decauville, perched on a pile of cocoa in one of the trucks hooked up to a small steam engine. When the bell struck at six, at sunset, the workers began to converge on the big open yard from every corner of the plantation. They came alone or in groups, walking slowly, backs bent, blades dangling down. They slumped to the ground and stayed sitting or lying down, mute, every limb exhausted. At six-thirty, the overseer ordered them to line up for the afternoon headcount, in case someone, in a sudden attack of madness, had bid farewell to his contract, to legality and 'security' in life, and had exchanged all that for the darkness of a jungle bristling with danger and offering no future happiness. After the headcount they lined up to get the food they cooked in their huts: dried fish, rice and bananas, for themselves and for their families – if they had any.

From his observation post on the plantation veranda, Luís Bernardo recalled the idyllic description, penned by one São Tomé plantation owner, that he had read somewhere:

Once the signal is given to disperse, they withdraw to their huts, where they eat, chat and dance away until the bell rings to mark bedtime. On their days off, when they are allowed to go to bed much later, they often organise a big song-and-dance, and give vent to their feelings of happiness by dancing and gesticulating. They harbour no worries relative to their subsistence or families, since that is the responsibility of their employers, who supply them with food three times a day, as well as clothes, accommodation and medical treatment, wages paid in cash and a return ticket to and from their port of departure . . . With these advantages and privileges, plus the interest and paternal support they receive from their employers and the Crown Commissioner, these labourers enjoy a relatively enviable existence, and consequently when their contracts come to an end, because they enjoy a well-being they could never find in the lands of their birth, these Angolan natives prefer to stay on the islands rather than return to Angola . . .

Luís Bernardo smiled as he remembered the quotation he knew almost by heart, but what he saw were hundreds of exhausted, dejected men dragging themselves back to their barrack huts, knives in hand, and he wondered whether the author of those words perhaps wanted people to believe that the heartbreaking chant he had heard in the early morning expressed 'feelings of happiness'. He imagined the man in Paris, at that very moment perhaps lounging in the Hotel Bristol or Créteil, getting ready to spend a night at the Folies Bergère with some chorus girl; an experience no soul working on a plantation, showered with 'advantages and privileges' and 'paternal support' would get from a whole lifetime of working dawn to dusk, day after day.

Luís Bernardo was still leaning on the veranda balustrade, immersed in thought, when they had all left and the yard was almost deserted. The first smoke was rising from the huts and it now seemed as if the two worlds – black and white – had separated and peace and the natural order of things had descended over the plantation. But it was only a short-lived illusion of peace: a silence rising from the entrails of the earth, spreading through the forest took possession of the *óbó*, where all sound had disappeared, as if prompted by a hidden signal. In the distance, the song of the *ossóbó* went up and set off the night shift. The plantation bell rang immediately, desperately, and a crowd of women left the barracks and hurriedly began collecting in the wooden trays of cocoa. A wind from the sea blew across the *óbó*, and the foliage and even tops of thirty- or forty-metre-high trees shook as it hit them, as if tragedy had struck. Three minutes later, raindrops as big as stones started to fall and suddenly the whole sky was rent by thunderclaps and lightning flashes that lit up the jungle as if it were daytime, and a deluge was unleashed upon the red earth. Old trees shattered in the storm, cracked apocalyptically and fell into the undergrowth, fell to the earth brushing against the trees still standing, as if bidding them farewell. The whole sky, forest and earth moaned and lamented, battered by the wind and savage storm. The *óbó* was filled with the sound of rivers forming and rushing down, violently disturbing sleepy waterfalls. Luís Bernardo was awestruck by the beauty of the spectacle: if someone had said the world was coming to an end, he would have believed them.

The terrible battle in the heavens between water and fire lasted little more than half an hour. Divine wrath was gradually appeased, the rain became scattered, the bright flashes receded and the thunderclaps were now heard far off out to sea. Suddenly it was all over: silence quickly possessed everything and the *óbó* was home to screaming night birds, panting animals hidden in the undergrowth and the sound of water gently running down the mountainside. Smoke again curled from barrack chimneys, the voices of men and women and shouts of children increased and a chant soon went up in one of the huts and spread to others, a low chant enveloping everything else. A sudden, numbing sadness overwhelmed Luís Bernardo. He turned his back on the yard and went in to dress for dinner.

Early next morning, he left the Porto Alegre anchorage for another plantation. Every single day in subsequent weeks his life was regulated by plantation bells, meals with strangers, visits to workshops and hospitals, and the gloomy chants of blacks plucked from Angola to guarantee the prosperity of these islands and a wealth enjoyed far away by their owners.

Mr Feliciano Alves, the Porto Alegre plantation administrator, had finally asked him, 'Well, Governor, what did you think?'

Luís Bernardo had sighed and answered half-smiling, 'I find it all quite astonishing, Mr Alves.'

'Really? And do you think they are as badly treated as they claim in Lisbon?'

'That depends. I expect you and I might possibly think they aren't so badly treated. There's worse in Africa, to be sure. But if you ask them, you might get a different answer.'

'What might that be, Governor?'

'I don't know, Mr Alves. Can you not imagine yourself in their place?'

'In their place . . .?'

'Yes, imagine yourself working ten hours a day on the planta-tion, getting up when the bell rings and going to sleep when the bell orders you to, and earning two and a half réis a month?'

'Governor, this is not a fit subject for conversation between gentlemen. Each man has his place; it was God who made the world, not us. As far as I know, he decided the lot of black and white, rich and poor.'

'Of course, you are right, Mr Alves. However, my faith has hardly been strengthened of late.'

And he'd embarked in the steam packet while Mr Alves looked on, visibly apprehensive.

He went to the capital three times in three weeks, to sleep in the Governor's Palace, change his clothes, deal with urgent business and read official communications from Lisbon. There was also private correspondence waiting for him, a letter from João giving him news of his friends and repeating his promise that he would visit 'as soon as your solitude is so unbearable I will no longer be able to bear the remorse I feel for persuading you to go to this exile and serve the Fatherland'. And the Lisbon newspapers had also arrived to bring news seemingly from another planet. Political agitation, rumours of conspiracies, complaints from the provinces filled the front pages, while the London correspondents reported on Dom Carlos's visit to England: he'd spent three weeks between Windsor, Balmoral and Blenheim, the Duke of Marl-borough's residence, hunting, going to the theatre, to concerts and bridge parties, a schedule only interrupted by the odd visit to a regiment. His Majesty's diary had no entry recording a working lunch with the Prime Minister, with Lord Balfour at the Foreign

Office, with those in charge at the Ministry for the Colonies, with financiers, importers or journalists – anything that might help Portugal. Luís Bernardo could not help thinking that between his hunts and concerts Dom Carlos might have remembered the mission with which he had entrusted him and its implications for relations with Britain.

The most comforting aspect of his return visits to the Palace was to see how Sebastião and all his staff seemed to miss him, and treated him like a soldier returning from the front to recoup energies in the rear guard. Mamoun and Sinhá in the kitchen kept asking the Governor to say what he 'would really like to eat', and whatever he mentioned was immediately transformed into his next meal, as if they'd anticipated his desires. Doroteia smiled at the pile of dirty washing he threw on his bedroom floor and neatly lined up a selection of washed, starched shirts on the top of his drawers for him to take the following morning. And smiling silently she slipped through his bedroom, dressing room and bathroom like a black gazelle, dressed only in white and ever more tempting, and he wanted to pounce on her as she walked by, pull her towards him, feel her firm, straight body against his, run his hand through her jet-black hair and whisper in her ear, as if giving orders but with other intentions.

At night, after dinner, as soon as he headed to the terrace with his glass of brandy or port, Sebastião would enquire knowingly, 'Would His Honour the Governor like me to put on the record of the singing Italian gentleman or the German gentleman's record?' and he would reply, highly amused, 'Giuseppe or Wolfgang?'

He visited thirty plantations in three weeks, some in the interior, embedded deep in the jungle, way up the mountain, and only accessible via long tracks and paths that had to be cleaned and cleared of undergrowth almost every day, since nature engulfed them so quickly. But that allowed him to get to know the jungle as few did. He climbed to peaks from which you could see the sea on a clear day, crossed rivers on horseback, descended steep valleys into the darkness of the *óbó*, passed under waterfalls and once bathed in the cold, transparent waters of a pool at the foot of a fall. The map of the island now held no secrets for him and he knew by heart the whereabouts of plantations, points to embark, beaches, rivers and mountains.

He had started in the south, and consequently left almost to the end the one he thought would be among the most unpleasant and difficult – the trip to the Rio do Ouro plantation, administered by Colonel Mário Maltez, whose exchanges at the Palace dinner had forewarned him of the animosity he could expect. But, to his surprise, when he reached Rio do Ouro in the early afternoon, the Colonel wasn't there to welcome him: he was informed that he'd had to go to the city on urgent business. Even stranger, he'd delegated the Crown Commissioner Germano Valente to stand in for him, who until that point had made no effort to accompany him or be present at any of his other plantation visits. Luís Bernardo didn't know what to think, but it struck him that the Colonel's absence was a mark of disrespect. No business in São Tomé was so urgent as to warrant a plantation administrator not personally welcoming a new governor visiting his plantation for the first time. On the other hand, the presence of the Commissioner, either representing or substituting for the administrator, sent out a clear message: that both stood shoulder to shoulder in any possible conflict with the Governor and that the Commissioner would personally defend the working conditions on that plantation.

Luís Bernardo didn't show his real feelings; he was seething with rage and hurt pride. He hesitated between leaving immediately or carrying through his visit as if nothing were amiss. He finally opted for a compromise, and allowed himself to be guided round the plantation, without making comments or asking questions provoked by the explanations given by the head overseer. The Rio do Ouro and its thirty-kilometre perimeter was the biggest and most impressive of the plantations he had seen so far. Its installations were exceptional, its machinery, including the recently installed Decauville line, were the most modern available; the plantations were perfectly organised and designed. It was not surprising the plantation produced two hundred and thirty thousand *arrobas* of cocoa a year, and amassed the astronomical amount of one thousand two hundred *contos* a year, which its owner, the Count of Valle Flor, ensured he spent sparingly in Lisbon or Paris.

The overseer fired off statistics as if he were reciting blessings, described the state of each plantation, the yield from each hectare, the total production from each work front. The Commissioner walked two paces behind, remained silent, as did Luís Bernardo, who looked always ahead, as if he already knew it all by heart or wasn't really interested. The numbers, however, pounded in Luís Bernardo's brains like truths that could not be refuted. The heat had reached maximum and he now looked forward to the redeeming rain of late afternoon as he felt more intensely that doubt or angst was futile, and that he should seek a truce, an honourable surrender: shade, a chair and a glass of fresh lemonade; if necessary, a request for an apology in exchange for a truce.

In the afternoon headcount, an endless black army lined up in the central yard and stood there neither happy nor defiant, and certain the two hundred and thirty thousand *arrobas*, twelve hundred *contos* a year were part of the world God had created like that for blacks and whites, and another day came to an end for the minuscule scrap of humanity that was the Rio do Ouro plantation on the accursed island of São Tomé.

After the workers had lined up, Luís Bernardo gathered all his remaining energy and pride and asked for his horse and Vicente's to be saddled up so they could ride back to the city. And now it was *his* turn to enjoy the shock on the faces of the Commissioner and the overseer.

'What? Won't Your Excellency have dinner with us and stay overnight?'

'No, thank you very much: I also have urgent business to attend to in the city.'

'But dinner and Your Excellency's rooms are all ready, on the express orders of Colonel Maltez . . .!'

'Well, you know, I didn't have the pleasure of meeting the Colonel . . . Tell him I am very grateful for his offer, and perhaps next time, when the Colonel can be here as well.'

'And does the Governor intend leaving at night to go back down the mountain?'

'Indeed I do. We still have half an hour of light, so please arrange for someone to accompany us with a lantern and then return tomorrow. It will be an easy enough journey.'

They set out, accompanied by two blacks, who walked on ahead, carrying two oil-lamps and pointed staves. They proceeded silently for some twenty minutes without light, until the rain hit them as they were preparing to climb the Macaco peak by cutting right along a path that came out on the other side on the road to the village of Santo Amaro. The jungle finished there and it would be easy to make headway to São Tomé, even at night.

But with the rain pouring down so hard it was difficult to follow the path; Luís Bernardo decided to call a halt. They dismounted, tied their horses to a nearby tree and took shelter under some bushes by the side of the track. Vicente unrolled an oilskin sheet he kept for such emergencies and stretched it over the top of the bushes to create a precarious shelter for himself and Luís Bernardo. The two blacks from Rio do Ouro continued to stand out in the downpour. Luís Bernardo beckoned them to come under the shelter, but they didn't seem to understand.

He shouted to one of them above the racket from the cloudburst.

'Hey you, what's your name?'

The black hesitated, but finally replied, 'They call me Josué, Boss.'

'Josué, come under here.'

They both stared at him dumbstruck, as if Luís Bernardo were speaking to someone else.

'I said, come under here!'

They looked at each other and tried to decide whether it was an order or an invitation. But Luís Bernardo stepped back to one side to make space for them to go in and sit down. They were silent and cringing as they crouched down and looked out into the undergrowth, as if they didn't belong inside. Luís Bernardo noted a deep scar running down Josué's bare shoulder and across the back now turned towards him. Drops of sweat, mixed with raindrops, ran down his bare torso and the smell given off, together with the stench from the drenched undergrowth, almost stifled them in their scant, improvised shelter.

Thus Dr Valença, the Governor of São Tomé and Príncipe by royal appointment, who, in an interlude in the royal hunt in Vila Viçosa, had been charged to abandon his Lisbon life and comforts, found himself huddled under a dirty oilskin sheet, sheltering from a torrential downpour, devoured by mosquitoes, streaming in sweat, with three black men he'd nothing in common with. But at that moment in the middle of the jungle, the only mission of any importance was to wait for the downpour to stop, mount his horse and disappear up the mountain into the darkness of the forest, with its shrieks, lianas and deep shadows, to reach the nearest village and a more secure path, where he'd ride for another three hours until he was able to wallow in his bath and stretch out in bed in his island home.

Exhaustion exacted by an infinite burden of sadness and lethargy had come over him, threatening to prostrate him there for ever in defeat, his mission a failure, his pride forgotten. He'd return to the Governor's Palace, sit down at his bureau and write a letter to the King: 'I give up. What Your Majesty ordered me to do is beyond my strength.' And would take the next boat back to Lisbon and the life he knew and loved. The press and the King's coterie would lambaste his reputation. The Fatherland, or what saw itself as that, would register his desertion. But at least he'd be intact and ready to live again. He'd have fled that green inferno, the solitude of the tropics and the unassailable sadness of those people. *He* would return from Africa.

Darkness now shrouded everything. The forest was a pitch-black stain buffeted by gusts of wind. One of the Rio do Ouro blacks lit a lamp and the smell of oil flooded their shelter, which he found absurdly consoling and familiar. It was the smell from nights fishing in the open sea off Sesimbra, in Antonio Amador's boat. The smell from his grandfather's house and his childhood, when he heard the servants' voices in the kitchen, his father's coughs in the bedroom, heralding the death that stalked him, the smell left in the passageway when his mother walked by holding a candlestick, beside herself with grief, between the room where death dwelled and the life in the kitchen that nobody ruled any more. His mother, distant, lonely and bewildered in the dark *óbó* of his jumbled childhood memories. A whiff of oil, a man dying of tuberculosis, a woman who had lost the meaning to her life wandering down a passageway, and voices from the back of the house, where life was hiding. Swaddled in a linen sheet and heavy flannel blanket, sheltered from every ill and storm in the protective darkness of his bedroom, the child Luís listened to everything.

'Is anyone there?' He repeated the question several times, on several nights, when he thought everything seemed even darker and more remote. But nobody ever replied.

He took a cigarette from his jacket pocket and lit it with his oil lighter. The light briefly lit up the face of Josué, who'd turned round when he heard the lighter. It was a hard, still childish face, the whites of his eyes a mixture of suffering and incomprehensible happiness; he had a deferential but loyal way of looking down as he swung round to listen to the rain. Luís Bernardo felt a sudden frisson of tenderness towards him. In the whole world, at this moment, there's nobody I am closer to. No friend, woman, lover or family. Only this man sharing two square metres of shelter against the rain.

He held his hand out and touched Josué's scarred shoulder, prompting him to swing back round.

'Where are you from, Josué?'

The same panic-stricken face. The same hesitation. And fear.

'I'm from Bailundo, Boss.'

'And when did you leave there?'

He lowered his head, as if in denial. Would he reply?

'A long time ago, Boss.'

'How long?'

'A long . . . long time. I've forgotten.' His white teeth gleamed in a sad smile.

'Have you always been here on the Rio do Ouro plantation?'

Josué nodded. His response was apparently so obvious he didn't need to speak. Luís Bernardo noticed how his companion remained still, didn't turn round and was still staring out at the rain. Josué was sideways on, uncomfortable and visibly wanting the interrogation to end. He also noticed how Vicente was equally ill at ease, sitting next to him and swaying like a nervous child.

But he didn't relent.

'And did you sign a work contract?'

He nodded again, so quickly it was as if he'd anticipated the question.

'Did you sign it yourself, Josué?

'Yes, I signed it, Boss.'

'Do you know how to sign your name, Josué?'

This time he didn't sway, as if he hadn't heard the question.

Luís Bernardo felt almost sub-human as he put his hand in his pocket, took his pen and small notebook out, looked for a clean page, and handed him pen and pad.

'Sign your name here, Josué.'

He shook his head and stared silently at the ground.

'Do you know when your contract ends, Josué?'

Another shake of the head, another silence. Only the patter of the rain now.

'Have you got a family here?'

'I have a wife and two children, Boss.'

Luís Bernardo came to the end of his questions. He had one remaining question he found difficult to ask.

'Josué, do you know that the contract only lasts five years – when it runs out, you could leave, if you wanted. Would you like to return to your land when your contract runs out?'

The silence weighed like lead. The rain had stopped: life, which had been suspended, seemed to return to the forest. Josué's black companion began to get up and Josué made as if to follow, but Bernardo gripped his arm and forced him to look up at him.

'Well, Josué, do you want to return to your land?'

He finally looked up. In the half-light, Luís Bernardo saw a tear muddy the whites of Josué's eyes as he stared him in the face.

The reply came so softly he had to listen hard to hear it.

'I don't know, Boss. I don't know anything about any of that. With your permission . . .' Relieved and anxious, he left their makeshift shelter, as if freedom were outside.

9

T HE ENGLISHMAN HAD postponed his arrival: he would now come at the end of June. Luís Bernardo had taken longer than expected to visit all the island plantations, so this gave him extra time to see what he hadn't yet seen on São Tomé and sail to the Island of Príncipe, where three days would suffice to get to know the town and the half-dozen plantations there. Meanwhile, the Ministry in Lisbon asked him once again to arrange proper accommodation for the British Consul, something he'd already dealt with, by ordering a government house, once residence of the Mayor, to be cleaned, painted and minimally redecorated. It was a small house, situated on the road out of the city, not very far from the Governor's Palace, but it had sea views and the privacy of a beautiful garden, where the house's colonial architecture, simple, straight lines, gained a dignity that surpassed its actual size.

The Ministry informed him the Englishman would come accompanied by his wife, but that he didn't have any children or retinue.

Strange, thought Luís Bernardo. Who can this Consul be, who travels here straight from India, where he's been previously in post. With his wife as sole company and travelling round the Cape in an English steamship?

Other news also arrived from Lisbon that he thought politically important: Major Paiva Couceiro, another of Mouzinho's men and a companion in arms of Minister Ayres d'Ornellas, had been appointed Governor of Angola, to replace the little Napoleon he'd met on his stop on his way from Lisbon. He had yet to exchange any correspondence, private or official, with the new Minister. It was also true he'd only sent two reports since his arrival, apart from short telegrams with very succinct information. The first report related, as it were, how he'd settled in and his initial contacts with other local people in authority. The second related his impressions after visiting nearly all the plantations on São Tomé and after his first formal encounter, held at his request, with the Crown Commissioner.

This was a tense meeting that he called when still feeling the after-effects of the humiliation and rage he'd experienced on his visit to Rio do Ouro. As soon as Germano André Valente, looking as smarmy as ever, sat down opposite him, he launched in without more ado.

'First of all, Crown Commissioner, I would like to know what you thought you were doing on the Rio do Ouro plantation?'

The other man looked at him as calmly as possible, as if it was just the question he had been expecting.

'I already explained why on the occasion of the Governor's visit: I was there to welcome you, at the request of Colonel Maltez, since he could not do so personally.'

'But do you represent the government or Colonel Maltez?'

At last Germano Valente shifted uneasily in his chair. That was going much further than he'd anticipated.

'Why do you ask, Governor?'

'Now I'm the one asking questions and I would prefer you to answer mine first,' Luís Bernardo spoke very softly and deliberately.

'Obviously, I represent the government.'

'Excellent, at least we can agree on that much. Because when I saw you there substituting for the plantation administrator, I thought for a moment that the Commissioner had forgotten what his real position was.'

He saw the Commissioner bite his lip and stifle his response. He clearly had to make a very great effort to restrain himself. It was a frontal attack and he had momentarily lost the defiant tone he always adopted towards Luís Bernardo. Instead, there was a silent hatred in his studied deadpan expression. This man, he thought, hated me from the moment he saw me. I hated him from the moment he laid eyes on me.

'As you must know, over the last month I have visited some forty plantations.' He paused so his interlocutor would understand that the Governor believed the Commissioner did what he could to check on his various excursions. 'And I had the opportunity on all these plantations to speak from time to time to some of the black labourers.'

'Really?' Germano Valente pretended to be unperturbed.

'And,' Luis Bernardo continued, as if he'd not noticed the interruption, 'none of those I spoke to possessed a copy of the contract they'd agreed with the plantation. I found some who swore they'd signed one but hadn't kept a copy, others who also swore they'd signed, but then I soon discovered they didn't know how to sign their own name, and that others plainly didn't know what I was talking about.'

Luís Bernardo went quiet: he was playing a game of poker with his opponent and wanted to gauge his reactions.

'Well, if there are any doubts, I have in my possession, as is my right, copies of all the contracts signed by plantation workers on São Tomé and Príncipe, since that became a legal requirement,' he retorted.

'Very good, just what I wanted to know! And could the Commissioner provide me with these copies so I can dispel my doubts?'

Germano Valente remained silent for a few moments that seemed interminable to Luís Bernardo. He was an expert poker player weighing up his hand before playing his cards and, when he replied, after an almost imperceptible sigh, he was like a gambler carefully considering his options.

'Governor, I will not do so.'

'You won't? Why on earth not?'

'It forms part of my duties and only mine. Your Excellency is politically my superior, but not my superior in the administration. Therefore, in terms of my specific functions, I have no hierarchical reason to obey you. If I did as you request, I would be allowing you to inspect my work, and, as you know, I am directly responsible to the Ministry and not to the Governor.'

'Very well, I can't force you to comply and, consequently, will just communicate to Lisbon that I cannot adequately appraise the labour situation of plantation workers because you refuse to collaborate.'

'Your Excellency the Governor will communicate with Lisbon as he thinks fit.'

That night, Luís Bernardo sat down at his bureau and wrote a long report to the Minister. It was his first political report, his first substantial evaluation of the situation he'd found and which, he emphasised, he could only relate now he felt in a position to speak with first-hand experience of the realities.

He began by reminding the Minister that his impressions were entirely free and independent, since he was no career diplomat and had never aspired to the post he now filled.

On the contrary, as Your Excellency must know, it was a personal, urgent request from His Majesty, and his appeal that I should serve my country led me to abandon my life and interests in Lisbon to take up a post I in no way desired, coveted or even imagined. I will remain here only as long as it is thought my role can serve my country: not a single day more. Consequently, if Your Excellency will allow me to tell you candidly and loyally, all you will hear from me will be what I think and what I witness; nothing will be held back or kept secret, influenced by opportunist considerations, by any need to protect third parties or, even less, my own position.

He then went on to relate the considerable marathon he'd engaged in since his arrival: getting to know every local organisation, plantation owner or administrator and visiting every island plantation and settlement. 'São Tomé now holds no secrets for me, or at least none that are visible,' he concluded.

With regard to the most important part of my mission, namely the situation of the black labourers on the plantations – which is in the end what drives the controversy threatening the islands and is the reason for my visit – I cannot, unfortunately, say as much: what is visible is not enough to establish definite conclusions. I went, saw, asked, enquired but, as was to be expected and is completely understandable, I found a natural distrust on the part of the Portuguese on the plantations when it came to facilitating scraps of information that could be used against them. I find it more difficult to understand the same reticence in the person of the Crown Commissioner, whose hostile attitude towards me and refusal to give me sight of the contracts signed between employers' organisations and plantation workers makes it difficult to reach a comprehensive understanding of the workers', legal position, which constitutes, as Your Excellency knows, the nub of the dispute we have with some sectors of British society and His British Majesty's Government.

From what I could see personally and must now report to Your Excellency, I can state it is evident that the conditions of life and work on the São Tomé plantations, given the extremes of the climate, the harsh nature and long hours of the work when compared with the benefits, namely wages received in kind, are barely tolerable for humans: no Portuguese peasant, however wretched and desperate his situation on the land, would want to emigrate here and do this work for this remuneration.

It will be said that – and one has to agree – it is certainly worse in other African or South American colonies belonging to the European powers. It is true, for example, that a fair number of São Tomé plantations possess their own hospitals, some with their own doctors, and that the labourers receive medical care, food and accommodation in their place of work. In this respect, there are even some who exclaim, 'And on top of that they get paid!' If one accepts, in fact, that such conditions are sufficient horizon for a human being, even if he is black, then I can tell Your Excellency we have nothing to worry about. But I don't think I was chosen to carry out my duties to sustain such ideas, quite the contrary in fact.

However, that is not what is at stake. What is at stake is not ascertaining whether the plantation bosses judge the conditions they provide their workers to be adequate, but finding out what the workers think. Do they stay on the plantations of São Tomé because, despite everything, they don't consider their situation to be so intolerable or their pay so meagre, and because they know they won't find a better alternative on the whole continent when it comes to work and quality of life, or are they there purely and simply because they have not the means to go home? Putting it as bluntly as I can: Are they here of their own free will or under compulsion, and, if the latter is the case, are they in fact slave labour?

It is true that there exists, as Your Excellency knows, a legal framework that removes the very possibility of slave labour. The law of 29 April 1875 decreed an end to slavery in all the dominions of the Portuguese Crown. The Law of 29 January 1903 created, here on these islands, a Repatriation Fund whereby half the pay of all plantation workers is deposited in order to pay for their passage home; at the same time it established contracts of five years' duration – which means that, in two years from now, contracts agreed under this law will terminate and its usefulness can be tested. The problem is that the majority of the workers came here before this law was promulgated and do not have contracts. Yet another issue is whether half of their wages docked to cover their passage home at the end of five years will be enough to pay the passages for themselves and the families they have naturally created here in the meantime?

It is also important to ascertain whether the workers currently covered by work contracts as the law requires signed of their own free will and are fully aware of the following: when their contracts terminate and whether they are free to return home, should they wish, and can draw on sufficient funds. Because if at the end of a five-year stint on the plantations (for the majority it will most likely be ten, twenty or thirty!) the Angolans don't realise they can leave, and are not free to go or don't have the money to pay their fares, then it will be difficult to reach any conclusion other than that the conditions of work amount to slave labour, even if it is with pay.

Luís Bernardo finished by making a direct appeal to the Minister. Since everything hung on the application of the law in respect of contractual conditions for plantation labour, and its application depended on the Crown Commissioner, the government should ask the latter to take responsibility for effectively implementing the law. If this were not done, he suggested, it would be difficult for the Governor by himself to carry out the mission with which he had been charged.

And my mission, if I correctly recall the words the King used when he gave me this post, is to guarantee that it cannot be said throughout the world that slavery survives, in any form, in the overseas territories under Portuguese administration.

It was a long report so he sent it by normal steamship and not by telegram. It would take much longer to reach the hands of Ayres d'Ornellas, but Luís Bernardo sensed this would be balanced by the benefits of spelling out to the new Minister exactly what the rules of the game were. He was there, not from self-interest, but from a wish to serve his country. He had come, not to change his ideas in relation to a form of colonial exploitation he deemed unsustainable, nor to compromise with the existing situation by avoiding all conflict, but to put an end to what was intolerable. If this was not also the government's understanding, it was clear he was not the right person for the post and they should quite rightly replace him. If, on the other hand, he did not receive the support and collaboration that was his due, he could not be held responsible for the outcome of his mission. He knew the tone of his report verged on the unacceptable in a communication to a superior. It was almost as if he were saying, 'These are my conditions: if you are in agreement, fine, if you are not, then please inform me.' But otherwise what sense did it make for him to stay on? If nothing needed changing, why had they sent him here? Any idle colonel or general, any overseas administrator eager to progress in his career could do the job and better.

He also received in his post from Lisbon a cutting from *O Século* with a translation of an article published in the Liverpool *Evening Standard*, where one Colonel J.A. Wyllie held forth on the conditions of blacks on the São Tomé and Príncipe plantations. This Colonel had retired from service in India, and had been funded by the Foreign Office to go on a 'study visit' to São Tomé. Great hopes had been placed on the outcome of that trip. The Colonel's visit led to a conclusion that was so pathetic it was quite counter-productive: 'The Angolan black is by nature entirely animal. He is like a monkey transported to a Zoological Garden, except that he is not placed in a zoo but in a climate more fatal for simian life.'

Luís Bernardo didn't know whether to laugh or cry over that indicator of political strategy. Whoever paid for this Englishman to get sodden on gin and tonic on the verandas of Casas Grandes did Portugal no good, he reflected. His liberal – indeed sceptical – spirit recalled time and again that farewell remark from the administrator of the Porto Alegre plantation, the first he visited: God made the world, not men. It was he who decided the lot of rich and poor, black and white. It was not within the power of men to change the divine plan, then. In effect: certain things could never be changed.

He knew he was the first Governor to throw himself so whole-heartedly into his work. He'd seen little of his office at the Government Palace in his first two months on São Tomé, but conversely had closely scrutinised the whole island on his tireless marathon to plantations and villages down the byways of São Tomé. He was sure no government functionary before him, no plantation administrator, no passing visitor had tried to familiarise himself so quickly and exhaustively with that slice of tropical jungle adrift in the Atlantic. He was motivated by curiosity and the conviction that it was simply the best way to carry out his mission; and he was driven by a kind of obstinacy, wilfulness or vanity. Whenever mention was made of a plantation or corner of the island, he could say that he'd been there and knew what he was talking about. Many could say that they knew the island well; few, if any, that they knew it as well as the Governor: that was his first political victory, no mean feat after only two months.

Even if the landscape and the atmosphere on the plantations came to assume a monotonously familiar sameness, he was perpetually astonished by the buildings and particularly by the Casas Grandes. He wondered at the clean white lines, the spot-lessly whitewashed walls and thatched roofs, which recalled Portuguese villages, as did the brass guttering running along the eaves to drain the rainwater off, the hard-wood floorboards, and the dark, heavy wooden doors, aged by polish and time. He imagined how many boat journeys from Europe had been necessary to bring all that was visibly not made on the islands, the porcelain door handles, dinner services, sets of glassware and cutlery, canopied beds where he slept on several occasions, the jugs and china basins in bedrooms, crucifixes and paintings of saints or absurd, remote landscapes, iron and copper pots in kitchens, glass mirrors in sitting rooms, velvet or faded leather sofas, chandeliers hanging from ceilings, vases or jugs from Canton, black Indian filigree wooden furniture, two grand pianos he found in two sitting rooms and even a gramophone he saw in a drawing room, which proved his was not unique on the island.

When, as was always the case on the big plantations, the administrators were not the owners, the Casas Grandes were uninhabited, except when the owners visited in the summer. The administrator and his family lived in a nearby house, the second in importance on the plantation, and on Luís Bernardo's behalf they opened up a Casa Grande dining room or reception room, when he stayed overnight, a guest room, invariably on the top floor. Some houses retained signs of their owners' last fleeting visit – old magazines in the reception room, headed notepaper on the bureau in the study, bottles of port and cognac lined up in the pantry, children's games abandoned in bedrooms, and men's linen or white cotton garments hanging in the wardrobe in the room where he slept.

Before dozing off, Luís Bernardo would try to imagine what the family and absentee landowners were like. How did they feel waking up to the rigours of the morning headcount, going to sleep to the racket from the *óbó*? How did they cope with the heat, and each day's hourglass monotony? Did they go riding, explore the nearby forest, listen to its birds, swim in cold pools by waterfalls, go down to the sea, swim among turtles and barracuda in the warm water off the beach, meditate on the veranda at night, smell the smoke from the barrack-hut fires, half dazed by their own reeking oil-lamps where night-time insects dizzily flitted. Did they think occasionally about the army of shadows sleeping in the huts who from dawn to dusk plucked the magical cocoa bean, which guaranteed the plantation owners Lisbon schools and mansions, gentlemen's club and Paris haute couture?

Thus by inhabiting their absences he made their acquaintance. He saw what they saw, imagined what they imagined and felt what they felt. And it wasn't just the plantation owners he knew so well. He saw the blacks and their sad resignation; he saw their bodies, their muscles stretched to breaking point, their exhaustion; he saw their childish gaze, neither fearful nor forlorn, occasionally defiant, the distant remnant of pride preserved deep within; he saw their gleaming, open smiles when suddenly greeted by name and treated as one more human being. He saw the 'resident' whites – civil servants, priests, military, administrators, overseers and their women, with their overbearing self-importance and mediocrity, their world-weariness or vanity. He saw and interpreted the signs of passage of these absentees, men who were the masters of those islands, in whose name everyone else abandoned any shred of optimism and hope they retained in the subhuman enterprise that was São Tomé and Príncipe.

He saw and recalled everything with the awareness and lucidity of a newcomer whose mind had yet to be clouded by island fever and who was still aware of the purpose of his presence there. In that stifling climate and prison of sleep-inducing odours, in that vision of the Inferno, his body was exhausted by the violent sensations. But his spirit stayed alert and faithful to all he'd left behind and focused on the mission that had brought him there. Otherwise, the upheaval would have been so much wasted effort.

But there was just one day when Luís Bernardo came up against the force of circumstance. After all, no man, not even the Governor, is made of iron. It happened when he visited the Nova Esperança plantation, belonging to widow Maria Augusta da Trindade, who'd given him the honour of the opening dance at the ball. It was one of his last plantation visits. The Nova Esperança was next to the village of Trindade, which he passed through early the previous day, after the eventful, tense visit to Rio do Ouro. He arrived for lunch, in the heat of the day, out of sorts and ready to explode at the least sign of obduracy. He was in no mood to visit more buildings and plantations, to listen to more lectures on innovations in seeding and harvesting, more complaints about the uncertainties surrounding the crop, prices on the international market or the expensive, lazy labour force. However, the widow welcomed him as if he were a friend of long standing.

She took him straight into her kitchen and poured him a glass of fresh lemonade to soften the pain of the journey and pointed to a chicken and pepper stew bubbling on the fire. She introduced Mr Albano her overseer, a jaundiced man in his fifties who oozed malaria, he'd lived there so long. He was a taciturn, irritable fellow who eyed Luís Bernardo suspiciously. Maria Augusta related how she inherited him from her father, how he'd stayed on as overseer for six years, when shortly after her marriage to an officer from the local garrison who'd come from Lamego, she unexpectedly lost her father. Her mother died when she was three and, as an only child, she'd always looked upon Mr Albano as a kind of older brother. He took her to primary school in Trindade every morning, fetched her in the afternoon, waited with two horses in the shade of a tree, and protected her from her father's rages. At Christmas, he would remember to collect a young tree he had uprooted and which they both decorated as if they had an inkling about what Christmas ought to be like in their tropical exile.

Mr Albano, she continued, as Luís Bernardo listened, staring silently into his bowl of soup, was best man at her marriage and her most reliable source of support. Especially when Lieutenant Matos from Lamego succumbed to an agonising death from a deadly strain of diarrhoea, after six years of married life on the plantation, and left nothing – no children, no fortune, no pension worthy of the name, no house, no place in the whole of Portugal to justify her final return, when all her family was dead, to the place where her grandparents once lived. When her search for relatives yielded nothing, she hotfooted it back to her Nova Esperança plantation, home of the only person who'd accompanied her from childhood, where she knew the song of every bird and where, to Luís Bernardo's astonishment, she also knew every black worker by name. All that was hers was here and she stopped looking for a world that didn't exist. But, as he also soon discovered, contrary to all appearances she didn't live in isolation from the outside world: she subscribed to French and Portuguese magazines, had learned French as a young child from a Frenchwoman, the wife of the then Governor, had imported several of the latest literary works from Lisbon book-shops, and read Eça, Antero, Camilo, Victor Hugo, Molière and even Cervantes. The local society ladies loathed her and con-stantly invented intrigues around her person, though she clearly didn't intend being buried alive like so many other ladies on the island.

While they lunched, she initiated these little conversations with visible pleasure. Luís Bernardo listened and thought how out of place she would be in Lisbon. She spoke more at the dining table than was the rule for a society lady. She was too physically 'on display' for a lady of her age, which he calculated to be thirty-seven or thirty-eight. She was tall and her abundant bosom provided a luxuriant haven for a medallion with a portrait, perhaps her deceased husband's, which she absent-mindedly pulled out and plunged back in as she talked. Her neat black hair had been summarily combed and fixed with a tortoiseshell clasp on the top of her head, while two loose tresses hung down each side of her face. Her gestures, as she ate and talked, didn't display the restraint required of a woman of respectable reputation. And her white, full-length cotton dress, with its red-rose pattern, had a brazenly square neckline dipping from shoulders to cleavage that would have looked just ridiculous in Lisbon's Chiado or Baixa. Her face was simple but pleasant, coarse-lined and dark-eyed. In a word, she wasn't a lady to walk on your arm down the high street or to pay polite visits.

But on this island, far from usual standards of comparison, her figure, manner and conversation struck Luís Bernardo as a most agreeable distraction. There was something relaxing and familiar in her demeanour, as if she were a distant cousin one visited in her provincial retreat: healthily elemental and mercifully uncomplicated.

After lunch, accompanied as always by the silent Mr Albano, they went for a ride round the plantation. The dry season was nigh and it wasn't as hot as in the previous month and the humidity didn't run straight from the sky down your body. Maria Augusta frequently stopped to speak to women or workers. She asked about their illnesses, their children, or requested a pitcher of water. Sometimes they rode deep down lines of cocoa trees so she could point out a feature of the landscape or panorama or recall with Mr Albano an incident long ago that they'd both experienced there and which only they remembered. The arrangements on her plantation were less modern and industrialised than others he had seen. There was no railway and the barrack huts and agricultural installations were much smaller. The rhythm of work was evidently less intense: Maria Augusta didn't long to visit Paris every spring or buy a house on the Príncipe Real Square.

At her prompting, Luís Bernardo told her about his family, life and work in Lisbon. They even talked about the political situation and he explained in general terms what the country was like, the one that was hers, though she hardly knew it at all. He didn't feel for one moment like a governor making an inspection. From the first half-hour he begged her to stop calling him 'Mr Governor' and if it weren't for the awkward presence of the third person whom he still continued to address as 'Mr Albano' and who answered as 'Mr Governor', anyone seeing them return to the Casa Grande would have thought it was a group of three friends coming back from a relaxing ride.

They attended the afternoon headcount, after which Luís Bernardo went for the first time to the bedroom where he would spend the night, the first in a series of six rooms occupying the whole of the top floor. As he'd anticipated, it was a very simple bedroom with no luxuries, looking over the back of the square with views to the mountains where the sun had just set. He took a cold bath in the only bathroom on the floor, dried his hair quickly on a towel, perfumed himself with a little eau de cologne he'd brought with him and donned a pair of plain trousers, a white shirt and a beige, ivory-buttoned linen jacket. He placed a cigar in his top-jacket pocket and went down to the veranda.

It was another half-hour before Maria Augusta put in an appearance. Meanwhile he passed the time drinking gin and tonic and attempting to talk to Mr Albano. He didn't dislike the man, though the reverse wasn't true either: there was a hint of suspicion in his eyes and conversation, and Luís Bernardo couldn't decide whether it was aimed at him in particular or at humanity in general.

'Do you have your family here, Mr Albano?'

Mr Albano looked at him askance, upset by such an intrusion in his private life.

'No, I don't.'

'Are you married?'

No, Mr Governor, I am not.'

Luís Bernardo sat and pondered the acid tone of the reply and of the man himself: what really was Mr Albano's present status on the Nova Esperança plantation in relation to its owner? For example, where did Mr Albano live – in the Casa Grande as a member of the family, or in an adjacent building, as befitted an overseer, if he was just that?

He resolved to probe deeper.

'Tell me something, Mr Albano: what led to the death of Lieutenant Matos, Dona Maria Augusta's husband?'

'He died of fever.'

'How long ago was that?'

'Five years come November.' Mr Albano was like a keeper of the Civil Register reading out entries. Like a court witness, he only answered the obligatory questions and no more.

'And she has never considered remarrying?'

'I don't know, that's her business. Perhaps Mr Governor could ask her during dinner.'

By the time Maria Augusta finally appeared, the atmosphere between the two had become very strained. She was wearing a yellowish pleated dress, transparent lace under a bodice tied in bows that hugged her bosom. The model was in line with present fashions that she must have discovered in the magazines she received from Lisbon: the colours and finish were in dubious taste. Nonetheless, she did smell of bath salts and had obviously dressed for the occasion. Only Mr Albano had not washed or changed his clothes: for him it was a day like any other.

But she visibly wanted to lend the dinner a sense of occasion. It was the first time, she confessed, that she'd had the honour of dining with the Governor of São Tomé and Príncipe in her home, and only regretted it was such an informal, low-key affair. She lit the candles, asked two maids in starched aprons and caps to serve at table, poured a very decent wine to accompany a plate of prawns in piquant sauce and snapper cooked in the oven, with *matabala* and fried onion.

After pudding and fruit salad, she asked for coffee and port and cognac to be served on the veranda. It was a calm, cloudless, starry night, with an occasional very light breeze that rustled the leaves on the trees on the other side of the square and suddenly filled Luís Bernardo with nostalgia for a Portuguese summer. Relaxing against hand-stitched cushions in his wicker chair, languidly smoking a Partagas, Luís Bernardo sighed softly, a sigh redolent of well-being and physical comfort.

But Maria Augusta must have heard him because she asked, 'Missing home?'

He smiled, reluctant to admit to this frailty.

'Sometimes . . . It is the nights that are so different.'

'One gets accustomed to them in the end, you just see.'

Silence fell on all three. Or rather, silence on two of them, because Mr Albano was always quiet, apparently absorbed in the contemplation of something out of the ordinary he'd discovered on his boots. Mr Albano was in the way: they all felt that, even Mr Albano, and after twenty minutes during which he contributed nothing to the conversation or to enliven the night's entertainment he spoke.

'Mr Governor will excuse me but I do have to get up at four o'clock. Tomorrow is another day. . .'

Luís Bernardo stood up to bid him goodnight and noticed him silently shaking his head in Maria Augusta's direction: a private, disapproving, resigned or protective gesture.

When left alone, they remained silent, savouring the absence of the individual who'd been in the way, yet not knowing how to take advantage of such an unexpected moment.

He broke the impasse.

'How do you usually spend nights like these?'

It was her turn to sigh. He saw her breast rise beneath the bodice, and her eyes shine in the light from the nearby lamp. He felt her body relax, a sense of release and ill-concealed desire rise up her legs, belly and bosom and bring a flame to her eyes.

Her voice was hoarse, coming from afar.

'I think of life. What was, what couldn't be and what might still be. What else do you think I might do?'

'And does it make any sense?'

'What? Life, my life?'

'Yes.'

'Don't ask me. You can't ask such questions here. What would be the point? You are just passing through. In a year or two, you'll go back to Portugal, Your life is there: here you're in transit. But I'm not: I live here and I will always live here; it's what destiny has decided for me. I chose nothing and am in no situation to choose. I cling to what passes by, whenever I can; things that come to me, that I don't seek out. Are you with me?'

Luís Bernardo looked at her in the half-shadow. He felt sorry for her. In effect, destiny had abandoned her there, although it was clear she deserved and aspired to much more than that exile. He felt attracted to her. She had welcomed him without pretension, drama or suspicion. She herself saw to the lunch and dinner with which she had welcomed him, and told the story of her life, with no frills or desire to be centre stage. She'd spent the whole day as if it were a pleasure to welcome him, not as another plantation owner receiving the Governor, but as a woman receiving a man and striving to please him.

Nothing, but nothing, he thought, is the same here. Everything seems more urgent, more direct and straightforward. How often had she worn that pleated dress and bodice restraining a bosom that was ready to leap out? How often did she light those candlesticks? How often did she order her maids to wear starched uniforms? How often did she bring the vintage port out of the drinks cabinet? How often did she have a civilised man to talk to, on a tranquil, star-filled night, on the veranda of the house she inherited, as one inherits a prison?

'Yes, I think I so.'

She got up and stood in front of him. 'I cling to what passes by, whenever I can.' That sentence stood as her goodbye.

'Luís, it was an honour to receive you here on Nova Esperança as the Governor. I really mean that. It was also a pleasure to welcome you as a person. I would like to see you again . . . today, or whenever you wish. Goodnight.'

She left and Luís Bernardo stayed seated in the big wicker chair, legs stretched out on the balustrade, cigar glowing in the darkness of night. Bats flew silently across the veranda, drawn by the light from the lamp, swerving away at the last moment. He listened to the crickets in the pitch-black jungle and the shrieks of nocturnal birds patrolling their hunting territory. Then he thought he heard muffled footsteps padding beneath the veranda and quietly got up to take a look. Indeed he had: at that very moment Mr Albano was walking under the veranda. Their eyes met between the light and the shadow.

'Everything in order, Mr Albano?'

'I think so, Mr Governor.'

He finished his cigar and his glass of port. The light from the lamp was flickering: she'd left the bathroom. He got up to see if he could smell the sea, however distant. But there were no marine fragrances, only the odours of night shutting down in the middle of the jungle, a stench of cocoa and congealed sweat; and there was the repressed longing for a man, far down the corridor.

He blew out the lamp, walked inside, and without stopping listened to the noise of his own footsteps on the floor of the passageway. He halted briefly by the door to the end bedroom. His hand gripped and turned the cold door handle. He took a deep breath and tiptoed in like a thief.

10

'M R JAMESON, SIR! The Captain sent for you: we are there, sir!'

To tell the truth he wasn't asleep when he heard the knock on his door and the cabin boy calling him. A presentiment had woken him minutes earlier, when he'd guessed it was time to confront the fate chance had brought his way. He got up, trying not to make a sound to avoid disturbing his wife Ann, sleeping like a child at his side in the berth. For the thousandth time in seven years of marriage he contemplated Ann asleep oblivious to everything, and for the thousandth time he thought how beautiful she looked: her blonde hair cascading down her neck, her, nose neat and straight, her large mouth opening in a half-smile, one long, slender arm lying in the space he'd filled a moment ago, the perfect roundness of her bosom showing under the low neckline of her white linen nightdress. He felt like getting back into bed, curling up in her arms and waking much later on that murky day.

In the dark he quickly slipped a rainproof cape and trousers over his pyjamas and left the cabin, shutting the door quietly behind him. After he'd climbed two flights of stairs to the deck of HMS *Durban*, the early-morning cold hit his body that was still warm from Ann. Captain McQuinn was leaning on the ship's side, gripping his pipe between his teeth, holding two steaming cups of coffee in each hand. He looked up and offered him a cup as he heard him approach.

'Well, this is it.' He pointed the hand holding the cup in an easterly direction. 'Land ho!'

Jameson looked, and initially could discern nothing through the mist floating over the sea that a feeble rising sun was hard put to chase off. Gradually, as he gazed at the horizon where McQuinn was pointing, he saw the outline of a mountain, then another and another: that was all. He felt his heart contract. Here was the sum total of São Tomé and Príncipe, three mountains side by side, afloat in the middle of the ocean and wrapped in mist. Here lay his destiny for the years to come, the filthy hole where his actions, lack of insight and restraint, had brought his marriage and brilliant career in India.

He looked on appalled, sipping the hot coffee, at a loss for words. In Bombay he had minutely studied the position of the São Tomé and Príncipe islands on the map, had read the description of the archipelago in the latest edition of the *Geographic Universal Encyclopaedia*, had read everything, which amounted to almost nothing, he found on the islands in the reports from the Navy and the Foreign Office. He discovered the essentials and hadn't expected anything different. However, as the HMS *Durban* drew closer to land, its desperate smallness and solitude was revealed in all its wretchedness. David Jameson couldn't help feeling a profound, harrowing sense of defeat. A small totally speculative light of hope had sustained him on the long twenty-day voyage, with stops in Zanzibar, Beira, Lourenzo Marques and Cape Town: the hope that things wouldn't be as bad as anticipated, that the islands would at least offer an exuberant image of tropical life, and a reasonable posting for a time to recuperate. But the city he now glimpsed more clearly seemed to offer no scope for self-deception. It was a place for deportees. Deportation, it is true, with the honorary title of Consul on behalf of His British Majesty, a house – hopefully a decent one – and the duties that went with the post. But what somebody beginning their career might have thought a mere place of transit, an assignment in an exotic paradise, was for him, a man who had had the Raj at his feet a humiliating blow he couldn't soften.

He felt a presence on his right. Ann had come silently to lean on the rail and look at land. She spoke not a word, and her eyes were expressionless. She'd slipped a dressing gown over her nightdress and her hair was dishevelled, as if the occasion were too serious to worry about appearances. The early-morning light – the only time of day in the tropics when the sun shines gently – emphasised the purity of her features, the liquid green of her eyes, her face's inner and outer radiance. Such beauty dazzled David, as if it were the first time he'd seen her in that light, and he was moved by her serenity.

He wanted to speak, but couldn't find the words, didn't know where to start.

'Ann . . .'

She turned round to face him. The green of her eyes was blinding. He wanted to cry, throw himself at her feet, beg forgiveness for the hundredth time, ask her to leave, beg her to stay.

Before he could say anything, she gripped his hand and whispered so softly he was almost afraid he hadn't heard her properly.

'I won't leave you, David. I did promise I would never leave you.'

David Lloyd Jameson was not born with a silver spoon in his mouth. He had got to where he was thanks to persistence, his own courage and effort. His father owned a small shop in Edinburgh, an unexceptional emporium of products from the East, carpets from Shiraz and Bukhara, lamps and silks from India, screens from Japan and painted wooden chairs from Nepal and Tibet. Orientalism was not yet the vogue and it wasn't easy to sell anything that wasn't Tudor or Victorian in the conservative society of Edinburgh. The business could only support a modest, decent life and David's education. From an early age the etchings, watercolours and drawings of India his father received fascinated him and gradually the mythical idea of the Raj turned into an obsession, a project, a destiny that, by the time he was eighteen, no argument or force could rebuff. India became his only aim in life, his only horizon and thought for the future.

He presented himself four times as a candidate to enter the Indian Civil Service – for a position in the public administration of the Viceroyalty – and for four years on the trot he was rejected. Others, not of his stripe, would have desisted, would have seen how the places available were allotted according to family, connections or influence. He never did: each year, with each rejection, he redoubled his efforts, tried to work out where he'd failed and tried to accrue more qualifications. He became a walking encyclopaedia on the history and geography of India. He contracted a teacher of Hindi and became fluent in the language and in the interpretation of the Upanishads. He learnt Urdu and the basics of Arabic and studied the Koran.

His persistence was finally rewarded: one cold December morning, the postman delivered the letter he had so longed to receive from the Indian Bureau. He had been assigned to Bangalore in the south Indian State of Mysore, as a third-tier officer in the local government, which, in the terms of the accords agreed between the British Crown and the five hundred and sixty-five principalities of India, belonged to the Maharajah of Bangalore. He was twenty-three and had been dispatched, quite unawares, to the heart of mythical India, that fantastic land evoked by the texts and engravings in the books in his father's shop. It was as if he had entered straight into those books like a character from one of their stories.

David Jameson fell passionately in love with India from the moment he set foot on dry land and entered Bombay through the renowned Viceroys' Gateway of India, which symbolised the possession of India and through which any servant of the Raj should pass, for good fortune and to mark loyalty and dedication to the task ahead. British India, devotedly protected and loved by Her Majesty Queen Victoria from Buckingham Palace's dismal corridors, was an immense and, by its very nature, ungovernable territory, extending from the Himalayas to the Straits of Ceylon, from the Sea of Bengal to the Sea of Oman. It was a land inhabited by a hundred and twenty million Hindus, forty-four million Muslims, five million Catholics and four million Sikhs, and governed by sixty thousand British, who administered directly two-thirds of the territory and four-fifths of the population, the rest being under the aegis of five hundred and sixty-five autonomous potentates, governed by their rajahs, maharajahs and nabobs, to whose loyalty Britain owed the success of its quite demented mission to govern the Indias. There were potentates whose lands were smaller than the Borough of Chelsea and others that were bigger than Scotland, though the political importance of the principalities was measured not in land but by the number of subjects, elephants and camels and by the number of tigers hunted by the ruling prince and, in particular – from the British point of view – by the number of soldiers in the private armies they maintained, which could, in times of need, line up alongside Her Majesty's Army.

In Bangalore, the British legation was a real embassy on allied territory. Its duty was essentially to keep the Maharajah's loyalty firm, draw on his generosity in relation to the financial needs of the administration of the Raj, nurture his good neighbourliness with the contiguous principality, thus avoiding the evil of fratricidal war that India seemed so fond of and which so greatly taxed the management of the territory. And finally, its duty was to perform the prime role of the coloniser: to arouse in the Maharajah and his court a liking for the values of the English race and English civilisation, an appearance of impartial justice, a sense of hierarchy and obedience to its common law, English education with lots of history and geography and portraits of Queen Victoria in classrooms and an equal enthusiasm for sports like polo and cricket. England asked for little in return. It closed its eyes to the application of local laws and customs, unless the disputes involved English subjects and interests. The English were as racist as the French in Pondicherry, but on the other hand were liberal in religious matters, never cherishing absurd pretensions about converting Indians to the Christian faith like the Portuguese in Goa. In exchange for their generosity and loyalty to the British Crown, which was regularly tried and tested, the English would confer, every now and then, the title of 'Sir' or some other glittering prize on one of these maharajahs who had all else that money could buy.

David stayed three years in Bangalore. He killed two tigers and innumerable lesser game on hunts organised by the Maharajah, shooting with a couple of Purdeys he'd bought second-hand from the second-in-command of the Queen's Lancers. He won the State polo championship with a mixed Indian-British team, riding horses borrowed from the stables of the Maharajah of Bangalore. He experienced – as was the wont of officers in the Indian Service – some of the incredible positions for sexual intercourse portrayed on the frescos in temples and practised in the Maharajah's harem, and travelled everywhere within the

State, carrying out the administration of good, pragmatic, reliable British justice.

His fascination for India grew still further, as did his admiration of the wise management of the Raj's business, as he himself implemented it in the British administration. As regards a future commission, his high work rate, knowledge of the language and local milieu and his youthful ambition did not go unnoticed in internal dispatches, and he was summoned to Delhi and given a post in the Viceroy's central government, precisely to deal with the area of relations with the Autonomous Principalities.

He initially hated Delhi. Tied to a desk and the duty to loom large at official receptions for the maharajahs, he was nostalgic for what he had enjoyed in Bangalore: hunting, adventure, nights camping in the forest, conversations with village wise men, sexual orgies with the Maharajah's concubines, and the direct or almost direct exercise of power and influence. But they soon began sending him on visits to principalities, on missions that were a mixture of diplomacy and espionage, where his facility for observation and foresight began to be duly appreciated and remarked upon at higher and higher levels, right to the Viceroy's Office. He travelled throughout India on missions that could last five or six weeks, by train, boat, camel, elephant or horse. Wherever he went he was the voice of the Viceroy, who in turn was the voice of the Queen and the Empire. He was equally at ease in reception rooms as hunting tigers or playing polo, in the officers' mess or in discussions in Hindi with local authorities. He belonged to a rare species of imperial Englishman who possessed the facility to be hybrid and conscious of his imperial superiority, but attentive and respectful towards local customs. If the Maharajah's favourite dish was cobra, he would eat it, with the same relish as he would down partridge pie at Raffles; if a local dignitary's custom was to vomit at table after eating, he wouldn't bat an eyelid, as if the man were a gentleman filling his pipe in his London club. When the Maharajah of Bharatpur invited him to the execution of a wretched bandit hung before an ululating mob, he put in an appearance, and showed no emotion or compunction. He'd learned from his superior in Bangalore right at the beginning of his time in India a maxim he had made his personal rule of conduct: 'Our mission is not to change India; it is to govern her.' His attitude towards India, his philosophy, his ability to analyse and reach a judgement he then laconically reflected in reports to central government were increasingly noticed, appreciated and quoted. At the age of twenty-nine, David Jameson was already a somebody, a household name in Delhi and the Viceroy's inner circle. There was the prospect of flying even higher, and he knew it. He gazed at the map of that huge possession and felt an entire continent bubbling with life, tragedies, adventures, conflicts to be resolved, crucial decisions to be taken, difficult missions to execute and glory to be won.

It was then that he met Ann. One Sunday afternoon, on one of those tediously English afternoons at the All India Cricket Club in Delhi, where conversations had been exactly the same for two hundred years, and generations changed but not the family names of the individuals mentioned in conversation. Unlike David, Ann came from a family that had been a member of the All India Cricket Club in Delhi for four generations. Ann's future did not lie in India, but in England. Colonel Rhys-More had in mind a special, different future for her with some lord who, passing through India, would not fail to be attracted by his daughter's beauty, intelligence, impeccable education and social graces, which handsomely compensated for lack of dowry or noble title. Four generations of her family devoted to the service of India and two brothers in the Army fighting on the frontiers of the Raj in the treacherous ravines of the Khyber Pass, and her virtue and natural gifts made her, in the eyes of the Colonel and his wife, a very acceptable marriage prospect. Ann was brought up to know and love not India, but a distant England where she'd never set foot. Her parents had taught her that the land where she was born and grew up, where she became a woman, was only a staging post to the mythical city of London she only knew from the magazines the Colonel subscribed to with the deferential devotion of a servant who wants to keep abreast of news of his master.

All that collapsed the day she met David Jameson. Her in-bred aloofness, her decorous façade dissolved like a sandcastle before the fury, ambition and life that poured from his eyes, voice and gestures: his unbridled vehemence. In the five hours they conversed, danced, ate and tried in vain to imagine they were interested in anything or anyone else, she learned more about India than she'd learned in twenty-five years of living in that country.

He was a gambler, a compulsive card player, a vice that had been plentifully nourished in the British officers' mess in Bangalore, and he gambled with his own life as well. India had given him the taste for outlandish gambling, and he hoped fate would be on his side when going for all or nothing. It was as if he had no time to waste, as if everything had to be played in each round, at every opportunity. He was in a hurry to live, to force things to happen; he couldn't wait for fortune to knock on his door. That was what made him attractive, the reason why so many women felt compelled to seek out his company, what disarmed some men and left others – those competing against him in their careers, amours or at the card table – not knowing how to parry his blows or match his bets. And that placed Ann at his feet from that very first night. In the rickshaw he had suddenly grasped her hand, urgently stared into her eyes and said, 'We can follow convention and leave it for now, or can decide not to waste any more time. One way or the other, you are the woman of my life and I never want not to be part of your life. The choice is yours whether or not to defer the inevitable'. She saw he was right, that it was futile to put off what was the only possible outcome in sight. She surrendered herself on a hot, humid night in Delhi reneging on everything she'd been taught about caution, reserve and planning for the future. It was as if she had been born again that night, as if everything in her previous life had been a futile attempt to thwart destiny. And he reaped all. Not like someone delicately plucking a single rose from a garden, but voraciously, as if he were devouring the whole garden.

Within two months, under the threat of a scandal in the making, Ann Rhys-More and David Jameson were married. And, as the months passed, the much feared prenuptial pregnancy that had terrified her father the Colonel showed itself to be a danger without substance: David was sterile, as a routine medical check soon confirmed. The syphilis contracted in the Maharajah of Bangalore's brothel that he'd thought cured with no aftermath except for the memories of the horrific pain and humiliating treatment had indelibly marked his body and his self-esteem. Nevertheless, it was Ann who best faced up to the news: 'I won't exchange the man I love and most admire for a potential father,' she explained to herself, her friends and parents. That was the first time Ann promised she would never leave her husband.

The Colonel was the one most distraught at the news. First, because he realised his daughter would never give him grand-children ('the only grandchildren we can have certain they are ours', as he liked to say). Then the knowledge of his son-in-law's past sexual shenanigans ('a maharajah's whores into the bargain!') only increased the negative impression he'd formed of his son-in-law's habits and wayward behaviour. He didn't like the tempestuous way he had entered the family's life, presenting them with a *fait accompli* that wrought havoc with all the plans he and his wife had legiti-mately made for their daughter. He didn't like his haste, the quick way he jumped fences in the race to become a top servant of the Indias, reaching a position of influence close to the Viceroy before the age of thirty. He was particularly irritated by having to discuss with his son-in-law whether the family had sufficient social standing to dare to invite the Viceroy to his daughter's wedding – and to register, as a result of Jameson's subtle wording, that the invitation could be sent and that Lord Curzon would come, not because of her family, but because of Jameson's own status. In six years in India, that young intruder had reached a point he had never dreamed of in a whole lifetime of service to the Crown in those lands, and which his sons, busy defending the frontiers of Empire, far from the corridors of power and the salons of maharajahs, could never aspire to. It was all the more annoying because young Jameson had neither name nor fortune to recommend him. And that made his style more suspect and frustrating in the Colonel's eyes.

'Tell me something, daughter,' he once asked, unable to restrain himself. 'Your husband must have a fortune of his own, put away somewhere?'

'I don't think so, Father. Not one I know anything about.'

'Not one he inherited from his father in Scotland?'

'No, Father, his father – who is still alive, as you know – is a shopkeeper with a reasonable standard of living, but that and no more. David had to wait four years to get a place in the Civil Service, though he was one of the most highly qualified candidates. But why do you ask, Daddy?'

'Because your husband, and I don't know if you know this, plays poker for very high stakes at the Regent's. People are talking about it: how come a man with no money can play for such large amounts?'

'But he is earning, isn't he, Daddy?'

'He earns money, to be sure. But there are very few who can match his stakes. It's as if someone's covering his back . . .'

Despite her father's insinuations, Ann couldn't repress a smile.

'What he lacks in money he makes up for in courage, Father.'

'Perhaps you're right. Or he is strong on audacity and weak when it comes to humility.'

'Come, Father, this is envious gossip, and you know it. David will go far because he is intelligent, enterprising and has the ability to take risks that others don't possess. And because he is able to understand India and its people in a way others don't bother to attempt: how many officers in the Indian Civil Service can speak Hindi and Urdu as well as he can? You know that is why a great career awaits him and why the envious can never forgive him. But you should be proud to have him as a son-in-law and happy he is your daughter's husband.'

The Colonel pondered silently, as he looked out from the veranda at the small garden of roses his wife tended devotedly far from England. Yes, he'd been in India for almost sixty years and didn't speak Hindi or Urdu. He'd never hunted tiger, or visited the Viceroy's Palace, never been to a maharajah's banquet, and certainly never come into contact with a prince's concubines. But who would dare to say that *he* did not know India!

For many men in the India Civil Service, whether posted to Delhi or passing through, Ann Rhys-More was the Jewel in the Crown. Her beauty was as gentle as a Hertfordshire morning, and as luminous as a Rajasthan twilight. She had an adolescent's smile and features, a luscious female body, and the moist green eyes of a woman beyond any period or fashion. She could be happy or serious, extrovert or reserved, warm or distant, genuinely spontaneous or intelligently observant. The first man she yielded to would enjoy all the brilliance of that body, her eyes, fire, tranquillity, and her captivating smile. That man was to be David Jameson. She was born anew through him, surrendered herself from the very first, without reservations, fear or sense of shame.

Ann became David's shadow and his light, his queen and his slave, like Mumtaz Mahal, two hundred and fifty years before her, to whose memory the Emperor Shah Jahan dedicated the extraordinary Taj Mahal in Agra. If he could, David would have built such a monument for her to demonstrate his happiness and the meaning she had brought to his life. In drawing rooms, at the club, official dinners and garden parties of that colonial society, even in church on Sunday mornings, their passionately physical relationship, providing apparently inexhaustible pleasure, was a magnet for all eyes and cause for myriad whispered conversations. It was worse behind the walls of their own home.

David was a gambler who liked all games, in bed or on beige, from the instinctually primitive hunt to the intellectual subtlety of drawing-room word games. He introduced Ann to a knowledge and enjoyment of Hindu stone engravings. By the light of candles scattered round the bedroom floor and in an alcove covered by a mosquito net that distinctly heightened the erotic ambience, they'd start to experiment with sexual positions they'd seen on temple façades and in his collection of antique books. Ann came to know intimately every inch of his body, exploring it surreptitiously as she'd been instructed with half-closed eyes, pushing her own pleasure to limits she had been taught would be non-existent.

As for David, he knew his colleagues viewed him with a mixture of cursing and envy when he said goodbye at the end of the day and headed home to sexual pleasure and abandon a man of his class was supposed to find only outside the home with women specially trained for the task. But the domestic concubinage that sent him to work every morning with a broad grin on his face, far from destroying his usual gusto, seemed to rekindle it. He continued to volunteer for all inspections or missions to government states that kept him far from home and Ann for long periods; he continued to be detailed and insightful in reports that soon became cabinet doctrine and to waste night after night playing poker at his club, until exhaustion led everyone, except himself, to give up their brandy and bad luck at cards. And he continued to accept all invitations to hunt, whether big game or small, whether for a day or a whole week. The opinion in the corridors of Government House was that his talents and ambition went beyond Delhi, and that he would soon undoubtedly have a distant mission where he would be master of his own decisions. He expected nothing less, and never hid his eagerness.

British India, excluding the territory governed directly by the Autonomous Principalities, was divided into seven provinces, each of which had its own governor. But if the governors were essentially representatives of the Viceroy in the provinces with important political and juridical duties to perform, the real government of the Indias rested on the shoulders of almost eight hundred district officers or collectors, who governed the districts into which the provinces were subdivided. They were all English – the elite of the Indian Civil Service. They were often advised by locals and lived in direct contact with their peoples and problems, with responsibility for all issues, from tax collection and the administration of justice, to public works, irrigation projects and the water supply. At the age of thirty David was still too young to aspire to an appointment as District Officer, though his three years of experience in a principality and four years with central government, with missions carried out in almost the whole territory of India, gave him a rich curriculum few could rival.

Consequently, when he was summoned one morning to the Viceroy's Office and knew he had an interview alone with Lord Curzon, he realised his future would be decided there and then.

'I have a task for you, Jameson,' Lord Curzon always spoke in the tone of somebody who harboured no doubts regarding what he was about to say, but was pained to be always so definitive. 'But this time it is not a mission with a return ticket, but rather one where I need you to excel yourself.'

David stayed silent, hands anxiously clasped.

'As you know, I decided to redefine the frontiers of the State of Bengal, the area and population of which were becoming virtually ungovernable. I have yet to meet a governor who has visited all the frontiers of Bengal. So I resolved to trim its borders, and give a piece to all of the neighbouring territories. The one that grew most was Assam: it went from one hundred and thirty-nine thousand square kilometres to two hundred and sixty thousand and from six million inhabitants – nearly all Hindus – to thirty one million, of which almost thirteen million are Hindu and eighteen million are Muslim. I took from the giant to give to the dwarf, so they would both benefit. But as you will appreciate, with your knowledge of this country, major opposition has been stirred up: an internecine conflict between the two communities and a revolt by both against us.

'I took advantage of the redefinition of the frontiers of this new state – now to be called Assam and Northeast Bengal – to terminate the commission of the present Governor. I am of the opinion that it will be useful to have a fresh, younger person in post, someone with experience and an understanding of both communities, a speaker of Hindi and Urdu, who has given proof, albeit at a different level, of his ability to deal with local conflict. After much thought and discussion with members of my cabinet, I reached the conclusion that that person might be you – if you think yourself up to the task. I know people will object, saying you are perhaps too young to occupy one of the top posts in the hierarchy of the administration of India, one immediately beneath my own, and that it would be more appropriate for you to start your career in the interior at district officer-level. But we considered all these objections to your selection and, if we did not see them as such, you should not either. As I told you, the only valid objection you could raise is to claim that it is beyond your capabilities. Am I right?'

It wasn't a question to ask a gambler. The proposal represented a career leap of some ten years, a once-in-a-lifetime opportunity with the corresponding risks if it turned into a fiasco. But if he refused, it implied the loss of the Viceroy's favours, and stagnation in Delhi waiting for a post to come up as District Officer in some far-flung spot. And, given his character and ambition, a decision he'd regret for the rest of his life. As he knew very well, there were times when one must take a gamble, because a hand with a couple of aces may not be dealt again, though experience had taught him that a pair of aces is also a treacherous hand that rarely wins.

David Jameson replied as quickly as his state of shock would allow.

'I believe you can count on me, sir.'

'Splendid. I expected as much of you, Jameson. But I trust you have considered what lies ahead, the difficulties awaiting you?'

David took advantage of that single occasion Curzon allowed him to guard against minimal damage in the future.

'I have given them due consideration, sir, and am not daunted. The only thing that worries me is my lack of direct experience of local government.'

'I understand your anxiety, but you have no reason to worry. In terms of the work of the administration and application of justice, you know the law and it is merely a question of implementation. As for everything else and the day-to-day business of government, you can depend on the help and experience of an excellent team comprising the District Officer and two members of his advisory council who will remain in post. What is essential is political and diplomatic vision, firmness and, at the same time, impartiality in the exercise of power; you must have clear aims and considerable common sense and persistence in carrying things through to a proper conclusion. It was precisely for such reasons I wanted someone with your profile. You will see. It will work out just splendidly, young man!'

And that was that. Lord Curzon got up, patted him on the shoulder and accompanied him to the door. This was the real door to India now opening before him. At the age of thirty, he was to govern a territory bigger than Belgium and Holland put together and with as many inhabitants as the whole of England. On his way home, his shock at the news transformed into euphoria, from euphoria to ill-restrained pride and from pride to apparent serenity, as he entered their living room and looked into Ann's anxious eyes.

'Well, then . . .?'

'Assam.'

'Assam? What?'

'Governor.'

She gave a shout of amazement and delight, leapt to her feet and threw herself round his neck.

'We will be happy, won't we?'

'Very, very happy.'

Lord Curzon had not got it wrong: David Jameson was the right man in the right place. Within a month of his arrival, he had identified all the pressing problems and taken the pulse of the situation. He attended to the main conflicts, spoke to the right people at the right time and removed the frictions. He left it to Ann to deal with the details of setting up home and the organisation and planning of their first official dinners and introductions into local society. He spent whole days closeted in his office or working in the public arena, visiting the police barracks, courtroom, hospital and local institutions, while she stayed up into the early hours, not to renew their interrupted marital life, but to inform him of matters of protocol that she took charge of quite naturally and instinctively. He approved everything on the nod, contently exhausted, too happy to ask questions or raise doubts, too drained to attempt a return to those times of sexual licentiousness that had defined the first phase of their married life. But they were also wonderful times, when, though they went whole days without seeing or speaking to each other, they both worked for a common goal. She was happy and proud to think she was of help to him; he was immensely grateful to her. At the end of three months, after he'd established the framework for the central governing of the state and asserted his authority in a natural, visible way on British Hindus and Muslims alike, David began to travel through the twenty-five districts of the now grandiose state of Assam and Northeast Bengal.

He spent entire days away from Goalpara, the capital and seat of government and almost the only city worthy of the name in the whole province. While he visited the territory, Ann performed in exemplary fashion the tasks of a First Lady in provincial government in British India: she visited schools and hospitals, opened shelters and orphanages, invited to tea the socially important ladies from local Hindu and Muslim society and the British colony. In the Governor's Palace, on a terrace overlooking the impressive Brahmaputra in full flow from the Himalayas, she imposed a style that was light and unpretentious, a realm of wicker, glass and crystal, and put into storage the heavy dark-wood patterned furniture and elaborate silver tableware. She treated equally delicately her guests, staff and the rose trees in her garden that grew down to the river's edge.

Her great indulgence was music. There were two resident musicians who played the tabla and the sitar. They lived in a remote corner of the house, where they remained unseen. At midday or teatime one would hear a gentle melody emanating from the entrails of the Palace, mingling with the scent of the jasmine on the terrace and the fresh, still dewy flowers picked every morning and placed in vases in the different parts of the house. When it was hot, thin bamboo drapes were drawn over doorways and windows, creating a play of light and shadow on the varnished wooden floor and on the white walls in each room. It was as if the whole house was in motion, stirred by the subtlest of breezes that suspended time and dramas elsewhere.

David loved his homecomings. After days sweating in the dust and stifling heat; after the tension of extreme situations where he needed all his cool and tact to defuse irrational hatreds that threatened to ravage some small community for no logical reason; after the horror of having to dispatch to slave labour in the coal mines a man guilty of theft, with a wife and children who threw themselves at his feet begging for mercy that he couldn't dispense; after the turmoil of the senses brought on by days and nights pursuing the tracks of a tiger that was terrorising a village; after nights sleeping in the open on the sand with a stone warmed in the fire for a pillow, listening to invisible serpents or snakes describing slippery circles around the fire he would melt in amazement and tender desire when he returned to take possession of the shadows, music and scents and the fearsome goddess with the long blonde tresses, green eyes and ample, panting bosom waiting for him. After a relaxing bath, he would drink a gin and tonic on the terrace, before entering the dining room where half-opened wooden shutters let in the cool of night, the perfume from the garden and the song of night birds. Like any officer or gentleman in the Raj he always wore a white dinner jacket to dinner, and Ann wore a tight-fitting dress, with a neckline as low as was acceptable, her eyes glinting in the candlelight.

He dreamed of everything and had everything: the huge territory of Assam and Northeast Bengal and its thirty-one million souls to govern. He was the direct, personal representative of the distant Emperor of India, Edward VII, the incarnation of wisdom, honesty and justice. He had to be living proof of the truth of Kipling's dictum: that the task of governing India had been placed, by a strange design of Providence, in the hands of the English race. And, as a consequence of this formidable task, he was treated like a prince, was welcomed at the end of the day or end of a trip by a princess who waited for him on their palace terrace, in the shadowy cool of their home and between the purest cotton sheets of their nuptial bed.

It was arguable whether Providence had chosen Great Britain to direct the destinies of India: after all, the Portuguese had got there first and, after them, and before the English, the French. Bombay, the British entrance into India, only became British when the Portuguese offered it as part of the dowry for the marriage of Catherine of Braganza to Charles II, and the Crown only established itself officially in the Vice-Regency a few decades before, attracted by the prosperous business of tea traders in the city. It was equally doubtful whether a large number of the British dispatched to India, in the Army or the Civil Service, felt that call from Providence, now supposedly summoning them to meet such a vast challenge, in the same way. But no one who'd had dealings with David Jameson could doubt that he was cut out for the work and duties that now fell to him. He displayed an eagerness to learn and an enthusiasm for every aspect of his post, even those aspects others in his position might have scorned. He inspired those around him and his deeds were soon news and the stuff of legend in the whole of Assam and Northeast Bengal.

The first year of his rule was a success story for David Jameson. The British officials admired him, trusted him blindly and strove to imitate him and did everything he asked, however demanding the task. Local worthies respected him and recognised his sense of justice and impartiality that was tested several times in real situations. The poor saw him as their last port of call and a human face of authority to which they were not accustomed. His wife Ann drained him of any desire for the company of other women: she looked after things in his absence, made each return an unforgettable experience, was his friend, adviser, lover, discreet and private when he only wanted her for himself, exuberant and dashing when he wanted her brilliance to shine for everybody's eyes.

When his style and authority were definitively established, when the government of the state obeyed pre-set rules that everyone knew and no one dared contravene, when even emergencies or unforeseen crises almost resolved themselves, David began to give himself space to breathe and become less immediately involved.

An extraordinary caste like the princes of India had never existed before and perhaps will never exist again. Whether they were Hindus – maharajahs and rajahs – or Muslims – nizams and nawabs – each was renowned for his absolute extravagance, the likes of which had never been seen before. At the end of the nineteenth century, the Nizam of Hyderabad, with his sixteen names and seven noble titles, was considered to be the richest, most avaricious man in the world. He presided over a country of fifteen million subjects, of which two million were Muslim like himself, and, among his fabulous hidden treasures, was the Koh-i-nor, the fantastic two-hundred-and-eighty-carat diamond that was the jewel in the crown of the Mogul Empire of India. He had twenty-two dinner services, each for two hundred guests, including two in silver and one in solid gold, but gave only one banquet a year and ate every day from a single brass plate as he sat on the ground. He had a private bathroom decorated in gold, emerald, marble and ruby, where he never bathed, in order to save on water. He had a private army the British could always call on and, for that reason, the tunic he wore for months on end sported the Star of India or Most Distinguished Order of the Indian Empire. Because of the Koh-i-nor, the symbol of the Mogul Empire, a young prince, descended from the Nizam, would be exiled to England for ever, entrusted to the protection of Queen Victoria – along with his diamond.

Buphinder Singh the Magnificent, the seventh Maharajah of Patiala, was not the richest, but was surely the most impressive

Indian prince, over two metres and weighing some forty kilos. Every day he would consume forty pounds of food, including three chickens at teatime. To satisfy his two main passions – polo and women – his palace gave shelter to five hundred British thoroughbreds and three hundred and fifty concubines. The latter were served by an army of perfumiers and beauticians, to keep them ever desirable for Sir Buphinder's voracious appetite. He also employed his own private corps of aphrodisiac specialists, to keep his sexual prowess in peak form. But as he advanced in years, his sexual appetite diminished and every concoction was tried to reinvigorate him: concentrates of gold, silver and spices, the brains of monkeys beheaded live, even the use of radium. His Supreme Excellency died, laid low by that most incurable of diseases: boredom.

The Maharajah of Mysore also lived a life controlled by his potential for erection: legend had it that the secret of his power and prestige with his subjects was owed to the quality of his princely erections, and thus once a year, during the Principality's festive celebrations, the Maharajah, on the back of an elephant, would display himself in a state of full erection to his people. To that end, he also explored every manner of aphrodisiac that local specialists could recommend. His ruination was to listen to a charlatan who guaranteed that diamond dust was the best spur to achieve an erection: His Most Exalted Majesty bankrupted the royal exchequer by gulping down cups of diamond tea on behalf of his sturdy sceptre.

The Maharajah of Gwalior was obsessed with hunting: he killed his first tiger at the age of eight and never looked back – by forty he'd killed one thousand four hundred and their skins lined every inch of the rooms in his palace. When railway trains appeared, he and other princes of his caste became intrigued by that European invention. Some ordered whole trains to be built in Birmingham, with carriages lined in French velvet, furnished in English mahogany and lit by Venetian chandeliers, for a line a mere three kilometres long that ran from palace to winter pavilion.

The Rajah of Denkannal was more visionary in transport matters, and constructed a two-hundred-kilometre-long railway within his kingdom, which had the distinctive virtue of deploying silver carriages. The Rajah's entire armed forces had to be detailed night and day to keep the Denkannal railway intact.

As for the Maharajah of Gwalior, he devised the shortest, most extraordinary railway in the whole of India: it was a miniature train, with carriages made of solid silver that started in the palace pantry and entered the dining room via a hole in the wall. Seated in front of a dashboard studded with buttons, the Maharajah would drive the train along his dining table, tooting, switching on lights and braking in front of each guest so that he could serve himself from the whisky, port or tobacco wagons.

Compared to such potentates and many others who governed huge autonomous territories in India, Narayan Singh, the Rajah of Goalpara, was the discreet prince of a discreet principality. He inherited from his father a taste for hunting, luxury and women, but with the restrained style of someone who'd benefited from an Oxford University education and a French mother who took him to spend the summers of his adolescence on the Côte d'Azur, while his father stayed in Assam hunting tigers and luxuriating in his barely concealed harem. At the turn of the century Narayan was someone one might call a modern Indian prince. He spoke English and French with a perfect accent. He subscribed to magazines and received books from Europe, and liked to live in between the hybrid culture of elemental, instinctive India where he enjoyed all his privileges and the refinement of a civilised world where good taste and discrimination reigned. He was equally at home on the back of an elephant, on a tiger hunt in the forests of Assam, or in a tearoom among English officers and visiting foreigners. His own kingdom was virtually limited to his beautiful palace in Goalpara, a few thousand hectares around the city and a similar amount of land in the north of the state. This spared him the tasks of government or diplomatic wheeling and dealing with the British. He was a loyal subject and in his home a proud gentleman. His wealth and tastes did not allow him the absurd extravagances of the others, but gave him the luxury of travelling the world, collecting art works, sleeping in the best hotels, always a guest of honour, eagerly sought after or viewed with interest or with envy in London,

Paris, Venice or New York. He was the same age as David Jameson, handsome, with dark brooding eyes, a light skin colour and an exquisitely twirled moustache. He was particularly fond of shocking people with his clothes: one day he'd appear dressed like an Indian prince in a light-coloured tunic with ivory and mother-of-pearl buttons over pleated trousers, the next day in the rough, simple outfit of a hunter from the Assam jungle, or in a tasteful three-piece Savile Row suit, flourishing a silver-topped chestnut cane. He was debonair and urbane, drawing the best from every aspect of his life. But as so often happens with such men, his real defect was his deep cynicism.

'Beauty conquers royalty. However, I must say in this case it is a most unequal struggle. Your dazzling beauty Lady Ann, was always going to defeat my brittle royal veneer. The important thing is that you should know it is my honour and pleasure to have you and your husband dine at my table.' Narayan Singh got up, raised his glass of port and made a circular gesture to welcome the whole table, lingering a moment to gaze at David Jameson on the other side of the table, and then, with a slight bow, he brushed his glass against Ann's.

'It is our pleasure,' she replied, 'to be welcomed by a host as splendid as Your Highness.'

He waved his hand vaguely, as if to say, 'Let's forget polite formalities – the key object is my enjoyment of your company.'

And Narayan Singh was in fact the perfect host. He hand-picked his guests, preferring quality over quantity. The atmosphere and decoration of his rooms and table were always subdued in their refinement and luxury. He never served more than four or five delicious courses, and the conversation was always useful and instructive, whether it was about the local situation, wider India or the news from Europe. The Rajah orchestrated his guests, measuring the time he spent with each in conversation, the time they spent mingling, the appropriate moment for the gentlemen to retire to smoke cigars after the meal. The music struck up right on cue, the card tables were brought out as soon as he sensed a desire for a game of whist. His servants flitted like shadows, never allowing a glass to remain empty for a moment, and from eleven at night there was a cold buffet on offer in the small room next to the main drawing room. Palace gardens and terraces were always lit by candelabra and torches until the last guest decided to leave of his own free will, never prompted by any sign of impatience on the part of the Rajah. When welcoming him on return visits to the Governor's Palace, Ann and David strove to match the level of the Rajah's entertainment but never quite could.

Narayan Singh spent half the year – the monsoons and deep summer – travelling abroad. His return to Goalpara was always celebrated with receptions that functioned as the official opening of the season. By the end of two years in Goalpara, David could tell the time of year according to whether the Rajah was in town or not. He went from being the Governor on official invitation to a frequent visitor to the Rajah's palace, from guest to friend. When routine took over his administration of public affairs – a sign that he'd carried out his mission successfully – when even the most important current business was entirely predictable and he could delegate almost every day-to-day task, Narayan's company became David's antidote against boredom. Both shared the conviction that India – that huge continent of three hundred and fifty million beings, divided by community, religion, race and caste – could not govern itself and required another centralising, imperial power. Left to its own devices, India would succumb fatally to its demons, hatreds and fanaticisms. It was essential for the association between the local aristocracy, made up of Hindu, Muslim and Sikh princes, guardians of tradition and the immutable nature of things, and the British administration, with its dash of justice and democracy, to be kept firm and unbreakable, to guarantee civil peace in a country that was by definition ungovernable.

In Goalpara, the capital of the state of Assam and Northeast Bengal, that association depended largely on the friendly relations between the Rajah Narayan Singh and the Governor David Lloyd Jameson. The two men, born on different continents, were of a similar age, shared tastes and a fascination for the other's culture, believed in the same ideas about the government of a territory where one was an authority by birth and tradition and the other by merit and imperial right.

Outside official ceremonies or protocol dinners, it became normal for the Governor to participate frequently, almost daily, in the soirées at the Rajah's. After a day's work and supper alone with Ann at the Governor's Palace, David would drink a brandy on the terrace and then ask his wife's permission to go to the Rajah's palace, about a quarter of an hour away by carriage. To begin with, Ann was surprised by, even apprehensive about, such systematic absences, but she rationalised them as a kind of male ritual, vaguely connected to matters of state, but nothing serious or important. She read it as a way for him to expend his apparently inexhaustible energy. He always returned in the early hours, but it was not unusual for him to wake her and for them to make love, as the light filtered through the white silk curtains of the window overlooking the gardens. Sometimes, he came back exhausted and she barely heard him struggling to undress, then dropping on their bed at her side, like a dead weight. On such occasions, she didn't talk to him, pretended to be sleeping and let him fall asleep straight away. But she never saw him come in drunk or distraught and, whatever time he returned, he would always be up at six-thirty and in his office punctually at eight.

Like all the women in the British colony in Goalpara, Ann had also heard about the Rajah's harem, which was small by Indian princely standards, but selected with the refinement of a connoisseur, so it was said. She also realised that, during the male parties at the Rajah's, the harem was there to be visited by the few hand-picked guests. Strangely it didn't worry her, for David continued to love her, not as in their first phase, but with an ever more subtle passion that led her to scorn and not want to know what happened in the private male gatherings to which David disappeared almost every night.

As it happened Ann had nothing to worry about: nothing happened in that respect. It is true women from the harem were there, serving the guests drinks, listening to their compliments, and occasionally dancing for them. From the very first night Narayan had hinted unobtrusively to David, as he did to other select guests, that the women in his harem, even his own favourites, were at his disposal. Some took up his offer, occasionally or systematically, always respectfully. In nearby candlelit bedrooms, with velvet cushions and satin sheets, the concubines from the Rajah of Goalpara's harem saw to the guests who desired them, massaged them with cedar oils and exotic essences and then, delicately, enquired after their sexual preferences. David never withdrew to such a room. Occasionally, he'd agree politely, not wishing to offend his host, to one of the harem's prettier young women lying next to him. She'd gently caress him and he'd reciprocate, feeling breasts under the fine silk of a sari, or rounded haunches or silkily-skinned legs, a gentle heartbeat or wet tongue. And it stopped there – because the dignity of his post required him to restrain himself before others, or, even more to the point, because he was proud that he was married to Ann, and it was his way of showing the others that, despite the splendours of sampling the harem, nothing there could better what he had at home. In the presence of his guests Narayan never retired with any of his concubines either. He didn't need to in their presence and maintained his harem because he enjoyed it. His dignified status imposed on him the restraint he visibly admired and respected in David.

That small gathering – which would usually comprise two or three British men, a well-known local Muslim trader and seven or eight representatives of local Hindu high society – assembled at the Rajah's to drink, smoke, talk and above all to gamble. They played for high stakes night after night, winning and losing considerable sums, but always in good humour, with the in-difference of those who gamble to idle their time away and never to turn the wheel of fortune. They entered, left and re-entered the game on the big octagonal poker table, chancing their good or bad luck. At midnight there was always a break for dinner and they would all retire to the adjacent room to eat and converse, while the servants cleaned the ashtrays and spruced up the gambling room. After dinner, each guest had to decide whether to stay for the second session of cards or remain to chat to others who had dropped out, or retire to an inner room to seek consolation from a woman selected from the harem, or simply go home after deciding the night was over. The gentlemen's rules they'd established stipulated one could not leave mid-session unless one was losing heavily; but to leave if one was winning was a serious offence and meant that one was there to win money from friends and not to spend a civilised evening among gentlemen.

Alistair Smith, Goalpara's Superintendent of Police, had lived in India for fifteen years, four in that post. It was a good place and he liked his work and the city. He couldn't imagine living in a country that wasn't India, but he hoped that, after Assam and Goalpara, he might be sent to a more pleasant posting, perhaps Bombay, or even the capital. It wasn't that work there was particularly onerous or that crime was widespread: there were not many serious cases, nor were there attacks from bandits from other states. When Assam joined Northeast Bengal, as determined by the Viceroy, there were moments of great tension between Hindu and Muslim communities. Alistair Smith feared the worst and lived with his forces on a twenty-four-hour daily alert. But the arrival of the new Governor, the firmness and impartiality he showed towards both communities and the diplomatic skills that Alistair Smith rapidly came to admire in David Jameson calmed tempers and normality was restored very quickly. Alistair thought the choice of Governor a wise and successful one. Even though Jameson had seemed too young and inexperienced for the job, he had a quality rare among the higher echelons of the Indian Civil Service – he could speak Hindi and Urdu fluently. Alistair Smith respected and trusted the Governor, as did most members of the British administrative community in Assam and local dignitaries.

On this particular Sunday in his office at Central Police Headquarters in the upper part of the city, Alistair Smith was unusually apprehensive. Even though it was a non-work day, he had come to the office carrying a bundle wrapped in a burlap sack with which he locked himself up in his room, asking the duty officer to ensure he wasn't disturbed. He placed the contents of the sack on a table opposite his desk, then sat down behind his desk and stared at the objects he himself had collected from a jewellery and antique shop in the Jewish quarter. Before him was a pair of solid-silver candelabra, each for three candles, encrusted with gold and rubies. Each bore an inscription on its base that, when put together, read '*Aeterna Fidelitas* – Shrinavar Singh,

1888'. Shrinavar Singh was the father and predecessor of the present Rajah of Goalpara and the phrase '*Aeterna Fidelitas*' no doubt implied a pledge of loyalty to the British Crown. The pair of candelabra, the value of which he dared not estimate, could only have come from the Governor's Palace. And when he thought that, a cold shiver ran down Alistair Smith's spine. He tied the candelabra back in a bundle, carefully packed them into the burlap sack, ordered his car be brought and, defying all the norms of good manners and deference to hierarchy, decided to inconvenience his Governor at home on a Sunday afternoon.

Ann and David were in their garden enjoying the late-afternoon breeze blowing lightly across the damp from the nearby river. A servant had brought out a tray of tea and scones for Ann and a jug of fresh lemonade for David. He was lying on a bamboo chaise longue, a glass of lemonade on the floor by his chair, reading *The Times of India*, occasionally skipping a line or two, feeling drowsy and languid like a cat basking in the sun. She sat on a simple bamboo chair, where she'd been reading a book she'd now closed and put on the table, and was listening to the sound of the running waters of the Brahmaputra, sacred waters that, in her metaphysical reveries, she also believed protected her marriage and the eternity of magical moments of peace like the present. She gazed at him absent-mindedly, tenderly, and for the thousandth time regretted that he, her husband, couldn't give her a child to play with her now on the grass and complete the perfection of the afternoon.

It was two and a half years since they'd arrived in Assam. Time passed quickly at the beginning, when David travelled from one side of the state to the other, frantically getting to know and organise all that kept him away from home for weeks on end. She sometimes accompanied him on these trips and felt as tired as he did, sensed the importance of his mission and learned to admire him even more – for the energy, determination and tenacity he brought to each task. Things began to settle down. David's trips became less frequent and they had time to be together and make friends in Goalpara, despite his frequent absences when he visited the Rajah's palace. Time passed more slowly and Ann occasionally imagined he might be transferred elsewhere in two years, and she tried to guess what the future held in store. It was certain he'd never leave India and that she'd never leave him. However, between commissions, there'd certainly be time and opportunity to travel to England so she could finally get to know the country that was hers by baptism. Retrospectively Goalpara would then become a time of transition, of apprenticeship, when alone together, far from friends and family in Delhi, they'd also quietly consolidated their marriage.

It was lonelier for her as she had few true friends in Goalpara. She was too liberal for local conventions, didn't have the patience and didn't identify with the conversations of the English ladies, the sighs and asides with which they lamented, though never really saying as much, the tedium of marriage and lack of spark in their conjugal relations. David had a state to administer, problems to solve every day, hunts and excursions throughout the territory, and male soirées at the Rajah's. She had none of that. She amused herself by reading or walking in the garden and her great solitary moments of pleasure were the massages given by her maid, Ariza, which touched the borders of bearable sensuality. At night David reaped the fruits of that controlled trance and wondered at his wife's almost animal, unbridled sexuality. No woman ever aroused him like Ann: besides, she was his legitimate wife, something rare, and he thanked the heavens for that gift.

Ann looked at him nodding over his newspaper as one might observe a wild beast relaxing. Her gaze carried a glint of guile and possession that made her shiver, like the breeze rustling the willows on the banks of the Brahmaputra. And it was at that moment as he dozed and her thoughts blurred that Joghind, the Palace butler, came to announce the arrival of the Honourable Alistair Smith, who craved permission to interrupt their Sunday rest on a matter requiring immediate attention.

David woke up, put down the endless pages of *The Times of India* and almost shouted at Joghind, 'Tell him to come in right away!'

'Do you want me to leave, dear?' asked Ann, slightly taken aback.

'No, that won't be necessary – it can't be any state secret.'

Alistair Smith came in, cap in hand, apologising profusely and shaking the Governor's hand in his sweaty paw.

David pulled up a chair opposite his and said, 'Do sit down. Would you like a drink, tea or lemonade?'

'I would be pleased to accept a glass of lemonade, sir.'

Ann gestured towards Joghind, who hurried off to get another glass and then disappeared, dismissed by a wave of David's hand.

'What brings you here today, Alistair? And what's that mysterious bundle you're holding there?'

Alistair Smith downed a gulp of lemonade, as if trying to embolden himself. He gazed at the toecaps of his regulation shoes, wondering whether they were sufficiently polished to put in an appearance at the Governor's Palace. He was like a young boy come to apologise for some folly he had committed.

'I'm brought here today, sir, by the contents of this bundle.'

And he started to undo the burlap sack and roll of newspapers that concealed the valuable candelabra. He did it clumsily, his hands shaking, and that only made David more impatient and Ann more apprehensive. He finally managed to remove all the paper from the bundle and held a candelabrum in each hand. Ann stifled a cry of surprise.

'Do you recognise this, sir?'

'Of course,' answered Ann, not waiting for David to react, 'they are the candelabra from the Red Room, a gift from the previous Rajah, during the government of Sir John Percy! Where did you get them, Mr Smith?'

David gestured to her to be quiet.

'In the shop of a Jew who deals in antiques, silver, gold and precious stones. One Isaac Rashid, a man who is very well known in the city.'

'Indeed, I know Mr Rashid very well. I've bought things from his shop.' Ann couldn't restrain herself. 'And how did objects that are the property of this palace and the Crown come to be in Mr Rashid's possession?'

'Please, Ann!' David was beginning to turn livid from rage, Alistair thought. 'Let the Superintendent say his piece, without interrupting him.'

'Sir, the first thing I must ask is if you noticed these candelabra were missing.'

Now, despite his previous contrary order, David looked questioningly at Ann.

'No . . . no. Perhaps . . .' she began. 'I haven't walked through the Red Room for days. Or rather, if I have, I didn't pay it any particular attention. You know, we don't expect things in the rooms to go missing, unless they've gone off to be cleaned. Wait a minute. Joghind! Joghind, come here!'

'Yes, madam.'

'Joghind, did you notice these candelabra had gone missing from the Red Room?'

The servant looked down and was silent for a moment.

'I think so, madam.'

'You think so? When?'

'The day before yesterday.'

'The day before yesterday. And you said nothing to me?'

Joghind, the butler to the Governor's Palace for fourteen loyal, unblemished years, looked down again and said nothing.

Ann stared at him, refusing to believe what was happening.

David now spoke up.

'Come on, Joghind, tell me why you said nothing to madam when you noticed they were missing?'

'Sir, I imagined the Governor or his lady had taken them to be valued or restored. For whatever reason.'

'And did it not occur to you' – Ann was getting more and more upset – 'that they might have been stolen by a member of staff or by someone who'd got in unnoticed?'

'No, madam, I checked that neither of those things had happened.'

'You checked? How? And how did the candelabra end up in a shop of a dealer in the Jewish quarter – presumably on sale, is that not so, Mr Smith?'

'Yes,' came the reply, 'they were indeed on sale and it was a British subject who visited the shop, recognised them and informed the police.'

'Very well, Joghind, you may leave now.' David seemed to want to deal with the matter. 'From what I can see, Alistair, this is straightforwardly a police matter, the only difference being that it involves the property of this palace. But I'm sure your services will get to the bottom of this very quickly. Given what is at stake, I would advise the maximum discretion. We two can deal with it. Come to my office tomorrow when you have any news. Have I made myself clear?'

'Yes, sir, there's only one thing . . .'

'No, Alastair, in my office, tomorrow. Just the two of us . . . Do you understand?'

The sweat poured down Alistair's face and scant hair: he still held the candelabra, one in each hand, as if he wanted to throw them into the river to be rid of that mess. He swallowed twice, but though David held his hand out, he made no move to leave.

'And . . . what about the candelabra, sir?'

'Well, what about them?'

'They are proof of the crime, sir . . .'

'Of the crime?' David was beginning to get nervous. 'You don't yet know that there was a crime.'

'They are proof of the incident, sir.'

'Of the incident? And so what?'

'So I must take them with me, sir. And keep them as proof, until the facts are cleared up and the case is closed.'

For the first time, David felt distinctly uneasy. The word 'case' sounded a warning shot in his brain. He stared at Alistair Smith: from the first day he met him and saw him at work, without any need to read his individual file, he'd been convinced Alistair was a serious man, zealous of his duties and faithful to him and all the necessary protocols, obedient to authority and loyal to his superiors. An exemplary policeman in times that had been turbulent and might become so again.

'Let's see, Alistair,' he said with real composure. 'There can be no doubt those candelabra belong here in this palace, am I right?'

'You are right, sir. There can be no doubt they belong here. They have already been identified by four people as such and dozens more could have done the same without a moment's hesitation.'

'So then, their ownership is not in question: and this is their home and is where you should leave them now, independent of whether they may be requisitioned temporarily, for identification and evidence, if necessary. Do we agree?'

The Superintendent gazed at him sadly, hesitantly. Then handed the candelabra silently over to David, bowed towards Ann and his governor and said goodbye.

'We will meet tomorrow, then, sir.'

David watched him cross the garden on his way out. The Superintendent of Police seemed to have aged too quickly in those two and a half years: his shoulders drooped slightly and his step was not as firm as he remembered.

He sighed and gave the candelabra to Ann, put a hand on her shoulder and said, 'Very well, let's go indoors. What an unpleasant business!'

Something had changed in the attitude of Superintendent Alistair Smith when he entered the Governor's office the next morning. He was the same loyal, conscientious policeman obedient to his superior, but was no longer a man afraid to carry out his duties.

'Sir, I want first of all to apologise for coming to the Palace yesterday. I now understand, as you the Governor said, that it is a matter for the two of us.'

'Apologies accepted, Alistair. Don't give it another moment's thought. Let's get straight down to business. What have you got to tell me?'

'Well, sir, don't you *know* what I have to tell you?'

'No, Alistair, I'm waiting for *you* to tell me. What conclusions have you reached?'

Alistair sighed deeply. He really felt for David Jameson, as man and as Governor. He admired what he had done in Assam and Northeast Bengal, his personality, his qualities as a leader and statesman. But now there was this wretched business and he'd been thinking all night how he could sidestep it but had come up with no solution. There was no more leeway for subterfuge. He wondered how the Governor would react and sincerely hoped he wouldn't make things even tenser.

'Sir, there are only two hypotheses: either someone stole the candelabra and tried to sell them to Mr Isaac Rashid, or someone sold them who had not stolen them.'

'And which of the two hypotheses do you think the more likely, Alistair?' David lit a cigarette and gazed, apparently casually, at the smoke curling up towards the beam of light coming through the window.

'It is no hypothesis, sir, it is a certainty: the candelabra were not stolen from the Palace.'

'And what makes you so sure?'

'Several reasons I could explain to you, if it were necessary, sir. But the main one is that nobody would ever dare to do that and Isaac Rashid, a reputable merchant in the market, would never dare to be the receiver of goods stolen from the Governor's Palace, if he were perfectly aware of the source.'

'In that case, they were sold to him – and by someone with the power to do so.'

'Exactly, sir.'

'By whom?' David now stood with his back turned on Alistair in front of the window from where he could see the central square of Goalpara. He didn't flinch when he heard the reply aimed at his back.

'By you, sir.'

David turned on his heels and faced up to his Superintendent of Police.

'And how much did I sell the candelabra to Mr Rashid for?'

'For fifty thousand pounds, sir. Equivalent to the debts you accumulated gambling at the Rajah's palace.

'I see you are well informed as to my private life, Alistair.'

'It is a part of my duties, sir. Not your private life as such, only that element that might compromise the government of the state or British interests.' Alistair Smith's voice trembled slightly and David thought a tearful shadow darkened his eyes.

He himself felt sunk in a kind of irrational fog, as if floating in a nightmare. This man is serious, he thought – but that didn't clear the fog. Nothing could now clear the fog, the nausea that engulfed him.

'Alistair, I don't think there's any point in continuing to be evasive. As I would expect, you are carrying out your duties efficiently. I can only appeal to whatever feeling of personal sympathy you might bear towards me. As you will understand, when this incident becomes public knowledge, it will tarnish my reputation and end my career. Can I count on your help and friendship to try and avoid such a disaster?'

'Sir, I feel the utmost admiration and loyalty towards you. I believed your appointment to be the best thing that could have happened to this area. I will do everything I can to help, so this business does not dishonour or discredit either of us. Tell me what you want me to try to do.'

'What proof does Rashid have that I sold him the candelabra?'

'The receipt for payment you signed, sir.'

'Blast, I had forgotten that! But we also signed a paper to the effect that I have a month to buy back the candelabra at purchase cost.'

'That is true, sir, I have read the documentation. But the problem is that Rashid is demanding the candelabra be returned to his shop and he wants to keep them on display during that month if, in the meantime, you do not buy them back. That way, the whole city will know he is selling perfectly legally the candelabra that were presented to the British Crown by the former Rajah of Goalpara as a gesture of loyalty.'

'Very well, Alistair, all I ask of you is to persuade him to allow them to remain in the Palace for this month while I attempt to scrape together the fifty thousand pounds.'

'I tried to do so this morning, sir, before even coming here. I spent an hour trying to persuade him, but he wouldn't give in.'

'Why not? What is it to him? Does he want to destroy me?'

'Sir, he says an Englishman reported him for handling goods stolen from the Palace and he is now accused of that crime. He says his reputation as an honest dealer is at stake and that the only way to save it and show the accusation is unfounded is precisely to have the candelabra back on display. Additionally, he has threatened to take the Goalpara Police to court on a charge of theft, because they took from his shop items that belong to him, for which he paid fifty thousand pounds; and he has the necessary documentation to prove the sale was legal. And – I do apologise for repeating his exact words – he is also threatening to go to the newspapers to denounce the Goalpara Police for falsely accusing him of a crime in order to protect the real criminal' – Alistair

Smith paused, embarrassed – 'who, in this case, would be you, sir . . .'

David felt the world had collapsed at his feet. In his desperation, he had foreseen everything, except that an Englishman would go to the Jew's shop, recognise the candelabra and report the incident to the police. But even so, it ought to be possible to do something. His involvement with the history of India couldn't be terminated like this, because of one lunatic night at the gaming table.

'Alistair! Isn't there anything we can do? He has to accept some kind of compromise, give me time to resolve the situation, to find the necessary money and put an end to this nightmare!'

'I've done what I can, sir. Believe me. If I had fifty thousand pounds, even if it were all the money I'd saved in thirty years in India and the whole of my pension, I swear I would lend it to you right now. Nothing saddens me more than to see the most brilliant Governor I have ever known destroyed by a paltry Jewish antique dealer.'

'But how long will he give me? He must give me some time.'

'Twenty-four hours, sir.'

'Twenty-four hours?'

'Yes. He wants fifty thousand pounds or the candelabra back by tomorrow night.'

'And how long will you give me, Alistair?'

'Sir, I very much regret to say this, but I can't offer you anything better. If you don't manage to rake together fifty thousand pounds by the end of tomorrow night, I will have to come to the Palace, recover the candelabra and hand them back to Mr Rashid's shop. I have no alternative, otherwise roles will be reversed and it will be the police that will be accused of theft. And that would constitute two scandals rather than one.'

'And when will your report be sent to Delhi?'

'In two or three days.'

An embarrassed silence descended on both of them. Everything that England tried to symbolise in India, in terms of virtue, seriousness and a sense of service, had been shattered in that room, by two men who were equally lucid about the drama and inexorably separated by the consequences. Assam's most brilliant

Governor, the most promising cadre in the Indian Civil Service, had been defeated at a gaming table and was now supine at the feet of an antique dealer. The immensity of the catastrophe dispensed with the need for more words.

David flopped into an armchair, distraught. He finally found strength to conclude the conversation with a minimum of dignity.

'Alistair, I am grateful for your discretion and what you have done to try to save my skin. You will have my reply within twenty-four hours and, unless miracles exist, I give you *carte blanche* to act according to the call of duty. And now, if you don't mind, I would like to be left alone.'

'I can't believe it, David! How could you gamble away fifty thousand pounds at the Rajah's?'

'I just lost, Ann. It's true, unfortunately.'

'And who did you lose to?'

'That's irrelevant. What's that to you? I lost, the money's lost.'

'Lost to who, David?'

Ann was now screaming so loudly David was afraid the servants would hear.

'Lost to who, David? Tell me, I have a right to know the names of the men who are about to destroy my life!'

'Ann, it is irrelevant: I was the one who destroyed your life. I am the only guilty party.'

'Tell me, David, you're going to have to tell me, or I will go out and ask people.'

'That's enough, my love: on that wretched night, I lost to everyone, unfortunately – to two Englishmen and three Indians from Goalpara. I lost to everyone: it was a night when I played every card wrong. It was a nightmare: I tried to save myself, I thought my luck would change, that I couldn't go on like that, game after game, that I'd have a stroke of luck and would at least reduce my losses and get them to a reasonable level so I could negotiate payment. But it didn't happen: every game brought the same nightmare, as if it were predestined, and when I was fifty thousand pounds in hock the Rajah forbade us to play on.'

'Oh, did he, he forbade you? And how much did he win?'

'He didn't play that night.'

'What, you mean His Highness just watched you head for disaster, and merely said, "Enough is enough," when he thought you were sufficiently deep in the mire?'

'No, Ann. He didn't play because he wasn't in the mood. It happened to us all.'

'My poor idiot! So brilliant at so many things and so ingenuous at the card table! Can't you see he was playing the whole time, even when he was only watching? It made no difference to him if he won or lost fifty thousand pounds on one night. His real game was playing with you, doing or undoing your life. And he was your undoing: that was his game.'

David stared at her in dismay. He'd never thought of that.

'Do you know what you must do now, David? Do you know what's the only thing you can possibly do now?' Ann had leapt to her feet and was walking up and down the huge bedroom they had in the Governor's Palace. 'You will demand the Rajah of Goalpara, the Honourable Narayan Singh, His Esteemed Highness, loyal subject of the British Crown, your hunting and gambling companion, and whatever else, covers the gambling debts you contracted at the clandestine casino he set up in the palace of his respected ancestors for twenty-four hours. That's what you must do!'

A long silence followed Ann's angry words. She waited for a reply and David waited long enough to know he wouldn't go back on the only reply he could give.

He sighed deeply and replied so softly she thought she must have misheard him.

'No, Ann, that's certainly one of the things I will not do. The others are ordering the killing of the filthy Jew who is black-mailing me, or forcing Alistair to resign and attempting to halt the investigation he has opened. I won't do any of these things.'

'And why not, pray?'

'Because it is a question of honour.'

'Of honour?' Ann reacted as if throwing a filthy rag on the floor. 'Your honour is worth zero. Or rather, is worth fifty thousand pounds. Invent them somehow or get them to forgo your debts, if you want to reclaim your honour.'

David felt the humiliation pierce his chest like a fine blade. He'd been humiliated by a despicable Jewish trader, by the

Superintendent of Police who served under his orders, and now by his own wife. He had to draw a line, stop the rot.

'Ann, I won't do one thing or the other. I won't ask the five people to give me my money back and forget the debt, because gambling debts are debts of honour. And I won't ask the Rajah of Goalpara, nominally a subject and ally of the British Crown, to give or lend me fifty thousand pounds, which I'd never have any way of repaying, in order to save my career and reputation. If I were to do that, I'd be betraying my obligations anew and whoever followed me here would represent a government eternally in debt to the Rajah and his descendants. I prefer my own shame to such an act of disloyalty.'

'What *will* you do then?'

'Nothing. There is nothing I can do to avoid this disaster between today and tomorrow. Unfortunately, miracles don't exist. Tomorrow I will inform Alistair that it is impossible for me to pay off my debts and I will send my resignation to Delhi with a covering explanation.'

'And after that?'

David stared at her silently. Two huge tears ran down his face, but he kept staring straight at her. He saw yet again how beautiful, how extraordinary she was and felt a *frisson* just to think she was his. His wife.

'After that, my love, everything depends on you. If you stay with me, I'll spend the rest of my life trying to earn forgiveness for all I've done to you, and whatever way you hurt me, whether to exact revenge, or from simple coldness, I'll accept it as the price to pay for the dishonour I have visited upon you and your family. I don't say this lightly or with any hope that you will immediately forgive me. On the contrary, I've thought a lot about us in the last hours, and my only wish now is to fight to hold on to what I have left, namely you. If you stay by me, we will begin our life afresh, somehow, somewhere. If you leave me now, I will understand and accept your decision. I'll raise no objections and face my destiny alone. I think there's nothing more I can say at this point. I have nothing else to offer, no promise I can make to you, nothing. I only want you to know I love you more every day, and feel wretched and miserable about what I've done to you.'

Ann walked out of the room and through reception rooms dimly lit by half-melted candles and couldn't avoid an ironic smile at the sight of the six candles still burning on the candelabra of their tragedy in the Red Room. She crossed the terrace and walked into the garden, where the glow of the full moon cast enigmatic patches of light and mysterious shadow. She heard as in past years the sacred river flowing at the end of the garden and breathed in the nocturnal scent from the damp rose trees. She thought of the peace of those years, the familiarity she'd developed with each tree and each scent; she thought of her sadness at not having a child to swaddle, to whom she could confide the secrets and anguish David didn't hear in his sleep; she thought about her sterile hero whom she loved and admired despite all his defects and weaknesses; she thought about the emptiness of a life in which nothing could be shared with him and, when she felt a cold shiver under her dress, she turned round, went back to their bedroom and found him still sitting on the sofa, head in hands.

'I am not going to leave you, David. I'll never leave you. Do whatever you think you must.'

The rest was simple and straightforward. The next morning he sent a telegram to Delhi offering to renounce his post, for the reasons set out in the accompanying factual report from the Superintendent of Police in Goalpara. And, as soon as he had received the reply from the Governor General accepting his withdrawal with immediate effect, they packed their things, and rewarded as best they could their palace servants. He wrote a letter of farewell and thanks to all those working in the government of the state and they left on the night express for Agra and Delhi, getting into their carriage hand in hand, as if they weren't two outlaws fleeing the city.

In Delhi, David Jameson went to the Governor General's office, where he was received by a department head who couldn't avoid a glint of malice when he asked, 'So, my dear fellow, come to present your resignation from the Service?'

'No, I have come to present myself and await orders. If it is a case of resignation, I'll decide whether to defend myself or not. Until such a time, I still consider myself as ready to serve.'

He was sent home, decisions pending. He spent a long, painful month in the house of his parents-in-law, unable to go out into the street, to stand the oblique looks and leaden silences of the righteous Colonel Rhys-More. At the end of that period, which seemed like an eternity, to his great consternation he was summoned to an audience with the Viceroy.

After three years he walked back into that office, from where India was governed and which he had left before with the ineffable feeling he was now part of the select elite whose destiny it really was to govern India. Either from absent-mindedness or to mark the difference between the two occasions, Lord Curzon received him now without even getting up from his desk.

'Come in, David. Sit down there and let me get straight to the point. To spare the detail or grandiloquent statements that, in your case, would be a futile waste of time, I will only say, as you must understand, that I feel personally betrayed in the huge trust I placed in you and the extraordinary opportunity I granted you, which so many others coveted and equally deserved. But, despite the circumstances of your departure from the government of Assam and Northeast Bengal that tarnish you and every one of us, I have made an effort to be just and to opt for a course that will best serve the interests of our country. I had two alternatives: either to subject you to the due investigation of your behaviour and expel you from the service for dishonesty, or to conclude that, in spite of your vices, it is undeniable that you, whether now or before, have shown spasmodically that you can serve competently and with talent. I chose the second alternative, but as you must also understand, there is no place for you in India, not even as a cleaning-boy in this palace.'

Lord Curzon paused, so his insult could make its impact, as it indeed did. A man stood before him, his career in shreds, and Lord Curzon felt he had meted out the most hurtful of punishments and could now pass on to the next phase.

'In the meantime the Ministry for the Colonies,' he continued in that same tone of weary contempt, 'has just circulated an announcement throughout its domains asking for someone to present himself to go to a place called São Tomé and Príncipe. Do you know where that is?'

'No, sir, I don't remember ever hearing of such a place.'

'That is right, and for the same reason there do not seem to be any candidates for the posting. Some don't know where it is and others know and have no wish to go. São Tomé and Príncipe are two small Portuguese islands, situated somewhere off the west coast of Africa. I reckon they have some thirty thousand inhabitants, one per cent being white slave-owners and ninety-nine per cent being black slaves sustained by the lash and bread and water. And besides that, they have the worst climate on the planet and every sickness you can imagine.'

'Forgive my interrupting you, sir, but why does the Ministry want to have a consul there?'

'In order to guarantee, in line with some treaty, that the Portuguese stop their local slave-trading which, apparently, allows them to compete unfairly with our exports in that part of Africa. We want to send a kind of policeman there. In conclusion, this is your second, certainly your last opportunity: the position is yours, if you want it. If you do not, I hope you will spare me the tedious business of a public review to remove you from the Indian Civil Service. And do understand I am offering you the most generous of exits. Consequently, what is your response – do you want São Tomé or do you want to return home worse than when you came?'

'Sir, I will take São Tomé.'

11

L ONDON SENT A note to Lisbon, which the latter relayed to São Tomé to the effect that the British Consul would bring his wife, that the couple had no children and would bring no staff, and that Edward VII's representative would travel straight from India, where he'd previously been posted. In line with instructions received, Luís Bernardo tried to get a house ready that he felt to be perfectly adequate for a couple of their standing. He also contracted domestic staff on their behalf: a gardener, a cook and another girl to do housework. Obviously, none of the employees spoke English, but that was a problem Mr and Mrs Jameson would have to solve by using their initiative.

Out of curiosity he began to try to imagine what kind of person the British would send on such a mission, which required someone partly to spy on the Governor of São Tomé, and partly to be his ally in the supposedly common cause of guaranteeing there was no slavery on the island. He wondered what manner of beast this might be, a young man at the start of his career, a bureaucrat who'd soon be a real headache, whose career had been blocked in India, or an old colonel pensioned off from the army who'd agreed to São Tomé as a way to boost his retirement pay.

So he was quite amazed when he saw that young, luminous couple get off the gig that brought them from the vessel anchored out to sea, wearing light-coloured tropical clothes that were as elegant as they were apt, yet unusual in those climes. They were visibly tottering after twenty days on the ocean blue, but walked firmly on dry land, as firmly as David shook Luís Bernardo's hand. He smiled broadly at the welcome they were being given and seemed genuinely happy to be in São Tomé. As for Ann, the first thing that struck Luís Bernardo, of course, was her unnerving beauty. She was tall and straight-backed, her blonde hair loosely gathered under an ochre-coloured straw hat, a few strands of which fell down to frame a face that didn't have the typically faded finish of an Englishwoman, but a light tan from the Indian sun and the salt of the seas she'd just crossed. Her nose was straight and long and her large, well-shaped mouth bloomed into a half-smile, revealing her white teeth. Her bluish-green eyes gazed gently into her interlocutor's eyes and illuminated her whole face, as if imbued with all the innocence or boldness in the world. Despite the heat in the air, the hand Luís Bernardo shook was cool and soft: Like the woman herself, he thought.

Luís Bernardo sat at the table in the dining room he rarely used and chatted affably with the newcomers he'd invited to eat at the Governor's Palace the day they arrived, in accordance with the niceties of protocol. To break the initial awkwardness, he decided on an informal lunch for the three of them in that large room with the French windows opening on to the terrace to let in the scent of the sea. The dry season had just begun, and at that exact spot where the line of the Equator passed it was like a blend of summers from both hemispheres. Humidity, by day and night, fell to a tolerable level and, though the heat was more intense, it was less oppressive.

'You couldn't have chosen a better time of the year to get to know São Tomé,' he told them. 'You've got three months to acclimatise before the weather becomes unbearable. By that stage you'll be well prepared. I hope they told you that this place is as beautiful as it is sometimes frustrating.'

'And what is most unbearable about life here, Governor?' asked Ann, who kept butting into the conversation, ensuring it was a three-way affair, thus helping create a more relaxed atmosphere.

'You know, Mrs Jameson . . .' Luís Bernardo went on before David could interject. 'As we're going to spend a couple of years here together and friendship and business mean we'll see a lot of each other, why don't we use first names from now on?'

Ann smiled and so did Luís Bernardo. He'd no doubt that the couple were convivial and cultured, slightly younger than himself – he was thirty-seven, David was thirty-four and Ann had just celebrated her thirtieth birthday – and a rare injection of fresh air into the oppressive climate of São Tomé! It was a real boon to him as a man who so often dined alone with nobody to talk to, except for Sebastião, who had the diplomatic habit of only speaking when spoken to by his boss.

'I think that's an excellent idea, David. I believe it's the only sensible way to address each other from now on. I drink to that!' and he raised his glass of white wine and was immediately joined by Ann and David.

'So then, Luís, to return to my question.' She pronounced it 'Louiss' and dispensed with the Bernardo she apparently found too difficult, 'What's most unbearable about life here on São Tomé?'

Luís Bernardo hesitated before replying, as if he were considering the question for the first time.

'The most unbearable thing, Ann? No doubt that that must be the climate, which causes severe humidity, malaria, at worst . . .' With a sweep of his hand he seemed to indicate the interior of the island. 'The isolation, the swamps, the feeling time has come to a halt and the people with it.'

'The isolation you speak of must be even worse for you, living alone as you do . . .'

'Yes, you're right, though I came well prepared.'

'Aren't you married, Luís?' interjected David.

'No.'

'You've never been?'

'No, never.'

A polite silence descended.

No close friendship, however inhospitable the situation is that makes it appear a good idea, can be sealed on a single night. In his role as dutiful host, Luís Bernardo broke the silence and brought the dinner to a close by inviting them out on to the terrace to take a brandy and enjoy the light night-time breeze.

'I wouldn't like you to misunderstand or be the one to spoil your welcome to São Tomé and Príncipe: not everything, as you will see, is unbearable. The islands are beautiful, the beaches wonderful and the jungle is an extraordinary experience. The place lacks everything that we consider constitutes society in the world we know in Europe and civilised countries, but, to compensate, the purity of a primitive, elemental world exists here in the raw.'

That night, before falling asleep in a new bed, in a new house in a strange land, Ann rolled over towards David and asked, 'What do you think of him?'

'That it will be unpleasant to have him as an adversary.'

'Does he have to be an adversary?'

'I think so from the way I read the advice I received. Apparently, he's a gentleman on an impossible mission, fighting an indefensible cause. I've no idea what brought him here or led him to accept this task.'

'It might be a reason similar to the one that brought us here,' she replied cruelly, and David fell silent, unable to think of an appropriate riposte.

Aware of the harshness of what she'd said, Ann pressed against him and, without saying another word, they began their first night's sleep on the Equator.

In the weeks to come, Luís Bernardo did all he could to make life easy for the new arrivals. He anticipated that, if he won them to his side, it would enable him to carry out his mission, which was essentially to ensure the report the Consul would duly send to London was as lenient as possible, given that the future of São Tomé's foreign trade depended on it. And also, because he'd taken a great liking to Ann and David, who were the only decent companions he'd had for months. He helped them settle in, found Bennaoudi, an Arabic-speaking black from Zanzibar to act as an interpreter from Arabic into Portuguese, and persuaded a local schoolteacher with a smattering of passable English to drop by at the end of the afternoon to give the couple Portuguese lessons. He gave David all the information he asked for and that he thought they should reasonably share, and noticed how the latter was circumspect enough never to raise issues or ask questions he felt were solely for the Governor of the island. He arranged a dinner to introduce them to island dignitaries and plantation managers, though barely half of them put in an appearance – a fact that Luís Bernardo registered but concealed from David – and at which not one of those present, except for himself, spoke English. The evening was not helped by Ann's dazzling beauty, which stood out amid the few ladies who attended the dinner. Finally, he used his influence to convince the local press to publish a note about the Consul's arrival, not as if he'd disembarked as an enemy, but as someone who'd come to investigate local working conditions and who would necessarily, given the goodwill and good faith on both sides, recognise the effort made by Portuguese farmers in particularly difficult and harsh conditions, that otherwise, tucked away at a comfortable distance in his office, he'd never have been able to get to know or judge fairly.

Then, as was inevitable, the Consul wanted to visit on the ground. He wanted first-hand knowledge of the famous cocoa plantations the Fleet Street press swore flaunted the last vestiges of the barbarism of slavery in the so-called civilised world. Luís Bernardo had thus to confront his first dilemma: whether to accompany him or let him go alone, whether to suggest he could accompany him or let the suggestion come from David. After much dithering, he finally decided on a diplomatic compromise: he offered to go with the Consul whenever the latter thought it might be helpful or to let him go by himself, if that's what the latter wanted. As he anticipated, David also welcomed his proposal like a good diplomat: he would be pleased to accept the Governor's company on his first visits to the plantations, where he could be hugely useful as a guide and interpreter. After a period of adaptation, as soon as he thought himself capable of independent appraisal, he would be obliged to stop exploiting the Governor's time and availability to execute a task that, all said and done, was his business alone. It was true Luís Bernardo had other things to be getting on with and he'd only bother him if exceptional circumstances made his presence vital.

Before things reached that point and the Englishman started travelling by himself to São Tomé and Príncipe plantations, Luís Bernardo thought he ought to write a confidential letter to all plantation managers, which he sent by individual messenger, day after day, until all had been duly notified.

Most distinguished sir,
    As you know, Mr David Jameson, the British Consul to these islands, has the task – as agreed by our government and his – to appraise and inform the British authorities of working

conditions on São Tomé and Príncipe plantations. We hope he will see with his own eyes and give the lie to some of the accounts currently being spread by the British press that are damaging this colony and influencing the highest echelons of the British government.

I have made myself available to Mr Jameson in order to accompany him on each and every visit he intends making to plantations to carry out his mission. I feel I could act as mediator and I think this might be useful to our interests. But evidently, in line with the status his mission enjoys, he is free to accept or refuse my offer. I gather it is his wish to accept it initially and then subsequently dispense with it. It is not within my power to obstruct him in this and I beg Your Excellencies not to obstruct the visits he undertakes individually. I understand there will be no surprise visits, something I've gone out of my way to avoid, by asking him to give each plantation manager prior warning of his impending visit. I would, moreover, like to stress to Your Excellencies how important the Consul's visits are for the preparation of the final report he will eventually send to London and how the conclusions he draws will decide the future prosperity of the plantations Your Excellencies manage, which are the basis of the economy of these islands. Consequently, the impression he forms locally is fundamental and the way you welcome him is decisive, as is the sensitivity with which you answer his questions.

I trust I have been sufficiently explicit and that Your Excellencies will understand the importance of what is at stake. I beg you to keep the contents of this letter confidential and equally to keep me informed of any act or incident that should be brought to my attention. In any case I remain at your disposition should you wish any further clarification.

May God Protect Your Excellency,
Luís Bernardo Valença, Governor

Luís Bernardo and David were riding back together after a visit to the Água Izé plantation along a track snaking along the coast that allowed a constant view of the sea. It was the end of a magnificent summer's day and a short ride from the plantation to the city. They were cantering along, in no hurry, enjoying those rare moments on the island when the landscape seemed gentle and life itself slipped along even more gently. Luís Bernardo was thinking of the letter he'd received from João the day before announcing his imminent visit. He'd embarked four days ago, and within a week would join him on São Tomé. He was euphoric at the prospect of finally having his friend with him; he'd get the latest news, have someone to relax with at home, to eat with and spend time with on his terrace.

A question from David woke him from his daydreaming.

'Tell me, Luís, can you give me a straight answer to a straight question?'

'I expect so. I don't see why not.'

'What do you think of the work the blacks do on the plantations?'

'What do I think? From what angle?'

'The human angle.'

'You know, the human angle is what you saw: hard, violent, in effect work for animals. Work you and I could never handle. But what else would one expect in Africa and we are in Africa, aren't we? You must have seen similar, if not worse, in India.'

'Naturally I did, Luís. But the question, the essential question I want to put to you – as a man, not as Governor – is whether in your opinion this does or does not constitute slave labour.'

Luís looked at him askance. Was it a question from a friend or from the Consul?

'David, I can only refer to the facts and to the legal side of the matter. They're here on a work contract, are paid and are free to leave when it terminates.'

'And how many leave? How many left last year?'

That was the perennial question, the one he'd asked himself and the Crown Commissioner.

'My frank response, David, is that very few left. I can't say exactly, but very few . . .'

'None . . .'

'I don't know the numbers, David.'

'Come on, Luís, admit it, as a friend: not a single one left because they're only free to leave on paper. And you know that only too well . . .'

'David, the law on repatriation is very recent, as you know. The first contracts signed under its remit will run out in a year and a half, in 1908. Then, and only then, will we be able to begin to reach any conclusions.'

'And what will you do when you find nothing has changed?'

'I don't know if that will be the case. You're merely speculating. But I can answer, at least hypothetically. If I find the number of workers repatriated to Angola or other provenances is exactly the same as in previous years, I will investigate the reasons why, and, if necessary, speak to every labourer who renewed a contract to ascertain whether they did so freely and were fully aware of what they were doing. And, if I discover they've been deceived, I will take all necessary measures. At a personal level, I would like to think you trust me in that respect.'

They'd now reached a vantage point from which one could contemplate the entire small city in the sweep of the bay. Twilight was beginning to fall and David suddenly noticed a forlorn, rather than lonely shadow on Luís Bernardo's face. He was taking his punishment there because of a debt of honour, but why was Luís Bernardo there? Was it a challenge, prompted by his sense of honour, sheer wilfulness or an absurd need to atone? His mission was easy: he had to observe, draw conclusions and report on what he saw. He had to be honest; nothing more was called for. But Luís Bernardo's mission was to overturn a way of life long embedded in local customs, to change the mentalities of people who had nothing in common with him and didn't understand why he was there, so that in the end David would be in doubt and might refrain from drawing definitive conclusions, thus allowing São Tomé and Príncipe a breathing space. And if all that failed, as seemed more than likely, nothing of whatever had brought Luís Bernardo to the Equator would make any sense. They would be wasted years. But they both realised he couldn't promise to cheat, if that was necessary. He could only promise to express confidence in him.

'I know, Luís. I expect you to try to deliver. It remains to be seen whether the people here or in Lisbon will let you.'

'If they don't, my life will be much easier, you know.'

There was a sadness in Luís Bernardo's voice.

'I don't need São Tomé and Príncipe or any of this. That's my advantage and what makes me free in this prison.'

For a moment, David imagined Luís Bernardo resigning, giving up his post and sailing back to Lisbon. Nothing could be easier: he really had that freedom and was perhaps tempted. Then he imagined himself alone on the island with Ann, having to put up with whoever replaced Luís Bernardo, a prickly career colonialist he'd inevitably be in permanent conflict with and with whom camaraderie would be out of the question. They'd only been there a month and Luís Bernardo had become a lifebuoy for Ann and himself, an island within an island. He was well aware the feeling must be mutual, but the big difference was that he was being held prisoner there, a punishment that could end only when others decided, whereas Luís Bernardo was detained there by pride or a sense of duty he could renege on as soon as his mission proved to be impossible.

They'd reached the Consul's residence. Ann came to the door to welcome them as soon as she heard the horses. She held a gas-lamp in one hand and wore a dark-pink dress with a very open neck that revealed small drops of moisture on her dark skin.

She smiled at Luís Bernardo.

'So Luís, still chaperoning my husband?'

'Oh, Ann, he never gets lost without me. We do it to have company from time to time. I think rather he's the one chaperoning me . . .' and he looked at David with a subdued smile, 'to ensure I don't wander from the straight and narrow.'

'Hmm, I follow. Men's talk.'

'Men's talk with no mention of women,' interjected David. 'I reckon you're the only woman worth discussing in a radius of five hundred miles of ocean, dear wife.'

'You know, I do hope I'm not a topic of conversation.'

Luís Bernardo bowed theatrically.

'It wouldn't be a very enthralling conversation, Ann. Praise and yet more praise; it would soon get boring.'

She reciprocated, while her humorous expression gratefully acknowledged his compliment.

'Very well then, Luís, would you like to stay to supper?' asked David, walking towards the door and running his hand over Ann's shoulder.

'That's very kind, David, but I must go home and look at the file with today's business. Who knows what urgent, juicy bits of news Lisbon has for me!'

'At least come for a drink later after dinner,' asked Ann.

'I'll see. If I get done quickly and am not too worn out.'

'Listen carefully, Mr Germano, I will tell you again and would like you to get it crystal-clear.' Luís Bernardo was sitting at his office desk, his legs stretched over the table resting on a pile of papers he had to read and sign. 'In less than two years we will have to proceed to the first renewal of contracts and this time I want things done properly.'

'And what do you mean by "properly", Governor?'

'Don't act as if you don't know, Germano. You know only too well what constitutes a proper renewal of contract and what is mere charade.'

'You mean His Honour the Governor thinks what we've done up to now is only a charade?'

'If you want my frank opinion, that is right. And I want no repetition of that.'

'Then what does Your Excellency suggest?'

'I will spell it out. Each renewed contract must pass by my desk, with the worker's signature or fingerprints, and your signature and those of two witnesses who can read and write Portuguese. And these witnesses, you included, must swear under oath that the worker had everything explained and has fully understood that he has a right not to renew the contract, to reclaim the sum deposited in his name in the Repatriation Fund and to be transported to his land of origin at his employer's expense. I will reject anything that does not follow this procedure and will order the procedure to be repeated in my presence. Do you understand?'

'I am not sure that it is within Your Excellency's powers . . .' Germano André Valente's face seemed impassive, but there was anger in the way the corners of his mouth quivered and his face shook slightly, betraying the hostility he felt.

'What do you know about the powers I have? What authority do *you* have to decide what powers I do or don't have?' Unlike his interlocutor, Luís Bernardo didn't disguise or make any attempt to disguise the indignation in his voice and on his face.

'As you know, Your Honour the Governor' – Germano Valente loved repeating that phrase 'as you know' – 'negotiations over work contracts between plantation companies and their workers are a private matter, governed by civil law, and they fall outside the legal remit of the Governor, and fall within mine, and only come to the former if problems later arise.'

Luís Bernardo jumped to his feet. Red with rage he hammered out each word as if pummelling the other man.

'Listen, Mr Germano: why do you think I came here? For fun? To turn a blind eye to the abuses of plantation owners? To pretend I can't understand why a wretched worker transported from Angola, not knowing why he came, understanding nothing, decides of his own free will to stay on a further five years in that subhuman work, where he is treated worse than any animal? Perhaps you are not worried by any of this, not even by the need to carry out your duties properly. You've been here too long and have got accustomed to turning a blind eye as the best way to avoid hassle. But I'm different. I didn't come on the same premise. I wasn't sent here to be like you. Listen to what I'm about to say: you are here as a commissioner to safeguard the interests of workers and not those of plantation owners. You either fulfil your obligations or will find you face a stack of problems the like of which you never imagined. I am giving you a last opportunity to see to it yourself that things change. And things *must* change, Mr Germano!'

'Your Excellency, if you will allow me, is the one who seems slightly changed of late . . .'

Luís Bernardo stood his ground. He was livid but made an attempt to restrain himself. He bellowed if confronted by arrogance, but met veiled threats warily to try to see what lay behind them.

'What exactly do you mean?'

'I mean that . . .' Germano André hesitated momentarily, thinking he'd gone too far. But he couldn't retreat now. 'His Honour the Governor has recently become much more demanding in these matters, even more imprudent, I might say, since that Englishman arrived . . .'

'So that's what you think, Mr Germano?' Luís Bernardo now spoke surprising softly, almost normally.

'And I'm not the only one to think that . . .'

'Really? Who else does?'

'Everybody. People talk about nothing else.'

'What in fact are people talking about?'

'Just that.'

'What exactly do you mean by "just that"?' Luís Bernardo again raised his voice.

'That Your Honour the Governor's friendship with the Englishman – you're always going around together, visiting each other's houses – has led him to side with his arguments against ours.'

'What exactly are the Englishman's arguments?'

'As His Honour the Governor knows very well, he has come here to make a report to the effect that we employ slave labour on our plantations.'

'And what is our argument, Mr Germano?'

'That this is not true.'

Luís Bernardo smiled.

'It's not true or it suits us to say that it's not true? What is your personal opinion on the matter: is there or isn't there slave labour on the plantations?'

'I don't have to declare a view on this matter.'

'Oh, yes you do! This is where things have changed as far as you are concerned. It forms part of your duties: if there is slave labour or any other abuse on the plantations, you are the first person who must denounce it as such. Or could it be you've forgotten what your duties are, Mr Germano Valente?'

Germano André Valente stayed silent and Luís Bernardo understood that silence was his final word. That was as far as his courage and contempt for the Governor allowed him to go, without running the risk of betraying himself completely. He now washed his hands of the matter. Let those in power sort it out. He would try to survive the storm his lighthouse had long seen brewing on the horizon.

'Very well, Mr Commissioner. Quite frankly I don't think it's worth wasting any more of my time on you. When a person pretends to understand nothing, there's no point in persevering. I have also tried to explain to lots of people out there that things have changed, but nobody wants to listen. You should let it be known in these slanderous conversations you're so fond of that the arguments deployed by the Englishman are the same as ours and were negotiated by our two governments. It wasn't me, or you, or the British Consul, or the plantation owners and overseers who established the new rules of the game. The rules of the game call for an end, once and for all, to slave labour on São Tomé. If it doesn't happen, if this isn't what the Englishman can report has happened, then more than half of São Tomé's export market will disappear. If you all want to face ruin, that's up to you, but at least listen carefully and make an informed choice. This is your last warning. You may leave.'

João sailed in on the *Zaire*. On a Saturday morning, when summer was drawing to a close and the morning air was a heavy haze, at once sticky and hot. He disembarked bewildered and nauseous after his journey, overwhelmed by the climate and the feeling of distress experienced by all who came to São Tomé for the first time. Only then did he really grasp the ridiculous size of that scrap of land adrift on the edge of the ocean and the known world.

'My God, Luís, tell me the city, the "capital" of this land, isn't what the eye can see from here, for heaven's sake! You don't live in this hole, do you?'

Luís grinned gleefully. He was as happy as a young child to have his friend by his side. He hugged him for so long he felt the sweat dripping on his shirt-collar.

'My dear João, you were the one who sent me into exile here, or have you forgotten?'

'Forgive me, do forgive me, my poor Luís Bernardo; I hadn't the slightest idea!'

'Let's go home. I'll get my sensual Doroteia to fan you on the terrace, serve you fresh lemonade and prepare your cold bath, and by tonight you'll love all this. I guarantee you'll adore São Tomé, João. Three years is exile, but a fortnight is sheer luxury. You'll weep tears of remorse and sorrow when you have to leave the island and abandon me to my own devices!'

Luís Bernardo was right. João Forjaz fell in love with the island after the first night, when they enjoyed a dinner supplemented by things he'd brought from Lisbon and which hadn't gone rotten on the journey – a brace or two of marinated partridges, home-cured Serpa cheese, red wine from the Douro and cigars from Casa Havaneza. After dinner they sat on the terrace, catching up on the news from Lisbon and smoking their cigars, the tips of which they dipped in their glasses of cognac. Luís Bernardo was the first to ask interminable questions, wanting chapter and verse on the political scene, social life, the parties, the season at the São Carlos, changes in the city, technological innovations, café intrigues, love affairs, marriages and infidelities.

And almost reluctantly he came to Matilde.

'Matilde . . . ?' João Forjaz contemplated the glowing ember of his cigar, as if he'd made an extraordinary discovery. 'You know, Matilde seems well enough. There's been no fallout from the interlude with you. I don't know if you find that disappointing . . . But the fact is I often see her with her husband and they're always most affectionate to one another.'

'So you don't think he ever found out?'

'No, I don't think so and I've never heard any gossip. It was a brief fling and you were very careful. Four people are in on the secret, and, God willing, they'll take it with them to the grave. And, besides, she's pregnant . . .'

'End of story . . .' muttered Luís Bernardo, as if talking to himself. 'Much better that way.'

They stayed silent for a few minutes and then it was João's turn to want to know everything about his work on São Tomé. He was already well informed or had worked it out from the letters Luís wrote, but now he was there on the spot he understood things better. Luís Bernardo didn't need to be asked twice, he let it all unravel, told him about the island authorities, the men from the plantations, the Englishman and his wife, the people he could trust, a real minority, and those he considered definitive opponents or enemies. It was such a relief finally to have someone whom he could trust completely, someone who could advise and encourage him, someone who, coming from outside, could help him see things more objectively than he could himself. He only stopped when he saw that João's questions were beginning to dry up, a sign his friend was exhausted and had had enough for one night. He took him to the guest bedroom, checked everything was in order, the bed made, a jug and glass of water on the bedside table, enough candles for several days, his clothes hanging in the wardrobe, and only then did he leave him and go to his own room, to sleep the most tranquil sleep he'd had since coming to São Tomé. For once, he wasn't alone on that small island listening to the endless lapping of the ocean.

Luís Bernardo spent several days showing his friend the island. They rode out in the morning and visited the city or nearby villages and plantations. On the way back, they always stopped on a beach – in Água Izé, Micondó, the Sea Shells or Seven Waves – and had a long swim in the sea in those neglected paradises. Afterwards, they stretched out on the sand to enjoy the sun and their conversation, which would occasionally be interrupted by a sudden shower from the heavens. They always came home for lunch in the afternoon to the relative cool of the pantry and day by day João got used to and increasingly relished the dishes that Sinhá cooked and which Sebastião served with visible pleasure in the style of a real butler.

For the entire Palace staff the visit of Doctor João, 'a distinguished Lisbon gentleman, a friend of His Honour the Governor and a frequent visitor to the Court' (as Vicente, at Sebastião's suggestion, made sure the whole city knew), was cause for sudden excitement and renewed gaiety. A different, more relaxed atmosphere reigned, from kitchen to dining room, to reflect Luís Bernardo's mood. Even Doroteia, who preferred to slip silently round the house like an invisible shadow, now became more visible and daring, laughing lots, even smiling more at the constant, casual compliments João sent her way.

On one occasion Luís Bernardo bumped into them in the passageway; his friend was addressing her in gallant mode: 'I'll take you with me to Lisbon and make you Countess of São Tomé,' and she feigned embarrassment and disappeared with a shimmy that made her hips sway under her thin white linen dress, and he couldn't repress the pangs of jealousy that caught him by surprise.

'Really, João . . .'

'What?'

'Nothing, nothing at all.'

'A spot of jealousy, Your Honour?' The joking smile on João's face deliberately goaded him on.

'Scoundrel, abuser! You're abusing the privilege of a holiday romance.'

'Cool down, Luís. When I leave, you'll have your little Doroteia all to yourself. I'm just doing the groundwork for you, because, as I understand it, no doubt due to the rigours of your post, His Honour the Governor has yet to nibble this particular titbit, isn't that so?'

Luís Bernardo turned his back on him and mumbled something about loyalty to friends in times of stress.

After lunch Luís Bernardo usually went to the Government Secretariat downstairs, where he'd spend the afternoon dispatching business, catching up on news and receiving people who had concerns to raise with him. João took advantage of this to have a nap, or return to the city centre that he inspected with a keen anthropological eye, always finding a piece of wood or turtle of interest. At other times, he'd go off with Vicente, whom Luís Bernardo had put at his disposition, to go fishing in a boat he hired for the afternoon and which he'd leave exuberant and return laden down with fish, because on São Tomé a fisherman only has to go thirty or so metres out to haul in the catch of a lifetime. João was clearly radiantly happy on his holidays on the Equator, burnt by the sun and salt of the sea, fascinated or shocked by everything he saw and happy to feel that his presence brought cheer to Luís Bernardo's life.

He'd already visited two plantations with him in the interior – Monte Café and Bombaim – and they'd gone as far as Ribeira-Peixe, on the northernmost promontory of the island. They'd both penetrated the jungle and his skin had felt the mysterious call of the *óbó* and the secrets held in that dense, green world. One morning at sunrise they left in the coast-cutter that linked the islands, and a favourable current took them to Príncipe by the early evening, in time to hear the roll call of workers on the Sunday plantation, where they stayed overnight.

The following day they visited two more plantations and the island capital Santo António, a settlement of a mere thirty brick houses, built around the only square, where the inevitable church pontificated. João amused himself seeing the sights like an idle tourist, while Luís Bernardo spent the day embroiled in whispered conversations with the government representative on the island of Príncipe, the youthful António Vieira, of whom he retained a good impression from the day he landed on São Tomé, when he was introduced to him on the jetty and the man's obvious shyness and nerves immediately won his goodwill. It was only Luís Bernardo's second visit to the island and he thought he detected a vague mood of tension on the plantations. There was something different in the labourers' attitude, something beyond the usual resigned look in their eyes that always moved him deeply. He questioned António Vieira, who was evasive, commenting that he'd only noticed the usual conflicts that were always resolved locally and with no great drama.

'Keep an eye out! Keep an eye out and contact me the moment you notice anything strange or different.' Luís Bernardo looked at him out of the corner of one eye but he didn't seem at all anxious.

'You can trust me, Your Honour, nothing is ever completely secure, as we know, especially here, where it's even more isolated than São Tomé. But if there were any serious problem, I'd be sure to notify you in time.'

Luís Bernardo wasn't delighted by his response but didn't have time to investigate further any foreboding he might have had. The boat was waiting to take them back at sunset and they had hours of night-time sailing before them.

In the middle of the crossing, beneath a clear sky dotted with stars on a pitch-black night, João came and sat next to his friend, and broke the thoughtful silence he'd been immersed in ever since the last signs of life in Santo António had disappeared over the horizon.

'What's the matter, Luís?'

'I don't know. I hope God's not playing tricks on me, but I feel something nasty's brewing on the Príncipe plantations.'

'What, for example? I didn't notice anything out of the ordinary.'

'I can't say, João, but I felt something in the air. Something different in the way the blacks looked at you. If you want the truth, I thought they seemed like a gang of slaves on the verge of a general uprising.'

'Good God, Luís! This bodes ill! You really thought so?'

'Yes, I did. As you can imagine, it's always a potential danger here. And it would be a disaster if there were anything like a revolt now with David Jameson around to be an eyewitness. How then would we possibly sustain our view that there's no slavery on these islands?'

'But do you think there is, Luís?' João seemed genuinely perplexed by his friend's worries.

'João . . .' Luís Bernardo sighed deeply, contemplating the magnificent firmament, apparently home to a universe at peace. 'That's a question I have asked myself every day since I arrived here. When I came, I thought the answer would be self-evident. I thought I'd only have to visit the plantations, see the circumstances of the blacks, consider their hours of work, consult the register of births and deaths, see what medical care existed. Or not even that: look in their eyes and glean the truth. Impossible: I let myself be caught up in a tangle of legal arguments and explanations, laws and treaties, contracts signed or about to be signed, conditions for repatriation, you know, a morass where legal argument gets mired in the scrutiny of facts and I don't know what's more important: what I feel or what I must argue out of sense of duty, as if I were a lawyer in court.'

He went silent. João stared at him in the shadows feebly lit by two oil-lamps that illuminated the ship's gunwale.

'Come now, Luís. Try to be rational: if the law obliges workers to be under contract and if contracts are for a fixed period and they are free to leave at the end of the period, who can call this slavery?'

'Is that what you think, João? Is everything so straightforward? I didn't know you were such a stickler for the law.'

'You know very well, Luís, that we both studied in the same law faculty. As far as I know, while a law isn't broken – and, as you explained, the deadline that will allow you to know has yet to expire – it's not right to assume the law will be respected or not. I didn't see any workers fettered in chains or being whipped to work: I saw them being lined up and counted in the morning when they went to work and on their return at sunset. But, for heaven's sake, Luís, you can't be more Popish than the Pope. This is Africa, it's a colony and, for reasons we don't need to judge now, we are the colonisers and they are the colonised and, as far as I know, colonisation is not banned by any law or international treaty. Isn't it the case that Britain, France, Spain, Germany, Belgium and Holland have colonies that they exploit? Who works on the sugar plantations in the Caribbean? Who works in the gold mines of the Transvaal?'

Luís Bernardo said nothing. He was gazing at the trail of light behind the boat. As if an answer to his questions floated brightly there.

'Luís.' João moved closer, putting an arm round his shoulder. 'I'm your friend, you can tell me everything, even your darkest thoughts. Tell me honestly what makes you so worried.'

Luís Bernardo sighed deeply for a second time. It was an exhausted sigh, a silent cry for help.

'João, I'm worried that I'm not up to the task.'

'What do you mean? Up to what task?'

'João, David Jameson hasn't been posted here to be on holiday. He's not said anything to me and doesn't need to, because I know he's here on a very specific mission: to reach a rapid conclusion as to whether slave labour exists or not on São Tomé and communicate that decision to London. If he concludes there is, it means I've failed in the mission I was charged with. If he concludes there isn't, it means I've managed to deceive him, or at least distract his eagle eye, and I don't know whether I can square that with my conscience.'

'But how can you deceive him, Luís? Facts are facts. They do or don't exist!'

'What? Do you want examples? If a revolt breaks out on a plantation, and I discover that workers are forced to renew their contracts without understanding what they are doing, do you think I will run and let the British Consul know? No, I'm duty-bound to conceal from him anything that might damage our interests. Do you understand now?'

'I think you're making a mountain out of a molehill and, worse still, it's pure speculation. There are always incidents and abuses.

We have them in our farms and factories in Portugal, and don't know the half of it. But there's a big difference between that and slavery.'

'No, João, things are completely different. We've not had serfs of the glebe in Portugal for years and years. Workers may be mistreated but they are always free to leave, even if that means starving in many cases. But here they are five thousand sea miles from home. They don't originate from here, João. Can't you see the difference? If they wanted to leave, they'd have to avoid falling into the trap of putting their sign on an extension of contract they don't want and don't understand and we'd have to repatriate them to the lands where they were from. Now it's true everything may appear very legal, and that bastard the Commissioner, who should protect the rights of the workers and is obviously on the side of the plantation owners, can show me thousands of extension contracts and numbers that show that last year only four – just four, João! – wanted to return home. And what does that mean? In my view, it simply means that slave labour is hidden under a pile of pseudo-legal paperwork. And perhaps you seem to have forgotten one thing, João: I was invited to take on this posting because I'm against slave labour and have said so and put it in writing. Because you, among others, told me I was conscience-bound to put my ideas into practice once I'd been given this position. I didn't come here to compromise and deceive the Englishman. For heaven's sake, I could have stayed in Lisbon and done that and, believe me, it would have been much easier and more agreeable.'

João Forjaz was stunned into silence by his friend's passionate tone. Here was a Luís Bernardo he'd never seen in Lisbon. It wasn't really the emphatic way he defended his ideas and points of view – he'd seen him do that often enough, among friends, in armchair polemic, in the political debates they'd frequently indulge in during Thursday-night dinners at the Hotel Central. But now there was a different tone, something more personal, more radical. São Tomé had changed the Luís Bernardo he knew so well. He glanced at him furtively while his friend silently contemplated the dark waters of the strait across which the boat was making such painful progress. He suddenly glimpsed a gregarious society man who had turned into a loner; a tolerant man who loved controversy, who'd suddenly become intransigent; a man who was detached and aloof from so much, who now acted almost like a messiah, as if the entire world depended on his obscure labours at the ocean's rim, on that scrap of land and civilisation! Had he become obsessed by the importance of his own mission in order not to feel completely futile? Had he been transformed by solitude, by the many silent nights spent talking and listening to himself? Had he lost all sense of proportion?

'Easy now, Luís. We all know that theoretically the law is the same everywhere, but that's a pious fiction. No empire was built or maintained that way: who authorised Cortés to capture Moctezuma when he landed in America? Who authorised Dom Carlos to defeat and imprison Gungunhana, who was King of Mozambique as a result of rights much more ancient than his own? All such ethical positions constantly develop: what's normal today will seem horrendous tomorrow and what's criminal today will be commonplace tomorrow. You can't come here and after six months hope to convince all the Portuguese who've lived here for generations, suffering what you've been suffering for a few months, hoping their reward will be to make a fortune if they're lucky, that the entire basis of their lives, the whole edifice they've erected, upon which they depend, is flawed just because you've brought from Lisbon decrees, instructions or secrets agreements with Britain they should rush to obey in twenty-four hours . . . You may be right, but it needs time, Luís. Time and discussion.'

'No. João.' Luís Bernardo abandoned his contemplation of the sea and spoke as if he were alone, as in so many long-distance exchanges he'd had with João, as if the latter were listening. 'You don't know these people. They will never change, never evolve, and never accept that the surreptitious slavery they practise on their plantations isn't a natural right, a gift from Providence for their own enjoyment and profit. They're only waiting for David to write his report and leave, and for me to get tired and leave as well, and for someone else to come like the people they're used to, so life can return to normal. Is that really what we want as a nation, João? Why then do we call them Portuguese Provinces? Why don't we call them Portuguese Slaving Stations in Africa?'

They both went quiet. The monotonous chug of the boat's coal-fired engine shattered the quiet night on a star-filled sea. By the side and in front of the vessel reflections of light glinted marking the presence of flying fish following in its wake. Landwards, a very pale, almost imperceptible brightness heralded break of day on the horizon, and ahead, towards São Tomé, now only two or three hours away, a thin thread of light at water-level revealed the exact spot where night was ending in the city where they were headed as the morning sun rose over the Equator.

João shivered with cold and pulled tighter to his chest the overcoat he'd wrapped round himself. He looked at his friend again and saw his sad gaze, an almost physical forlornness that betrayed wrinkles he'd never noticed before and which now stood out on his face in the first light of morning. He felt a friend's tender love towards Luís Bernardo, something he'd never felt before: he must defend and protect him. Get him out of here as soon as possible.

David and Ann kept returning to dine at Luís Bernardo's house. From the moment João arrived in São Tomé, those meals at Luís Bernardo's or the British couple's had become so commonplace they almost dispensed with any prior notification. To begin with, they spaced the meals out with a modicum of ceremony, as if to maintain the appearance of the etiquette to which they were accustomed. But very quickly the meals became – the result of a tacit agreement – daily or almost daily, in one house or the other. Once the couple's liking for João showed itself to be reciprocal and immediate, the foursome, knowing they belonged to a unique sub-group in those parts, decided without comment to shelve all protocols that might prevent them, for no plausible, indeed for trivial reasons, from enjoying each other's company. For the 'residents', João's brief transit through their tropical exile was a rare opportunity to turn those dinners into foursomes and not threesomes – and it made all the difference.

As usual, Luís Bernardo had dinner served in the pantry and not in the dining room that he continued to regard as too big, unpleasant and formal with its heavy Indo-Portuguese wooden furniture he so heartily detested. Besides, the pantry enabled them to open the French windows to the terrace, and bring night and the garden into the house. And it was a beautiful night, with a full moon and quiet breeze, and a heat that waxed and waned bringing with it a scent of the sea when the tide was out and of flowers he couldn't identify, but which Ann named immediately. He used the extra work as an excuse to tell Sebastião (diplomatically, so as not to offend his good humour) that he should ask Doroteia to help him serve at table. He was making a sly dig at João, who was fascinated by her silent, undulating movements, smiling white teeth and dark eyes as she circulated around the table. The truth was none of the men could remain indifferent to her presence. Luís Bernardo felt an urge to put his arm round her hips when she came to remove his plate, a gesture to show the others he had proprietary rights to that lithe panther, carved from ebony, ivory and languid sweat. He was about to make his need tangible when he noticed Ann, seated to his right, watching the scene with the instinctive concern women have at such times. And he stopped there, hand suspended in mid-air, blushing like a child caught on the point of committing a terrible blunder.

Sinhá had prepared her fish soup that was unrivalled on those islands, following it with roast wild boar cased in banana-apple, which gave it an imaginative, refined taste, worthy of a French chef. A cocoa and nut dessert and mango sorbet provided a grand finale to the repast.

Prompted by the chilli hotness of Sinhá's soup, David remarked he'd never understood why piquant sauces were used so much in hot climates.

'After all, you Portuguese brought Indian peppers to Europe and it's only natural they were most appreciated in our cold climes in Europe in order to boost body temperatures. But nowhere in the world is food so hotly spiced as in the tropics – in Africa, India, Brazil and the Caribbean. Why do you need to sweat more when you are already dying from the heat?'

João countered that he'd read somewhere that spice helped fight the effects of the heat – a thesis that was ridiculous rather than scientific, as David explained. And then they both became engrossed in a conversation on life in the tropics, that soon developed into a comparison of the tropics and civilisation and what Kipling called 'the white man's burden'. Pointing out they could continue the conversation on the terrace, Luís Bernardo got up and invited the others to follow suit, but only Ann did so, while the other two stayed enmeshed in debate.

He and Ann sat on the bamboo chairs on the terrace facing the sea that was illuminated by the moon in a path of light from horizon to ground. Apart from the odd cry of a night bird or stray sound from the nearby city, all was peaceful and still. Luís Bernardo lit his cigar on one of the candles Sebastião always kept lit until he went to bed on the countless nights he spent gazing seawards, listening to music and smoking, alone with his thoughts. But tonight he was happy: happy, relaxed and in good company. He wore plain black linen trousers and a long white shirt open at the collar. The only trace of the life he'd abandoned was the silver Patek Philippe he'd inherited from his father and which he'd placed in his small front-trouser pocket, its chain hanging down his left leg.

Ann was resplendent: her blonde hair gathered up, a tress down each side of her face, a gleam in her eye, her skimpy dark-blue cotton dress with very high bodice and low neckline revealing an expanse of bosom, darkened by the São Tomé sun and moist with small, almost invisible beads of sweat. Her voice was hot, halting and sensual, and made him shiver as if unseen arms were embracing him, like Ulysses lured by the song of the sirens, lost on his journey home. It wasn't only now, that evening in the magic moonlight, that he'd noticed this. Day after day, night after night, he found her presence more and more unsettling; hopes that he might see her distracted him during the day and disrupted his sleep at night. But he never made the slightest gesture that might betray this to her.

'Luís.' Her voice abruptly ended that enchanted moment and he woke up at once, senses alerted. 'You've quite changed since João came. You're a normal human being, and no longer behave like a hunted animal.'

He smiled.

'Do you think I am a hunted animal, Ann?'

'Do you never look at yourself in the mirror, Luís? You're like a fakir about to walk on daggers, always expecting the next fall, the next blade!'

'You're probably right, Ann. I've been here almost a year: it's been a very hard year, a life different from everything I have ever known. With nobody at all I could trust, talk to, be like this with, relaxing as we are now. João's visit changed all that, but I know it's only a brief interlude: he'll be gone in a few days and then everything will be back to normal. And normality, Ann, is sometimes difficult to come to terms with.'

'I know, Luís, I guessed as much. But you know that at least you can always rely on David and me. We like you and have spoken about your situation often. We at least have each other, but you have no one. It must be very difficult to endure nights like this on your terrace.'

Luís Bernardo looked at her: she was beautiful, almost unreal. He was afraid to stretch out a hand to touch her in case she disappeared. He decided to try his luck.

'Ann, I don't doubt your friendship for one moment. But as you know David and I have very different, not to say opposed, missions. Maybe the day will come when our respective tasks will disrupt the friendship we've built so spontaneously. Perhaps the three of us or myself should have made sure we didn't become friends: if there is ever a crisis, it would make things easier.'

'You know, you men love to cultivate this kind of inner conflict. Driven by your consciences, you tolerate enemies and abandon friends. I've experienced this elsewhere . . . But listen, Luís, I'm a woman, I'm your friend and I don't experience this kind of conflict: if I have any say, I'll never abandon you.'

He was struck dumb. He didn't really understand what she was hinting. He felt groggy: perhaps it was from the wine and cognac, the full moon and her astonishingly beautiful skin, bosom, hair and eyes. He felt dizzy and got up, leaned on the balustrade and breathed in a little of the breeze from the sea the heat of night didn't stifle en route.

'Where will you go, Luís?'

'Me?' He noticed how he'd swung round unawares and turned to look at her, 'Nowhere!'

'Will you flee?'

'Flee? Flee from what?'

He did now feel abandoned, adrift, and unable to think or say anything sensible. But she wouldn't let up. Her voice resounded, soft, hot and sensual. And relentless.

'From me.'

The noise from the argument between David and João in the dining room grew louder. They were embroiled in a comparison of British and Portuguese colonisations and in the heat of debate seemed to have completely forgotten the couple alone on the terrace. Luís Bernardo took advantage of their raucous argument to avoid improvising a reply to Ann and noted in the meantime with a smile that João was passionately rehearsing all the arguments that supported the Portuguese position in relation to São Tomé. He was working on his behalf and apparently scoring points. And he pretended this was distracting him, but Ann would have none of it.

'I asked you a question, Luís, but got no reply, and that is a reply in itself. Well, given we are here, in a place so far from everywhere and in such unexpected circumstances, I don't believe there's room for hypocrisy. I will come straight out: you fascinate me, Luís. I've asked myself a thousand times what an intelligent, cultured, educated, attractive bachelor like you is doing exiled on this island. I asked João a few days ago and he gave me the response I'd expected: you have come from a sense of duty, a wish to feel useful for once in your life, to fill a void and meet an intellectual challenge. In other words, a classic bind, Luís. You're not the man for this job, and you know it. It's not your world and you don't believe in the values you are supposed to be representing and defending. But you feel trapped and don't know how to free yourself. But what crime have you committed that you need to flagellate yourself so?'

'And what crime did you commit to end up being sent here?'

'I didn't; my husband did. I promised not to be hypocritical and I'll tell you the gist of it. David did something terribly idiotic in India, an unforgivable *faux pas*, and was forced to come to São Tomé, the most obscure corner available to any servant of the great British Empire. Any other woman would have left him after the trouble he brought and the destiny that life by his side now opened up. But I really admire my husband, despite what he did, which can never erase or blot out everything else, the brilliant man he was and still is. I loved him a lot until he hurt me the way he did and now I love him in a different, more private, more distanced way I find difficult to explain. I could have abandoned him, but I thought I shouldn't, after everyone else had. As you can see, I am not at all above feelings of duty. It was clear to us that I am the constant presence at his side, I am his wife as far as the world and the law is concerned, but I am not his wife in practice, if I don't wish to be . . . That is the price he must pay to have me with him. I am a free woman, as if I were a traveller who'd just landed on São Tomé, where . . .' Ann stooped for a moment and looked him in the eye, 'Where I found you.'

They stayed there silently staring at each other. She was still sitting on the chair; he was still standing, leaning against the balustrade, his back to the sea and the moon. He was in the shadow and she was in the full light. Luís Bernardo held out his hands to her. Ann got up slowly and walked over to him, to the shadows where he remained motionless, hands outstretched in mute appeal. From where they stood they weren't visible from the inside, from where they heard the voices of David and João locked in endless argument. For a moment it struck Luís Bernardo that João had guessed what was happening outside and was pursuing the debate with David to give him time and opportunity to make that the most decisive of all past and future nights on São Tomé. And it was his final thought before feeling the softness of her face gently touch his, the velvet of her lightly perfumed hair brush against his cheek, her body lean into his, and her heaving breast press against his chest. He had time to look and see the liquid green of her eyes, where the reflected moon faded when she closed her eyes and surrendered an eager, moist mouth, her hot tongue running over his teeth, entwining with his own tongue, her body almost crushing his in a desperate passion or desire no other woman yielding to him had ever shown. And closing his eyes he melted into that mouth and passion for what seemed an eternity, at the frontier of what was bearable.

12

I SLANDS CAN BE desolate places and more so when the time comes to say farewell to visiting friends and relatives. It is almost always sadder to stay than to depart, and an island community gets divided into two kinds of human being: those who live there and those who come and go.

Two boats stopped every month on São Tomé and Príncipe, from Angola and Portugal respectively. There was no jetty, just a small beach where passengers and cargo were ferried to and fro from the boats anchored out to sea; all arrivals and departures were charged with a level of emotion that lingered over the strand and city long after the boat had disappeared over the horizon. The boats hooted stridently on arrival, after rounding the cape that led into the Bay of Ana Chaves, as if wanting to summon the entire city to the beach. And they would be spotted from far rocks perched on mountain tops. As the news passed from islander to islander, from mouth to mouth, to the city, people rushed to the beach, not just the few relatives or friends expecting visitors or those with cargo or merchandise aboard, but crowds of young children, married women with nothing to do, men in authority pretending it was their duty to be there, and idle bystanders, all lured by the silent, patient curiosity of those accustomed to living life watching others come and go.

The boat from Lisbon always came loaded with 'the latest thing' – fashionable clothes, agricultural implements, cures for strange diseases that were sometimes unknown there and magazines and newspapers that brought the world to the islands – and which that same night would be the talk of the town. Lisbon folk would come bringing their society airs, preening as they made the small crowd of onlookers move aside. When the vessel left for Lisbon, it took with it the plantation owners who had just spent *la gravana* between the beach and Casa Grande, surrounded by the scent of cocoa drying on wooden trays, soldiers or civil servants who'd finished their tours of duty and only wanted a calm sea and tail wind to blow them quickly back to the Tagus sand bar, and businessmen who felt every extra day was a nightmare. Those left behind on the beach stayed quiet, watching the gigs take on last-minute passengers and cargo, the heavy steamer activate its boilers, strike anchor with a farewell squeak, set off slowly then gradually pick up speed. Luís Bernardo rarely appeared at these ceremonies on the beach. He sometimes had to fulfil an official duty when the vessel was leaving or arriving with a high-ranking civil servant from the Angolan government or Lisbon Ministry on board. He hated departures and arrivals in equal measure but he did go to say goodbye to João the day he left for Lisbon. They indulged in a rather awkward embrace, each feeling the other's sense of loss. When would they see each other again? And in what state or circumstances?

When the steamer lifted anchor and began to head for the open sea, Luís Bernardo didn't wait for the customary hoot. He turned round and walked towards the carriage awaiting him.

Midway, he felt an arm link into his.

'Alone again, Luís?'

Ann. He'd caught a brief glimpse of her when people had begun to embark. She'd come with David to say goodbye. In the to and fro that ensued, he had lost sight of them and assumed the couple had gone home after giving their farewells. But there she was, and Luís Bernardo very quickly registered the absence of David.

Taking advantage of the unexpected private moment he teased, 'Someone told me the other day that, if she had her say, I'd never be alone . . .'

The setting sun was reflected in her eyes, and there he thought he saw a fleeting sadness. But her voice when she responded was warm and enticing, just as he always remembered it.

'Luís, there's one thing, only one thing you should know about me and you must believe it. I never lie, never pretend, and never forget what I've said, however easy it might be for me to use a situation or chance as an excuse. It's down to you. Luís, look at me: here we are on the beach where everyone can see us. We're not alone on the terrace at your house under a full moon, after we've drunk half a bottle of wine and a couple of glasses of port. It's down to you. The decision is yours.' And she moved away, as if she'd not said anything out of the ordinary.

David finally appeared and she went over to her husband and quite naturally slipped her arm into his. David waved him goodbye over his shoulder and he and Ann continued walking arm-in-arm to the waiting carriage.

When he got home he decided he didn't want supper. He dismissed Sebastião for the night and sat on his terrace, with a single candle burning and a cigar he'd lit from the candle's flame. He stayed up till past midnight with half a bottle of cognac, until the nearby cry of a bat woke him rudely. He staggered to his feet, walked to his bedroom in the candlelight and felt the presence of Sebastião, who watched to make sure he didn't set fire to the house and waited while he performed his ablutions. His emotionally exhausted body, still fully dressed, thudded down on his bed, sleep coming on. But it was not the restorative sleep he'd hoped for.

He woke up tired with a dry, unpleasant taste of fermented brandy in his mouth; his muscles ached and he looked simply dreadful. He shaved and showered, but that brought no relief to his deep moral and physical lack of well-being. João's room was empty and he missed the voice and friendly understanding of the man now sailing on the ocean en route to Lisbon. He remembered Ann's voice, the luminous green or blue of her eyes, and the taste of her mouth that wouldn't go away. He now had to go and join in the mundane routine awaiting him on the ground floor: obscure, threadbare civil servants nervously doffing their hats, begging a favour, to be recommended for a promotion they thought well deserved or to be granted permission for unwarranted holidays in the metropolis. There would be the post from Lisbon, statements to be approved and published in the colony's official bulletin, fines to be raised, the health of the local Ministry of the Exchequer to consider, decision on funds to allocate for the Christmas and New Year festive lights, the list of public works contracts to give out, complaints, petitions and applications to see to.

He looked up and down at himself in the full-length mirror, and saw himself as he was, naked, forlorn, adrift, unsure whether he'd been smitten by an obscure illness or had won a battle on behalf of an obscure cause.

He looked at himself hard and shouted, 'Luís Bernardo Valença, royal appointee to the Governorship of the Colony of São Tomé and Príncipe, wake up and go and do your duty. The story doesn't end here!'

He spent the next days shut up in the Government Secretariat, dispatching everything, answering his post, receiving those who'd requested an audience, catching up on the backlog of work. He even worked through one night, suddenly obsessed by the need to review all government accounts, now that the end of the year was approaching and final accounts would have to be closed and sent to the Ministry in Lisbon. It was a good year for the cocoa crop. São Tomé harvested four thousand two hundred more tons than the previous year and Príncipe one ton more. Customs creamed off more duties, the government more taxes and the Town Hall more rates: on that front, he could feel happy. The public works being undertaken were in budget, current expenditure remained at the same level as the previous year and the colony continued to be self-sufficient, paying on time every single import and even accumulating surpluses, whether in the balances of the plantations and local trade or in the match between receipts and expenditure in the local Exchequer. It was a real success. Besides, if that weren't the case, what was the point of having colonies?

One beautiful morning he noticed there were no papers on the top of his desk; his office was in order, and nobody expected an audience. He went up to his rooms, drank a glass of fruit juice and ordered his bay to be harnessed while he got changed. He rode out from the Palace entrance away from the city, then slowly along the coastal road, greeting informally the few passers-by he encountered. He rode on, not knowing for sure where he wanted to go, engrossed in thoughts that took him back to Lisbon, to dinners with friends, to debates, to stories and anecdotes that had become legendary. He thought about Matilde and what João had told him about her pregnancy and apparent conjugal bliss, remembered their two clandestine meetings in the Hotel Braganza. The memories excited him and made him drift so far in thought that by the time he returned to reality he'd ridden past the last houses on the city outskirts and was cantering along an empty sand path that led straight to the Micondó Beach. He spurred his horse on to a quick, syncopated gallop as if the empty stretch of road had frightened him. He'd intended to return along the track along the top of the cliffs and get back to the city in time for lunch, but when he reached the top of the hill overlooking the beach, he was transfixed. Before him stretched dazzling white sand, dotted here and there with fallen coconuts, bits of wood or fronds from the palms lining the conch-shaped beach, which sloped gently down to the quiet foam of the waves as they came to die on the sand. The water was so clean that he could make out the shadows of rocks, the sinuous shadows of turtles swimming close to the beach, the shapes of fish, anemones and seaweed. Drawn like a magnet he began to canter down to the beach. He dismounted by the coconut palms, tied his horse to a tree-trunk and walked along the deserted beach, listening to the chirping of birds in the palm grove, the sound of which hid the murmur of the waves splashing gently on the sand.

He sat down ten metres from the water's edge, took his boots off and lit a cigarette. Then he made a headrest from the sand, lay back and smoked, gazing into a sky that was unusually clear for that time of the year, with only a few clusters of almost motionless clouds scattered across the perfect azure. It was as if the whole universe had stopped and he'd come to rest there, a survivor from a shipwreck or a creature fallen from a cloud in his sleep to land on that virgin beach, where no other human seemed to have trod before. He closed his eyes against the blinding sun and felt the skin of his face tighten in the heat. He finished his cigarette, stood up, and looked around to check he was alone. Then he stripped off and entered the translucent water and began swimming slowly out to sea. After a while, he took a deep breath and swam underwater back to the beach. He saw some fish and a turtle moving away, saw the willowy shape of a barracuda, teeth as sharp as a saw, looking at him askance and then he was back on the beach with the waves splashing over his head and his body buried in the sand, like an alligator's.

He was about to stand up when a voice, very quiet and very close, filled him with consternation.

'Such a beautiful sight! The Governor of São Tomé and Príncipe, not working in his office, but bathing naked on his private beach! Who will ever take you seriously again, my dear Governor?'

Ann was sitting ten steps away where he'd left his clothes, and he noticed another horse now tethered next to his among the palm trees. He retreated instinctively, backing into the sea without a word, not knowing how to react.

'Luís, you've taken fright? Lost your voice?'

'No, I'm just wondering how I can leave the water now . . .'

'How? The same way as you entered: on foot. Or do you want me to come in after you?'

'No, I can get out by myself. The problem is that, as you may have noticed, I'm completely naked.'

'Oh, what a fantastic prospect, finding you alone on a deserted beach and quite naked in the water!'

'It's as if you've done this on purpose . . .'

'No, it's the hand of fate. I swear I didn't follow you and just happened to ride by when I saw a horse tied up in the palm grove and decided to take a look at the solitary beachcomber. I must confess I recognised you by your horse and not by the sight of your distant rump, diving and coming back to the surface!'

She burst out laughing, like a young girl who'd admitted playing a practical joke, and he couldn't stop himself from laughing too at her confession.

'Very well, I'll walk back then. Look away or prepare for the scene where the Governor of São Tomé lands naked before the wife of the British Consul's gaze.'

'Go on then.'

'I can't. Not now.'

'And why not?'

Do I, don't I? Do I go on and let God's will be, or don't I? Luís Bernardo tried to get some indication from her expression, but she just sat there, naturally and calmly, with only the hint of a mischievous smile at the corner of her lips.

'Well, Ann, the fact is, as you can perhaps imagine at this point in time, I'm not, how can I put it, in a state of anatomical innocence. I don't know if I make myself clear?'

'Yes, I think I understand, I can guess what your problem is. But there may be another solution.'

'You could pass me my clothes?' he asked, waiting anxiously for a reply.

'On the contrary, tell me what the water's like.'

'The water? It's excellent; it's really warm.'

She pulled off her riding boots with a struggle, sitting on the sand and cursing between her teeth. Then she stood up, un-buttoned her blouse one button at a time, took it off and threw it to one side to reveal a short bodice clinging to her bosom. She unbuttoned that garment, pulled the straps over her shoulders and brought her bosom into the light of day, large, voluptuous and firm, nipples round and pert. Then she unbuttoned her jodhpurs and let them slide down her thighs, pulling them over her feet. She had long, perfectly shaped legs, much darker-skinned than one would have expected. When she'd stripped off and begun to walk naked into the water, Luís Bernardo ceased his exhaustive investigation of her body. He started to look at her face and into her eyes: she also looked at him, bare, calm; only her mischievous smile disappeared and she observed him with a single expression, an air of silent determination, of almost the premeditation with which she'd stripped off and walked towards him.

Luís Bernardo finally got out of the water and received her standing up, body to body, her breasts pressed against his chest, her thighs melting into his, her mouth fusing with his. Ann gently pushed him on the shoulders and he lost his balance and fell backwards, pulling her with him. Luís Bernardo sought her mouth again, now a salty, honeyed taste, felt her tongue slip shamelessly along his and the passion of her surrender sent his head into a wild spin. He let go of her mouth and started kissing her neck and shoulders. Maddened by desire, he nuzzled her breasts, started to suck her nipples, while his hands explored her breasts, held each one in turn, as if measuring their weight and consistency, and now crushing them with his flattened palms. But Ann wasn't passive, didn't close her eyes, didn't moan, and didn't throw her head back like a conquered woman. She furiously sought his mouth as she slid her hand down under the water, grasping his stiff cock, squeezing tight as she ran her hand up and down. Luís Bernardo pushed her back on the wet sand burying himself in her breasts again as he felt his thighs crush hers and his cock press against her belly.

They rubbed against each other like animals on heat, thrown up on the sandy beach by a sea eager that they consummate their desire. Luís Bernardo was swept along by a devastating surge of desire but suddenly he felt he should speak.

'Ann . . .' he began, not really knowing what he wanted to say, but she stopped him.

She had a rapt smile and the same resolve in her gaze, her hands pulling at his neck and his body bringing them towards her.

'Shush, Luís . . . come. Come to me!'

Arching her body, she opened her legs and directed him inside. Then he surrendered himself, thinking no more, moving slowly in her, holding back, and he felt her moistness, a thick spume that wasn't just from the sea, and, sighing almost inaudibly, he went deep into her, so deep he felt the earth turn round his head. He felt her salty tongue, and something else open up, tearing itself to receive him, somewhere beneath the ground the roar of a dormant volcano and he roared with the volcano, with her, a hoarse sound when everything suddenly came together in an explosion and he saw only stars glinting in her eyes, the green and blue of Ann's eyes was a sky over all that chaos and, even when he felt himself go and let himself go in the deepest part of her and of himself, he still had time for a final flash of lucidity, and he encountered raw truth in all its radiant purity: he would lose himself for ever in the body, gaze and depths of this woman.

A long time after – an eternity for someone like him, who suddenly felt like a criminal on the point of being arrested – Ann freed herself from his arms, kissed him gently on the mouth, sighed and said, 'I must go.'

She began to dress slowly, and gradually he saw that perfect body covered up, disappear from his view, but never now from his memory. They walked to where they'd left their horses. Ann untied hers, walked towards him holding her horse by the rein, pressed her body up against Luís Bernardo's again and gave him a long, last kiss.

He had said nothing after possessing her on the sand. He stood there silently, and watched her ride away. He lit another cigarette, stayed on the top of the hill contemplating the sea, which was as transparent as it had ever been, and he felt a tightness in his chest as he gazed at the exact spot where the marks in the sand signalled the unbelievable moments he'd just lived through. If it hadn't been for those marks the sea would be quick to erase it would all have seemed a dream.

Luís Bernardo was sitting behind his desk at work reading the newspapers that had just arrived from Lisbon. The great sensation in the capital was the presence in considerable numbers of the first motor cars. The first car races, of cars 'with a combustible engine, powered by petrol, able to transport driver and occupants at a speed of fifty, sixty or even seventy kilometres an hour!' were being organised. He remembered the first motor car to be purchased a few years ago had been a Panhard-Levasseur by the Count of Avillez. The inaugural drive between Lisbon and Santiago do Cácem also recorded the first fatal car accident, when an Alentejo peasant riding his donkey was caught unawares by the appearance of that strange contraption, went to take a close look and was knocked over by the chauffeur: the donkey subsequently died. The Portuguese scientists the newspaper consulted disagreed about the future of the motor car as a means of transport: some saw the beginning of a revolutionary period that would quickly dethrone all other means – as happened with electric trams, which a few years before had made mule-driven coaches obsolete – and others predicted a short, stormy, accident-prone life. Others, like Professor José Medeiros, judged the combustible used – petrol – to be the primary reason for the engine's lack of a future: 'due to the scarcity of that fuel throughout the world, as the few sources existing on the face of the planet can only guarantee two years' supply for such a futile, transient discovery'. Such pessimism was not shared by Mr Henrique Mendonça, 'distinguished colonialist and estimable citizen of the islands of São Tomé and Príncipe', who had recently, so the newspaper informed, rented the stables of the Marquess da Foz's palace in Restauradores, 'where he intends to set up the first motor-car showroom in Portugal, on behalf of the Peugeot company'. The same Mr Henrique Mendonça, the newspaper reminded its readers, who had inaugurated less than a month ago a magnificent mansion in Campo Santo, which looked down on the whole city from the top of the hill where the house-warming party surpassed in pomp, excess and glamour anything Lisbon had seen for years. Luís Bernardo smiled inwardly, as he thought of the vision, pomp, glamour and distinguished merits of the master of Boa Entrada. Should he have sent two torch-brandishing São Tomé blacks to welcome guests at the entrance to the party to launch his 'magnificent mansion'?

He went through the newspaper with a fine toothcomb as usual, not missing a word, from the political manoeuvres in Parliament to the activities of the Royal Family, via the results of the horse trials at the Jockey and description of dinners at the Turf and main Christmas celebrations. He avidly read the reviews of the São Carlos opera season and scanned the names of all those who'd died, been born, baptised, married, travelled abroad or returned from their journeying. From a distance, even with that profusion of news – for someone like him living in a place where nothing ever happened worthy of inclusion in those pages – he thought how little had changed in the behaviour and ideas of his metropolitan contemporaries. The political atmosphere had become significantly tenser, from the day Dom Carlos instituted by decree the dictatorship of João Franco, who promised 'to save the country, the monarchy and the economy'. Violent hatred had been unleashed, and the Republican Party, which benefited from broad freedom of movement in spite of the word 'dictatorship', was visibly expanding, in Lisbon, Oporto and the provinces. King Dom Carlos made things worse by explaining in an interview with a French newspaper, employing his usual tone of unmitigated contempt, that he had instituted the dictatorship as a provisional measure merely to put the country back on the right track after years of incompetent government by the politicians available. When republished in Portugal the interview led to all manner of dispute, and outlandish insults were directed at the head of the House of Braganza.

Luís Bernardo was so engrossed in his newspaper he didn't notice the knocking on his door and his secretary heard an order to come in only at his third attempt.

'What is it?'

'The English Consul is outside and wishes to see his Honour the Governor.'

Luís felt a shiver down his spine. Could it be . . . ? No, Ann couldn't have said anything! Even so . . . Hadn't she suggested, in the conversation on his terrace, that she wanted to take revenge on her husband, felt free to take it and that he was even expecting it? No, it was impossible: if she'd done that, it would mean everything that happened that night and on the beach was only her taking revenge on her husband, he Luís Bernardo merely the instrument. He didn't believe that was the case. Perhaps someone had seen them on the beach and started to spread the word and in less than two days it had reached David's ears.

He couldn't keep conjecturing: David was out there and wanted to come in.

Luís Bernardo sighed and said, 'Tell him to come in,' and got up to welcome him as warmly as ever.

'Hello, Luís! I was just passing and thought I'd call in to see if you were about.'

They shook hands. Nothing betrayed anything unusual in David's voice or manner.

'Sit down, David, and tell me what brings you here.'

'Oh, nothing worth sitting down for. It's a quick visit and I don't want to disturb you at work.'

'I was only reading the Lisbon newspapers . . .'

'Well, anyway, it's not very convenient for me now. I just wanted to fix a meeting with you. There's a personal matter I want to discuss with you, a few questions I'd like to ask. How about if we had dinner tomorrow?'

'Tomorrow is fine. No problem. I'll be there.'

'At seven-thirty, as usual, all right?'

He shook hands again, turned half round and left as casually as he'd come.

Luís Bernardo stood there gazing thoughtfully at the door he'd shut behind him. A formal meeting arranged a day in advance –

didn't they issue invitations at less than an hour's notice when they wanted to meet up? A personal matter? A few questions he'd like to ask? A supper at their place, in Ann's presence? Was it a mere coincidence or just a perverse provocation *à trois*?

Whatever the truth of it, he realised that from now on he would have to live with that anxiety. David was a friend of his. He genuinely liked him and had taken to him from the first time they met. He and Ann had been incredibly supportive in helping him to come to terms with the loneliness of his existence. And it was true he'd pay them back whenever he could, but that only made things worse: gave David the right to trust in him as a friend. And the first thing one requires of a friend is loyalty – even if his wife falls into your arms, tells you she has the right to take revenge on her husband, a right recognised by the husband himself, and catches you naked on a deserted beach and, instead of disappearing, strips off and enters the water to be with you. The wives of friends can act as they please, but not the friends of husbands.

The fact was everything that shouldn't have happened already had. It was irrevocable and worst of all he felt passionately about Ann and that he had neither the strength, reason or will to resist her. And there they were, shut up on a tiny island, with no discreet hotels or cooperative lady friends to help. He'd landed himself in a real mess! Of course, he could always take flight: that was the price to pay and the usual solution in such circumstances. That's what he'd done with Matilde – fled to São Tomé. But the problem was he didn't want to flee from Ann. The mere idea of taking flight and leaving her on São Tomé devastated him. No, on this occasion, he had no desire to take flight. Did it mean he wanted to accept the consequences? No, it didn't. Destiny had set him a splendid trap!

The British Consulate in São Tomé was a small, two-storey house, surrounded by a wall, with a small but packed garden of begonias, mulberries, blackberries and banana trees, which brought shade in summer and cool in the rainy season. There were three rooms on the ground floor that opened out directly on to the garden, and on the top floor three bedrooms and the only bathroom. At the back of the garden an annexe, separated from the main residence by a kind of shed, housed the kitchen, pantry and wash-house, stables and servants' quarters. There were just two maids, apart from the gardener who looked after the garden under strict instructions from Ann and Bennaoudi, the black from Zanzibar, who acted as interpreter for David and who presented himself for work every morning, accompanying the Consul on his travels and returning at the end of the day to his thatched hut in the city. The main bedroom, where the master and mistress slept, led out to a wooden veranda looking out on the garden and a vine that twisted and climbed beyond the roof. Underneath the veranda, Ann, fascinated by the 'mad rose', strove to cultivate a bed of them; their changing colours during the day served as a clepsydra; their scent flooded the bedroom and transported her far away.

The small wooden door in the middle of the external wall, which gave entry to the Consulate garden, was always shut, though only on a latch, and guests would out of politeness ring the small side bell to announce their presence. But that night Luís Bernardo forgot the bell because he was distracted or for some unconscious reason and simply unlatched the door, walked in and closed it behind him. He walked to the front of the house and found Ann on a cane chair looking into the garden, deep in thought. She didn't notice he'd come.

'Hello,' he cried, halting in his tracks the moment he saw her.

'Oh, Luís, do come in!' She got up, went over to him, placed a gentle, welcoming hand on his chest and gave him a tender kiss on the cheek. He looked at her apprehensively, and Ann, reading his thoughts, said, 'David's late. He'll get here any moment. We can wait here. Would you like a gin and tonic?'

'Yes, that would be nice.'

Ann disappeared into the house and he noticed how, despite her apparent boldness, she seemed sad, and that a shadow muddied the usual luminous gleam in her eye. He sat down on one of the comfortable padded cane armchairs the couple had brought from India like so many other things in the house: cupboards, tables, chinaware, muskets and lances for the hunt. Photographs of India adorned walls and tables on the ground floor, as if to convince themselves they'd brought a bit of India with them and that one day they'd set sail taking all those things back over the same sea they had crossed, back to the life they'd once enjoyed.

He heard her enter the room and stood up. She was carrying two glasses; she handed him his and chinked hers against his gently in a silent toast. But suddenly she pulled him towards her and pushed him against the wall where they wouldn't be seen by either maid. She pressed her body into his, as she had on the beach.

'Luís, I've been so miserable. I wanted so much to see you and feel you close to me!'

'Ann, don't say that! No man has ever missed a woman as I've missed you!'

'Come, maybe we'll feel better and more in control if we sit down.'

Luís Bernardo wrenched himself away and sat down, leaving a prudent space of one chair between them.

'Ann, why does David want to speak to me?'

'I've no idea, Luís. He just told me he'd invited you to dinner because he needed to speak to you.'

'Does he suspect anything? Could he have found out?'

'No, I don't think so. But he is very intuitive, and maybe he's guessed something's happening, though doesn't know for sure.'

'You didn't say anything? You've not hinted at anything?'

'No, I swear I haven't, Luís.'

'And you're not planning to?'

She looked at him, as if that was the question she'd least expected.

'No, I don't plan to do anything. I've learned not to make plans. I just let things happen. I live from day to day. That way there are sad days and happy days. If I planned things, and my plans failed, there would be more sad days. No, Luís, I don't plan to tell him anything . . . to stop seeing you, or cultivate remorse.'

Luís Bernardo was quiet. They both were. The rain that had stopped half an hour ago sparked off the song of night birds coming out of the *óbó*. From the other side, from beyond the garden wall, came the soft cadences of splashing waves. The 'mad rose's' strong scent permeated the moisture in the air. Despite everything, the hopelessness that hung on them, he wanted to stay like that for ever.

They soon heard the garden door bang to and David's voice calling Ann.

'I'm here in the garden,' she replied.

David came in flushed and hot, soaked to the skin, boots covered in mud.

'Oh, Luís, I'm so sorry I'm late.' He kissed Ann and hugged his friend.

'My horse went lame when we reached the city and I had to lead it back on a rope. I see you have a drink. I hope you've not been waiting long,' and turning to his wife, he continued, 'Love, I must have a bath and change my clothes. Can you ask for dinner to be served in twenty minutes? I'll be down straight away.' And he went inside.

Ann got up to follow him into the house.

'I've just got to see to something, Luís. Wait for me in the living room. It's cooler there.'

The living room was immersed in half-darkness, barely lit by a candle-holder with two candles and a red table-lamp that bene-fited from two hours of weak voltage a day from the city. As usual Luís Bernardo stood and looked at the photographs of India in various silver frames set out on the tables. David had spoken to him so often about India that he almost recognised a country he was familiar with in those photos, one that fascinated him. Perhaps one day, when I leave this hole and board a ship to tour the world and not just return home, I'll have an opportunity to go to India, he wondered, and the idea suddenly seemed so impossible, so remote he smiled at his own ravings.

Ann hadn't returned and he started to feel like a ridiculous intruder, an unwanted guest. But she was back five minutes later and the sadness he'd detected in her eyes in the garden seemed to have vanished.

'We have a quarter of an hour to ourselves,' she said urgently. 'Come.'

She leaned against the wall of the passage between the two rooms and beckoned to him. When he came to her, she wrapped herself, wet with desire, around him. She grabbed one of his hands and pulled it to her breast. A shudder of desire ran through him as he felt the lack of garments between her flesh and the light cotton dress. Luís Bernardo touched her breasts, which felt soft in contrast to the hardness of her nipples. He felt her hand between his legs, gripping his cock that strained inside his tight trousers. Her fingers started trying to unbutton his flies.

'No, for heaven's sake, Ann! This is madness: one of the maids or David might come in. I can't! It's his house!'

'Shush!' Her left hand kept hold of his cock while her right struggled to unbutton him. 'David's in the shower, and I've just come from there and told the maids only to light the dining-room candles when he's ready. We've got time! I want you now, Luís. Now!'

With her free hand she lifted her dress up almost to her waist and guided his arm between her legs so he'd realise she was wearing nothing underneath. His fingers rubbed between her legs, searched for her opening, felt her wetness. He held her between two fingers, then let one slip inside, first slowly, then deeper and harder. Ann moaned softly. She grabbed his cock and pulled him into the centre of her desire.

It was all so incredibly stupid! He couldn't stop now, even if someone did come in and catch them. He imagined David rushing downstairs and them still at it, locked together opposite him. He pushed her harder against the wall and began to penetrate her, down, up, slowly, then shafting deeper, more intensely, almost brutally until he exploded inside her, just as her whole body shuddered against his. They stayed still, as long as their discomfort allowed. Then gradually he felt her breathing return to normal, felt his desire acquiesce in an ineffable, overwhelming tenderness. But that was the end: he couldn't continue to defy fate. He moved away from her as slowly as he could, gently repelling arms that still pulled him towards her. He quickly buttoned himself up, listened out keenly and pulled her dress down so she could do up her bodice. Kissed her gently on the mouth and each cheek before falling back on the sofa opposite, like a thief leaving the scene, whispering, 'I love you.'

She leaned against the wall for a few minutes more: still panting, her face red, in contrast to the intense, liquid gleam in her eyes. They could hear David's footsteps in the bedroom on the floor above them. The sound of voices and pans came from the kitchen annexe, and they could hear the San Niclá whistling in the garden to mark its presence. All the sounds of the house that had never gone away seemed to return.

When he came down to dinner, David found Ann busy lighting the candles on the dining-room table and Luís Bernardo in the small side room, absorbed in an edition of *The Times* that was already several weeks old.

Dinner was torture for Luís Bernardo. He drank more, much more than he ate. He found himself wandering as David spoke. He struggled to concentrate. What was he talking about? Ah, right, the visits he was beginning to make by himself to the plantations. He explained how he'd decided to go alone, even when it was far off and he had to stay overnight. He'd noticed the majority of plantation managers didn't bring their wives to dinner. So it would be pointless, even embarrassing to expose Ann to the discomfort of these trips and the very peculiar etiquette that ruled the meals. Nonetheless, Luís Bernardo – who was reasonably well informed on such matters – wanted to know what kind of welcome the English Consul was being given on the plantations.

'Oh, very hospitable, my dear fellow! And I suspect,' he added with a smile, 'something you've said has helped in that respect. I don't know *what* you can have said, but the truth is that so far I've been given very warm welcomes, and I now feel I'm so welcome that even my questions and attempts to wander round on my own don't upset them. Otherwise, I'm sure I would have been kept discreetly at arm's length or even ignored.'

David just talked and talked, comparing the methods of harvesting in São Tomé with those in India, or comparing styles of architecture or the mentalities of the respective colonisers. He was a scientist interested in the discoveries he was making, and curiously, as Ann remarked, of the three seated round that table, he seemed the one most suited to life on those islands and least prone to attacks of melancholy or frustration. Ann had always admired her husband for his extraordinary ability to adapt to the situations he faced, as if, on that distant day when he left his native Scotland, he had decided to meet the world with an open mind, wherever he was, whatever his task or status. How much was his strength and ability to deal with situations down to him and his own resilience, and how much did it depend on having her at his side, knowing she would never renege on the promise she'd made never to abandon him? And what would remain of his strength and resolve if he'd come down five minutes early for dinner to find her making love with Luís Bernardo?

For his part, seated between them, Luís Bernardo tried to follow David's conversation as attentively as possible. He didn't notice anything different in the way he felt towards David: he was the same intelligent, genuine man, who appreciated his company and friendship and whose company and friendship he would never scorn anywhere, under any circumstance. But there was a subtle difference now. Something – he recognised shamefacedly – that didn't stem from David, but from himself: a perverse, insidious rivalry, the obscene, illegitimate shadow of jealousy. He imagined himself later that night turning over memories of that scene in his solitary bedroom, while here, on the top floor of this house, David made love to Ann – as was his right and must be their custom. Ann liked sex, as he'd seen himself, and she'd certainly not discovered sex with him. A woman who surrendered herself as she did didn't do it from pure passion. Would she, even so, be capable of making love to two men on the same night, of making love to her husband while still feeling another man inside her? He looked askance at Ann, trying to read the answer in her eyes, but she smiled wanly at him, giving nothing away. Suddenly a feeling of panic started to rise up inside him. His chest felt tight and his throat dry. He wanted to flee, breathe in fresh air, even vomit.

Finally Anne seemed to notice he was suffering.

'Why don't we go outside now it's cooled down?'

They took coffee in the garden. Ann poured David a glass of port and Luís Bernardo a glass of brandy. She chatted for five minutes and then got up.

'I'm very sorry but I must leave you. You've things to talk about and I'm really short of sleep. I'll go straight to bed.'

She said goodnight to David with a peck on the cheek and goodbye to Luís Bernardo with a squeeze of the hand that was just slightly longer and firmer than usual. As if reassuring him that his fears were unfounded, Luís Bernardo thanked her silently with a look. It was enough to re-animate his spirits that a moment ago had been so low. And he needed to lift himself, now he was left alone with David.

'I'm tired as well and would like to leave soon, David. What is it you want to talk to me about?'

'Of course, Luís, we're all tired. We've discussed this before and you know I consider you to be my friend and not an adversary. We are men brought together by circumstances, who hold posts and play roles that might eventually set us at loggerheads, but I think we know and understand this.'

Luís Bernardo began to relax: what he most feared was apparently not on the agenda.

'Well, Luís, what I must tell you is straightforward and it's the voice of a friend you hear now. When the time comes to send my report to London, the main conclusion of which may be to confirm that there is slave labour on São Tomé, I'm unclear what the implications would be for you, whether it would imply the failure of your mission in the eyes of those who brought you here. Would I be right to think that?'

'Yes, more or less.'

'I see. I am also fully aware that you don't intend to follow a career as a colonial civil servant. You had and still have your own independent life in Lisbon and, for reasons of your own that I respect, you decided to accept this mission, whether out of patriotism or pride. But you are not typical in this world where I belong. You don't deserve to end this mission as a failure, thus opening yourself to facile criticism from people who know nothing of the difficulties you confront here.'

'In that case?'

'In that case, what I wanted to tell you is the following: when that moment comes I promise I won't send the report to London before telling you my conclusions and I'll give you time to step in first and offer your resignation – not as a result of my conclusions, but as a result of your own.'

'In exchange for what?'

'In exchange for what?' David looked genuinely shocked. 'In exchange for nothing, Luís! In exchange for the support and companionship you've given us, in exchange for the respect I feel for you as a person and friend.'

Luís Bernardo stared at his shoes. In the silence that ensued, he heard sounds from the floor above. From Ann and David's bedroom. He'd not anticipated anything like this. He was at a loss for words. He felt it had been a long night and that, curiously, he wanted to be alone. He crushed his cigar on the floor under the sole of his boot. Sighed deeply and got up.

'I'm really grateful to you, David. I know you are sincere and I don't know what I've done to merit this offer, but obviously I accept. I do miss home and that very different climate, space and life. I would like to be able to imagine my imminent return. Who knows, perhaps this offer of yours might be the solution!'

13

Luís Bernardo completed the first year of his assignment in São Tomé and Príncipe in March 1907 and decided to celebrate it with another dinner at Government Palace, not a ball, but a gathering of the same guests as the previous year. It was his first error of judgement: of the two hundred and twenty to whom he sent written invitations, only forty accepted. Half of the rest excused themselves on the pretext of urgent tasks on their plantations, sudden illness or prior engagements (as if such a thing existed on São Tomé!); the other half didn't even deign to reply, so he had to keep a few tables at the ready until the last moment. His second error was to invite the British Consul and his wife. In truth, he hadn't given this enough thought before sending out the invitations. He had hesitated over following the normal rules of protocol of a colonial governor, which would be to invite official representatives of a foreign country – or to go along with the unspoken expectation of the colony's stalwarts: that the occasion be celebrated among Portuguese, without the presence of the British 'enemy'. He had even considered asking David if they could reach a friendly agreement: he'd invite him, but the Consul would politely decline. He finally decided he couldn't act so hypocritically towards his friend or so feebly in his post. As nothing remained private for long in São Tomé, everyone knew the British Consul would attend the dinner accompanied by his wife.

Only ten of the forty present were women, accompanied by their respective husbands. Luís Bernardo divided the room into five tables of eight and, after concluding very sensibly that he shouldn't place the Consul and his wife at his table, to avoid hurting Portuguese sensibilities, he allocated them another table, where he was careful to put two guests who had some knowledge of the polite formulas of English small talk. But it was all in vain:

despite David's strenuous attempts and Ann's aloof serenity, masked behind a polite smile, the ladies on their table simply ignored her, feeling sidelined by her poise and beauty, which shocked perfectly in the simple elegance of her light-blue silk dress, restrained décolleté and sapphire pendant. The gentlemen at the table had at first thought it only courteous and opportune to converse with David, and had addressed Ann with pleasantries, but they soon withdrew after being glowered at by friends on adjacent tables and vaporised by the gazes of their respective wives whenever they dared to look up and address the dazzling woman.

Luís Bernardo was seated two tables away – purely by chance and not because he'd planned it – in a position where he could see Ann. He performed perfectly his role as host on his own table, but didn't miss a single move in the drama being played out on her table. He felt for them, for David, who seemed to be making an effort to play the game of diplomatic niceties, but above all for Ann, who was being scorned and humiliated out of the pettiest envy. It was the Count of Souza Faro who initiated every conversation on Luís Bernardo's table. He acted as a kind of dean at high table, because of his age, forebears and knowledge of the colony. After the previous year's gala dinner, Luís Bernardo had experienced a degree of empathy for the Count, the administrator of the Água Izé plantation and, previously, Public Works Secretary on São Tomé. He was the most civilised, cultured, worldly man in that colonial society.

When dinner, which Luís Bernardo had found distinctly disagreeable (how he regretted his menu of four dishes and three desserts!), was coming to an end, he tapped the Count's arm and said, 'I'd like a few minutes in private. Would be that possible?'

'Of course, my dear Governor! How about a cigar and a cognac?'

They went to the small room that served as Luís Bernardo's study and sat down in the armchairs there. They were like two gentlemen about to engage in a business conversation in their Lisbon club and Luís Bernardo momentarily felt for a brief moment he was back at home.

'My dear Count, I would like to ask you a direct question and would beg you to give me an equally direct answer: why are there people in this colony who are showing me such scant respect and regard?'

'You refer to tonight's absentees?'

'They are a great many, and some didn't even send apologies.'

Souza Faro puffed pleasurably on his cigar before replying. He was visibly enjoying his role as adviser.

'You do want the truth from me, don't you?'

'For once . . .'

'Well, the fact is this colony doesn't like you. It has always mistrusted you, even before you arrived, and through the year the mistrust has only hardened, making the hostility towards you beyond redress.'

'But why?'

'Because people believe you are more ready to hear and support the arguments and interests of our enemies than you are our own.'

'But why, I repeat?'

'Well, on the one hand, it is evident that you, my dear fellow, have been completely bewitched by the Consul and his wife: they are your best friends on São Tomé. Everyone knows this and you, to your credit, have never hidden the fact.'

'And do people think, do you think, Souza Faro, that my personal relationships might influence my opinions and the way I carry out my duties?'

'You want the truth again? Yes, we all think that is the case.'

Luís Bernardo looked thoughtful: he appreciated his guest's opinion, and saw it as a kind of barometer. Prudence told him he shouldn't ignore it.

'My dear Count, how exactly do you think I might be influenced or directed by the opinions of Mr David Jameson?'

'Well, for example, you told the Crown Commissioner that your view as to the existence or not of slave labour on these islands would depend on the number of workers who, at the end of the three years of their contract under the new law, asked to be repatriated to Angola . . .'

Luís Bernardo felt his anger surge when he heard that: Germano André Valente was an informer working for the plantation owners!

'Did he tell you that?'

'Not personally, but he put it around.'

'Souza Faro, don't you think it's a criterion we should endorse?'

'My dear fellow, I trust you're not that ingenuous.'

'What do you mean?'

'You're surely not expecting people to ask every one of the thousands of blacks whose contracts have run out, in line with the law, whether they want to continue on the plantations or be repatriated to Angola – with interpreters, individual negotiations and signatures in the presence of the notary. It this what you expect?'

Luís Bernardo was taken aback. Described thus, the procedure seemed impossible, if not absurd. But how could it be done any differently?

'Listen to me, my dear Governor,' Souza Faro took advantage of his silence, 'If we accept that a third, only a third of the plantation workers say they want to be repatriated, do you realise what the inevitable fate of São Tomé and these islands would be?'

Luís Bernardo continued to be silent.

'Ruination and inevitable bankruptcy. The plantations would end up with the banks and I know of no bank that can or wants to run an African colony on the Equator. The people you complain about not coming to your dinner are people who have sacrificed the best part of their lives here, have worked from dawn to dusk, have put up with the tedium, their wives' recriminations, the suffering of losing children killed by malaria and the lack of understanding and injustice of plantation owners, who each year ask them, from the comforts of Lisbon, why the harvest was a thousand tons less than last year's, that being all they ever want to know. Of course they're uncouth. You speak English and listen to opera on your veranda and are a prince compared to them. And you tell them their way of life and means of subsistence are out-of-date, outmoded by the power of new ideas, treaties and laws or by King Dom Carlos's wish to continue to receive invitations to go hunting from his cousin Edward in England. And you think they should be grateful, that they should admire you because you are the harbinger of modern times?'

The Count never raised his voice, never seemed overly committed to what he was saying. On the contrary, he spoke almost with irritation, as if he was explaining things that should be self-evident. As he listened, Luís Bernardo thought the man was right. It was a situation from which there was no escape: the perfect trap.

'So what would *you* do in my place, Souza Faro?'

'Fortunately, *I* am not in your place.'

'And if you were?'

'I would defend our Portuguese side. There will be no place in history for you if, rightly or wrongly, you defend the stance of half a dozen British cocoa traders who are afraid of competition from these wretched islands that belong to Portugal.' The Count got up and walked into the reception room. He left the scene unhurriedly, like a professional actor fully aware he'd performed his last lines.

Luís Bernardo saw him depart, and tried to blow life back into his dormant cigar. He was at least sincere, even if he wasn't honest. He believed what he'd said and that army of shadows, of black ants, was still lining up, still working on the plantation under the Count's eyes, and after a year's work they'd still find it difficult to earn enough to pay for a dozen Havana cigars imported from Cuba via Lisbon, to smoke during a gentlemanly armchair conversation, where their own destiny was debated so sagely and so easily.

When almost all the guests had left, Luís Bernardo accompanied Ann and David to the door.

David commented, 'Your dinner wasn't a great success, I believe?'

Luís Bernardo felt warmly towards him: he was an observant, considerate friend.

He put an arm round both of them and replied, 'No, David. I feel as if I was given a real drubbing this evening.' And then, as if talking to himself, he muttered, 'But it's one year down! One year!'

Three days later two workers escaped from the Rio do Ouro plantation and were caught by the police near the town of

Trindade, laid low by hunger and exhaustion. Luís Bernardo had given express instructions to the chief of police to inform him immediately in such circumstances and hand over the escaped workers to the court for trial, rather than routinely return them to the plantation they'd escaped from. Consequently, despite the protests and threats from Colonel Mário Maltez, the police refused to hand over the escapees to the Colonel and the District Judge fixed a court session in two days' time.

The morning of the trial, Luís Bernardo went to the Sessions House. He didn't wish to intimidate the Judge with his presence, but felt he was duty-bound to see personally how the law was applied in this case. The law decreed that the employer could opt to sack the worker, who would then lose the right to any payments pending, or else could extend his contract, from three to ten days – according to the Judge's ruling – for every day on the run. Luís Bernardo had more than enough reason to suspect that, before he'd insisted fugitives be given over to the courts for trial, custom and practice was to return them to their plantations, where they were very probably whipped or subjected to other physical punishment, after which their contracts would be extended by the plantation administrator, without the Crown Commissioner even knowing anything had happened.

Although he entered the courtroom discreetly and sat in the back rows set out for the general public, his presence didn't go unnoticed among the few people present. A mutter went round the room, and the clerk, waiting by his desk for the Judge to come in, hurriedly disappeared through an inside door. Colonel Maltez, seated in front, turned round and looked defiantly at the Governor. Luís Bernardo nodded in his direction and got no acknowledgement as the Colonel turned and started talking to the person next to him, possibly the overseer or someone else from Rio do Ouro. A few moments later the door at the back opened and the escapees came in, tied together by chains round their feet, and pushed along by two policemen who put them in front of the first row, some two metres from the Judge's bench. Luís Bernardo noted there were no chairs for the men, who seemed in their early twenties and looked pitiful, barefoot and scantily clothed in dirty rags. One had three big red welts down his back, where scars were beginning to form. The other seemed to have a lame left leg and found it difficult to stand: he kept leaning gently on his companion's shoulder.

The clerk reappeared through a side door, glancing fleetingly at Luís Bernardo, as if to confirm he was still there, and sat behind his table. A few moments later, the Public Prosecutor came in, looking as unpleasant and as pockmarked as Luís Bernardo remembered him, followed by Dr Anselmo de Sousa, the Judge. All present, including Luís Bernardo, rose immediately to their feet, and only sat down after Dr Anselmo had done so. Neither the Judge nor the Prosecutor showed any sign they had noticed the Governor's presence in the room.

Dr Anselmo placed his spectacles on his nose and rasped at the clerk, 'Do begin.'

'Trial Crime No. 1427, in which the Public Ministry in this District accuses Joanino, family name unknown, a native of Benguela in the Province of Angola, and Jesus Saturnino, native of the same District and Province, both agricultural workers, resident here in the service of the Rio do Ouro plantation, of taking flight and disappearing from their place of work, thus breaking the contract that they had signed with that enterprise and without providing any reasonable justification – a crime categorised and punished in article 32, section b, of the General Rules concerning Agricultural Work in this Colony, approved by the Law of 29 January 1902. Being present the Most Worthy representative of the Public Ministry, the plaintiff, in the person of Colonel Mário Maltez, and the accused – who have no defence. Being present also the witnesses called by the prosecution, Mr Alípio Verdasca and Corporal Jacinto das Dores and soldiers Tomé Eufrásio and Agostino dos Santos of the City Guard.'

After the clerk's preamble, Dr Anselmo Teixera, who seemed to have been listening quite absent-mindedly, started the trial formalities.

'I declare the session open, given that no element is lacking to prevent the case proceeding. And, since the accused have no defence, and there is no solicitor with a law degree or qualification present in the room, I nominate the Crown Commissioner of São

Tomé and Príncipe, Mr Germano André Valente, as official defence lawyer.'

It was only then that Luís Bernardo noted the presence of Germano Valente, discreetly seated in the second row from the front, on the opposite side to Colonel Maltez. But, as he got up to go to the lawyers' table, Luís Bernardo, driven by an impulse beyond his control and which a moment's thought would have probably indicated was a strategic error, stood up to address the Judge.

'I beg Your Excellency's permission to speak.'

Dr Anselmo Teixeira looked at him over his spectacles, betraying no reaction, or even change of tone as he replied.

'Your Excellency the Governor, your presence here today bestows great honour on this court, but does not, however, confer on you any rights above those enjoyed by other citizens present. At this juncture it is forbidden, on any pretext, to interrupt the progress of the work of this court.'

'I am aware of that, Your Honour, but it is a procedural matter.'

'A procedural matter?' The Judge arched his eyebrows, his curiosity now decidedly aroused.

'Yes. As Your Honour will discover or confirm by consulting my appointment as Governor to São Tomé, published in the Official Bulletin of the colony, I do possess a law degree. And consequently, I offer myself as official defence lawyer for the two accused, that Your Honour was delegating, there being, as you said, no one here better qualified for the task.'

A deafening silence fell on the courtroom. The sound of conversation could be heard outside in the street; passing carriages, a dog barking. Colonel Maltez turned ponderously in his chair and stared at Luís Bernardo as if he were a lunatic. The clerk's jaw dropped in shock, and the Public Prosecutor, who continued to act as if he were ignoring Luís Bernardo's presence, finally looked up from the pile of papers he was pretending to read and stared incredulously at the Governor. Dr Anselmo Teixeira removed his spectacles and began cleaning them with a hand-kerchief he'd taken from his jacket pocket.

'In other words: if I have understood correctly, Your Excellency wishes momentarily to put aside his responsibilities as

Governor of the Province and take on those of a lawyer?'

'I see no conflict between the two things, all the more so given that, as Your Honour has just stated, I cannot exercise my responsibilities as Governor in this room.' Luís Bernardo looked calm but his chest was a mass of nerves.

The Judge sighed. He took his handkerchief out again and wiped away drops of sweat that had formed on his temple and forehead. He was an old courtroom fox brought to São Tomé by two unsuccessful judgements that unfortunately for him had been widely reported in the press.

Dr Anselmo de Sousa Teixeira now tried to gain time by addressing an astonished Public Prosecutor.

'Does the Public Prosecutor have any objections?'

For his part, Dr João Patrício had had time enough to gather his wits. All things considered, that common crime, the sentence for which was straightforward and known to everyone in advance, gave him an unexpected opportunity to shine at the expense of that arrogant governor, towards whom he had felt extreme antipathy ever since he saw him disembark on dry land more than a year ago.

'Yes, I do, Your Honour. It is true that the Governor has a degree in law and that, as such, he possesses the legal qualifications to assume the role of defence he requests. But it is also true that, whatever position he may occupy before this court, he is also the Governor of the Province, and has sworn impartiality in the carrying out of his responsibilities. It cannot be said he is impartial if he decides to defend in court one side against another, as if a governor could practise as a lawyer in his idle moments. I believe we would be contemplating grave neglect in relation to the status of Governor, were Your Honour to agree to such an unusual and . . . how should I say, such a revealing aspiration on the part of His Excellency . . .'

Luís Bernardo felt his blood boil. He made an effort to remain impassive, and waited for the Judge to state his view.

'I believe your objection to be well founded,' the Judge began timidly. 'Does Your Excellency the Governor wish to respond?'

'I would like to ascertain whether deciding if I am breaching my duty as a governor to be impartial by offering to defend two inhabitants of this colony who haven't the power or the knowledge to defend themselves falls within the competencies of the Honourable Prosecutor or Your Honour. The Honourable Prosecutor is of this opinion and Your Honour may also share this view. I am of a diametrically opposed opinion. But this is not what is at stake here. What is at stake is the application of the law. This court has not the remit to judge the way I exercise my mandate. It is merely competent to judge whether I, citizen Luís Bernardo Valença, awarded a degree in law by the law faculty of Coimbra, possess or not the necessary qualifications to exercise the official defence of the accused. If Your Honour can cite any ruling of law that is against such an option, I will withdraw my request.'

And Luís Bernardo sat back aware he was possibly forcing Dr Anselmo de Sousa Teixeira to take the most sensitive decision in his period as a magistrate on São Tomé.

Dr Anselmo snorted and wiped the sweat away again. He looked around the courtroom, as if hoping some merciful soul would come to his rescue. As the only reaction was silence and several pairs of eyes staring anxiously his way, he sat straight in his chair and spoke to the clerk.

'I dictate for the minutes: at the request of Dr Luís Bernardo Valença, bachelor in law and Governor of the Province of São Tomé, he is appointed official defence of the accused, given that nobody among those in attendance has the necessary qualifications to do this and that nothing in law prevents him.' And he looked up and spoke to Luís Bernardo. 'From now until the end of the session, I shall address you as Doctor. Please be so good as to take your place on the lawyers' bench.'

Luís Bernardo crossed the room to sit behind the table at a right angle to the Judge's and opposite the one occupied by Dr João Patrício, who'd immersed himself in his paperwork again, as if preparing for the most complicated of trials. At this juncture, alerted by some anonymous flunkey, a crowd now flooded into the empty spaces in the courtroom, standing in passageways and crowding into the entrance. The din from whispered conversations was deafening.

After recovering control of events and feeling that so far things hadn't gone too badly for him, His Honour Anselmo Teixeira bellowed, 'Silence in court, the slightest noise and I shall have the room emptied. Police, please be so good as to close the door to the courtroom and ensure nobody comes in.' And turning to the clerk he now addressed him in a normal tone. 'Have all the windows opened, or nobody will survive this heat!'

And the trial began with questions to the accused. Within minutes it became crystal-clear that they understood only half a dozen words in Portuguese. The interpreter, who was standing by on duty in the office, was called in. But neither of the two said a word; both seemed completely alienated from what was happening around them. When the Judge asked, 'Why did you run away from the plantation?' they remained silent, even after the interpreter had translated for them. It was as if they'd understood nothing or weren't interested in enlightening the court. When it was Luís Bernardo's turn to question them, he repeated the same question, begging the interpreter to explain that they were there to defend themselves and shouldn't be afraid to tell the truth or explain their motives to the court.

But, before they could say anything, Dr Anselmo suddenly stiffened and interjected, 'The interpreter will ignore that request, which I consider an insult to this court. The Honourable Doctor should know that no accused, in a trial I have presided over, whether here or in any other district of this kingdom I have visited, has ever felt constrained when telling the truth.'

'My intention was never to doubt that in any way. I thought, Your Honour, the accused showed evident signs of not even understanding how the court works and what their own rights are. That is certainly not Your Honour's fault, but the fact is that this seriously undermines their rights to a proper defence, and is adequate motive I believe to provide them with a minimal explanation of their situation.'

'Just translate the question,' Dr Anselmo ordered the clerk, as if he'd not heard the objection.

The question was repeated and the accused remained silent, looking ahead at some spot on the wall behind the Judge.

Luís Bernardo returned to the attack.

'Ask them if they ran away because they were badly treated on the Rio do Ouro plantation.'

Another silence and another question from Luís Bernardo.

'Ask them if they worked too many hours.'

'Ask them if they didn't get enough to eat.'

'Ask them if they were whipped or beaten.'

No reaction. Not a flicker in the eye of either of the blacks suggested for a moment that they'd understood or wanted to speak.

Luís Bernardo sighed and insisted one last time, 'I would ask the interpreter to address the accused on that side – I believe he is Saturnino – and ask him to point to the marks Saturnino has down his back and ask him how they got there.'

Dr João Patrício, who had to that point listened to Luís Bernardo's efforts with the same air of quiet contempt, was now quick to react.

'I protest, Your Honour! The question is at once insidious and pointless, given that the accused have previously responded silently, that is, in the negative, to the question about whether they had been mistreated. Besides, if I have heard correctly, what the defence wants is for the interpreter not only to translate his question but also to complement words with gestures and physical contact with one of the accused – which is a singular way of putting answers into the mouth of the accused. I ask Your Honour to overrule the question and any gesture.'

'Before I do or do not overrule the question,' Dr Anselmo de Sousa Teixeira began warily, 'I would like to know, in fact, whether our distinguished counsel for the defence has any particular reason for requesting the question be accompanied by complementary gestures.'

Luís Bernardo paused before he replied. He had begun to sweat profusely. He felt stifled by the heat in the courtroom. But, beyond that, he felt corralled, a prisoner of his own ingenuity. In fact, he had a very definite reason for asking for those gestures to be made: he'd begun to suspect increasingly that the interpreter wasn't translating his questions, but was saying something that made no sense to the blacks – and, most probably, in a language that wasn't theirs. But how could he raise such doubts in that court? It would be tantamount to saying they were all of a piece and launching a frontal attack on the Judge's honesty. But could he retreat now, be sullied like the rest of them, abandon the defence he'd begun and leave the courtroom tail between legs to the delight of all his enemies?

'Honourable Doctor . . . ?' The Judge was waiting, rather anxiously, thought Luís Bernardo, for his reply.

'Your Honour: my question does not stem from the fact the accused haven't answered a single question, for that doesn't prevent me asking further questions, to which they may eventually provide answers. The question is not insidious and arises from a single concrete fact: I want to ask how the accused procured those welts but I in no way wish to suggest they were procured by a whipping on the Rio do Ouro plantation, as the prosecutor rapidly seems to have concluded,' and he looked directly at the prosecutor, who was now blushing a bright red. 'As for asking the interpreter to address the accused and point straight at the marks down his back, that is merely to make it clear that I – and the court too, undoubtedly – am unhappy with the lack of help from the accused in clarifying the facts.'

That was the best tactic Luís Bernardo could think up to get out of that mire without completely losing face. He immediately saw the Judge relax for he'd been afraid that Luís Bernardo would trample on the frontier line that allowed them all to keep up appearances. He read the clear message in Dr Anselmo's eyes: The man is arrogant, but, God be thanked, he isn't mad.

'Honourable Doctor, the accused are free to reply or not, as they see fit, and the court cannot force them to reply in any way, contrary to what you suggest. Consequently, I instruct the interpreter simply to translate the defence counsel's question and to remain seated where he is.'

After the predictable silence from the accused in respect of his controversial question, Luís Bernardo leaned back in his chair and retreated into a lengthy silence, as if he'd given up. He watched three guards come to the witness stand and describe the circumstances in which they had captured the accused and the 'humanitarian' way they'd treated them in the police station and cell while they awaited trial. With a nod of the head, Luís Bernardo indicated he had no wish to question any of the three – which was visibly a great relief to that trio. The last of the witnesses called by the prosecution came to the stand: Alípio Verdasca, who identified himself as deputy overseer on the Rio do Ouro plantation and the man responsible for the section where the accused worked. He answered the prosecutor's questions unfalteringly, like a good schoolboy: no, they weren't overworked on the Rio do Ouro, food was plentiful, they had enough time off and medical care was a priority; no, there wasn't punishment of a physical kind, which was strictly forbidden; one could say the Rio do Ouro workers received exemplary treatment, beyond what the law required, and, for that very reason, few ran away, few failed to turn up for work, and few faked illness. He couldn't for the life of him understand why the two men had run away.

'Would Your Honour the Doctor like to question this witness?' asked Dr Anselmo, who was already preparing for the summing up and could see a most satisfactory end to the case in sight, with no major damage inflicted. The Governor, who'd unexpectedly involved himself as defence counsel, could not accuse him of a lack of impartiality or find any excuse in the way he'd conducted business to criticise a sentence it was obvious he'd already mentally prepared and was ready to dictate. Moreover the Governor, after the first part of the trial in which he'd wanted to show off his talents as a lawyer, had descended into a state of conspicuous aloofness that led him to spend the last half-hour staring out of the side window, as if he too only wanted it to be over quickly so he could clear off.

But, much to the Judge's dismay, Luís Bernardo emerged from his prolonged silence and replied, keeping his eyes firmly on the window, 'Yes, I would like to, Your Honour.'

'Please proceed then.' The Judge stiffened his back. He felt the prosecutor shift nervously in his chair and saw the witness look at Colonel Maltez as if wanting to be told what to do, and the latter merely nodding, as if silently saying, 'Keep calm, nothing to worry about!'

Luís Bernardo finally looked away from the window and stared the witness in the eye for a few seconds.

'Mr Alípio Verdasca: given your persuasive description of the excellent working and living conditions on Rio do Ouro, one finds it difficult to fathom why anyone should want to run away. Isn't that so?'

'Yes, sir.'

'In fact, in respect of these two men, you still see no reason why they should want to flee?'

'No, sir.'

'How many years have they been working on the plantation?'

'Saturnino, four. And I think seven or eight in Joanino's case.'

'Have they ever run away before?'

'No.'

'Neither of them?'

'No.'

'Do you happen to know if either has relatives off the plantation?'

'No.'

'You don't know or they don't have any?'

'No, they don't have relatives outside the plantation.'

'How can you so be sure, Mr Alípio Verdasca?'

The witness hesitated for the first time. He coughed and began to say something in reply that Luís Bernardo interrupted.

'Could that be because neither has ever left the plantation since they arrived on the island?'

'Hmm . . . I don't know.'

'Is it usual, for example, for workers to leave the plantation and enjoy a stroll round the city?'

'No.'

'It's "no" again, is it not? And you don't know whether one of these men from your platoon of workers has ever visited the city?'

'No, I don't think so.'

'Good, let's continue. So they didn't run away from the plantation in order to visit relatives, did they?'

'No.'

'And do they have family on the plantation?'

'Yes, they do, sir.'

'Both do?'

'Yes.'

'Yet another reason not to run away, is that not so?'

The witness preferred not to respond and Luís Bernardo continued.

'Well, let's sum up, Mr Verdasca. Two workers who have been living for four and seven years respectively on the plantation, where they have been treated excellently and where they have family, who don't even speak Portuguese and who have absolutely no reason to leave the plantation to the extent that they have never left the place, suddenly, for no reason at all, for none whatsoever, take flight, face all the dangers of the jungle and risk being taken prisoner, as has happened, and being punished. They must have gone mad – both at the same time, wouldn't you agree?'

At this point, a wave of laughter swept spontaneously through part of the courtroom and the muffled chit-chat became perfectly audible. Colonel Maltez restrained himself in his chair, while his deputy overseer seemed to want to see the back of the witness's bench as quickly as possible and was looking askance at the Judge, as if begging him to put an end to his torture. At this point, Dr Anselmo looked at Luís Bernardo with considerably more respect. He recognised a good lawyer when he saw one.

'Silence in court or I'll empty the courtroom immediately. The Honourable Doctor may proceed, but I must remind him we don't have all day.'

'Your Honour, don't worry: even if we had, how would it advance us? The witness is so eager to explain to the court the reasons why the two accused ran away that he gives me the impression that if all the Rio do Ouro workers suddenly decided to run away he would still be incapable of offering a single explanation as to why a single soul would want to flee.'

A fresh wave of muted laughter rippled round the courtroom, but this time Luís Bernardo anticipated the Judge and continued.

'I have asked the witness, in relation to his statement, whether the only reasonable motive for the flight of the two accused might in fact be that they had suddenly gone mad, and I am still waiting for the witness to reply, "I don't know," and consequently, in the light of Your Honour's comment, I shall move on to my next and I suppose my final question: In the witness's view, what might have caused the welts on the back of the accused, Saturnino?'

'I don't know.'

Before more laughter erupted in court, Dr João Patrício raised his voice above the background hubbub.

'I protest, Your Honour: the witness cannot be questioned about actions he knows nothing about.'

'And how does the distinguished prosecutor know he knows nothing?' Luís Bernardo riposted immediately.

'Silence. The distinguished gentlemen cannot enter ·directly into dialogue. At any rate, the witness has answered the question, saying he doesn't know. Anything else, Dr Valença?'

'A simple question: could a whip have caused those marks?'

'I object, Your Honour!' João Patrício now seemed apoplectic.

'Objection overruled. Would you please finish your questioning, Dr Valença?'

'Or could they have been left . . .' Luís Bernardo now spoke as if declaiming poetry, to underline his irony. 'By tree branches as they fled, thus marking the accused's back so geometrically that the welts recall, most curiously, the effect of a whip and that . . .'

'I object, Your Honour! The defence is beginning to reveal a lack of respect towards the court!'

'Dr Valença: I am in agreement with what the Public Prosecutor has just said. I will allow you one final question before I move us on. But only a simple question related to a concrete fact; no questions calling for improper opinions, conclusions or speculations on the part of the witness.'

'Improper? Improper, Your Honour? Well . . . so be it! A simple question related to a concrete fact: I will ask Mr Alípio Verdasca, here under oath, whether the accused Saturnino was or wasn't whipped on the Rio do Ouro plantation, and whether that action provoked his flight.'

Total silence now reigned in the courtroom previously filled with background hubbub, and Alípio Verdasca's voice sounded more subdued than ever.

'No.'

'I didn't really hear your reply,' was Luís Bernardo's last twist of the knife, of which he made the most. 'Please repeat good and loud.'

'No!'

'No more questions, Your Honour,' Luís Bernardo started to tidy the papers on his table and the last thing he saw before turning to the window again was the look of pure hatred directed his way by Colonel Maltez.

'His Excellency the Public Prosecutor has the floor to give his summing up.'

Dr João Patrício predictably aimed his irony at Luís Bernardo, saying it was certainly the first time the court of São Tomé, or any other courtroom in an overseas province of Portugal or indeed in any colony of any civilised country, had seen its respective governor abandon his work, office and duties to come and amuse himself as a lawyer. 'It was the first time and I dare say it will have been the last.' Then he took it as proven that the Rio do Ouro plantation workers enjoyed all the benefits guaranteed by law, and more besides, which explained the small number of escapees from that plantation. Inexplicably, however, the defence had tried beyond the bounds of good faith to demonstrate the contrary: namely that, if two workers had run away for no apparent reason, it was because the thousands of workers on the plantation, who showed no desire to flee, were all being mistreated. In other words: two lousy black sheep were being taken as representative and he had done his best to transform these delinquents into heroes or victims. What was an aggravating circumstance in the behaviour of the accused – the absence of any plausible motive for their flight – was, for the defence, the basis of their innocence. And, as such an approach was quite invalid, in fact implied legal bad faith, the defence had tried, as an alternative, to force a witness to confirm his miserable insinuation, which was not backed by rumour, let alone proof, and which the very silence of the accused belied.

'And if the accused themselves have opted to remain silent it is because they know they have nothing to invoke in their defence and they prefer, at the very least, not to make their behaviour appear any worse. Consequently, as there are no extenuating circumstances in their favour, Your Honour should ignore the insinuations a very part-time lawyer today brought before this courtroom, and sentence the accused to the maximum penalty recommended by the law in such cases. In that way you will see that justice is done, as moreover, is Your Honour's custom.'

When his turn came to sum up, Luís Bernardo had already taken two decisions: to be brief and to ignore Dr João Patrício totally.

'As Your Honour put it so succinctly,' he began, addressing the Judge, 'I didn't appear today in this courtroom as the Governor of São Tomé and Príncipe, but as a lawyer, defending the two men before us. But an individual exists within both these skins and I am the man I am, with my ideas, whether mistaken or not, and my code of values, whether mistaken or not. And that led me spontaneously to offer to defend the two accused, who had everything stacked against them – the absence of a qualified defence lawyer, the absence of witnesses, their lack of knowledge of the right to a legal defence and even their lack of knowledge of the Portuguese language and of everything about to happen here. The very same ideas that led the government of Portugal and His Majesty the King to invite me to take up this post I have and which led me to accept. The reason why I offered to defend the two defenceless accused and the reason why I am here as Governor of these islands is one and the same: because I, along with many others, believe that the goal of Portugal must be to act both as a civilising and colonising power. We can and must reap the fruits of our labour and colonial wealth that we owe to our forebears, but that does not mean we can overlook progress and civilisation. And there is no progress or civilisation when the wealth produced is the result of the subjection of the natives to methods of working that would better suit the Middle Ages than the twentieth century. And if we tell those abroad who accuse us of using such methods that everyone is Portuguese in our eyes – both in the metropolis and the colonies – we cannot have free unions and freedom of contract for workers in the metropolis and for Portuguese workers in the colonies and still maintain the law of the whiplash and the status of serfs of the glebe – even if that may be the exception. The two accused men before us today are – because we wanted it thus, define it thus and proclaim it thus to the wide world – Portuguese citizens. It is true they are black and don't speak Portuguese, but they are as Portuguese as any of us here – from the metropolis – in this courtroom.

'My duty as Governor is to defend their rights, as well as those of all the inhabitants of this province. My duty as their lawyer is to attempt to ensure that they will be tried according to the same rules and the same rights as would be accorded, for example, to the witness Mr Alípio Verdasca or to Colonel Maltez present here. Perhaps you find it difficult to accept this, but this is what is at stake, and Your Honour the Judge knows this better than I and could explain this when he comes to give sentence. However, I wouldn't like to be in his shoes: the law establishes a sentence for cases of running away and the unilateral breaking of contract by plantation workers – that being the accusation hanging over these men. But the law also states that, in order to deliver a sentence and punishment, it is necessary to ensure the accused have no noteworthy reason, namely mistreatment, that led them to take flight. And when I say I would not like to be in Your Honour's shoes, it is because I understand there can only be a just sentence when all facts have been clarified. In this case, we see a combination of the astonishing silence of the accused, which I find totally incomprehensible and unprecedented, and the manifest lack of goodwill on the part of Mr Alípio Verdasca – the only witness who could enlighten us as to the motives of the accused – in order to obscure the facts. The court will thus have to reach a decision without having succeeded in clarifying why two workers, who were apparently so very well treated and had no reason to lament their lot, resolved to run away from the Rio do Ouro plantation. And it will have to reach a decision without having succeeded in clarifying why one of the accused bears the welts on his back, which seem to have been inflicted the day he fled from Rio do Ouro and appear – I said "appear" – to be marks made by the lash. I cannot see, quite candidly, how Your Honour can reach a decision in all conscience and with any sense of justice based on such a lack of evidence. But, whatever your decision may be, I cannot see how it can be in excess of the minimum advised by the law, if it is not total exoneration. In any case, I will allow myself to suggest to Your Honour that, if you eventually decide to return the workers to the plantation, with the due punishment imposed, you should remind the administrator he is expressly forbidden by law to add to Your Honour's sentence any other punishment, whether of a material, physical or any other kind. And, while about it, you should also remind the Crown Commissioner that it is his duty to ensure that the law and sentence are strictly upheld *in situ*.'

Luís Bernardo sat down after completing his summing up. He stared hard at Dr Anselmo de Souza Teixeira. The whole court-room also stared hard at the Judge. The clerk had his pen at the ready to write down the sentence: he knew Dr Anselmo was quick, almost immediate, in giving a sentence as soon as the summing up had been completed. But that morning nothing would happen as normal.

And the final surprise came from Dr Anselmo.

He took his handkerchief from his pocket yet again, cleaned his spectacles and face with the same handkerchief, and looked out of the window as he stated, 'Sentence will be given tomorrow, Thursday, at nine o'clock. Until that time, the accused will remain in detention, by order of the court. The hearing is closed.'

Luís Bernardo was one of the first to get up. He nodded to the Judge and ignored Dr João Patrício, Colonel Maltez, Germano Valente the Crown Commissioner and everyone else and began to make his way through the small crowd that moved aside to let him through. The air was equally scorching outside, but at least there was space, a horizon, not the physical oppression of the courthouse. He felt himself breathe as if he'd just left captivity. News of what had happened within those four walls must have spread through the city like wildfire: Vicente was waiting for him outside the courtroom with his carriage, and, quite extraordina-rily, Sebastião had also come and stood by the carriage door.

'Sebastião, what are you doing here?'

'I thought His Excellency the Governor would be tired so we came to fetch him.'

'No, Sebastião, I want to walk back through the city. You can wait for me on the outskirts.'

'Your Excellency the Governor . . .'

'Doctor, Sebastião!'

'Doctor, perhaps you should . . .'

'What, Sebastião?'

'Come with us.'

'No, Sebastião. I'm Doctor to you. Governor to them.'

And he started to walk by himself towards the Town Hall Square. He went down the rua do Comércio, where shops were shut for lunch. He noticed there were small huddles of chattering people in the entrances to some, groups who stopped talking when he walked by. Some rushed inside shops, others greeted him, doffing their hats and muttering, 'How are you, Governor?' Others looked at him silently. He greeted those who greeted him, and met those who stayed silent with silence but drew on his reserves of energy to force himself to look them all in the eye, one by one, and force them to declare themselves. He never stopped or slowed his pace, but walked briskly on as he had done so often before in that city.

He was near the Town Hall Square when he turned a corner and almost bumped into the familiar figure of Maria Augusta da Trindade. She seemed more surprised than he. But Luís Bernardo was happy to see her, almost relieved by a friendly interlude on a walk that seemed more like the Way of the Cross.

He held out a hand.

'What are you doing here, Maria Augusta? Come down from your estate to the city?'

She took his hand with no great enthusiasm. She had blushed, but he couldn't tell whether it was because she was embarrassed or because they had only seen each other once since he'd spent that night on the Nova Esperança many months ago, when he'd felt for the first time since he'd landed on São Tomé the warmth of a friend in her informal welcome. Later that night they'd come together spontaneously, like animals on heat, when their bodies joined in sweat and fire, fruit of long mutual abstinence.

And now she offered a limp and reluctant hand, as if she hardly recognised him.

'Yes, Luís Bernardo, I've come to the city and, it seems, by chance on quite a special day.'

'Why special?'

'The day you allowed yourself to be overcome by vanity, blindness, lack of awareness, . . .'

'What do you mean, Maria Augusta?'

'My poor fellow, you cut a sad figure in your performance in the courtroom.'

'How do you know? Were you there?'

'No, and that's hardly the point. It's the talk of the town and nobody is interested in whether you were any good as a lawyer. I thought you'd come to São Tomé to make a career as Governor, not as a lawyer. A new governor, with new ideas, but on our side. I've often defended you, Luís Bernardo. I've tried to explain to others how important and difficult your mission is. I swore as to your good faith and good intentions. But you denied my trust, and capped it today with your performance in court. You must be very proud of yourself, but if I were in your place I would resign now. You are finished as our governor: the colony is against you.'

'You too, Maria Augusta?'

'Yes, me too.'

'Why? What's changed?'

'You've changed.'

'Me? How?'

'Don't ask me how, because it's self-evident: you've gone over to the side of our enemies, to those in Lisbon and in Europe who are conspiring to bankrupt us here in São Tomé. If you like, ask rather why you've changed and I will tell you.'

'Why then?'

'You don't know, my dear fellow? Do I have to tell you to your face? Hasn't anyone told you yet?'

'I don't know what you're talking about, Maria Augusta.'

'Oh, *you* don't know? How can you not know what has made you change and discredited you in the eyes of everyone is the fact you have fallen madly in love with that whore of an English-woman, who deceives her husband in bed with you yet works for him by beguiling our Governor between the sheets?'

Luís Bernardo felt his blood run cold. Felt the ground give under his feet.

'*Entre nous*, Luís Bernardo, tell me, a woman who's also been to bed with you, whether it is the fireworks between the whore's legs that leaves you in such a state.'

Luís Bernardo was searching for words that eluded him. His mouth felt dry and was exhausted that morning. He made an effort.

'I didn't expect this from you, Maria Augusta . . .'

'There are so many things we don't expect from people we once trusted, are there not? Goodbye, Luís Bernardo. Enjoy yourself.'

He stood and watched her walk off, and tried to recover so he could continue on his way. But now he saw nothing, the people passing by his side, those who said hello or those who turned aside. Everything suddenly seemed irrelevant. He looked around, distraught, and saw his carriage on the other side of the square. He waved and called to Vicente, who broke into a trot and came to pick him up, as if he'd been expecting a signal. He got in and slumped on to the leather seat. Sebastião was sitting at the side in the shadow, and looked at him but said nothing.

It was only after they'd reached home, after they'd ridden in silence for ten minutes, that Sebastião said, 'Doctor, I apologise if I address you as Governor, but I just wanted to tell you one thing: it's an honour to serve you and have you as Governor of São Tomé.'

Luís Bernardo got out, saying not a word. Went into the house as if fleeing from a tempest.

Went straight up to his bedroom and bellowed to Sebastião, 'Sebastião, I am at home for nobody, until further notice. Nobody! Not even if the King himself were to put in an appearance!'

But instead of disappearing, Sebastião followed him into his bedroom, gripping a piece of paper.

'Doctor, excuse me, but I have a very urgent telegram the Secretary General brought here by hand, a short while ago.'

Luís Bernardo looked at the sealed telegram, which carried the inscription on the outside 'Confidential. Very Urgent', and pulled it to the top of the bed where he'd just collapsed. He stared at the telegram, wondering what to do. He felt like throwing it out of the window, putting it down the lavatory or burning it. He closed his eyes, tried to sleep and forget everything, but finally had a change of mind. He sat up on his bed, opened the telegram and read.

The Minister's Office, Ministry for the Colonies

To the Governor of São Tomé and Príncipe and São João Baptista de Ajudá

His Highness the Prince Dom Luís Filipe and myself will embark on a tour of the colonies of São Tomé and Príncipe, Angola, Mozambique and Cabo Verde next July STOP Journey will begin with a two-day visit to São Tomé and one day in Príncipe STOP Details in next dispatch, but tell populace of visit now and begin preparations for welcome at level of historic event STOP Minister Ayres d'Ornellas e Vasconcelos

Luís Bernardo stared at the telegram, as if he hadn't really understood. He crumpled it in a gesture of exasperation, then exclaimed, 'This is all I needed!' He turned on his side and tried to sleep.

14

THE SITUATION IN the city was volatile. First came the commentaries on what had happened in court, a more or less accurate account, which sounded more like fiction, of the intervention of the Governor-cum-lawyer defending the two black runaways from the plantation. Then came the posters the Governor had designed and printed in record time and which he ordered to be displayed at strategic points in the city to give notice of the surprise news of the Royal Prince's visit to São Tomé in July. Four sentences heralded the visit of the Prince and the Minister for the Colonies and called on the populace to prepare 'a welcome to match this historic event'. While the citizens of São Tomé were still digesting that extraordinary piece of news, another suddenly surfaced to oust it: that morning Dr Anselmo de Sousa Teixeira had decreed the release of the two escapees from Rio do Ouro, and ordered their return to the plantation, on express instructions that neither of their contracts could be extended, nor could they be punished in any way, given that there was no proof their escape was justified, or *vice versa*.

Some – who swore they'd witnessed the whole trial – put the Judge's astonishing verdict down to the Governor's brilliant legal defence, others claimed it was merely the result of his intimidation of the Judge. Others, however, linked Dr Anselmo's unexpected benevolence to the news of the royal visit – either because he'd decided this news warranted a show of benevolence from the authorities, or because the Judge had concluded the visit was only possible because of the manifest influence the Governor exercised over the Portuguese government and Royal House. In the wake of Dr Anselmo's ruling, public opinion was divided yet again on what to think of Luís Bernardo. One group believed he'd gone outside his remit and completely undermined the independence of criteria his post demanded – a view more than vindicated by the events in court and the friendship he enjoyed with the British Consul and his wife. Another group believed, on the contrary, that the Governor was merely following instructions he'd brought from Lisbon and the King that the colony could neither understand nor follow, and that represented a change in traditional colonial policies. Generally, this opinion was only expressed in the city and towns by a few traders, civil servants and army officers or police inspectors, and not by the Portuguese who lived and worked on the plantations.

Early in the morning the day after the sentence was announced Luís Bernardo had gone personally to the Tipografia Ideal print shop and written the text and agreed the layout and size for the posters announcing the Prince's arrival. He ordered they be given absolute priority and printed immediately. He wanted to be the first to announce the Prince's visit and didn't want anyone else spreading the news before him. He was spurred on by a sense of urgency he couldn't really fathom, and didn't rest till he saw the printed posters and had confirmation they'd been displayed at the strategic points in the city he'd designated. After that, he went to his office in the Government Secretariat to check whether the dispatch with details of the visit had arrived, but apart from two newspapers, his only post was a letter from João. A short letter, sent ten days earlier from Lisbon, that had arrived with the morning steamer.

It's rumoured here that Ayres will visit the African colonies, including São Tomé, early in the summer, and has invited the Royal Prince to accompany him. I write in haste to tell you. If it is confirmed, get ready to make what you can of what I deem to be an excellent, unexpected opportunity to enhance your position, internally and externally, that is, both here and over there. *O Século* published an article to the effect that São Tomé has a governor 'lulled to sleep by lethargy or a siren's song, who seems incapable of choosing between old and new policies, of neutralising the animosity of the British or winning the trust of the Portuguese colonisers'. This stinks and I beg you as a friend to take care. If this visit is confirmed, be at your most lucid and let it concentrate your mind – as I would expect it to. Greetings to Ann and David. Please listen to me: watch those closest to you. The most appalling betrayals can come from where you least expect. You know what I'm referring to and that I know how easy it is to give advice. But I want you back here intact. Your friend as ever, João.

That night when he got up from dinner he suddenly felt sickly: his head was spinning, his chest felt cold and clammy. He reckoned a double cognac was the cure, but despite the subdued heat of night and the fire of the alcohol in his throat, his body was racked by fever. At nine, he retired to bed thinking a good night's sleep would get him over his indisposition, but he woke up at midnight soaked in sweat and feeling incredibly thirsty. He groped in the dark for the glass of water and jug always left on his bedside table and downed three glasses rapidly. He felt weak and collapsed back on his bed.

Next morning when he hadn't woken at the usual time Sebastião decided to look in on him and found his master feverish and delirious. He was experiencing his first attack of malaria.

Dr Gil was called to examine him. He found Luís Bernard unconscious with a temperature of 43°. He injected quinine, ordered him to be stripped naked and wiped his head and chest repeatedly applying a cold wet towel. Within half an hour, his temperature had dropped to 40° and he seemed more rested, but was still delirious. He opened his eyes from time to time, uttered a few incoherent phrases, and sank back into a kind of deep sleep. Dr Gil agreed to come back in the late afternoon to see how the patient was and give him a further injection of quinine. Meanwhile, he recommended Sebastião take his temperature every hour and put a wet towel on him whenever it rose above 40° and call him if his condition started to deteriorate.

'There's not much one can do. Just wait till he gets over it. The first attack is normally the worst.'

Luís Bernardo spent the entire first day unconscious. He never showed any sign that he recognised anyone or even where he was. Sebastião, with Doroteia's help, spent the day changing drenched sheets, wiping the sweat away, taking his temperature, applying a compress and forcing him to sit up to drink water from a tube of bamboo he'd ordered to be cut from the garden. Doroteia put a chair at the foot of his bed and never left the room. Whenever he groaned or tried to speak, she tried to soothe him by stroking his head or face. After the doctor's evening visit, they decided to take turns during the night to be at Luís Bernardo's bedside. Doroteia took the first shift to 2 a.m. and Sebastião took over until the doctor's visit in the morning.

Luís Bernardo's temperature hovered around 40°, though now he shot above that less often. At midday they managed to get him to drink some fruit juice and eat half a mashed banana – his first intake of food in thirty-six hours. By the late afternoon, alone with Doroteia, he seemed to give the first signs of a return to life. He groaned and Doroteia placed her hand on his forehead and softly sang a Creole song her mother had sung to her as a child when she was ill. Luís Bernardo opened his eyes and appeared to listen attentively to the song she was singing. He took her hand that was resting on his head and placed it on his chest, next to his heart, under his own hand, shut his eyes again and returned to the depths of that shipwrecked world where he'd been marooned.

Later on when trying to recall what had happened during that period, and without the slightest notion of how long he'd been in that state, the first memory Luís Bernardo hauled to the surface was that moment alone with Doroteia. The memory brought him back from the shadows and he began to remember other things that had occurred after that. He recalled hearing Sebastião's voice several times in his bedroom and being aware of the presence of another person he couldn't put a name to: they said it was the doctor.

Late in the evening on the second day, the doctor confirmed the improvements he'd noted in the morning. His patient's temperature had dropped, and now rarely went above 40°. Whenever he opened his eyes, he seemed to remember who he was rather more frequently.

'It looks like he's over the worst,' he said to Sebastião. 'But we must remain vigilant until his temperature is back to normal.'

That night, when it was his turn to be at Luís Bernardo's bedside, Sebastião noticed he woke up several times, apparently making an effort to say something. He listened as carefully as he could but never heard anything that made any sense. At one point he thought the Governor spoke in English, the same language the Consul Mr Jameson used. He sometimes spoke calmly, at others became agitated, desperate because he got no reply or wasn't being understood. Until at another point a long silence followed a number of incoherent phrases, when he could only hear Luís Bernardo breathing, and that was suddenly broken by one word that was quite audible: 'Ann.'

On the morning of the third day, when the doctor arrived, he found his patient's temperature almost back to normal, though he was still prostrate and exhausted. Luís Bernardo woke up, opened his eyes, looked round and appeared to recognise where he was.

The doctor asked, 'How do you feel?'

But Luís Bernardo didn't reply, barely nodded his head.

Dr Gil gave him another quinine injection, got no apparent reaction from his patient, and only later did he speak wearily and with difficulty.

'What's been the matter?'

'A bout of malaria. A really bad one. But you're out of danger now: you've been improving over the last couple of days.'

Luís Bernardo closed his eyes and fell asleep again. Later on, Sebastião and Doroteia gave him his first proper meal for three days: a broth with rice and strips of chicken and fruit juice.

He woke up two hours later as the twilight sky sank into the sea and the last rays of light glimmered through his bedroom window. He felt a hand gently touch his head and mouth and, before opening his eyes, tried to recall where he was and why. He remembered the conversation with the doctor, though he couldn't locate it in time. He remembered he'd been sick with malaria and high temperatures, but didn't know for how long. He recalled his body overheating, the icy sweats, the presence of Sebastião and Doroteia, who'd caressed him and applied cool towels to his body. It was only remembering all this that he slowly opened his eyes and came back to life.

'Doroteia . . .' he called, his voice still weak.

'Shush! Don't talk now. It's me.'

He gave a start, looked round and saw the hand holding his was not Doroteia's but Ann's, who was sitting in the chair next to his bed. Instinctively, he looked round again to confirm they were alone. Two candles burned in the holders on the chest of drawers opposite his bed and the light from them, almost the only light in the room, was projecting strange shapes on to the ceiling.

'What are you doing here?'

'Your employee, Sebastião, told me to come. We'd known about your illness for two days but I didn't dare visit by myself. I called in yesterday with David and discovered you were on the mend. Today I was getting ready to come to find out whether you were any better, when Sebastião sent Vicente to our house to ask me to come.'

'Why, what did he say?'

Ann smiled. She continued to caress his face and support his head so he didn't attempt to lift it up.

'He said you'd asked to see me . . . last night.'

Luís was now wide awake. He couldn't recall the period he'd been sick, except for a few hazy details, but the memory of the days that preceded his illness immediately rushed to mind. He remembered the telegram announcing the visit of Prince Luís Filipe and the Minister for the Colonies, the court sentence, João's letter, and how that night he'd felt peculiarly fragile and giddy. Then he suddenly felt nervous.

'Ann, nobody must see you come here or leave!'

'If we're lucky, nobody will. But so what if they do? I've come to see a sick friend. Besides, I told David I was coming.'

He was about to say something in reply, but she didn't let him: she covered his mouth with hers, slipping her hand beneath the blanket covering him. She felt him react and quickly stripped off and slipped under the blanket.

Luís Bernardo feebly tried to hold her off.

'Ann, this is madness, not here!'

'My love, nobody will ever see me here until I leave. It's one of the few places we are safe.'

He made no effort to resist. He was too weak to take any initiative. He let her do whatever she wanted. It was all very quick and intense and she soon dressed, covered him over, smoothed the ruffled blankets and sat on the side of the bed staring at him.

'My poor love! It was either kill or cure!'

270

'I think you killed me!' he murmured with a smile she extinguished with a final kiss.

'I must be off or your servants will wonder why I've lingered so long. Make sure you get back to sleep. Tomorrow the doctor will still confine you to your bed, so I'll arrange to come to see you in the late evening.'

Luís Bernardo spent most of the following day on his feet. He took his first full bath for four days, read his post and dictated to his secretary whom he ordered to come up from the Secretariat. At the end of the day, when the Secretariat closed for business, he announced he was exhausted and retreated back to his bed, just as Ann appeared outside and asked Sebastião if he was in a state to be visited. He heard her coming up the stairs in his direction, like somebody waiting for a window to open and let in the bright light of a new day, dispersing the shadows that had gathered.

Malaria is like a black widow that catches the living and healthy by surprise and brings down a darkness that blots out the light of day. Suddenly, from nowhere, a female mosquito scores a direct hit that festers slowly and prostrates her victims, who are left defenceless, without a will of their own. In most of Africa and the tropics, malaria brings its victims to their knees, but in São Tomé and Príncipe, it kills as it does nowhere else. It attacks the brain, devours cells and, in a few days, without any antidote to restrain its insidious progress, it takes the life of those who a few days before were vigorous and hearty. Luís Bernardo realised from what Sebastião and Dr Gil told him that he'd journeyed very close to that frontier from which there was no return. Ann had restored him violently, fleshily back to life, via a route to which the body responded before the senses. But it was only later, when he finally left his bed, where he'd wrestled with fate for four long days and nights, that he gradually grasped how close he'd come to his end. He was moved when he read the notebook in which Sebastião and Doroteia had religiously recorded his temperatures hour by hour. He'd been absent and defenceless and they'd looked after him, every minute of the night and day, bringing him back – to Ann's body, to the scents from his garden, to the sound of the sea, to the humidity hanging over the city, to the cries of children tumbling out of school, to life itself.

When Luís Bernardo sat down in his office on the ground floor in the Government Secretariat, though the pile of urgent business made him feel anxious and behindhand, he immersed himself immediately, calm and lucid like a man who had just seen the difference between what is essential and what is superficial. But the telegrams screamed at him to take decisions: there was a telegram from the Deputy Commissioner on the Island of Príncipe, whom he knew didn't enjoy the best of relations with Germano Valente, and who, perhaps for that reason, had opted to communicate directly with the Governor, thus bypassing his immediate superior in the hierarchy. 'Tense, potentially dangerous atmosphere on the plantations requires Your Excellency's immediate presence to assess situation in person.' Luís Bernardo responded at once asking him to come to São Tomé for talks or, if he didn't think it advisable to absent himself immediately from Príncipe, to give more detail on the situation and justify the need for the Governor to travel there. He made it clear that arrangements for the upcoming visit of the Royal Prince were taking up his time on São Tomé. He also sent a telegram to the government representative on Príncipe, telling him that he'd heard rumours about a tense situation on the plantations and asking him to keep him informed. In reply, the Deputy Governor tried to calm the Governor down, agreed there'd been the odd isolated incident, but added that order had been quickly restored and that he was monitoring the situation closely by the day. Far from being soothed, Luís Bernardo became more apprehensive. He chided him for not telling him earlier, suggested he be more specific about the kind of incident and the measures he had taken and told him to communicate immediately the slightest change in the situation. Without saying as much to the government representative on Príncipe, he took the decision to visit the island as soon as he'd set in motion the preparations for the welcome for the royal contingent.

Two further telegrams from the Ministry in Lisbon gave details of the royal visit. His Highness and the Minister would sail aboard the packet ship *África*, thus taking advantage of its timetabled sailings from the metropolis to the African colonies. At a moment when the expenses of the Royal Household were the main hobby horse of the republican opposition, the fact that the heir to the throne was going to travel for three months on an ordinary vessel and mingle with ordinary passengers was evidently a political measure to influence domestic public opinion. That, plus the minimal nature of the retinue travelling: four people with the Prince and three with the Minister. A prince had never before travelled so modestly. And it was one of the rare visits a member of the Royal Family had made to a Portuguese colony after nearly five hundred years of colonial rule. Moreover, everything seemed to have been decided at the last minute and without too much thought.

The Prince and the Minister would arrive in São Tomé in a month or so. São Tomé and Príncipe had the honour of inaugurating the royal tour, which would continue on to the English colonies in South Africa and Mozambique and then, on the return journey, Angola and Cabo Verde. They would spend the first two days and nights on São Tomé and a day and a night on Príncipe. The Ministry specified that His Highness would sleep the first night in the Governor's Palace (where accommodation should be prepared for his aide-de-camp and his personal adjutant, and the second on the Rio do Ouro plantation, whose owner, the Count of Valle Flor, would sail directly from Paris in his private yacht to welcome the royal party to his plantation.

The Governor should arrange things so the party also visited the Água Izé and Boa Entrada plantations, the latter being the property of Mr Henrique Mendonça, who would also travel especially from Lisbon to welcome Dom Luís Filipe. Finally, on Príncipe, the Prince wished to visit the Infante Dom Henrique and Sundy plantations, intending to sleep overnight on the latter or, if that were impossible, aboard the *África*.

A third telegram came the following day, classified as Confidential, and which broached political concerns.

The Minister's Office, Ministry for the Colonies
    To the Governor of São Tomé and Príncipe and São João Baptista de Ajudá

273

I hope you have safely received my previous telegrams giving details of royal visit, I expect Your Ex has understood the political importance of this unique mission by HRH Prince of Beira and myself as Minister STOP São Tomé and Príncipe will have the honour and responsibility of being the first Portuguese colony in a very long time to receive a visit from a member of the Royal Family, Heir to the Throne STOP Decision determined above all by the intensified English campaign against our colonising of São Tomé, and redoubled accusations of slave labour, as Your Ex knows and has been constantly informed STOP It is thus imperative visit is a success politically and with populace, leading to press articles that can be publicised in Britain and help defuse such accusations STOP Attention to the detail of the visit, heavy involvement of populace and accompanying social and political tenor will be vital for success of mission, the achieving of which rests very much in Your Ex's hands STOP Please do not hesitate to ask for necessary help or suggest anything for proper execution of historic task STOP You must keep British Consul abreast of all protocol measures and make it clear we wish contact and have nothing to hide STOP Royal Prince and I will reaffirm in our speeches Portuguese sovereignty and loyalty to treaties signed, and our openness to criticism in good faith, restating rights and assuming obligations STOP May God protect Your Ex, most sincerely, Ayres d'Ornellas e Vasconcelos.

Despite the Minister's express offer of support, Luís Bernardo got no response whatsoever from the Ministry when he asked for an increase in allowances to cover the costs of festivities and the anticipated expense of the reception. According to estimates that he sent to Lisbon, the latter would cost between fifteen and twenty thousand réis, and he had a mere three thousand available in the Governor's chest, after other extra expenditure was accounted for. The absence of a response from Lisbon was, to his mind, typical of the government of his country: they wanted omelettes without cracking a single egg. They wanted the Prince to be given a euphoric welcome, but didn't want the opposition to be able to say the euphoria had dented the public coffers. 'The

Prince of Beira's picnic in Africa' – as it was dubbed by *A Lucta* the Republican newspaper – was expected to be mysteriously self-financing.

To that end, he summoned the Mayor, traders in the city, plantation administrators, the pillars of island society and tried to initiate a campaign to collect funds and support for the under-taking ahead, never hesitating to repeat verbatim phrases from the telegram so they grasped the political importance of the success of the visit for São Tomé. 'Dear gentlemen, more than anything else it's in your own interests it should be a success!' he repeated till they believed him.

He devoted the whole week to meetings and inspections related to the Prince's visit. He met the Bishop, the Commander of the Garrison and Police, the Mayor, the administrators of the three plantations the royal contingent were to visit (in the case of Rio do Ouro, the Secretary General represented him), the owners of the shops on the city's main thoroughfares, to persuade them to pay for the illuminations to decorate the streets and building façades. The Secretary for Public Works was encouraged to spend, if necessary, all the money he had available till the end of the year, to repair, paint and freshen up the landing jetties, public parks and squares and, at the very least, the façades of the main state buildings. 'Let us not forget,' he told everyone, 'it is likely we will have to wait another five hundred years before a member of the Royal Family again sets foot on the islands of São Tomé and Príncipe!'

Luís Bernardo, fully recovered from malaria, managed to fire all concerned with his energy. From the start, he had seen the unexpected development of the royal visit as an opportunity to reaffirm his authority and control. He also saw how the visit by Dom Luís Filipe and Ayres d'Ornellas gave him another im-portant opportunity: namely to clarify once and for all the status quo on the island, to speak loyally but frankly to the Minister and heir to the throne, without hiding any of his doubts and profound disagreements with many of the colonisers. He hoped, at least in private, to get them to understand his dilemma, trapped as he was between the economic and diplomatic interests at play. There were two possible outcomes: either he engaged them in the political options or forced them to free him from his responsibilities. He wasn't prepared to let the opportunity turn into a mere 'picnic in Africa', a 'royal tour' devoid of content and consequence.

Amid all the hustle and bustle, David made an appointment to visit him during office hours following the proper protocols. They'd all three had dinner at Luís Bernardo's house two days before he'd started back at work. Superficially, it was only a dinner with friends to celebrate the recovery of one of their group: David even brought a bottle of French champagne, a Veuve Clicquot that Luís Bernardo couldn't honour properly on medical advice. The three of them chatted on the terrace till almost midnight as informally and warmly as they had done ever since that day circumstances brought them together and they realised their friendship was a form of resistance and mutual support they badly needed. David talked about India, and, quite unusually, about his time as the Governor of Assam. Luís Bernardo was fascinated and at the same time quite distressed that he was able to sit next to Ann and yet maintain his friendship with David, knowing that a fire burned within him that could separate the two men most violently.

The following day Ann sent a note via a maid asking him to accompany her to the beach in the late morning. When they met and he berated her for her increasing lack of precautions, she held him tight.

'My love, I cannot live without you. It's stronger than I am! Find another way, another solution, whatever! I'm at the end of my tether! I soon won't be able to live in the same house as David, pretending everything is normal, when I only think of you, only think about what you're doing, only want to run away and live with you and abandon him. I can't stand this distance between us. It's as if my house were another island where I'm imprisoned, an island within an island, a double prison. I'm dying of despair, of life without you, of jealousy even!'

'Jealousy!' Luís Bernardo laughed. 'Jealousy of whom?'

'Do you really want to know? Well, of Doroteia. I saw how she looked at you when I visited your bedroom the other day. I saw the way she looked at me when Sebastião indicated she should leave. She's beautiful, a sweet seventeen, and you're alone at home every night.'

Luís Bernardo stared at her: she was irresistibly beautiful.

'No, I am not thinking of changing you for Doroteia. Or taking on the two of you. I was just thinking I'd like you to myself, and was wondering whether that might be possible one day . . .'

She dropped on to the sand next to some coconut palms, and beckoned to him. The horses tethered close by stood guard over their passion as they made love on the sand.

The memory was still vivid when David entered his office the following morning. He could still feel Ann's body clinging to his, the taste of her mouth, hear the sound of her moans. He had a sudden attack of terror and thought he might still be carrying her scent and, instinctively, kept a distance from his friend. David had started talking but Luís Bernardo wasn't listening. He was far away, looking way beyond him, trying to chase off unruly thoughts from his head.

'. . . basically I can't fathom what your prince wants to do here. Does he intend to set you free?'

'What?'

'Aren't you listening, Luís? I'm trying to ask you why he's coming here.'

'Well! Why shouldn't he?' Luís Bernardo was now fully attentive. 'Doesn't the Prince of Wales go to India and other British colonies?'

'São Tomé is hardly India . . .'

'Everyone to his own. He's coming to São Tomé, and also visiting Angola, Mozambique and Cabo Verde.'

'I understand Angola and Mozambique. But why São Tomé? It's such an insignificant little island.'

'David, don't be so snobbish. I know the British Empire has got thousands of little islands. We haven't. So we regard these little islands as being important: even appoint governors to them!'

David laughed, but didn't relent.

'Come on, Luís, you know very well what I'm getting at. There are other reasons for this visit and I'm sure the Minister must have informed you of the political rationale.'

Luís Bernardo remained silent. He thought he sensed a subtle change in his friend's attitude. But he thought it had nothing to do with Ann. It was something else he sensed forcing them back into their official roles and pushing friendship to one side: David was now the official representative of a foreign power challenging the policies of the government Luís Bernardo represented.

'Well, have you nothing to say?'

'What do you expect me to say, David? Of course, the Minister has been in correspondence with me as he would be with any other governor informing him of different turns in policy, asking that we try to respond as best as we can.'

'Yes, I understand but you know I don't expect you to reveal any state secrets. What I'd like to know is what is expected of me in the midst of all this palaver.'

'What palaver?'

'Look, my dear fellow, we are friends, no point pretending we can't see what is quite obvious.' David paused, stared Luís Bernardo in the eye, and continued in the same ostensibly unselfish tone. 'Sometimes, when one is a friend, it's better to pretend not to see what should remain invisible, however hard it may be. In the name of friendship and things that are more difficult to explain. But others ought to understand we are only pretending not to see.'

Those words chilled Luís Bernardo to the marrow. His heart thudded in his chest. He was going to end the agony, ask him point blank what he meant. Force him to be blunt. Force him to confront the consequences.

But all he said was, 'I don't know what "palaver" you are referring to . . .'

'Well, what is driving the madness that has struck São Tomé – the preparations for the Prince's visit they say you're responsible for? Evidently, the need to boost His Highness in the popularity and deference stakes, with political effects for internal and external consumption. Or am I mistaken?'

In the end it was a false alarm. Luís Bernardo took a deep breath.

'What's wrong with that? Don't all governments do the same? What's the point of state visits here or anywhere in the whole world?'

'I agree. But what I'm asking you, what I want to know is what is my role in all this palaver, in the great display of sovereignty where São Tomé will enjoy a front row in the stalls?'

'You know what your role is. It goes with the job. I will merely follow the express instructions from the Minister and give you the importance protocol requires for your post; that means, for example, sitting you next to the Prince at top table at the banquet to be given at the Governor's Palace the night he arrives. You happy with that?'

'No, Luís, you're still avoiding the issue. I don't want to know my place at the dinner table. As you can imagine, knowing me, I'm not worried about that at all. What does worry me is if I find I'm expected to sit down to dinner, clap hands and tell London that the Prince's visit was a huge success.'

'Which is what you intend doing, don't you, David?'

'In no way.' David stood up and started to head for the door. 'I leave it to your judgement and sensitivity to guess what . . .'

'David!' Luís Bernardo had also stood up now. 'I sincerely ask you as a friend: tell me what you intend to write!'

'Not a word, as your friend. I'm not fishing for favours, which would be absurd in this context. I'm now addressing you as the Governor: you are the Governor, you know what my role is here, you know the reasons why I am here, and the political reasons why our countries are at loggerheads over São Tomé. The heir to the throne and minister responsible for your policies are now paying a visit. Just think for a moment what my function and involvement should be at this point, if any. Nothing more.'

And he left, closing the door gently behind him. Luís Bernardo noticed he hadn't even said goodbye. In fact, something had changed in David's attitude. And Luís Bernardo reluctantly accepted he was right. Not just because of Ann. It involved something more and, with regard to that something more, David was right as well.

The *África* set sail from Lisbon on the 1st of July, carrying on board the Prince and the Minister for the Colonies and their small retinue. It would reach São Tomé in a little under two weeks. Luís Bernardo had got the machinery under way for the local festivities and inspected the three plantations the royal contingent was to visit. He saw equally to the preparations for the banquet to be held at the Governor's Palace on the day of their arrival, when he had to allocate two hundred table placements carefully and avoid causing offence. Yet another task was to confirm with Sebastião all the details for the Prince's accommodation on the night he would stay at the Governor's Palace. As only three bedrooms were available, it was easy to agree that Dom Luís Filipe would occupy the main bedroom, the Prince's adjutant, First Lieutenant in the Navy, the Marquess of Lavradio, would have Luís Bernardo's room and the aide-de-camp would be put up in the spare. Luís Bernardo meanwhile would move to the ground floor, where a single bed in his office in the Secretariat would allow him to deal with any unforeseen circumstances.

Time was speeding by. David was right: Luís Bernardo had taken on the organisation and detail of what his friend called 'the palaver'. He sensed that the success of the 'palaver' depended largely on his margin for political manoeuvre in relation to the Minister and Dom Carlos's son. He wasn't worried about his future as Governor, but about his ability to carry through his mission with due dignity and authority. He'd already given up seventeen months of life to São Tomé and Príncipe and that only made sense if it hadn't been time wasted, and if, on his return to Lisbon, nobody could accuse him of betraying his ideas or of not serving the interests of Portugal. Princes and men of power liked the applause of the rabble. He'd give them that and get his payback in terms of a strengthening of his own authority and legitimacy. He'd emerge enhanced or they'd call in someone else. João was quite right: it was an opportunity not to be missed.

Nevertheless, during those hectic days of meetings and inspections, the situation on Príncipe was never far from his mind. Something kept telling him he ought to bring forward his trip to the island to scrutinise local preparations for the great visit, and investigate the reasons behind the Deputy Commissioner's anxiety. The latter's subsequent silence and the local governor's insistence that everything had returned to normal didn't completely reassure him, but it did make him feel his trip could be deferred, one day after another, so he could tackle the more urgent matters requiring his attention on São Tomé. So when the dreadful telegram arrived in the late morning of 4 July, he blamed his own lack of foresight.

Signed by the Deputy Governor António Vieira, it had been copied to Lisbon that same day.

Five hundred workers in revolt Infante Henrique plantation. STOP Whites murdered STOP Fear general revolt STOP Most urgent warship sent

Luís Bernardo moved with speed and urgency. He asked his secretary to summon immediately the Mayor and Major Benjamim das Neves, the Commander of the Garrison, and to locate the coast-cutter the *Mindelo* – the only vessel that regularly went between the two islands – and which they should bring to the capital as soon as they'd tracked it down.

No sooner had his secretary disappeared at top speed, than Agostinho de Jesus Júnior peered round his door. From that first conversation, when he landed in São Tomé, he'd realised the man was a cynical enemy he couldn't trust, and Luís Bernardo only dealt with him when strictly necessary. Otherwise, he saw to day-to-day business through Caló, his secretary, whose importance increased for the Governor in direct relation to the rate at which he became targeted by the Secretary General's subtle snooping.

Now, however, after he'd seen Caló race out of the Governor's office, Agostinho de Jesus, who was used to being marginalised in everything, couldn't repress his curiosity.

'Is there any way in which the Governor would like me to help him?'

'No, Mr Agostinho, everything's under control. I must urgently go to Príncipe, because of the royal visit, but Caló is seeing to that.'

'I don't know whether Caló can manage everything: there are a lot of things to see to at the moment.'

'Everything is under control, Mr Agostinho. And if Caló needs reinforcements, I will see to it.'

'As you wish, Governor. I merely came to offer my services.'

Half an hour later Caló came rushing back. The Mayor had been summoned as well as the Major: both were on their way. As for the *Mindelo*, it was returning from Príncipe and was expected towards the end of the day. Luís Bernardo asked him to wait on the jetty and summon the Captain to the Palace as soon as he landed. Then the Mayor arrived and Luís Bernardo explained how the preparations on São Tomé were well in hand, while he was aware that very little had been done on Príncipe. He'd therefore decided to go there as soon as possible, leaving the Mayor in charge of operations until he returned. He would be away two or three days at most.

When Major Benjamim das Neves arrived, Luís Bernardo shut the door behind him to check nobody was eavesdropping.

'Major, I ask you to consider the following information as completely confidential: a revolt has broken out on Infante Dom Henrique on Príncipe. I don't know whether Captain Dario, who heads the local detachment, has enough troops to control the situation, as I don't know the details. Consequently, I want you to accompany me today on the *Mindelo*, with as many soldiers as the boat can take, and you will be in command. We will sail at night as discreetly as possible to avoid causing panic in the city. I will send you a note with the exact time of departure. Needless to say I expect the soldiers to be sufficiently armed.'

'Yes, Governor.' The Major stood to attention, saluted and left without reacting in any way.

If only I could function like the military! Luís Bernardo thought. He sent a telegram to Príncipe, to the Deputy Governor António Vieira.

Coming as soon as *Mindelo* available with Major Benjamim and troops STOP I forbid any direct communication with Lisbon STOP Keep me informed of situation hourly until I arrive STOP I forbid use of military force unless absolutely necessary, against armed civilians or uncontrolled actions of plantation managers against workers STOP You must immediately assume personal command of situation on plantation till I arrive STOP

An hour later, he received the first reply from Príncipe:

Situation still very tense but stable STOP. Captain Dario and thirty-five soldiers on plantation STOP Workers cornered STOP

At 4 p.m. an urgent telegram arrived from the *África* sent by Minister Ayres d'Ornellas, asking Luís Bernardo for details of the situation on Príncipe and the actions taken. Luís Bernardo responded with the information António Vieira had just sent saying he hoped to have more detail once he was there. At six, the *Mindelo* anchored opposite the city and its captain was ordered to disembark immediately and go to the Governor's Palace. Once there, Luís Bernardo requisitioned his boat and crew in order to sail back that same night to Príncipe with twenty-five soldiers from the Garrison and Major Benjamim. It was agreed they would load up at nine. Luís Bernardo went home, had a bath and packed a suitcase with two changes of clothes and his revolver, had a quick bite to eat and went downstairs to give Caló two telegrams to send from the post office, one to Príncipe and one to the *África*, via Lisbon, informing them he was on his way.

By ten o'clock he was on the prow of the *Mindelo*, contemplating the lights of São Tomé moving away on the horizon. It was an almost moonless night and the boat glided across the tranquil sea as if it were a pond. A slight breeze made for a pleasant night and the cool airiness was a sign that there was no humidity and that summer had returned.

15

I N THE FIRST light of morning, the city of Santo António do
Príncipe appeared in silhouette to the prow of the *Mindelo*,
emerging from the mist like a green raft floating across the
desolate surface of the ocean. No system of public lighting
allowed one to discern from that distance the outlines of a small
settlement they called a city. A few bonfires lit up the hill above
the houses and the rising smoke vanished in the haze covering the
whole island almost on a level with the rooftops. Luís Bernardo
was shocked by the peaceful vision of an island in revolt, if not
already aflame. Indeed, from a kilometre out to sea, one might
almost say it was just another peaceful day dawning.

The *Mindelo* hooted as it rounded the sand bar and progressed
smoothly to the anchorage by the beach, where a few people
were already gathered expectantly. As soon as Luís Bernardo
stepped on land he was greeted by José do Nascimento, the
Deputy Commissioner, who'd been the first to warn him of the
tensions on the island. He reported there'd apparently been no
worsening of the situation during the night: at least no news of
anything had drifted down to the city. Following orders from Luís
Bernardo, the Deputy Governor had stayed on the Infante Dom
Henrique plantation, and had been joined the day before by
Captain Dario and thirty-five soldiers, almost the entire garrison
on Príncipe. Captain Dario had remained in the city on the
express orders of the Deputy Governor, who felt that his presence
on the plantation would only inflame tempers.

'You mean he suspects you of instigating the labourers' revolt
on the plantation?'

'No, Your Honour the Governor, I'm accused of wishing to
defend them.' He didn't flinch at Luís Bernardo's quizzical gaze.
There was fear, but also serenity and strength of mind in the way
he waited for the Governor's response.

'So tell me what really happened.'

'Several weeks ago,' José do Nascimento began, 'we heard rumours of extreme tension on Dom Henrique, growing as a result of the physical punishment being meted out by the foremen and the overseer, Ferreira Duarte. I decided to go to the plantation to see with my own eyes what was going on, but was practically run off the property by the administrator, Engineer Leopoldo Costa, who denied that anything unusual had happened, or that anybody had been mistreated. When I got back, I informed António Vieira, who reassured me that if anything unusual did happen, he'd be the first to know. But I have my own informants on the plantation – that's part of my job – and they told me the situation was explosive. That's when I sent Your Excellency that telegram.'

'It's true, but then you never confirmed events in any detail,' Luís Bernardo interrupted.

'It was difficult at that juncture to confirm anything: there were only rumours and scattered bits of information. Anyway, last Tuesday, the labourers refused to leave for work after the morning roll call. One born here – third generation, I think – was their leader, a Gabriel, who explained to Engineer Leopoldo that the men would only return to work after the overseer and two of the foremen accused of whipping them had been removed from post. Engineer Leopoldo made no response and the situation remained unchanged until the following day, when the labourers stayed in their huts refusing to go out. The next morning the administrator summoned Gabriel, a fluent Portuguese speaker, and told him he wanted to negotiate with him, on the proviso that the men went out to work. It seems it took Gabriel a long time to convince them to resume their labours in the bush. When they returned that evening, there was no sign of Engineer Leopoldo or of Gabriel, who hasn't been seen since, and nobody knows whether he's dead or alive. I don't know what happened next. Four labourers ambushed the overseer Ferreira Duarte when he was off guard and slashed him to death with machetes. Silva, the foreman who'd come to help him, met with the same end. The whites started shooting and five blacks were killed or wounded. Later, they all retreated into the carpentry workshops and barricaded themselves in, armed with machetes and knives. It was then that Engineer Leopoldo alerted the city and Deputy Governor Vieira went to the plantation, accompanied by Captain Dario and his troops. I wanted to go as well but he expressly forbade me. All this happened yesterday afternoon and, as Your Excellency is now here, I assume that from then on he has kept you informed of developments. I've heard nothing since; we've had no more news.

Luís Bernardo said nothing for a few moments, turning over what he'd just heard.

Then he said, 'Very well, you will now come to the plantation with us. If there are problems with labourers on a plantation, the place of the Commissioner for Labourers is there, to get information first hand, and not here, waiting to hear things from third parties. When this is over, you must send me a full report and one to the Ministry in Lisbon. Major Benjamim! Send two or three of your men to get whatever transport is available for us. We also need food that I will pay for. I want to be on the road within the half-hour. And with minimum fuss.'

But news of the Governor's landing and of soldiers come from São Tomé had rapidly spread through the town, and early risers and a small crowd of bystanders soon gathered to inspect from a healthy distance the group that had just landed on the beach, blacks who looked scared and whites who now seemed more relaxed talking in hushed tones. Fear was troubling the whites, that much was obvious, although Luís Bernardo, who kept walking one way then another, pretended not to notice anything abnormal. He ordered the Captain of the *Mindelo* not to sail without them and to be at the ready to leave at a moment's notice. He instructed Major Benjamim das Neves to put the local forces of Captain Dario under his command as soon as he reached Dom Henrique.

Very shortly a frugal meal arrived for the contingent, freshly made bread, manioc potatoes, fruit and coffee. Major Benjamim's men also returned with several carts, each harnessed to a pair of mules, requisitioned from the municipal stables. They ate quickly and Luís Bernardo gave the order for them to leave.

The climb up to the Infante Dom Henrique lasted almost an hour and a half as they crossed rudimentary tracks hewn out of the jungle by machetes over ground partly flattened by stonerollers. Progress was so slow and uncomfortable that after a while Luís Bernardo got down, preferring to walk for half an hour, and was joined by Major Benjamim and several soldiers, their weapons slung across their backs. En route they bumped into a couple of blacks from the Sundy plantation who, when interrogated by the Commissioner on Luís Bernardo's orders, replied fearfully that they'd been sent on an errand to the city and knew nothing of what was happening on the Infante Dom Henrique.

It was 8 a.m. when the perimeter of the plantation's buildings came into view. Luís Bernardo ordered Major Benjamim to tell all his men to get off the carts and line up in marching order. The Major placed himself at the front, with Luís Bernardo and the Commissioner behind the soldiers, followed by the empty carts. A quarter of an hour later, they entered the plantation's main square. At first glance, Luís Bernardo noticed a big building along one side surrounded by soldiers waiting expectantly: it was a sign that they'd not arrived too late.

As soon as they'd come to a halt, Captain Dario ran over, looking as if he'd had a sleepless night.

Luís Bernardo held out a welcoming hand and asked, 'What's the situation, Captain?'

'Nothing has changed since yesterday, Governor. Following your instructions, as conveyed to me by the Deputy Governor, I merely stationed my men around the carpentry workshops where the labourers have been corralled since yesterday. They have made no effort to leave and we have made none to force them out.'

'You mean your men haven't fired a single shot?'

'Correct, Governor.'

'And how many victims were left by the skirmish between whites and labourers before you got here?'

'As far as I know, we must regret the death of Mr Ferreira Duarte the overseer and the foreman Joaquim Silva, as well as three blacks and one wounded man, who is in the infirmary. All were victims of defensive fire from plantation employees.'

'Very good, Captain. From now on, you and your men are under the orders of Major Benjamim and at my disposition.'

287

'Yes, Governor.'

'And now tell me: where are the Deputy Governor and the plantation administrator?'

Captain Dario had no need to respond because the door to the Casa Grande swung open and Engineer Leopoldo Costa hurried out accompanied by António Vieira, Deputy Governor on Príncipe.

'Your Excellency the Governor, here at last! How are you, Major?' The plantation administrator didn't wait for a reply to his blandishments and ignored any protocol about who should speak first. 'How many men have you brought with you, Major?'

'We have brought twenty-five,' interjected Luís Bernardo, 'and why do you ask?'

'Well, twenty-five plus the thirty-five under Captain Dario's orders and the twenty I have armed constitute a fire power of eighty men.'

'And to what end, may I ask?' riposted Luís Bernardo.

'To what end?' Engineer Leopoldo seemed genuinely shocked by the question. 'To put an end to this riot, naturally, what else do you think?'

'Have you got your strategy in place, Engineer?' There was a hint of irony in Luís Bernardo's tone that the other didn't detect.

'We'll give them a deadline by which they have to leave and . . .'

'And if they don't leave, we'll launch a full-blooded attack on the workshops?'

The administrator of Dom Henrique finally understood that he and the Governor didn't see eye to eye on how to bring the situation under control.

His expression and tone of voice changed when he replied, 'Well, I thought if they don't leave in the time we give them, we'll torch them out.'

'And then?'

'Then?' Engineer Leopoldo looked visibly annoyed by this interrogation. 'Then they come out and give up their machetes and knives and we'll decide, or else if they're crazy and come out fighting, eighty guns will put paid to them.'

'Indeed, I don't see how they'd stand a chance,' retorted Luís Bernardo pensively. 'And how many do you want to kill, Engineer?'

'I don't want to kill anybody, Governor. But if there's no choice, we will kill however many it requires to end this revolt. We've been over-patient as it is!'

'It's strange, Engineer: wherever I go, plantation administrators complain of a lack of workers. You quite clearly aren't worried about liquidating however many it takes!'

Engineer Leopoldo recoiled as if he'd been punched in the face. He went red with the rage and desperation accumulated over the last few days that he'd suppressed with difficulty.

He now addressed Luís Bernardo.

'Perhaps His Excellency has a better plan?'

Luís Bernardo looked at him with undisguised contempt.

'Yes, I have another plan that will possibly not be so appealing to you. Do you think I came here to join my forces with yours and launch them into indiscriminate slaughter of the wretched people corralled in that hut? Look at me: is mine the face of a murderer?'

Engineer Leopoldo made no reply, stifling his silent rage.

'My plan couldn't be simpler: find out what happened, punish those responsible on both sides and put an end to the riot, as you call it, but without shedding blood. You must understand the troops are here to buttress the authority of the state that I represent, and are not here to serve you or your blood lust, disguised as a ridiculous military strategy.'

'And who will avenge the deaths of Ferreira Duarte and Silva? I saw those animals hack them to pieces with their machetes. Your Honour doesn't know what happened and what might happen here in the future if nobody avenges these deaths.'

'Justice will avenge these deaths. Courtroom justice, not yours.'

'Your speeches, dear Governor' – the Engineer spoke as if spitting his words out – 'are all well and good in a Lisbon gentlemen's club. But this is Africa, and one hell of a shitty island where Your Honour deigns to set foot only when there's an emergency!'

Luís Bernardo decided he'd already shown Engineer Leopoldo too much regard and turned his back on him in order to address the Deputy Governor.

'I'd like to know, in your evaluation of the facts, what really happened here.'

'Well, I believe Your Excellency knows the essentials: the day before yesterday, during morning roll call, the labourers refused to go out to work.'

'And why did they refuse?'

'I don't know, I wasn't there.'

'And didn't you try to find out? Do you think it's likely they refused to go out without good reason?'

Before António Vieira replied, the administrator interjected once again.

'I can tell you the reason they invoked: they were calling for the removal of the overseer and Silva the foreman, the two they murdered, and Encarnação, another foreman.'

'And why should they want to do that?'

Now it was the turn of Deputy Commissioner José do Nascimento, whose presence had been ignored until that moment both by Engineer Leopoldo and the Deputy Governor of Príncipe.

'They'd been mistreated by them. Had been whipped and left without food and water.'

'Is that true, Mr Vieira?'

'I don't know.'

'You don't know? Had you no idea? Weren't you familiar with working conditions on this plantation?'

'I was but I'd never heard of anything like that happening.'

'Hadn't the Commissioner informed you weeks ago of the complaints circulating among labourers on this plantation and of the potentially explosive situation this could provoke?'

'Yes, it's true he mentioned that, but this information wasn't confirmed.'

'And what did you do to get confirmation?'

António stayed silent. He looked into space, as if distracted, as if the matter was of no concern right then.

'Do you mean, Mr Vieira' – Luís Bernardo spoke quickly, emphasising each word, as if underlining his slanderous accusation – 'that you were informed by a person of authority, namely the labourers' commissioner, that there was a situation that could deteriorate in this way, due to the mistreatment of which labourers on this plantation complained? And, though informed, you did nothing, not even to find out if there was any truth in the allegations and whether the situation could in fact become dangerous. You investigated nothing. You told me nothing. And then, when the revolt breaks out and you're caught with your trousers down, without even consulting me, you send a panicky telegram off to Lisbon, asking them to send a gun boat no less to come to the rescue! Am I right or have I misunderstood what you told me and what you didn't do?'

'That is your interpretation, Your Excellency . . .'

'It's mine? And what is yours, sir?'

'I'm more interested by the facts of the situation here than by any interpretation.'

'The facts of the situation here!' Luís Bernardo's tone was wearily ironic, of someone hating to state the obvious. 'Do you know what the facts of the situation are? There have been five murders and a revolt that, if it hadn't been checked, might have spread to the other plantations and even to São Tomé. And all this a few days before the arrival of the Prince of Beira and the Minister for the Colonies, whose visit to Príncipe will obviously now be cancelled, because of the climate your negligent inter-pretation of the facts of the situation has generated. Be in no doubt that I hold you personally responsible for this and whatever else might happen!'

A crowd made up of all the whites living on the plantation surrounded them. The atmosphere was clearly hostile to Luís Bernardo. Bloodshot, angry, malaria-weary eyes stared at him, openly contemptuous and angry. The air was charged with repressed violence, a smell of blood about to be spilt, unremitting harshness, exhaustion and frustration long held in abeyance. At a time of confrontation and danger, they might have expected the Governor to be on their side: whites against blacks, Christians against savages, with no thought of law or ethics. But they'd got a jumped-up Lisbon politician, with his glib, demagogic rhetoric, speaking in the name of justice and the state, as if those words meant anything to them, the people who lived there, not in transit, but sentenced to what seemed like permanent hell. And now he was going to deprive them of the fleeting pleasure of the day of festivities to welcome the Prince of Portugal, with the facile declarations of a man who wielded power and humiliated the island governor and the plantation administrator in their presence. They knew they didn't face a situation of eighty armed whites against five hundred mutinous blacks, but something much more dangerous and slippery. The will of a single man, backed by a military force compelled to obey him.

Major Benjamim das Neves seemingly remained aloof and indifferent to the general feeling emanating from the group: nothing in his attitude or gestures betrayed his own opinion or judgement. He placed his men around the workshops and took Captain Dario's under his command, following Luís Bernardo's orders, and now seemed to await fresh instructions from the Governor, which he would obey, whatever they might be.

Luís Bernardo turned round and confronted Engineer Leopoldo.

'Where is the labourer they say headed this revolt? Gabriel is his name, I believe?'

The administrator looked round, shamefacedly, as if his eyes were searching out the black. Luís Bernardo realised he hadn't been expecting that question, and didn't know the Governor had information on that front.

Luís Bernardo insisted,

'Where is he? Is he dead?'

The administrator looked the Governor in the eye, quite fearlessly.

His mouth scowled contemptuously as he replied, 'No, he isn't dead: we're not murderers here. He's merely injured.'

'Injured? Injured, in what way?'

'He was injured in the skirmishes here,' he rasped equally defiantly.

'What skirmishes, Engineer? Isn't it the case that he was taken off to negotiate with you on the morning of the day before yesterday, and that the skirmishes took place in the afternoon when he was in your care? How could he have participated in the skirmishes?'

Engineer Leopoldo was unable to stifle a look of shock. Then he ran his eyes over those standing before him till he came to the Deputy Commissioner on Príncipe, José do Nascimento: there was the informant, the traitor who had given that information to the Governor.

He glared angrily at him, then turned back to confront Luís Bernardo.

'He threw himself upon me when we met. We had to hold him down by force. He is now under arrest.'

Luís Bernardo withstood his gaze and replied surprisingly calmly, 'Then order him to be set free immediately and brought here.'

Engineer Leopoldo didn't budge. He stood legs apart, one hand on his belt, where a revolver was lodged. He spat on the floor and said nothing.

Luís repeated his order, emphasising every word.

'Did you hear what I said? Bring him here immediately or I'll have my troops search the whole plantation till they find him. And start praying that he is still alive.'

Engineer Leopoldo still didn't budge. He was weighing up how far he could possibly resist that iron fist. He looked at Major Benjamim, who was smoking a cigarette and maintaining the same silence and the same impenetrable expression as when he arrived. Luís Bernardo also glanced at the Major: the same thought that had gone through the mind of the administrator of Infante Dom Henrique now occupied his – could he rely on the loyalty and blind obedience of Major Benjamim? From the moment he'd summoned him on São Tomé to accompany him to Príncipe, he'd hung everything on that officer's loyalty and obedience. Instinct told him he could be trusted and there was another factor in his favour: the imminent arrival of the Royal Prince and Minister Ornellas. No person in authority on the islands would dare defy the power of the Governor and welcome rulers from Lisbon in a state of revolt against the man Lisbon had appointed. He might have rebelled in other circumstances, but not now.

Engineer Leopoldo spat at the ground once more. He waved his left hand at two of his men on the periphery of the crowd listening to these exchanges and pointed them in the direction of one of the houses surrounding the square. They nodded and went off. The others waited in silence.

Luís Bernardo sat down on a stone bench set against the Casa Grande, lit a cigarette and savoured his first moment of relaxation that morning. He didn't know when he would have another moment to himself; he couldn't predict when and how this would all finish. He only knew there could be no retreat or compromise.

He'd finished smoking his cigarette, and was crushing it under his boot, when all those present shifted silently, including the soldiers on guard outside the workshops, and he looked up and straightened his back against the wall. Everybody was looking silently at the two foremen the Engineer had sent to fetch the black they considered to be the leader of the revolt. They'd emerged from a lean-to, dragging between them a body that was doubled over like a sack of *matabala*. They marched him into the centre of the group and dropped him on the ground. The black didn't move but sat doubled up over his unshod, swollen feet. His clothes were in tatters, his shirt no more than a bloody rag stuck to his body. Bluish marks from the beating and dried blood covered his legs and back exposed to the sun. Several wounds were still bleeding and the broken tibia showed through the skin on his left leg, a fracture for all to see.

Luís Bernardo walked slowly into the centre of the group as the others reluctantly separated out to let him through. He reached the black, put a cheek near the ground to be level with his shoulders and stretched out a hand to lift up his head that was slumped on his chest. What he saw made him shake with horror: the black's face had been beaten to a pulp. One eye was completely shut, pus ran from between his eyelids, three front teeth had been shattered, his right ear looked as if it had been sliced down the middle by a random blow from a knife, black bruises and dried blood turned the expression on his face into one huge wound and an immense blow had torn the skin under his scalp, from where two streams of blood still trickled down. It was difficult to gauge for how long he had been beaten and if the intention had been to beat him to death or simply let him gradually agonise. Luís Bernardo turned round to look at Engineer Leopoldo, whose face was fixed in the same defiant expression. It was now the turn of Luís Bernardo to spit ostentatiously in his direction.

Then he looked back at the black heap on the ground, and held his face by the chin so they were eye to eye.

'Gabriel . . .'

The other man's face didn't react, and nothing indicated he'd even heard someone call him by name.

'Gabriel, can you hear me? I'm the Governor of São Tomé and Príncipe. I've come to investigate what happened and to make sure justice is done by everyone: blacks and whites alike. You don't need to be afraid because nobody else will hit you and those who did will pay for what they have done. I need to speak to you alone and for you to tell me what happened. Can you hear me? Do you understood what I'm saying?'

A deep silence followed and he showed no signs of reacting. Luís Bernardo thought he must be in a coma or had lost consciousness and that was preventing him from understanding. But suddenly he realised his only open eye was staring at him and that he was nodding imperceptibly, showing he'd understood. Luís Bernardo got up and gave orders to Major Benjamim for two soldiers to carry him to a place where they could talk confidentially.

They lifted him up and carried him to a spot under a tree some twenty metres away from the main group. They leaned him against the tree and offered him water from a small cup he drank with difficulty, helped by one of the soldiers.

Luís Bernardo pulled over a small wooden bench and sat down opposite.

'Gabriel, can you hear me now?'

He nodded very slightly.

'Do you understand what I'm saying?'

Another nod.

'What happened when you were taken off to speak to Engineer Leopoldo?'

Gabriel struggled to speak. His Portuguese was fluent enough but his mouth struggled to shape words. He spoke very slowly and from time to time broke off to have a sip of water, helped by Luís

Bernardo. But he didn't have much to tell: it all began, he explained, when foreman Joaquim Silva, the one most feared and hated by the labourers, violently lashed a worker who was only eleven years old and had left his work under a merciless sun to get a drink of water. The labourers saw what happened, rebelled and went after the foreman, who ran off, only to return with Ferreira Duarte the overseer and five other whites, all armed with revolvers or shotguns. The overseer listened to the labourers' explanations, looked at the whiplashed back of the young boy and threatened them all with something similar if they didn't return to work immediately. That night, all the older blacks met in the compound after dinner and it was decided that the following morning, when they were ordered to break ranks after the headcount and go to work, nobody would move and it was agreed that he Gabriel would ask for the administrator to be summoned, and would tell him they would only return to work if the overseer and foremen Joaquim Silva and Custódio 'Pilão' were removed from their posts. He would also ask for the Commissioner to be summoned from the city so they could inform him of their complaints.

That was what they did the next morning, and when Engineer Leopoldo came into the square, he ordered Gabriel to come to his office and said he was prepared to listen to the labourers' complaints and discuss a solution with him, Gabriel, but not under the threat of a riot. He would only negotiate if Gabriel could persuade the labourers to go back to work, while he negotiated on their behalf. Gabriel went back to talk to his companions, who believed it was a trap, that he shouldn't stay back and that they shouldn't compromise on their demand that the overseer and two foremen be sacked. Finally, he managed to convince them and was himself led back into the administrator's office where they threatened to end the riot by force of arms if necessary. They tried to get him to sign a paper to the effect that the labourers on the plantation had no reason to rebel. He refused and immediately four or five whites, armed with clubs and cudgels, began attacking him in front of Engineer Leopoldo. He tried hopelessly to defend himself, but the battering continued till he lost consciousness. That was all he remembered; subsequently, he knew he'd woken up that morning in an empty, windowless lean-to.

Luís Bernardo listened to his every word without interjecting. Occasionally, he had to wait for him to recover his energy after a sip of water and resume his account, punctuated by moans that weren't complaints, but the manifestation of pure physical pain. Despite his battered and swollen features, his face bore an unmistakable air of pride and intelligence that made it plain why his comrades had chosen him as their spokesman and why the plantation people considered him to be the leader of the revolt. And, in spite of the hideous bruises over his whole body, one could see he was handsome, some twenty-five years old, with a lighter-toned skin than the blacks from Angola, which revealed that his forebears had lived several generations on the island and that there'd perhaps been some mixing of blood with whites or mulattos. He looked like a wounded, panting animal, prostrated at Luís Bernardo's feet. But he wasn't asking for mercy and didn't seem afraid: it was as if he'd accepted his fate, with no recriminations. But Luís Bernardo felt the fate of the wretched labourer on a plantation on Príncipe had become a question of honour for himself on that mission.

'Gabriel, listen to me,' he began, 'I trust you and believe everything you've told me. But you must also trust me. I'm not the same as them and I won't leave you in their hands, because they would kill you as soon as my back was turned. You'll come with me to São Tomé and, given there is no crime they can accuse you of, you'll remain under my protection; if necessary in my own house. I will also take your two companions with me, the ones accused of killing the overseer and the foreman. They are accused of a serious crime and will be tried in São Tomé. Overseer Ferreira Duarte and foreman Silva, whom you wanted removed from post, are dead. "Pilão" is still with us and I will insist the administrator takes him off supervision of labour contingents. In exchange, I want you to accompany me to the building where the labourers have barricaded themselves in and I want you to persuade them to go back to work. What do you say?'

Gabriel looked at him, trying to detect any hint of deceit. He'd rarely known a white keep a promise made to a black. God hadn't made the world for whites to take pity on blacks and recognise they had any rights.

'I don't know . . .'

'What don't you know?'

'I don't know if I can trust you.'

'You have no alternative but to trust me. If I leave you and your two companions accused of murdering the overseer here, you'll be dead by the end of the day. And if I take the troops I brought from São Tomé with me without resolving this situation, the whites on the plantations and soldiers on Príncipe will set the workshops on fire and, when your companions run out, they will be shot to pieces. Those who survive will have to agree to be whiplashed back to work.'

'I don't know if they will trust you.'

'Perhaps not, but they do trust you. If you go and tell them you've agreed this with me, they'll trust you. But first you must trust me. Listen to me hard, Gabriel: it is as much as I can do for you and your people!'

Before Gabriel could reply, they heard two horses trot round the corner of the Casa Grande and ride into the plantation's main square. The whites immediately stopped talking and stared at the newcomers, one black, one white, riding on their respective steeds. Luís Bernardo also looked their way and the profile of the white man seemed familiar from a distance. When he stopped, dismounted and gave the reins to the black, fear ran through Luís Bernardo, who trembled when he recognised the figure of David Jameson, jumping off his horse as if he'd just joined a friendly social get-together.

Luís Bernardo leapt to his feet and ran over to him.

'What are you doing here, David?'

'Well, the same as you, I expect . . .'

'No, I am here as Governor, carrying out my duties.'

'And I'm here to carry out mine. Or have you forgotten that visiting plantations is part of my duties you should be facilitating?'

Luís Bernardo was too tense and too tired to take any pleasure from his friend's unsubtle irony.

'David, don't tell me, you've just happened to drop by on a routine visit?'

'No, I wouldn't say that. I don't like being hypocritical, particularly with friends. Obviously I'm not here by chance. I heard rumours the day before yesterday that something serious was stirring here and came over yesterday on the normal sailing made by the *Mindelo*. I tried to see the Deputy Governor but he'd already left, and yesterday I couldn't find anyone to guide me here. Foolishly, I slept in too much this morning and, when I woke up, I discovered you'd arrived, had requisitioned the boat and landed with a small army, and that you'd all come here. I had to shell out a few pounds to hire these horses and this guide to bring me here. And that's the truth of the matter.'

Luís Bernardo had to admire his friend's instincts and at the same time he felt constrained by the situation. Nevertheless, the British Consul had read the signs more quickly than he had and managed to get to where it was all happening before the Governor himself! How?'

'How did you find out, David?'

David Jameson looked down, like a child wanting to keep a secret.

'Oh, Luís, I can't tell you. It's all part of doing my duty. Or do you think I only came to São Tomé for the social life?'

Luís Bernardo sighed softly.

'*Chapeau*, David! But that's as far as your perseverance and initiative will get you. I'm sorry, but I must now insist you go back to the city, and then take the same boat as me back to São Tomé.'

'Is that an order, Luís?'

'Yes, it's an order from the Governor.'

'You don't have the power to do this, Luís!'

'Yes, I do, David, you know I do. This is an internal matter for the government of the colony and I have the right to forbid the eyes of strangers to see anything – note how I said strangers and not foreigners.'

'I believe this to be a decision determined by *force majeure* and not guided by law . . .'

'David, think what you like. I won't allow you to stay here and I know you'd do the same if you were in my place.'

'How can you know, Luís?'

'I know you'd do the same in my place.'

'It's not true: when I held a post similar to yours – one, do forgive me, that was immeasurably more important, in fact – I never compromised in matters of law . . . even when it would have favoured me.'

Luís Bernardo looked at his friend: he still believed something had changed between them and that something stemmed from his friend. Or perhaps he was doing him an injustice.

'We can debate this at another time – as friends or whatever. But, forgive me, David, I must insist you leave now. I have more urgent matters to see to.'

'It's a great pity, Luís. Not wanting witnesses is always a bad sign. The way you deal with this situation is important for my report. Once you send me away, I'll have no choice but to think you're seriously compromising yourself over crucial issues.'

Luís Bernardo didn't hear what his friend said, or at least pretended not to. Once more he was being guided by instinct. During his entire conversation with David he had been conscious that the group of whites was following the dialogue sufficiently near by to hear what they said. They were waiting to see how he managed this sudden interference by the Englishman.

He turned round to Major Benjamim and raised his voice so everyone would hear.

'Major, be so good as to select two men from the local contingent to escort His Honour the British Consul and his companion back to the city. Once they've arrived, you should ensure he doesn't leave the city till you receive fresh orders from me.'

David remounted, lifted his hat in farewell to those gathered there and cantered off, his guide by his side, followed by two soldiers on horseback, who caught them up just as they were leaving the plantation.

After they'd disappeared, Luís Bernardo walked determinedly towards Gabriel, who was still sitting in the shadow of the tree, keeping out of the sun blazing high above.

'Well then?' he asked, suddenly wanting to get it all over. 'Will you or won't you come with me?'

'Let's go,' replied Gabriel, struggling to his feet.

Luís Bernardo ordered a walking stick be brought and insisted Gabriel lean on his shoulder for additional support. And that was how the leader of the revolt tottered precariously into the workshops, leaning on the Governor's shoulder, where five hundred pairs of white eyes set in black bodies against a backcloth of semi-darkness welcomed them full of silent expectation.

The stench was dreadful, the stench of sweat and excrement the rarefied air wouldn't ventilate. Coming from the harsh light of midday into that darkness, Luís Bernardo could make nothing out at first, except for a black mass bubbling slowly up like larva inside a volcano. It was a dark, shapeless mass of bodies undulating slowly and breathing heavily. Gabriel quickly imposed silence on the growing chatter prompted by his arrival. He started talking to them in a Creole dialect that was incomprehensible to Luís Bernardo, and he only understood a very few words: Governor, São Tomé, and the names of the dead overseer and foreman. Afterwards, Gabriel responded to several voices that spoke from the depths of the crowd; there were angry exchanges, discussions conducted in strange, syncopated rhythms, as if they were being sung. Then a deep silence descended and Gabriel spoke once more. He spoke very slowly and softly, as if talking to children. When he finished, another silence descended and then an old man spoke, his beard glinting in the dark, and two young blacks set themselves apart from the indistinct mass of sweaty bodies and walked to the front, near to Gabriel. Luís Bernardo thought for a moment the whole dark crowd might get up and step forward crushing him against the wall of the shed. He panicked for an instant from pure fear, realising the extent to which he was defenceless in the face of that array of sweaty bodies seething with a rage as ancient as it was repressed. Sweat also ran down his body, soaked his hair and glued his clothes to his skin. His heart was beating loudly and he breathed in short, rapid bursts: he didn't want anyone to see him like that.

He felt Gabriel tap him on the shoulder.

'Well?'

'These two killed the overseer and foreman. They have agreed to give themselves up to you and be tried in São Tomé. Order your soldiers to withdraw now and, if "Pilão" is removed from the area of work, everybody will return home to their huts and will be there for the headcount tomorrow before going to the plantations.'

Luís Bernardo took a few moments to regain his composure. He wiped the sweat from his face with his shirt that was already sopping wet, ran his fingers through his hair, took a deep breath and walked outside.

He conferred with the administrator, the Deputy Governor António Vieira, the Deputy Commissioner José do Nascimento, Major Benjamim and Captain Dario in the administrative offices of the Infante Dom Henrique plantation. They were all standing up and all eyes stared at him as they waited for him to pronounce. Luís Bernardo was still sweating, his nostrils still filled with the stench of fear and tragedy. His eyes came to rest on a ridiculous calendar on the wall that had come to a stop in March of the previous year and which displayed a snow-covered Alpine landscape and a couple skiing, hand in hand, down the mountainside, above the legend 'Saint Moritz, season for winter sports'. He didn't know whether to laugh or cry. He wanted to forget all that, run away to the snow and the cold, light a fire in the hearth and, lulled by its heat, eternally make love to Ann.

'Engineer, the agreement I have reached with your labourers is as follows: I will take Gabriel with me, and he is accused of no crime, rather the contrary, and I will also take the two blacks accused of killing your overseer and foreman, who will be held and tried on São Tomé. The other foreman of yours, the one they accuse of a fondness for the whip – "Pilão" – must be transferred from the area of work to other duties. On your part, there must be no punishments, no reprisals or settling of accounts of any kind. In exchange, they will return to work tomorrow morning and all will continue as before. The military detail will leave now with me, and the Deputy Commissioner here present will prepare a report – for me, for the Deputy Governor António Vieira and for the Ministry – on everything that has happened here, the causes, those responsible and the measures to be taken so that situations of this kind never occur again here or on any other plantation. We either seize the moment or leave: do I have your agreement and word of honour that you will do what has to be done?'

Engineer Leopoldo had followed each movement and attitude struck by the Governor with the same mute rage he'd felt in the morning. He watched him enter the workshops full of rebellious blacks with an admiration he couldn't hide, but at the same time he hoped he'd be given the lesson of a lifetime. And now he'd seen him emerge with a solution that defused all the violence and merely demanded he remove one of his foremen from his post. He found this infuriating and it was even more difficult to acquiesce before the Governor's triumph.

His rage led him to miscalculate and think he could issue a final defiant challenge.

'I can't just accept this. As you know, Your Excellency, this is a private estate and I don't give the orders. They come from my boss in Lisbon. I must consult him.'

Luís Bernardo almost took pity on him. He had opened the path to his own humiliation, and it came quickly.

'You mean your boss in Lisbon, the Count of Burnay? I know your boss very well and you've just given me an idea. I should write directly to him and tell him what's happened. I wonder what he will think if I tell him that, because of the mistreatment suffered by the labourers on his plantation, a revolt erupted that caused the deaths of five people, including the overseer. That this led to the intervention of the local garrison, and the Deputy Governor of Príncipe had to send a telegram to Lisbon asking for a navy man-of-war to be dispatched immediately. The Governor of São Tomé was obliged to rush here and it meant the cancellation of the visit by the Prince of Beira and the Minister for the Colonies to the Island of Príncipe. Of course, all this can be published in the Lisbon newspapers, at a juncture when Portugal is looking to convince the whole world, and Britain in particular (whose consul also put in an appearance) that we treat our plantation labourers like ordinary Portuguese citizens! How do you think your boss would greet this news?'

As Luís Bernardo spoke, Engineer Leopoldo's face went from pink to white and from white to livid. When Luís Bernardo stopped talking, he wasn't at all inclined to continue the confrontation. The Count of Burnay was the richest man in Portugal and owned the Infante Dom Henrique plantation with the same indifference that he owned so many other things he sometimes didn't even remember he owned: banks, mines, vineyards in the Douro, estates in Angola, palaces in Lisbon, art collections and, above all, the negotiation of almost the entire loan from international banks to the Portuguese state and the monopoly of tobacco sales throughout the country. As Rafael Bordalo Pinheiro had written, his motto was; 'Buy, sell, exchange, lend. Propose, dispose, impose. Credit, sell it, profit.' Dom Carlos made him a count – out of gratitude for the constant loans he made to the Royal Household – but he was the true symbol of the mercantile bourgeoisie, hated by the old aristocracy. The Count had everything except for two things he couldn't control and which he wanted more than anything else: the respect of the press and the support of public opinion. Luís Bernardo had touched a raw nerve and concluded by demanding the other man's outright surrender.

'So how should we leave it, Engineer? Do I have your word of honour, before these four witnesses, that you will abide by what I have suggested, or do you prefer to wait on the views of your boss?'

'You have my word. But listen to me, Your Excellency: you've not been long here on São Tomé. You are but a wretched blackmailer, a jumped-up Lisbon intellectual, only too sure you are more intelligent, wiser and more of a gentleman than most. I have seen others like you fall from much greater heights.'

Luís Bernardo didn't respond. It was all over. He felt calm and relieved. He only wanted to go home, see Ann again and lose himself in her body.

'Major, Captain, sirs: rally your soldiers and we will leave immediately. Get the two prisoners and find a stretcher for Gabriel. Deputy Governor and Commissioner, you will stay here to ensure the agreement is kept and will start collecting statements from witnesses for your reports. I expect to receive them by telegram within three days at most.'

It was less than twelve hours since the Governor and his small military force had landed on the island of Príncipe and the *Mindelo* was already setting off on its return voyage to São Tomé, carrying the men it had brought, plus the two prisoners from the Infante Dom Henrique plantation, Gabriel – who received some rapid medical treatment from the doctor in Santo António – and David Jameson, whom Luís Bernardo summoned from the only lodging house in the town, where he'd been accommodated. They left in the light of day, but, as is usual in the tropics, night fell quickly. Luís Bernardo made a space for himself astern, in the small steam-packet that had now exceeded its capacity. He had drifted into a physical torpor, releasing all the tension experienced over the last twelve hours. He felt relief at the way things had turned out and confident he had acted in the best possible manner. He was smoking a cigar and enjoying victory. Only one thing distressed him: he couldn't run to Ann's arms when they arrived, to tell her all and then forget everything in the softness of her skin. That privilege was reserved for David – whether he exercised it or not. He was suddenly overcome by feelings of grief, jealousy and above all a sense of powerlessness.

He looked at David, who was smoking a cigarette on the bridge and conversing amiably with the Captain in his erratic Portuguese. He really admired David in that respect: he was a man who seemed to adapt to any circumstance, wherever he found himself. He'd never heard him complain about exile in São Tomé or about fate taking him from his glorious career in the British Raj to the most obscure posting the British colonial administration could offer. What did occasionally surface was that David found it difficult to accept that the cataclysm in his life had also fallen on Ann and he deeply regretted it. But, apart from that remorse and grief, David was essentially an optimist who managed to find profit everywhere and who considered nothing a waste of time. In fact, everything seemed to interest him, even in São Tomé, where so little was of interest. He had only been there a just over a year, and already knew everything about the cultivation of cocoa, the government of the islands – even the budget available to Luís Bernardo – the geography of the islands, the mountains, rivers, bays, predominant winds and beasts of the jungle. At that precise moment, he was discussing the currents between São Tomé and Príncipe with the *Mindelo*'s Captain, and even sneaked a look at the engine under the bridge. Luís Bernardo was quite sure that he now had all the information necessary to steer the boat back to São Tomé.

The two men hadn't exchanged a word on board. David had slipped on to the bridge to talk to the Captain and Luís Bernardo had settled down astern to enjoy his favourite pastime, namely the contemplation of the stars in the sky while he smoked a *Partagas*. Exhaustion from the events of that day and the previous sleepless night had taken their toll and he soon stretched out his legs and rested his head on coils of rope to get some sleep.

'Sleeping after mission successful?'

Luís Bernardo sat up. In the dark he couldn't make out whether David's expression was ironic or not.

'Luís, I wanted to tell you that I don't harbour any resentment. Here, between ourselves, I can acknowledge you were right to do what you did: I would have sent you packing if I'd been in your place. Consequently, I shouldn't have said what I said about not wanting eyewitnesses.'

'No hard feelings, David . . .'

'Seriously, Luís, I think you did what you had to do and I've no criticism of the way you acted.'

'But this won't soften the tone of the report you'll send to London . . .'

'Perhaps. I will write what I genuinely think: that there are still many people here who don't consider slave labour or the rule of the lash to be things of the past. But also that São Tomé has a governor who doesn't go along with these ideas and who, unless the contrary is proven, represents and has the support of his government.'

Luís Bernardo sighed. It was the kind of conversation they used to have some time ago. Each from their respective positions, separated by their missions, but united by the same ideas and by the personal affection they felt for each other.

'You know, David, neither of us knows how all this will end. Whether I'll have my way or they will have theirs.'

'Or what position your government will adopt at the vital moment . . .' David added as Luís Bernardo retreated into himself.

'Luís, there's one thing I can tell you,' David continued, 'the situation must be resolved soon. I've been informed that in six months, in November or December, a key meeting is to be held in Lisbon of British cocoa importers and owners of plantations on São Tomé. The British will decide there and then whether to impose a boycott or not on produce from São Tomé.'

Luís Bernardo looked ahead into pitch blackness.

'I suppose your report will be decisive in shaping the attitude of the importers, so it means I have less than six months to convince you I'm going to win the wager?'

David smiled and it was now his turn to stay silent. He took a cigarette from the silver case he always carried with him, handed it to Luís Bernardo and lit one for himself. They smoked in silence and then Luís Bernardo declared he was going to try to sleep.

But David still had things to say.

'Luís, I was thinking about that black, who'd been half beaten to death, the one you rescued from the claws of those savages. What's his name?'

'Gabriel.'

'Gabriel. You know, what are you going to do with him?'

'To tell you the truth, I hadn't given it much thought. If I can't think of any better idea before we land, I'll take him home and then decide.'

'Luís, you can't do that! You can't take the leader of a plantation rebellion to your house, even though he's not accused of any crime. It would mean, in the eyes of everyone, that the Governor had openly taken sides and that would totally undermine your position, on the eve of the Minister's visit.'

'You're right, but what's the alternative?'

'That's where friends can be of help: I'll take him to our place. They can say that I'm the one protecting the rebellious labourer. It won't make me any better or any worse in their eyes. Send him along and he can join my staff: I'll find him something useful to do, even if it's only to accompany Ann when she goes out for a ride. I sometimes worry when she rides around the island by herself.'

'David, I'm very grateful to you.'

'No need to be; it doesn't cost me anything. And, as I said, I'll feel much happier if Ann has an escort.'

Luís Bernardo pondered his friend's last remark. He hesitated for a moment, then decided to ask him a question, the answer to which he both imagined and feared.

'David, can I ask you a personal question?'

'Of course.'

'Could you tolerate life here without Ann?'

David didn't reply immediately, as if weighing his words carefully.

'It's difficult to say . . . life has shown me that our ability to resist and suffer is always greater that we suppose. Yes, I think if absolutely necessary I could tolerate life on São Tomé by myself, as you yourself do. What I couldn't have survived would have been her abandoning me after India. If she'd left me then, I wouldn't have endured it.'

'And if she left you now?'

'It wouldn't make any sense for her to leave me now. But if she did I would pursue her. To the end of the world. Why do you ask?'

'No reason in particular. It's what I expected you would say.'

Luís Bernardo turned round to go to sleep. Before closing his eyes, he looked back at the stars in the sky. They were pointing the way home.

16

THE ROYAL VISIT to São Tomé was arranged with the precision of a military operation. Luís Bernardo discovered he had a talent for organising popular festivals and events, and spared no effort to that end. But he was also annoyed that the achievements of his eighteen months of governance on São Tomé would largely be endorsed by the Minister according to his success in staging these festivities. He managed to mobilise the enthusiasm of the Mayor – with whom he had always had good, if formal relations – and, with his support, they sparked off a kind of collective rivalry among the traders, inhabitants of the city and population in general. Stores such as Casa Vista Alegre, Casa Braga & Irmão, Casa Lima & Gama or the Elite Brewery tried to outdo each other in terms of decorating their respective façades. In the city's main streets – Matheus Sampaio, the Conde de Valle Flor, Alberto Garrido or General Cisneiros – Town Hall and local tenants combined forces, money and labour to create a fairy-tale décor that included a triumphal arch at the entrance, adorned with the royal coat of arms and a profusion of flagpoles, balloons, drapes and arches mounted together and garlanded with flowers from one corner to another. The streets had been levelled, cleaned and lined with flower borders the morning the Prince arrived. However, lack of funds left the façades of public buildings less spruced up, starting with the incredibly ugly Sé Cathedral where the Prince would begin his visit.

The *África* arrived, as scheduled, on the morning of 13 July, and the transfer to land was completed in the packet's rowing boats, with Dom Luís Felipe acting as helmsman in his. From the day when King Dom João VI had fled to Brazil a hundred years ago with his entire court to escape the invading French army led by Junot, no member of the Royal Family had ever set foot on Portuguese territory overseas, with the sole exception of a short journey made by Dom Luís, as a child from nearby Madeira to distant Timor.

The heir to the throne of the Braganzas landed on the jetties of São Tomé dressed in the so-called 'colonial uniform' of the navy – white shoes and trousers, white jacket with gilt buttons and epaulettes and a white kepi. Dom Luís Felipe had recently celebrated his twentieth birthday, but had the face of a seventeen-year-old, his Northern European blood evident in his blue eyes and fair hair. He landed with a smile and an eager interest in everything around him in line with his reputation and character. According to previously agreed protocol, the Prince was welcomed on the jetties by Minister Ayres d'Ornellas and his small party, Luís Bernardo, the Mayor and those who would be the Prince's hosts on the plantations he was going to visit – the Count of Valle Flor, who'd arrived on his own boat the night before, directly from Le Havre, and Mr Henrique Mendonça, who'd arrived the previous week.

The group walked to the cathedral, flanked by the crowds, cordoned off by army and police as they shouted, 'Long live the Prince! Long live the King!' Monsignor Atalaia celebrated with a *Te Deum* in the Cathedral, and gave thanks to God and the peaceful sea that had brought His Royal Highness. It was a short ceremony that the ladies of the colony appeared to find very moving, as they sniffed and wiped away tears with their hand-kerchiefs. When the retinue left, they mounted six flower-bedecked carriages, their horses' harnesses glinting in the sun, and headed towards the Governor's Palace slowly and with difficulty through the crowds, escorted by a contingent of local cavalry that opened and closed the procession, under the personal command of Major Benjamim das Neves.

The servants and all the staff in the Government Secretariat were lined up in the Palace gardens dressed in their Sunday best. Dom Luís Filipe nodded in their direction and acknowledged their shouts of 'Long live the Prince!' with a wave of the hand. Sebastião waited by the entrance in his white, gilt-buttoned uniform that was curiously similar to the Prince's, except for the absence of rows of medals. Luís Bernardo made a point of introducing him personally and Dom Luís Filipe smiled when he heard the name Sebastião Luís de Mascarenhas e Menezes. He held out a hand and shook the white-gloved hand of that black-skinned nobleman. Tears streamed from Sebastião's eyes. 'What a strange thing monarchy is!' the Governor thought, as he followed the Prince of Beira into the house.

Drinks were served in the garden and everybody relaxed for half an hour, sitting informally on the chairs set out there. Dom Luís Filipe had inherited from his father a captivatingly open manner and curiosity about the natural environment. He asked Luís Bernardo the names of the trees, the fish that could be fished, and the animals that could be hunted on the island. The Prince was welcomed one by one by the great and good on those islands: forty men paraded through, representing military and legal spheres, government functionaries and merchants. Nobody could complain of being discriminated against by the Governor, whether in this welcoming ceremony or at the official banquet that evening.

After the round of welcomes, and after the Prince had gone up to his rooms to change, the Prince, Minister, Governor and Dom Luís Filipe's adjutant had a private repast. Sebastião served an excellent light lunch of warm lobster salad and *poulet au citron* that Luís Bernardo had demanded of his chefs, to the protests of Mamoun and Sinhá, who would never contemplate fewer than than six or seven courses for a Prince. Dom Luís Filipe continued to initiate most conversations, and displayed an indefatigable curiosity about everything related to the island.

Ayres d'Ornellas, known to Luís Bernardo only by name and from the three or four telegrams he'd received from him since he'd been appointed Minister, said little and seemed to be weighing up the Governor with his small beady eyes. He was a veteran of Mouzinho's campaigns and had already allocated two of his previous companions-in-arms to the governorships of Angola and Mozambique. He had inherited Luís Bernardo from the previous minister, mainly as a result of the personal designation of the King. But he was well informed about Luís Bernardo from the few faint echoes of praise that had reached him from the colony and the considerable criticism and hatred he appeared to have aroused locally. However, as a man of some intelligence, he wanted first to get to know Bernardo personally, before fully accepting what seemed to him to be well-founded criticisms published by some Lisbon newspapers 'of the erratic policies that seemed to have no purpose and to be of no apparent benefit to Portugal' pursued by the Governor of São Tomé. When he joined in the conversation, the Minister referred only to small details about the governance of the colony, and seemed deliberately to sidestep sensitive questions of a political nature. Or else he was waiting for Luís Bernardo to raise those issues.

In turn, Luís Bernardo was also hesitant and uncertain about the approach he should take. When he returned from Príncipe five days earlier after quelling the local rebellion, he sent the Minister on board the *África* a telegram updating him on the difficult situation and, at the same time, advising him against sending the gun boat the Governor of Príncipe had requested, and against continuing with the royal visit to that island, after the entourage left São Tomé. The Minister had sent his response cancelling the visit to Príncipe, and asked that every effort be made to ensure the matter didn't enter the public domain on São Tomé. And now Luís Bernardo didn't know whether he should wait or whether he should take the initiative and raise the issue.

The young Prince interrupted his flow of thoughts.

'You cannot imagine what pleasure it gives me to be here! What it means to me, my father and, I believe, to the whole country, to be here representing them in this outpost of Portugal that is so remote and different, but which is, from what I've seen, so very Portuguese!'

'I am very aware of this, because I know the views of your father concerning the importance of the colonies, which I am sure Your Highness shares. This is a historic day for São Tomé and for Portugal – we are all most conscious of this.'

'Governor, you know what high esteem my father holds you in. He spoke to me about you before I left, and of how difficult, delicate and important for our interests was the mission you have been charged with. We all hope and trust you will carry it through successfully, that you are the right man for the job. Don't you agree, Minister?'

Ayres d'Ornellas seemed to have been caught off guard but reacted quickly.

'I am sure that is so. We all expect Governor Valença to bring the boat safely into harbour.' He paused deliberately. 'With tact, common sense and carefully weighing up all the interests in play.'

He looked at Luís Bernardo, who blushed slightly and nodded in agreement.

'But we will speak of these matters later,' the Minister continued, completely master of the situation. 'The Governor and I have to find the time, during the programme of the visit, to have a conversation about work.'

'Very good, now let us go into the streets and meet the people. They must be keen for us to finish lunch!' Dom Luís Filipe concluded jovially, getting up from the table, followed by everyone else.

The city had come out in force to greet the Prince of Beira on its streets. Dom Luís Filipe and his retinue got out of their carriage and walked amid the throng. Accompanied by the Mayor, who was preening himself with pride and emotion, they slowly strolled along the streets that had been garlanded with so much expenditure of time and money by the Town Hall. The Prince halted to greet people, to respond to someone welcoming him, to speak to shopkeepers in the doorways to their livelihood. After two hours of promenading through the streets, Dom Luís Filipe visited the Town Hall, where he drank a glass of port and received the keys to the city from the Mayor, signed the Book of Honour and listened to a brief, confused speech of welcome from the aedile. He then wanted to visit the open-air market, where he bought several items of local handicraft, before the retinue took to their carriages once more to visit the Fortress of Saint Sebastian overlooking the Bay of Ana Chaves.

At around six o'clock, the Prince and his adjutant and aide-de-camp returned to the Governor's Palace to rest, take a bath and get dressed for dinner, while the others, including Minister Ayres d'Ornellas, went back to the *África*, where they would spend the night.

Luís Bernardo took advantage of the two-hour gap in the official programme to check on the preparations for the banquet that would take place in the ballroom. On this occasion he had decided to hold a banquet without a ball for two hundred people, practically the whole white community on the island and half a dozen blacks. All the local figures of authority had been invited from both islands, all plantation administrators, the main businessmen, army and police officers, bishop and priests, doctors, magistrates, public works engineers, in a word, everybody who was anybody in that remote piece of Portugal.

The Prince and Luís Bernardo headed top table at respective ends. There were just two women seated at the table, namely the Mayor's wife and the English Consul's wife. Following protocol Dom Luís Filipe was to the right of the Mayor's wife and to the left of the British Consul. Luís Bernardo was to the right of Ann and to the left of Ayres d'Ornellas. The Count of Valle Flor was on Ann's right and Mr Henrique Mendonça sandwiched the Mayor's wife between himself and the Prince. The Bishop, the Judge and the rest of the Lisbon contingent made up the table together with the Count of Souza Faro, administrator in residence of the Água Izé plantation. Dom Luís Filipe was the focus of attention for everyone, but it was Ann who attracted all the male looks, especially those of the young officers in the royal entourage. She was resplendent in a thin white silk dress, shoulders and arms naked, with an astonishingly low neckline where a blue-sapphire pendant glinted on a gold chain. Blonde curls cascaded down her shoulders and the modest parting above her eyebrows heightened the glow in her eyes. Everyone, Luís Bernardo included, was spellbound by her presence and beauty. The Count of Valle Flor swore you wouldn't find in Paris, from where he'd sailed the day before in his private yacht, a woman as well dressed as she. All the eyes were on their table: first, the Prince was observed out of eager curiosity, then it was Ann's turn to be stared at. All the ladies present, exiled from high society and its subtle demands, had spent time and money, had suffered endlessly planning their attire for that evening. They had thought to find in the Casa Parisina, or on rua Matheus Sampaio, their solution – the latest models, fabrics in fashion, styles of the moment from distant Europe. And suddenly there was Ann, in her dress with its white silk straps, her bare back and shoulders, the blue-sapphire pendant in a swooping neckline. It was enough to cast all their artifice to the wind. Because no artifice can resist the challenge of a pair of firm shoulders, the gentle allure of a straight back and an exuberant, ample bosom.

Ayres d'Ornellas, seated opposite her, was the single exception. He appeared to observe her, but not with the eyes of a slavering male.

Meanwhile, the Count of Valle Flor was trying to satisfy his curiosity about Ann. How did she, he asked, someone evidently out of place in that neck of the woods, fill her days of exile in such a remote spot, where there weren't even four hands to play a round of bridge.

'My dear Count,' Ann replied, disarming him with the sweetest of smiles, 'I've never lived in Europe, only in India. I learned that one must adapt to circumstances and that wherever you are there's always something of interest. People make places and not the other way round.'

'Ah, Ornellas, what can one say to such a response? When beauty unites with intelligence, what can we mere mortals do, but breathe in the passing scent?'

Ornellas pondered the question with all the seriousness required by a matter of state.

'All *I* can say, Count, is that Britain asked permission to have a resident consul here, but didn't inform us he would be accompanied by a lady of such beauty and intellect.'

'If they had, the government would have raised no objections, I suppose?' The Count continued laughing, though now rather strangely.

The Minister continued as seriously as ever.

'I think not: we could not have foreseen the danger.'

Luís Bernardo felt his body go into a cold sweat, all the more so now it was time for toasts and, following the protocol for the evening, time for his speech welcoming the Prince. He'd rehearsed it, but had decided to speak without notes. After dispensing with formalities, he reaffirmed the fact that Prince Luís Filipe was representing his father, the King, whose political views on the African colonies he Luís Bernardo knew, shared and tried to put into practice. It was the political heart of his speech, and despite the need to remain ambiguous, he looked round at the Prince, the Minister and the gathering of dignitaries from the colony, as he came to the nub of the question.

'I hope and trust that throughout this tour, and not just here in São Tomé and Príncipe, Your Royal Highness and Your Excellency the Minister understand how all the Portuguese residing in these African colonies make efforts that many would find unimaginable. Scraping a subsistence in very harsh conditions, they are very conscious that by living thus they also serve Portugal. They are the heirs and continuers of that huge labour of discovery, defence and settling of territories by our ancestors. But today, at the dawn of the twentieth century, in an era of such wonders as the telephone, electric light and automobile (wonders that have yet to reach here) empires can no longer justify themselves by the rights given by the act of discovery but must do so by the effort to civilise, and not by sword and gunpower, but by reason and justice. But I am sure, as is Your Highness, quite rightly, that nobody can lecture us in this respect. I am sure that, despite differences in questions of strategy or other matters, here, for example, in your colony of São Tomé and Príncipe, everybody – from the humblest civil servant to the Governor – is aware that his main task is to defend the interests of Portugal, in the light of what is accepted as international law and recognised by civilised nations.'

After the toasts and national anthem, when they all got up from the table, Ornellas gripped Luís Bernardo by the arm briefly and, though Luís Bernardo was unable to tell whether he was being ironic or sincere, commented in hushed tones, 'A fine speech! It's inevitable, my friend, after this, if you so wish, that a political career will await you in Lisbon!'

The Prince didn't let on whether he'd interpreted, for better or worse, the coded messages in his speech.

Ann took advantage of the confusion as everyone got up to hold his hand tightly for a few moments, before David came over to him and surreptitiously whispered in his ear, 'I don't think what you said was much appreciated by the half of those present who understood what you meant. As for your Prince, I still don't know whether anyone has told him what all this is about . . .'

The guests now scattered through the garden in small groups, chatting animatedly until about ten o'clock. Then the Prince, followed by everyone else, climbed into the awaiting carriages and visited the city's night-time illuminations that had cost the city purse and the Governor General's budget so much effort and money. But it hadn't been in vain: from the bay, where hundreds of boats, from canoes to coast-cutters, bobbed up and down all lit up, to the jetties of the Customs House and all the main squares and streets of the city, illuminations, the like of which had never been seen before in the whole of Equatorial Africa, welcomed Prince Dom Luís Filipe. A sea of coconut-shell lights, barrels of burning oil or bonfires improvised on street corners turned São Tomé into an illuminated raft floating between heaven and ocean. Dom Luís Filipe decided to go down and walk among the crowd, who were euphoric in their welcome, and the police struggled to open a path for the royal entourage.

Ayres d'Ornellas was now clearly delighted and turned round, grabbed Luís Bernardo by the arm and exclaimed, 'Congratulations, my dear fellow! You and the Mayor are to be congratulated!'

It was long after midnight by the time Luís Bernardo could accompany the Prince and two officers in his retinue back to the Governor's Palace. Luís Bernardo was still up at three, getting the house ready, sorting out breakfast and the logistics for the royal visit to the plantations that would take place the following day. He slept little more than two hours and was up again and dressed at six, supervising arrangements once more.

The second day of the visit by the Prince and the Minister for the Colonies began with an excursion to the Boa Entrada plantation, situated to the north of the city, next to the village of Santo Amaro. They travelled with difficulty the short distance to the plantation, along the coast around the bay and Lizard Beach, in carriages and on horseback, a contingent of some thirty people, greeted by an enthusiastic populace that lined the path. The choice had been carefully made: Boa Entrada, the property of Henrique Mendonça, who was waiting for his visitors by the entrance to his plantation, could be seen almost as exemplary in the way it was managed and the way he treated his workers. Henrique Mendonça, who'd come to São Tomé some twenty years earlier as a customs officer, married the woman who owned the plantation and rapidly made it prosper, making him one of the richest men in Lisbon. Although his wealth was as visible as the

Count of Valle Flor's he was more cultured and was the first plantation owner to show any social concern for his labourers. He had a hospital built for them that was exclusive to the plantation, and built them whitewashed, thatched brick houses. The plantation was one thousand seven hundred hectares in area, and cultivated coffee, cocoa and rubber as well as extensive plantings of bananas, coconuts, avocados, jack and mango. The visit lasted more than three hours, with the ever enthusiastic, endlessly curious Prince Dom Luís Filipe dragging his retinue behind him at a swift pace. Henrique Mendonça had erected a huge canopy of palm fronds over the main square and it was there in the shade and open air that lunch was served for sixty people. At the request of the Prince, a generous selection of São Tomé fish was served, washed down by an excellent white wine from Colares that he'd brought from Lisbon.

Luís Bernardo sat next to the Minister who discreetly asked him various questions about the state of the plantations, the relations between local government and administrators, the situation on Príncipe and the prospects for renewing contracts with the labourers, something that, according to the 1903 Agreement, should start at the beginning of the following year.

'This is the great test of our colonisation and we must not fail!' commented the Minister.

At another juncture, Ayres d'Ornellas asked him how many plantations were like Boa Entrada, in terms of social concern for their labourers, to which Luís Bernardo responded frankly, saying it was the best, if not the only one where the management could be deemed acceptable in that regard. The Minister looked at him askance but said nothing.

After lunch, they remounted carriages and horses and travelled further north, to Rio do Ouro, the jewel in the crown of the properties on São Tomé owned by the Count of Valle Flor. Rio do Ouro covered a total area of seventeen kilometres from Monte Macaco to the Beach of Fernão Dias. The four plantations of the Valle Flor domain on São Tomé employed more than five thousand labourers, making this man, who had landed on the island as a humble shop assistant, with a number of lucky breaks, the colony's principal owner of land and labour.

After visiting several buildings on the plantation and some of the cocoa groves, the Count offered the royal contingent, according to a later report in the *Ilustração Portuguesa*, 'a noble repast, to be sure, like the man's mind, and dazzling, as one would expect from his huge fortune'. In fact, it was just as had been reported. The Count served, whole on the spit, pigs, lobsters, huge prawns, groupers, turtles and shark followed by desserts made from coconut, mango, papaya, banana, pineapple and even chocolate. There was French champagne on the tables, white wine from Palmela and red from Cova da Beira, vintage Quinta do Vesúvio port and genuine Havana cigars brought straight from Paris. The two thousand labourers on the plantation sat by bonfires on the main square surrounded by the reception rooms in the Casa Grande where the banquet was being served, and also ate well, though not quite the same menu. Finally, the order went up for a fireworks display that could be seen from the Bay of Ana Chaves and the city itself, which left all present, particularly the blacks, half dazzled and half frightened.

Luís Bernardo was impressed as much as anyone and couldn't help comparing his modest reception the day before with the conspicuous luxury of the Rio do Ouro dinner. It was the difference, he reflected ironically, between the state coffers of the colony and the private coffers of the Count. Nor could he prevent himself from thinking that the two wretched labourers from Rio do Ouro, who he'd the occasion to defend in court, must be seated somewhere thereabouts, won over temporarily by the substantially improved food on offer and by the fireworks the Count had offered them as entertainment, in sharp contrast to the daily grind they suffered under Colonel Maltez.

During the toasts, the Prince got to his feet and gave thanks for the day's hospitality, to Henrique Mendonça, and the Count of Valle Flor.

He declared, 'I have often been proud to be Portuguese, but never more so than now when I see the fruits of Portuguese colonisation.'

He was given a standing ovation, with lots of 'Long live the Prince!', 'The King!' and 'Portugal!' Two months after the visit to

Africa, His Majesty the King, at the suggestion of the Prince and his Minister for the Colonies, gave due thanks to his son's hosts in São Tomé. The Count of Valle Flor would gain, thanks to his unforgettable party, the title of the Marquess of Valle Flor. As for Henrique Mendonça, it was more complicated: he refused the title of the Count of Boa Entrada because he felt the ennobling business quite absurd, but he finally accepted to become peer of the realm and receive the Grand Cross of Christ.

The Prince, Minister and retinue spent that night on the Rio do Ouro plantation. Luís Bernardo had to travel two hours at night in the Governor's carriage, which was only the second time he'd used it, lit by two feeble oil-lamps on the coachman's seat. David took the opportunity to ask for a ride back to the city and thus turned the journey back into even more of a torture. He was closeted in that dark, tiny space with David and Ann, so near yet so far from her that a mere brushing of cheeks caused by the potholes on the path became almost unbearably painful. Fortunately, they were so exhausted they travelled almost the whole way in silence. As his bedroom and guest rooms were still occupied by the Prince and his two companions, Luís Bernardo slept one more night on the ground floor, on the bed set up in his office in the Government Secretariat. He was up again with the sun, in order to reach Água Izé at half past eight, when the royal retinue was expected.

On Água Izé, the plantation belonging to the Viscount of Malanza, they were welcomed by the Count of Souza Faro, on behalf of the present owners, a consortium known as the Island of Príncipe Company, which included some creditors left by the massive bankruptcy of the deceased, ruined Baron. After visiting the plantation and lunching on a beach adjacent to the buildings, where the entire product from the plantation's seven thousand hectares was washed, the Count of Souza Faro made the most directly political of the speeches heard so far, homing in, quite unceremoniously, on the issue of the Angolan labour force. After detailing the benefits enjoyed, as he saw it, by all those plucked from the Angolan jungle, where 'they were subject to the most savage outrages, and defenceless under the iron rule of local potentates', the General, Count and administrator, whom Luís

Bernardo had respected as a liberal, concluded his speech to the Prince, Minister, Governor and British Consul.

'In such conditions, one easily understands why the compulsory repatriation of our workforce, as demanded by the entirely self-interested opponents of our immigration, would be an act of indescribable violence no government could lightly sanction. We assert before Your Royal Highness and the Noble Minister, that of all our Angolan labourers, from those who have established families here – that is, nearly all – not a single one would willingly abandon this their adopted land, for the simple reason that here they have everything they could possibly wish for. And as the saying goes, your home is where you are happiest.'

Enthusiastic applause from almost all the whites present greeted the speech given by the administrator of Água Izé. The Prince applauded without showing any sign that he disagreed. Luís Bernardo thought the Minister applauded most warmly. From his seat on the opposite side of the table, David Jameson looked at Luís Bernardo and smiled. As for the latter, he sat straight-backed, his hands clearly visible on the table.

As soon as they got up, Luís Bernardo rushed after Ayres d'Ornellas, asking to speak privately to him. The other man moved several steps away from him and looked at him quizzically.

Luís Bernardo seethed within but maintained the same restraint he'd shown at dinner.

'I would beg Your Excellency a private audience in order to comment on this speech and everything else in a way one cannot in public.'

'Very well, dear fellow. As you know, we leave at seven. We can speak in the Palace at six.' And he walked off to where the Count of Souza Faro stood being congratulated by several guests.

At 6 p.m., Luís Bernardo was summoned by the Minister's secretary to his own office on the ground floor of the Palace, when he was in a state of nerves fit to explode. He turned the corner of the building to go in through the main door and bumped into David, who was on his way out.

'David, what are you doing here?'

'Doing my duty.' He bowed ironically. 'I came to speak to your Minister.'

'What? The fellow met you without my being present and without even informing me?'

'Come on, calm down! You've not been betrayed: I was the one who asked for him to see me alone.'

'You asked! And you think I wasn't betrayed? Wasn't betrayed by you? You, my friend, who knows the situation I endure here, who heard Souza Faro spit in my face! I wasn't betrayed? Then why did you want to speak to my Minister without my being present?'

They stood at loggerheads by the door. Luís Bernardo was practically beside himself.

David kept calm, appearing to feel sorry for him.

He looked him in the eye, gently pushed him away and said, 'Who are *you* to speak of betrayal, Luís? Forgive me.'

Luís Bernardo stood and watched him walk off and leave via the garden gate. That's the end of our friendship! he thought. The Minister's secretary called to him again: His Excellency was waiting.

The Minister was alone in what was Luís Bernardo's own office. They were his paintings, his books, his photographs, his gramophone and his records. This had been his small, very small world over the last awful seventeen months. It was a peculiar sensation being received by the other man as if the latter owned what was his.

Ayres d'Ornellas gestured to him to sit down.

'Well, then, dear Valença, what was it you wanted to talk to me about?'

'On my way in I bumped into the British Consul. First of all, I would like the Minister to tell me what private matters you talked about that excluded me from this meeting.'

Ayres d'Ornellas gave him a studied look. Once again it was the cold, quizzical gaze of someone used to trying to read others before they themselves speak, or decide to remain silent.

'It was your friend, Mr David Jameson, who asked for a private audience and I could see no reason to deny him one. But rest assured I am not one to forget the need to support those under my command, particularly in the presence of foreigners, and similarly your British friend betrayed none of your secrets. Indeed, he told me nothing I didn't already know.'

'So what did he say, Minister? Might I be informed?'

'Of course, there is nothing secret in any of this. What the British Consul came to tell me is that, in his opinion, slave labour does exist on São Tomé. That labourers are held on the plantations by force, that they don't have the wherewithal to run away, and that, if there were a proper renewal of work contracts, as the law requires, they would all, or almost all, have gone by now. Quite the opposite of what we were told by General Souza Faro and many others.'

Luís Bernardo stayed silent. He remembered how David had promised him one day that he would never take such a step without informing him in advance and giving him the honourable opportunity to present his resignation. Times had changed.

'I presume' – Ayres d'Ornellas spoke slowly – 'that it is your opinion too?'

The moment of truth had come. Luís Bernardo felt the tumult of ideas and emotions in his head, but thought there was little he could salvage now. Perhaps his honour; it was too late for his pride, and far too late for him to claim any success.

'Not in every case. But in general, yes, that is my opinion as well.'

The Minister sighed. He too was exhausted after three days of visiting São Tomé. He wanted to return to the peaceful, even monotonous life aboard the *África*, the voyage over calm waters to Mozambique, and the time to be by himself in his cabin writing to his wife and writing his diary.

'Well, if that is the case, my dear Valença, I really don't know what more I can say. We trusted in you to change the situation slowly, so things would become more reasonable, without bringing on the economic ruin of the plantations, for, as I think you know, they are not in a position to cope with a mass exodus of labourers. I agree it is a difficult balance to strike, but we understood that, if anyone could do it, that person was you. Now you tell me nothing has changed . . .'

'It is difficult to change anything when there is resistance to any change, and when the man first in line, namely the Crown Commissioner, who should look after the rights of the labourers, works hand in glove with the plantation owners. As you will recall, Minister, I included all this in a report I sent, shortly after Your Excellency took up his position.'

'Yes, indeed, I remember your report. If I might say so, it was very well written, but hardly practical, in terms of concrete solutions.'

'But what concrete solutions would you like? I don't live on the plantations, I don't administer them, I don't monitor the work conditions of the labourers – that is the Commissioner's responsibility. If neither he nor the plantation administrators see the need to change anything whatsoever and the only thing worrying them, as we just heard from the Count of Souza Faro, is the repatriation of labourers to Angola, what can I do? I received them here, visited them on their plantations, talked to them, wrote to them, explained that, whatever their opinion or mine, the key issue was the opinion the British Consul would form. After all that, I had to take urgently to Príncipe a military force I scraped together, to put an end, without bloodshed, to a revolt by labourers who had been whipped on a plantation. And as if that was not bad enough, I find the British Consul is there and has seen everything.'

'Quite so, Valença, that was the one thing people told me: and why was the British Consul there?'

Luís Bernardo felt insulted.

'Your Excellency isn't suggesting, I hope, that I was the one who tipped him off?'

'I wasn't suggesting anything at all. But the mere fact that someone might have suggested that shows to what extent you, Valença, have allowed the opinion to circulate that you are on the Englishman's side and against our settlers. In other words . . .'

'Your Excellency, this' – Luís Bernardo felt his blood boiling – 'is unfair and even insulting. I never put myself on anyone's side. I put myself on the side of the proper execution of my mission as described to me, in Vila Viçosa, by King Dom Carlos, namely to convince the world, starting with the British Consul, that Portugal does not employ slave labour in São Tomé and Príncipe. That was what was asked of me and that was what I accepted to do. Nothing else.'

'Not true: you were also asked to take into consideration the actual economic conditions on São Tomé and the fact that the colony's prosperity cannot survive without its labour force.'

'Slave labour?'

'No, it is not slave labour!' Now it was Ayres d'Ornellas's turn to get irritated and raise his voice. 'It is not slave labour! There is the greatest difference between this and the humanitarian hypocrisy of the British, who, as you must be aware, are only worried about the way we compete with their colonies. And that is the difference you should have exploited with the Englishman and not posturing about a perfect world that doesn't exist here, doesn't exist in Africa and doesn't exist in any of his Gracious British Majesty's colonies. We demanded you be sensitive and sensible but you preferred to invoke immediate revolution and wanted the Englishman, seduced by your charms, to wait till you performed your miracle!'

Luís Bernardo was appalled. He'd finally understood what was expected of him. It had taken an intelligent politician, with a strategic colonial vision, to come from Lisbon to clarify to him what his mission was really about.

'In that case, Minister, it only remains for me to tender my resignation, which I request you accept, with immediate effect.'

Ayres d'Ornellas removed his spectacles misted by the humidity, blew on the lenses and began to clean them slowly with a handkerchief he'd taken from the top pocket of his cream-coloured jacket.

'Listen, young man: I will be quite candid. We have a serious problem on our hands, and no obvious solution, but that doesn't mean I want you to resign or be humiliated. I will not accept your resignation because it would resolve nothing and would not change things at all in our favour – yours or ours. As far as you are concerned, it would be a dishonourable surrender; for us, it would be futile to try to find someone who, from now till the end of the year, could be in a better position to try to exert influence on Mr Jameson so the report he sends his government is less damaging to our interests and can give us an opportunity to negotiate and reach a compromise. Your mission here is not over. It's teetering on the verge of failure and I'm giving you one last opportunity for damage limitation.'

'Minister, I doubt that I can in any way influence Mr Jameson's conclusions . . .'

'Perhaps you can, perhaps you can't. The Prince's visit was a palpable political success, and that is down to you. That favours you here in the colony, even among your enemies, and favours us at an international level. This narrow margin for manoeuvre is something you can draw on – if you are able to cultivate the right relationship with Mr Jameson, given the situation.'

Luís Bernardo had been listening carefully: the Minister was no novice. Perhaps in the end he was showing a way out that only arrogance on his part could lead him to scorn.

'What kind of relationship is Your Excellency suggesting?'

'You won't be offended if I answer frankly?'

'I have nothing to lose, Minister.'

'Yes, you do. But you should hear me, however you feel later. I can understand how a cultured man like yourself who led a gilded, comfortable life in Lisbon, finding yourself here, in this leafy wasteland, became a friend, even a very close friend, with the only person you met at your level. The fact he was the representative of interests contrary to our own wasn't even, in principle, an obstacle. Quite the contrary, seducing the Consul sent by Britain to spy on us here seemed like a good policy.'

'Where did I err, then?'

'My dear Governor, you erred when you didn't limit yourself to seducing the enemy: you also seduced, quite literally, his most beautiful wife.'

Luís didn't move a muscle in his face. He let the Minister continue, like a father chiding his son.

'By doing that, you transformed your friend into your enemy. I spoke to him just now and I can assure you that is the case. You must know the reasons why, rather than shoot you – which would, in the end, be an honourable way for you to die for your love – he preferred to threaten me with a report that will devastate both our interests and the prestige of your mandate.'

Luís Bernardo had entered that room to talk to the Minister feeling an anger he thought would override anything. He now left like a criminal hoist by his own petard. All things considered, he preferred to surrender to the Minister in the privacy of that room than surrender to the whole world by the light of day:

'What, then, does Your Excellency suggest?'

'That you see your mandate through to its completion, as you pledged to the King. That you continue to defend what you think is just and right before the settlers. And that, as far as your former friend Mr Jameson goes, you should have a loyal, man-to-man relationship with him, that means he has to accept his moral duty to relate facts, not feelings, and to reach conclusions on a rational basis, and not out of spite.'

An hour later, Luís Bernardo was on the jetty to bid farewell to the Minister, the Prince and the other five member of the entourage visiting the African colonies.

When the moment came to leave, Dom Luís Filipe gripped him by the arm and said, 'Governor, I will tell my father of the wonderful welcome you arranged for us on São Tomé and Príncipe. I am sure he will be pleased and happy to know he made the right choice for this difficult position. In the name of Portugal, I would like to thank you for being so capable and for exceeding the expectations for these historic days when, for the first time in almost a hundred years, a member of the Royal Family stepped foot on national territory overseas.'

Luís Bernardo wondered once more at the Prince's almost childish manner. His speech mirrored his age and the royal education he had received almost from the cradle, but not his youthful face that seemed to be thanking him merely for the party he had staged on his behalf.

'I am the one who should thank Your Royal Highness, in the name of all the inhabitants of São Tomé and Príncipe, for the unforgettable honour that you conferred on us as well the tremendous joy everybody experienced and which Your Highness witnessed for himself. It is a source of immense pride for me that good fortune and the designs of your father, my King, bestowed upon me the unforgettable honour of welcoming Your Highness in my capacity as Governor of these isles. I beg you, on your return, to convey to His Majesty that a single day does not pass when I do not remember the conversation we had in Vila Viçosa and the mission he charged me with.'

'Your message will be passed on. I promise you that.'

Dom Luís Filipe held out his hand and shook Luís Bernardo's vigorously. He raised his arm and waved round a final goodbye, climbed down into the small boat and, as on their arrival, positioned himself to steer before giving the order to leave. Ayres d'Ornellas nodded and waved to him from the boat that Luís took to be a wave of encouragement. And, finally, those three days in hell were at an end.

Luís Bernardo stayed on the pontoon and watched the *África* making its preparations and manoeuvres to up anchor. The sun was setting on the horizon when the black-and-white vessel set sail to depart the bay, hooted three times and turned west, out into the open sea. Luís Bernardo stayed to the end, alone, more alone than ever, as if suddenly the whole island had been depopulated and, among the signs of abandon and solitude, he searched for a trace of Ann's presence so as not to be driven mad.

17

Luís bernardo's last hopes disappeared in the wake of the *África*. If he had expected explicit, enthusiastic support from the Minister or even from His Royal Highness for the implementing of his policies as Governor in the teeth of hostile opposition from the settlers, that expectation had faded. Not that the Minister had condemned his governance in any way, in private or in public. But silence in this matter was tantamount to lack of support. It allowed the deadlock to survive, for the standoff between himself and the plantation administrators, abetted by the Crown Commissioner, to continue as before. Luís Bernardo required a decisive victory he could present as proof of the success of his policies, and that victory could only be sealed by the expectation that, as a result of his efforts, the report David was about to deliver wouldn't entirely undermine the Portuguese government's strategy. But David had pulled the carpet from under his feet. Out of spite and his wish for personal revenge, according to the Minister. Such a possibility never occurred to Luís Bernardo: he'd always believed that David, even if he delivered a negative report, would always do so from conviction and never from personal motives. Not so much in the name of their previous friendship, but rather in the name of a kind of 'gentlemanly honour'. Of course, it was true he'd betrayed his friend by seducing his wife. But, for once in his life, he'd not been driven by lust or a passing fancy, vanity or mere desire, but by passion. He had fallen madly in love with her, in a place where everything was so different, from the pre-eminence of the senses to the rules for social behaviour, in a place where instincts were voracious, where desire grew like the small plants that transformed into trees in just a day, where blacks walked around almost as naked as animals, where heat, lethargy and remoteness soon dissolved what would be protected elsewhere by rules and convention. Of course, a distance existed between desire and consummation, and that depended on morals more than on conventions. But David knew his relationship was special – something Luís Bernardo couldn't explain to the Minister or his other detractors. David had surely intuited, anticipated and understood that it was Ann who had provoked the relationship. She didn't feel fettered by any matrimonial ties, and it was her freedom that had swept Luís Bernardo along. It was the price David paid to be near her, because, if the criteria were moral, he'd lost the high ground when he dishonoured her in India. She'd not left him – as she had promised she wouldn't – and he, in exchange, could make no move to oppose her relationship with Luís Bernardo, for that was the implicit contract between them, the very basis of their marriage. Why should Luís Bernardo renounce Ann? In the name of what, in exchange for what – the vague hope it might make David feel more benevolently towards the political interests of Portugal and the professional goals of Luís Bernardo?

The day after a party is always painful. Those who'd come from the metropolis went straight back to Lisbon, while the Prince's retinue continued its long three-month tour that would take it to Angola, Mozambique, and South Africa, and then back to Angola and finally Cabo Verde. Nostalgia reigned on every front in São Tomé as the city cast off its finery after three days and nights of festivities. It returned to a darkness lit by the scant oil-lamps on the façades of a few houses and street corners; the ground was cleared of a sea of sun-rotted flowers; the wooden arches embellishing the entrances to the main streets were dismantled and stored away. The island was alone again, in the grip of the Equator, waiting for the next boats to drop anchor, at the mercy of its perennial fate.

Luís Bernardo sank into a gloomy torpor. He was happy enough to reclaim his bedroom on the top floor, which had been the temporary home of the Marquis of Lavradio. He watched the house revert to a normal daily routine, its hours of light and shadow, its sounds, silences and limpid summer nights. He was in the grip of a viscous sadness. He never left the house, but wandered around it like a soul in limbo, stifled by the slow passage of time, and not even his terrace at night gave him the breathing space he craved. If everything followed its course, he had eighteen months of his term left, was exactly halfway though his period of exile: that was what he had to survive.

One night, after dinner, he sat behind his desk and decided to send an SOS across the seas to João.

Dear friend,

In my whole life I don't think I've ever needed a friend by my side so much. Forgive me for beseeching you in this way, but you must believe I only do so because I have reached the end of my tether. Eighteen months of exile remain and my mission is heading towards the most disastrous failure, the woman with whom I have unfortunately fallen in love, as never before, is now beyond limits because of the higher interests of the nation. The island now holds no secrets or mysteries, only pain and the minimal reassuring knowledge that she is still there, breathing the air I breathe and desperate for the same air that I need. Please, João, I beg you, if you can find a way to take some of your holidays, even if it represents a great sacrifice, come quickly, in a fortnight or a week, in one boat or another, to resurrect my hope in a life after this death. Don't worry about money: I'll pay for your ticket and, believe me, it's a small price to pay.

Tell me by return whether I can look forward to this relief or should throw myself to the sharks on one of these anguished nights when I can no longer stand the sight of this endless sea opposite my window.

From your ever more equatorial and lonely friend,

Luís Bernardo

The mere act of writing the letter cheered him up and the following morning he woke up in a much better frame of mind. Just as he'd been succumbing to resignation, he was now suddenly consumed by a desire to do things and make use of the time left so he could leave his tour of duty with his name linked to the history of the islands. Two projects, which he'd considered in the past albeit fleetingly, now came back to mind, and he genuinely wanted to put them in motion: to supply the city with electric light and construct a new hospital to replace the dismal workhouse now serving that purpose. He realised he had in the Mayor an enterprising fellow who was keener on doing things than dedicating himself to local political intrigue. He summoned him to a meeting, together with the Secretary for Public Works, and told them of his ideas. Unfortunately, the Republican press in Lisbon hadn't lied when it spoke of the cost of His Royal Highness's trip: in the case of São Tomé, it had exhausted the coffers of the provincial government and Town Hall. Nevertheless, Luís Bernardo wasn't going to be defeated at the first hurdle: he ordered architectural and engineering plans to be put in hand, and that costings be prepared for the future hospital and the electrification of the city from the landing jetties to the Governor's Palace. Then he began to pester Lisbon with weekly telegrams, demanding his government be repaid, at the very least, the enormous expense the Prince's welcome had incurred. He simultaneously made direct contact with Lisbon banks and the Electricity Company, in order to explore the possibilities of opening up a credit line for the colony to enable it to electrify its capital, which could then be paid off out of the profits from supplying electricity to individuals and companies. He discussed possible locations for the hospital and electricity power station with the Mayor, met with the health inspector and two of the town's doctors to plan the future hospital, and demanded quick, palpable progress be made with architectural and engineering plans. He also dealt swiftly with all pending business, signed and endorsed all bills and invoices that were the government's responsibility, studied and took decisions on all matters relating to staff, management and customs tariffs. He soaked up work like a sponge, and every case he received in his office in the morning was dispatched by the afternoon at a speed that outpaced his own Secretariat. When he'd cleared his desk, he ordered Vicente to saddle his horse and went out for a ride to the north of the city, where he knew it was likely he might encounter Ann.

In the meantime, she'd sent him two notes, the first asking him to meet her on their usual beach. He replied via the black maid who'd delivered her message: he couldn't, due to pressure of work. Three days later, she sent a second, asking him to say when and where they could meet. He replied he would tell her as soon as he could. Then one evening, at twilight, he bumped into her as he turned the corner of the square in front of the Governor's Palace. Ann was on horseback, in jodhpurs and riding boots, with Gabriel on another horse a few paces behind. Luís Bernardo couldn't decide whether she was waiting for him, or just happened to be passing by. They stopped opposite each other, he on foot, she on horseback.

Ann smiled, ironically, if not a little sadly.

'The city isn't such a big place, Luís! How long did you think you could avoid me?'

She spoke in English and, before replying, Luís Bernardo glanced at Gabriel, who'd stopped a short distance away. His wounds seemed to have healed. He looked well treated and healthy. Luís Bernardo noted again what a fine-looking man he was, his torso rippling with muscle under a half unbuttoned shirt, his eyes, large and intelligent, with big black pupils against the brightest of whites.

'How are you, Gabriel? I see Mrs Ann and Mr David are looking after you . . .'

'Very well, thank you, Governor. They've treated me really well. I am grateful you allowed me to stay in Mr David's house.'

Luís Bernardo nodded.

But Ann interjected.

'Go back to the house, Gabriel. I'll ride back by myself . . . or His Honour the Governor will accompany me.'

Gabriel seemed to hesitate briefly, then turned his horse round on the rein and said, 'Good afternoon, Governor.'

'Goodbye, Gabriel.'

Meanwhile Ann had dismounted, and was holding her horse by its bridle. She waited till the black labourer was far enough away and then faced up to Luís Bernardo:

'What *is* the matter, Luís?'

Luís sighed deeply. At that very moment he wished she wasn't so incredibly beautiful, that she hadn't loved him as passionately as he had loved her, and that his body didn't carry the traces and memories of her body like indelible scars. But it was too late to wish that now.

'You want the truth, Ann?'

'Yes, I think I deserve the truth, don't you, Luís?'

'The truth is I love you more than ever. The truth is I can't not. The truth is not one day, morning, evening or night goes by when I don't miss you desperately. And the truth is that there's only one solution: you must jump on the next boat and escape with me. But you will never do that, will you?'

Ann looked at him as if she no longer recognised him.

'Is this the price I have to pay, Luís? Are you blackmailing me?'

'No, Ann, it's not blackmail. It's the end of the line. It's the only thing that makes any sense; the only thing that can save us.'

'Luís, I've never lied; I told you the situation. You know I promised my husband I'd never leave him.'

'I've made lots of promises, Ann. Promises to myself and other people I'd be prepared to break for you.'

Three people walked by and greeted them in the almost pitch dark that had now descended. Luís Bernardo replied so distractedly he didn't register whether they were black or white, acquaintances or strangers. He saw only tears welling in Ann's eyes, the sun setting over the sea behind her, the light of sunset giving her hair a golden hue.

'Yes, Luís, I can leave David for you. I know I can. I know I love you enough to do that. I know it's what I want, every day and night, as you say you do. But not yet. There's a difference between leaving him and abandoning him. I can leave him when he finishes his tour of duty, when his punishment is at an end, and when, in India or in England, he can resume a decent life, and once again be a person respected and admired for his own qualities. I can leave him when I feel he's regained his self-esteem and can defend himself. But if I left him now, if I jumped on this boat with you and left him alone in São Tomé, I'd be abandoning an entirely vulnerable man, and I know it would break him. If you truly love me, Luís, please understand!'

'And continue to be your lover, greeting him as if nothing had happened, knowing full well the whole city gossips behind our backs about our betrayal of him, knowing full well I betray him by day, now and then, on our beach, and that he betrays me every night or whenever he likes, in your bed?'

'Stop, Luís, shut up, you've no right to say this. You don't realise what you're saying.' Ann now cried, spoke in sobs and he saw her for the first time in a different light, completely beside herself, as he'd never seen her before.

'I don't know what I'm saying? Did I say something that wasn't the truth?'

'Truth, Luís? Forgive me for saying so, but you and David are very similar: strong on principle, weak on sentiment! What do you know about truth? Do you think you're the only one to suffer? Do you think I don't suffer? Do you think David's not suffering, though he keeps more quiet about it than I do?'

'He's suffering. Of course, he is. I even know he's suffering so much that he came and suggested to my Minister that our relationship is the reason he will deliver a report to London that states slave labour exists on São Tomé. And he knows such a report will sentence me to return to Lisbon as a defeated, slandered man. Were you aware of that, by any chance?'

'No, I wasn't. But I'm not surprised: it's natural he should fight for me with the weapons at hand . . .'

'Ann, what about me? What weapons should I use to fight for you?'

'You have my love.'

'Your love . . . You know what use your love is? So your husband can insinuate to the Minister that he will sink the lot of us, so the Minister can suggest I should distance myself from you, for the good of the Fatherland and my reputation, in the hope your husband might then change his ideas and give us a more favourable profile? So the outcome of my mission, the outcome of a year and a half rotting on this island, hangs on your husband's jealousy?'

'No, you don't know him. David would never do such a thing. He would never write a report that was not based on conviction.'

'The issue isn't whether he would or wouldn't: that's what he suggested to the Minister and the latter believed him. Just reflect for a moment: if we lose the battle with Britain, it won't be because David sincerely believes slave labour exists on São Tomé, as I too believe, but because I am his wife's lover. In other words, I'll have cut short my posting here and disappointed the trust placed in me all because of an amorous fling.'

Ann looked at him in amazement. Suddenly, everything was crystal-clear.

'So that's why you are avoiding me?'

'Yes.'

She turned round without saying a word. Seized her horse by the mane, put her left foot in the stirrup, jumped up and hoisted herself on to the saddle in a perfectly synchronised movement.

She faced up to him again from on high.

'That's your problem, Luís. David has his. I have mine. I can't help you. I won't take the next boat with you, though perhaps one day I might take a boat to you. But, Luís, if you love me, you'll have to put up a fight.'

She turned her horse and began to ride away. First trotted, then cantered, and finally galloped across the square, soon vanishing into the darkness, her horse's hoofs beating like muffled hammer blows in Luís Bernardo's breast.

João answered by return as Luís Bernardo requested. However, he couldn't come that summer. The backlog at the office wouldn't allow him more than a week's holiday, which he'd already set up in Praia da Granja, hotel booked and everything. Besides, a week wasn't even enough time to get to São Tomé. Perhaps at Christmas, he wrote, adding, 'Stick at it till then!' From the Lisbon newspapers, Luís Bernardo concluded that, despite constant political intrigue, the country he knew was peacefully on holiday, as ever. Some were swimming in the sea, others had gone to their country residences where servants, family furniture and petty local dignitaries awaited from one year to the next, while others were taking a cure at thermal springs. King Dom Carlos, on whose behalf he was lingering and suffocating in the tropics, was, as usual, spending the summer of 1907, a mere month of tranquil holidays, in the spa at Pedras Salgadas, lodged with his entourage – which didn't include the Queen or their children – in the local hotel, enjoying cures, pigeon shoots, outings in his new car, a 70 horse-power Peugeot, and bridge parties, piano recitals and the occasional village dance. The monarchist press praised the King's 'natural simplicity' as he mingled with the people and the sons and daughters of the glebe; the Republican press didn't miss an opportunity to draw attention to the King's natural predisposition to concern himself with everything that was banal and frivolous. Luís Bernardo tended to think they were right. Despite the farewell words from His Royal Highness the Prince on his departure from São Tomé, he felt his father the King had ordered him there, then quickly forgotten him.

Summer dragged on for Luís Bernardo, more desperate and senseless than ever. Even trips to the beach, which had always acted as a tonic against anxiety, reviving a childishly instinctive cheerfulness, now seemed full of grief and longing. He started talking to himself, as if he were talking to Ann, seeing himself from the outside, as if she were watching him, performing a kind of theatrical spectacle for an invisible audience, diving into the water, only to return suddenly to dry land, in the vain hope she might be sitting on the sand, watching him, like that first time. But, when he got back to the beach, it was empty, with no footprints of hers on the sand, no horse tied to the tree next to his, no voice breaking the silence, nothing at all, except for a distant image, clouded by tears that attracted salt from the sea and blurred his vision.

One sentence flew round his head from morning to night; pursued, haunted, distracted, paralysed and overwhelmed him at every moment. A cry disappearing down a bottomless pit, getting fainter and fainter by the day, like an echo fading – the sentence uttered by Ann: 'If you love me, Luís, you'll have to put up a fight.' But how should he fight, how long, craving what over the horizon? São Tomé was so small it seemed unthinkable they could go weeks, months without crossing each other's path. But the fact was they did: there was no daily promenade; there were no restaurants, clubs or soirées where people met, no opportunity for love for two officially clandestine lovers. After a few weeks, Luís Bernardo could no longer stand the void, the silence, the deserted beach, the rides past Ann's house in the hope – continually dashed – that he might see her. He imagined his frankness with her had ruined things for ever, and that he'd tried to force a decision on her and she'd refused, out of fear. That she'd opted for peace and quiet and decided to renounce him and resume her marriage with David. He imagined her pacified, sad perhaps, but finally reconciled with herself, after settling accounts, exacting her personal revenge, and now back to the only thing she recognised as solid and secure, namely her marriage. He represented folly, a fleeting adventure offering a vague possibility of happiness that could only be consummated by bringing pain to others. David represented a happy, exciting past and a secure future, where he'd always be at her side, and whenever she said 'my husband' life would seem meaningful. He could stand it no longer and wrote her a short letter, in which he drafted and redrafted every word countless times, so she would read it as a declaration of love and not a prayer, a veiled threat and not an ultimatum.

Ann,

You said that if I love you I would have to put up a fight. I love you, am desperate to see you, now and for a lifetime. I know and understand why you won't take the next boat with me, but I need to know whether at least you will board the last boat with me – the one that will carry me far from here to a life that will only make sense if it is lived with you. If I'm sure of this, I can accept whatever you decide: for us to continue seeing each other for a temporary period on the way to a relationship that won't be lived in hiding, or to stop seeing you, on behalf of a better future than the wretched present, until the day you board that boat with me. The decision is yours.

He entrusted Sebastião with the note, and expressly ordered him to deliver it to her hand alone. He received a reply the next day brought by her maid to Sebastião.

Dear Luís,

I am also desperate to see you – every day and night. Sleep affords no respite. I'd like to be able to say 'Come!' or 'Go away!' but feel unable to say either. What I desire most fervently is peace – peace from irrevocable decisions, from which there's no turning back, from feeling the choice one has

338

made is the only one possible. But that decision cannot only be mine – or perhaps I can't envisage making it or don't want to. That's why I told you I will leave my husband one day, but can't abandon him now. To my mind the two things are different and the difference is the moral ground without which I can never start afresh with you. That's also why I told you that you would have to put up a fight, even though I couldn't tell you how or even guarantee that I will jump in a boat with you, even if it is the last one. I know this doesn't help you decide whether it's worth putting up that fight, but you must understand it is only a reflection of my own confusion, the turmoil in my life, and where, if I keep silent, I will lose my self and all else. Forgive me, my love, but it's the only help I can offer. I loved you and love you as a rational as well as a passionate being – and this at least is real, exists and can withstand all else.

When the first rains came, Luís longed to go back to the plantations, to see the *óbó* again, to hear the sound of the brooks that formed overnight, to breathe the scent of the wet forest, to take a dip in the dark, awesome waters in the middle of the jungle, to the singing of birds and slithering of cobras, which frightened his horse and made every hair on his body bristle. He wanted to ride on tracks where his horse faltered painfully, as tree branches hit him in the face, as if welcoming his return to that dark, mysterious world. He wanted to ride out again to the plantations, to their big open spaces, to bonfires lit at twilight and the smell of cocoa drying in trays, the smell of roast coffee, and of fresh wood clippings feeding the ovens.

So he rode back to the plantations to satisfy his nostalgia for all the smells of Africa that he now knew would live with him for ever, every day of his life, wherever that might be. He revisited the precise, clean geometrical lines of houses on the plantations, the familiar Portuguese tiled roofs, the white from the bottom of the whitewashed walls splattering the damp, brown earth, the sound of his steps on wood-plank walkways, the songs of the black labourers at the end of the day, returning to their thatched huts after evening roll call, the meals in the Casa Grande on pink Sacavém crockery with embroidered napkins from Castelo

Branco and brandy drunk on the veranda, surrounded by the mysterious night-time noises of the forest, which began right there, at the corner of the Casa Grande.

He revisited several plantations, and was received with suspicion, aloofness, if not ill-disguised hostility. And one day, not quite understanding why, he decided, on the spur of the moment, to return to the Nova Esperança. He arrived, as on his first visit, in the late morning and found Maria Augusta busy helping to shoe a horse in the stables. She turned round, shocked to see him standing in the entrance. Her face was flushed from her exertions and the heat: beads of sweat ran down her skin and straw hung from her dishevelled hair.

She didn't seem pleased to see him in such circumstances.

'Just dropping by, Luís Bernardo?'

'I'm revisiting plantations and my journeying brought me as far as Nova Esperança. But remembering the tone of our last meeting, I can appreciate you might not want me here. One word from you and I'll leave.'

She looked at him intrigued. She seemed to be trying to guess what had really brought him there, and by the way her expression soon relaxed, one imagined she'd understood why.

'No, do stay for lunch. It will be my pleasure.'

Just like the first time, she welcomed him as if she was expecting him and improvised a lunch that made him recall the noble, unpretentious hospitality one finds in northern Portugal. In the afternoon they rode round the plantations and visited the areas where labourers were working. They came back to the house and he accepted her invitation to have a bath, change his clothes and stay for dinner. Maria Augusta, on the other hand, didn't change or smarten up for his benefit. She merely served up a fine dinner and a good glass of port, and led the conversation against a prolonged, hostile silence from her overseer, Mr Albano. When the latter withdrew, they were both alone on the veranda again.

Luís Bernardo was in no rush, felt comfortable and was clearly – as she perceived – more solitary, more at a loss than ever. He inspired compassion and tenderness in her, but she wasn't prepared to fall into the same trap a second time.

And so she asked ironically, 'Well, then, Governor, how's your love life these days?'

'I don't know, Maria Augusta. What about yours?'

She laughed. And her laughter, like everything else about her, was genuine and open, in the manner of someone who's in debt to no one.

'Oh, my love life will never be news or a subject of conversation!'

Luís Bernardo looked at her as if seeing her for the first time. It was a coarse look, undressing her, sizing her up. The gaze of a male on heat, but also – and this is what annoyed her most – the gaze of a little boy lost in the jungle.

'Good for you, Maria Augusta! That's why – and because I know I've no big secrets to hide from you – I dare ask a straight question I'd never dare ask normally: may I stay and sleep the night with you?'

She guffawed in a slightly forced way, but – and he did notice this – her bosom rose several centimetres above her neckline.

He recalled her ample bosom that promised so much, and suddenly, desperately, hoped she wouldn't slip away now. If only she'd hold him now as she had before, with stifled moans and rising lust, allowing him to forget all else, even Ann's incomparable, unforgettable body.

'Poor Luís Bernardo, what's the Englishwoman done to you? Did she take her pleasure of you then go back to her husband? It's a tale as old as the hills! Do you want me to erase the memories? Fair dues: you satisfy my desire and I'll anaesthetise your longings? What do you take me for: a stand-in for the Governor's married lover?'

Luís Bernardo made no reply and she was the one who took hold of the situation.

'In the grand scheme of things, why not? Who will ever know apart from us? We've nothing to lose, and in spite of all else, it's a better prospect than the frustration of seeing you depart without having benefited from the situation. Come, let's drown our respective sorrows in an act that will leave no trace.'

The great political showdown got under way. The result of Luís Bernardo's strenuous mission, almost two years on São Tomé and

341

Príncipe, was drawing to a conclusion. Equipped with the information collected on the islands by Mr Joseph K. Burtt and the report presented by British Consul David Jameson, the representative of the British firms that imported cocoa from São Tomé, Sir William A. Cadbury, set up a meeting in Lisbon with a delegation of plantation owners from São Tomé and Príncipe. The Ministry informed Luís Bernardo of the meeting and, from over the ocean, he waited, impotent and anxious, for the final decision, which would decide the fate of São Tomé and his own.

The first encounter took place on 28 November 1907, in the Colonial Centre, and comprised a presentation of the combined reports of Mr Burtt and David Jameson the Consul, made by Mr Cadbury, accompanied by Burtt himself, to a delegation of Portuguese plantation owners including the Marquis of Valle Flor, Alfredo Mendes da Silva, José Paolo Monteiro Cancela, Francisco Mantero, Salvador Levy and Joaquim de Ornellas e Matos. The meeting began with Cadbury's presentation and the Ministry subsequently sent its main conclusions to Luís Bernardo.

The vast majority of natives from Angola taken to São Tomé are shipped to the islands against their wishes.

The fine laws that insist on repatriation are dead on the page, because, if we except Cabinda, natives are never shipped back from São Tomé to Angola. Considering the statistics and hard evidence we now possess, there are and will always be, until Your Excellencies introduce free labour, innumerable offences against these natives that will never be recorded, but which are the inevitable consequence of the present system.

We are unanimously agreed that there is no repatriation of workers to Angola, given that the packets that sail laden with natives to São Tomé never take anyone back. As long as this situation obtains, no argument will ever persuade the world that this labour is free.

Nevertheless we would like to emphasise we were pleased to to note that the treatment of labourers on many plantations, like the Boa Entrada, is excellent. However, even on that model plantation, the death-rate is high, despite the owner's

342

efforts. Thus with this death-rate and an extremly low birth-rate every year thousands of workers have to be imported to replace those who die. We would also like to emphasise that, as noted by the resident British Consul, the policy espoused publicly by the present Governor of the islands, Mr Luís Bernardo Valença, is to put an end to this state of affairs by defending the rights of the indigenous workers against the abuses of which they are victim. We are sure the abuses still in evidence are the last vestiges of an evil system that Your Excellencies all deplore and that we believe must be vigorously eradicated so that never again can the word 'slavery' be associated with the glorious name of Portugal.

We have always bought cocoa from São Tomé and, in the hope that we will continue our business accord for many years, we would advise Your Excellencies yet again to implement the necessary reforms, beginning with the effective repatriation of workers who will come to the end of their five-year contracts from January next, under the provisos of the Repatriation Law of 1903. However much it will pain us to stop buying the excellent cocoa Your Excellencies produce, and, being fully aware it will damage our own interests, speaking at least on behalf of my company, our consciences will not allow us to continue buying unless we have assurances that in the future the cocoa will be produced by free labour.

The following 4 December William Cadbury received in the Hotel Braganza where he was lodged the official response from the cocoa producers of São Tomé to the report he had presented. The Ministry sent it to Luís Bernardo almost twenty days later. It contained not a single concession in relation to what Cadbury reported, and showed no obvious wish to make amends: their counter-arguments repeated the usual legal formulas. After refuting distinctly minor detail, the essential argument from the Portuguese was as follows:

One cannot compare the rate of mortality on São Tomé with Great Britain's, particularly if one takes into account its location on the Equator and compares it with similar countries.

It is untrue that the physical punishment referred to by Mr Joseph Burtt's report is applied, and when he was asked to state what these punishments were and on which plantations he'd witnessed them, he refused to give any concrete data or the names of his informants.

The fact that the workers only received two-fifths of their wage was because, in line with the Law of Repatriation, the remaining three-fifths is deposited in their names and can only be released at the end of their contracts to finance their repatriation.

Plantation workers, as well as their monthly wage, enjoy remuneration in kind as foreseen by the law: food three times a day, two new sets of clothes every six months, hygienic accommodation, medical treatment, medication and special diets, paid passage to the islands and the return journey for those who wish to return. They are not subject to military service, don't pay taxes, are exempt from expenses and have the right to a free lawyer in criminal trials, namely the Crown Commissioner, who is legally bound to do this. Given all these benefits and advantages, these workers, at the end of their contracts, after enjoying a well-being they could never find in their places of birth, prefer to stay on the islands rather than return to Angola, and this and no other is the reason for their non-repatriation.

The above exposition shows that the labourers from Angola, who renew their contracts in São Tomé, do not stay against their will and are not slaves in any way. It is a fact that next year, from January, the first contracts terminate signed under the remit of the 1903 law, and that, legally and openly, as always has been the case, the growers will allow them to choose freely between returning to their lands or staying on the islands.

The growers also reaffirm that they too sincerely embrace the same humane, liberal sentiments as Mr Cadbury and genuinely hope that some labourers will want to return to their country with the good news about how they have been treated on the islands.

Luís Bernardo read the dispatches sent from Lisbon with mixed feelings, ironic laughter and annoyance.

'The idiots! Idiots quite beyond redemption! They will lose everything!' and thumped the top of his desk.

He summoned Germano Valente to his office and went straight to the point.

'How many labourers' contracts run out in January, under the provisos of the 1903 law?'

'I don't carry the number in my head, Governor.' The Commissioner's attitude was an undisguised mixture of indifference and contempt.

'But you must have some idea, surely?'

'Right off, like that, I have none.'

'How many, Commissioner: a hundred, five hundred, a thousand, five thousand?'

'I couldn't make an estimate . . .'

'Give me an estimate. You're duty-bound . . . Or give me the files and I will make one.'

'As we said before, I cannot, must not and will not do this. Unless I get express orders from Lisbon.'

'Very well, keep your information secret. But I am the Governor and have the duty and obligation to know how I will implement the process of repatriation. I've just received from Lisbon the report on the meeting between the British importers of São Tomé cocoa and the Portuguese owners of the plantations, in which the Portuguese agree to set up a fully free and fair system of repatriation. And it falls to me to inform the Ministry if it was thus or not. Hence, I must ask you yet again: how many workers' contracts do you estimate will run out in January?'

Germano Valente hesitated, looking for a fresh argument to support another refusal to comply. But couldn't and had to concede.

'Five hundred, perhaps?'

'No more?'

He got no reply: he had given sufficient response. But Luís Bernardo didn't give up.

'Very well, you estimate that five hundred finish their contracts in January and I estimate that at least half will want to return to Angola. And it is likely that in the months following your estimate of the numbers will rise substantially, or else we would have to

345

conclude that there aren't thirty thousand Angolan labourers on the plantations of São Tomé and Príncipe, but a mere six thousand, which we know is a ridiculous number. But, based on your January estimate, I shall requisition the steam packet *Minho*, with a capacity for eighty people, from the second week in the month, to proceed to repatriation. I sincerely hope the boat doesn't return empty . . .'

Germano Valente got up, nodded vaguely and left without saying another word.

It was particularly difficult for him to get through Christmas. However much he tried to avoid the symbols of the season, they pursued him and deepened his feeling of loneliness. Nevertheless, he made an effort to cheer himself up. The steam-packet from Lisbon brought him a Christmas hamper that made up for the absence of João, who hadn't been able to come after all: two kilos of dried cod, a bottle of French champagne and another of vintage port, a bag of nuts, two recent issues of *Gramophone Company* and a blue silk tie from Casa Elegante on the Rua Nova do Almada. He asked Mamoun to track down a turkey in the city, which he did with some difficulty. Then he planned a Christmas party, instructing the kitchen to prepare cod cooked with kale from the garden and oven-roasted turkey stuffed with giblets and dry pineapple, garnished with slices of fried *matabala* and a kind of fritter that had a horrendous taste. He ordered, insisted and finally had to get annoyed before all his domestic staff sat down to have Christmas dinner with him. Six pairs of eyes shining against black skin stared at him in embarrassed silence: Sebastião, Vicente, Tobias the coachman, Doroteia to his right and more tempting than ever, Mamoun and Sinhá. They all shamefacedly turned down the champagne he wanted to pour out so he downed the whole bottle by himself.

By the end he was hovering between melancholy and champagne-induced lucidity and got up to make a speech, tears welling, but the only thing he could say was, 'This is a table that has served a prince, a minister of the realm and several governors, a table where you have so often served me alone, and now I want you all here on this Christmas night because, like it or not, you are my only family in this world.' And after saying this, he burst into tears and fled to the terrace, leaving them all dumbfounded, sitting and looking at each other.

At ten o'clock, someone rang the doorbell and Vicente went to open up and returned with a sealed letter, which, according to the existing hierarchy, he handed to Sebastião, who placed it on a silver tray and took it to the terrace. It was a note from Ann.

Luís,
  As on every night, but especially tonight, I think of you and what must be going through your head and heart. I wish you a Happy Christmas, my love, knowing that one way or the other this will be the last Christmas you will have to spend alone.

He saw Ann again on New Year's Eve at the magnificent party he organised with the Mayor. He had ordered what remained of the public illuminations from the Prince's welcome to be lit, for fireworks to be let off over the bay when the cathedral bells rang at midnight, and persuaded the band from the Garrison to play in the bandstand for a dance in the square. The Elite Brewery manned a bar so that the ladies and gentlemen could get refreshment from the heat of night and the exertions of dancing. Luís Bernardo leaned on a corner of the building, holding a glass of beer, watching the spectacle and returning the greetings of those who greeted him as they walked by.

Then he saw Ann walking towards the Brewery arm in arm with her husband, but she stared at him, as if they were alone.

She spoke first.

'Well, then, Luís? Not dancing?' The question was meant ironically, but her tone betrayed her. She wasn't dancing either and seemed to float about, pulled along by her husband's arm, above everything, above the fake gaiety and vapid celebrations.

'I didn't organise a partner,' he said, looking at her directly, making no effort to disguise his own anguish. And only then did he look round and add, 'Hello, David.'

'Hello, Luís.'

They both stayed like that for a few moments by the door to the Brewery, as if frozen in time, but aware that everyone was staring at them.

David reacted and pulled Ann inside.

'You know, we should go in and get a drink.'

Luís Bernardo bowed his head slightly and continued to stand there, back to the wall, looking ahead as if something vitally important had caught his attention. Then he put his glass discreetly down on a nearby table and slipped away before disappearing round the corner and down a dark street.

On its first trip in mid-January, the *Minho* sailed to Angola with seventy-eight Angolan labourers, whose contracts had terminated, along with their respective families. It made a second trip a week later repatriating a further twenty-five. On its third trip, Luís Bernardo came down to the jetty in the morning to see it set sail with five labourers, three women and four children aboard. Luís Bernardo turned his back on that sight only to find himself face to face with Germano Valente, taking notes in a black notebook, apparently quite engrossed in the pursuit of his duties. He acknowledged Luís Bernardo with a nod and immersed himself in his notes, as if he, the Governor, counted for nothing.

Luís Bernardo felt the blood rushing to his brain.

'I thought we'd at least got this clear: it must be a proper repatriation and not one of your little games.'

Germano Valente looked up from his notebook and replied quite serenely, 'What do you expect me to do? Drag them on board by force?'

Luís Bernardo was incensed. He took two steps forward and stood threateningly close to his adversary.

'You're playing games with me, aren't you?'

'What do you mean?'

Luís took another step, while Germano Valente stood there impassively, and squared up to him.

'I can guarantee one thing: Lisbon must make a choice, without prevaricating, between you and me. One of us will have to go.'

'Perhaps that will be you, Governor . . .'

Luís clenched his fists till his fingers went white, then spat out his reply.

'Tomorrow you'll get the reply, you bastard puppet of the plantation owners!'

He turned his back on him, unhitched his horse from the post on the jetty and galloped back to his house. He immediately ordered Sebastião to bring his lunch, and shut himself in his office to draft the text of the telegram he would send to Lisbon that afternoon, a personal missive to the Minister containing a straight-forward ultimatum: either the Commissioner was sacked forth-with or he would present his irrevocable resignation, on receipt of the Minister's decision.

He wouldn't go along with Valente's charade a single day more. Lisbon would have to choose, as it had chosen a few months ago, when, at the request of the plantations owners on Príncipe, it had sacked the Deputy Commissioner there, who they accused of instigating the instability and latent rebellion among the island's labourers. All he had done in reality was to take his duty seriously and follow the call of his conscience.

Luís drafted four or five versions of the telegram, tearing each one up in succession, because they didn't seem sufficiently hard and irrefutable. He needed wording that, if it were released discreetly to the Lisbon press, would leave no doubt in any mind that he'd fought for the national interest and good name of Portugal against boundless stupidity and bad faith that he couldn't defeat. That he'd fought a lone battle and been betrayed by the government's hypocrisy and lack of support. Lunch interrupted his unsuccessful attempts to find the perfect balance and he decided to take a break from the exercise, calm down and clarify his ideas.

He was just getting ready to resume work after lunch, when Sebastião came to announce an unexpected visit from João Patrício, the Public Prosecutor. After that long morning in court they had only spoken on official duty during the ceremony to introduce local dignitaries to Prince Dom Luís Filipe. The only thing uniting them was mutual hatred and contempt.

After he'd been ushered into the small room that served as his study, Luís Bernardo signalled to the Public Prosecutor to sit down and, with a wave of his hand, indicated he was ready to hear what he had to say.

He cut to the quick.

'As I believe you know already, I consider that Your Honour the Governor has betrayed your mission and the interests of Portugal in the way you have conducted your mandate here. Many people think as I do, people who live here and really love São Tomé and Príncipe, who are not simply in transit, looking down on all this arrogantly and contemptuously.'

'Am I supposed to applaud?' After his argument with the Commissioner, Luís Bernardo felt like enjoying himself with this unexpected attack from another source.

'No, I merely came to say that we . . .'

'We?'

'. . . that we are not prepared to tolerate any more your arrogance, your treachery and the damage you are trying to inflict on us. We have had enough: your performance in court, your charade on Príncipe, the reports you sent to Lisbon slandering those who oppose your wishes, your irresponsible liberal fads . . .'

'So what have you decided – to eliminate me?'

'No, to put a stop to you and the damage your irresponsible behaviour is inflicting on the plantations and the whole economy of these islands.'

'How interesting . . . And how will you try to put a stop to me?'

'Our plan is simple but depends on your collaboration, and is for the common good: you must persuade your English friend to send a report to London saying the repatriation of labourers, according to the terms of the 1903 Law, is being carried out. Let's say that thirty to forty per cent – no point exaggerating – of the plantation labourers are being shipped back to Angola, after receiving the repatriation money that is their due. And you'll send a similar message to Lisbon. That is all.'

There was something in the Prosecutor's threatening, confident tone that put Luís Bernardo instinctively on high alert.

'That is all? And, even if I were prepared to do your business, how do you think I could persuade the British Consul to agree to such deceit? Do you think he doesn't know how many labourers have been repatriated so far?'

'Of course, he knows. He knows everything that happens here. I don't know how, but the fact is he doesn't miss a thing. Even so, with your collaboration, he could perhaps be persuaded to forget he knows what he knows.'

'Indeed? So your intention is to convince me first, so I can then persuade him?'

The Prosecutor looked at him witheringly, like someone enforcing a harsh sentence and feeling little sorrow for his victim.

'The alternative would be very unpleasant for all concerned . . .'

'Stop trying to frighten me with all your insinuations: just tell me once and for all what your blackmail amounts to!'

'If Mr Jameson doesn't send this report to London tomorrow, I will return and arrest you.'

'Arrest me?' Luís Bernardo laughed uneasily.

'Indeed, as you know, I have the legitimate power to order the arrest or impose a court order on anyone in this territory, including the Governor himself.'

'And what accusation will you use to attempt to justify my arrest – don't tell me charges of treason?'

'No: charges of adultery.'

'Adultery?' Luís Bernardo felt his head spin.

'Yes, adultery. As you know, adultery with a married woman is a civil offence: there only has to be an accusation and sufficient evidence for the Ministry of the Interior to be able to demand imprisonment without bail and the trial of the suspects – in this instance, Your Excellency and the wife of the British Consul. I would have to arrest both of you. The whole island can bear witness – perhaps even the husband himself could be summoned to give evidence . . .'

Luís Bernardo took a long time to regain his composure and articulate a few words.

'You're threatening to imprison the wife of the British Consul and me for adultery if her husband and I don't give into your wretched blackmail? Did I hear correctly – was that what you said?'

'Precisely.'

'Get out of here, you bastard! Get out, before I shoot you in the snout! Get out, you filthy swine, get out of my sight!'

Luís Bernardo came round from the back of his desk so quickly the Prosecutor had no time to react. He grabbed him by the collar, dragged him outside, opened the door and threw him out with so much struggling and shouting that Sebastião and Doroteia came running to see what was happening.

Luís Bernardo banged his office door shut and locked himself in. He lit a cigarette and paced up and down like a caged animal. He shook with impotent rage; he'd never imagined hatred could be so devastating. The 'we' the Prosecutor João Patrício had referred to would be: the Commissioner Colonel Maltez, Engineer Leopoldo from the Island of Príncipe and perhaps António Vieira, the Deputy Governor over there. And no doubt several plantation administrators: he had made enough enemies. And so they had organised and coldly hatched a plot to put a stop to him, one that was very efficient because it didn't just involve him but Ann and David as well. It wasn't merely a question of putting him out of action, but of doing it in the most shaming, sullying way, and humiliating the woman he loved and her husband, who was completely innocent.

It was a perfect plan. The Public Prosecutor could arrest him and Ann and, even if an appeal to the Lisbon Registry found that imprisonment was not legal and ordered their release, it would take months for their case to be heard. Even if the Minister or the King himself intervened politically and ordered the prosecutor to release them, it would take at least a week, and one day in prison was enough to drag them through the mud of the streets of São Tomé. After coming out of prison, the only step he could possibly take would be resignation in the most shaming of circumstances. David would see his career destroyed yet again by a scandal, for which he was in no way to blame, and it would be left to Ann to stay by his side to expiate the humiliation she had inflicted on her husband. They'd hatched all this painstakingly and unscrupulously, while the furthest he'd gone had been to confront the Minister with a choice between his resignation and the removal of the Commissioner. How stupid he'd been to think it would all be played on the level, that he alone called the shots and that his appointment by the King protected him from devious attack!

He chain-smoked, trying to calm down, attempting to see a way through the chaos into which his life had fallen and to clinically elaborate a way out of the trap. There had to be a way out, a last-minute counter-attack, as at war, when a platoon is surrounded by a superior enemy and only two options remain: to sit tight and await annihilation or launch a desperate fight back that sometimes triumphs because there's nothing else to lose. But no miraculous solution came to mind; he was still in a rage and unable to think rationally.

He ordered his horse to be saddled and decided to go for a ride to try to cool off. It was already late afternoon; rain hung in the air waiting to pour down on the island and bury the merciless heat under its freshness or drown those already afflicted. He instinctively turned left as he rode out and headed along the path leading to the Micondó Beach, guided more by the cantering of his horse than any criterion of his own. He trotted along for half an hour and met no one on the small earthen track through shadowy trees that seemed to bow their branches compassionately before him. Sparrows flitted from one tree to another on either side and the familiar intoxicating smell of chlorophyll finally had its usual pacifying effect on him. Despite everything, despite his loneliness during those years, his boundless hatred of his time there and the suffocating climate, despite it being the land of his anguished love for Ann and the land where he'd learned to discern loathing in the eyes of others, he loved the island, the green of the jungle, the blue of the sea and the translucent grey of the mist enveloping him, as if their embrace sheltered him. Now that his other world had become such a distant memory, fed only by newspapers or scant letters from his friend, that island landscape had become his familiar, innermost territory. Now that everything seemed to be nearing its end, he understood for the first time something he had never understood before: the bond felt by so many white men for Africa, who thought idly of leaving, but could never in fact cut loose.

He cantered down to the beach. Dismounted, didn't worry about tethering his horse to a tree, and let it roam among the palms. It was then he heard voices in the distance and realised that he wasn't alone: down below, where the waves were breaking, two men, one white, one black, were busy loading up a small sailing boat anchored in the sand. He thought he recognised David and tried to get a better view, when the man spotted him and waved to him vigorously. Luís Bernardo walked over the sand dotted with bits of dry palm fronds and coconuts until he was sure it was indeed David he had seen. He reached the boat and they shook hands. Suddenly he was struck by how much he really liked David. They could have been the best of friends, if he hadn't spoiled this – and everything else – because of Ann. David's face was sunburnt, his eyes glinting with an unusual delight and resolve and there was a childish glee to his gestures and in the way he gave orders to the black labourer accompanying him. He wore thick flannel trousers, high canvas boots over the top of his trousers and an old salt-stained nightshirt, and had an oilcloth at his feet, as if he were in his native Scotland.

'What are you doing here, David?'

'I'm going fishing, as you can see. I'll spend the night fishing with Nwama, who's from Namibia, by the Moçamedes desert, and who knows more about fishing than anyone on the island.'

'Are you leaving now?'

'We'll sail out two hundred metres or so. Then drop anchor, light our lamps, eat the lunch in that basket and then fish through the night till dawn: barracudas, groupers, turtles, maybe the odd shark. It's become my favourite pastime of late.'

Yet again, Luís Bernardo looked admiringly at his friend. Yes, 'friend' was the right word. A friend is someone whose presence one enjoys, whom one admires, and in whose company one learns. Luís Bernardo admired everything about David: his ability to make the most of any situation, the zest with which he lived life and all it brought, the calm determination with which he handled blows from fate and faced up to them. He admired the linear simplicity of his moral code, his absolute lack of anguish at the passing of time, because he had no concept of wasted time – every day was a gift that no unpleasantness could cloud. If he was in India, he hunted tigers; if he was in São Tomé, he fished barracudas or sharks. If he was the Governor of Assam, responsible for thirty-one million souls, he executed his duties unceasingly and single-mindedly. If he was the Consul on São Tomé and bored to death, he did his duty and paid serious attention to petty detail. If he was at war, he fought; if he was at a gambling table, he gambled – to the bitter end, to the point of bankruptcy if necessary. Now, however, though he was unaware of this, David's destiny was in Luís Bernardo's hands. There was no distraction or task that could enable him to treat lightly the shame of seeing his wife dragged through the streets of São Tomé and imprisoned for adultery in the law's humiliating turn of phrase. Was he duty-bound as a friend at least to inform him of the deal that had been proposed? Or should he spare him this latest insult and let him leave for a night's untroubled fishing and return in the morning to the most humiliating, damaging day of his life?

'David, can I ask you a question that's not really to the point now?'

'Of course, go ahead!'

'Have you sent a report to London about the number of Angolans being repatriated?'

David gazed at his friend: he tried to imagine what he was thinking. It was a last cry for help.

'No, not yet. I was waiting to see how things developed. I'll send it tomorrow.'

'And what will you say?'

'Come now, Luís! What do you expect me to say? What I've seen, what you've seen, what happened. I was on the jetty early this morning: eight adults left, and four children.'

'Were you? I didn't see you . . .'

'But I saw you . . . I saw you arguing and shouting with that puppet of a commissioner, and I think you've grasped how impossible it is to change these people. They've had time to choose and have chosen the bed they wish to lie on.'

'All right . . . There's nothing to be done. We must let destiny take its course . . .' Luís Bernardo seemed elsewhere, as if the subject no longer interested him.

'Right. Very good, I must go before sunset. Goodbye, Luís.'

'Goodbye, David, good fishing!'

David now leapt quickly into the boat after Nwama had hoisted the sail. He sat by the rudder, while Nwama pulled in the anchor and gave the small vessel a shove, before jumping, ducking to dodge the boom and settling down in the prow. David pointed the boat towards the waves breaking half a dozen metres from the beach. The boat bobbed impetuously and gracefully over the first two waves and then sailed into quiet waters. Luís Bernardo watched the manoeuvre from the beach as if watching sand slip through an hourglass. Time was speeding by; the boat had already moved some twenty-five metres from the beach: soon everything would be irrevocable.

'David!' he shouted out above the din of the breaking waves. But David didn't seem to hear. He shouted again and waved his arms.

David turned round on his seat in the poop, but kept steering ahead.

'Yes . . .?' His reply sounded as if it came from far, far away and it was obvious that it was too late now.

Luís Bernardo waved his arm, indicating it was unimportant. Then nodded a farewell to his friend. He saw David's right hand wave goodbye before he turned round and looked ahead, his back slightly bent, the prow cutting through the open sea, while the sun suddenly disappeared in a rain-filled sky and Nwama lit the first oil-lamp on board. They soon disappeared into the sheet of water hanging in the air and beyond the waterline.

Luís Bernardo splashed his face with sea water, cupped his hands into a shell, and drank a mouthful, as if it were sacred water that cures illnesses and wounds, sicknesses spiritual and physical. He walked slowly over the sand in the pitch-black night, found his horse waiting quietly where he'd left it and mounted. This time, as if he wanted to leave the Micondó Beach behind him for ever, he burst into a long gallop home, his horse foaming at the mouth, flanks streaming with sweat.

He left him with Vicente, told Sebastião he wasn't hungry and dismissed him till the morning. He shut himself in his study and dragged his leather sofa in front of the balcony window that was open to the sea. Out to sea, the lights from fishing boats shone weakly through the rain; one must have been David's. He stayed like that for a long time, one or two hours perhaps, smoking in front of the window.

The more he looked out to sea, the clearer it became that his only path to salvation lay there. São Tomé was over and done with. He must leave, escape, and not fear these words. Now, right now. Tomorrow the steam-packet would leave for Lisbon – that was the last boat. There wouldn't be another; there wouldn't be another chance. He and Ann should embark at dawn. Before David returned, before the Public Prosecutor arrested them as criminals. All else was lost: duty, pride and honour, friendship, loyalty and a sense of mission. All that remained was their love and that was all there was to save. They would reach Lisbon en route to somewhere else – to India, Ann's birthplace, or to England, to the Fatherland she'd never known. To Paris, to Brazil, to wherever. Even if he found no work, he had enough money to see them through several years without having to worry. He would recount his failed mission to the King by letter. He would explain his soiled pride or name to his friends and those who understood would be the only ones who interested him. And David would cope. At least he wouldn't have to suffer the shame of seeing his wife arrested on accusations of adultery in an obscure Portuguese colony in equatorial Africa. He'd have the strength to resume his life and career without her, hunting tigers or fishing barracudas, wherever his extraordinary ability to survive and surge back led him.

There was no other way out. Now, tonight. The last boat. The last opportunity to be free and happy again.

He got up and tiptoed down the stairs, trying not wake up Sebastião or Doroteia, who slept on the ground floor of the main house. He carried a candlestick with one lighted candle and went out though the front door and walked towards the stables. He put the candlestick on a bench and silently harnessed his horse, patting him to calm him down and whispering in his ear, 'Come, my friend, we must go out again. This is a special night. I've an appointment with destiny and you must take me there.'

He led his horse by the reins out of the stable and through the front gate, making the least noise possible. The sentry was asleep in his turret and didn't notice them leave. He led the horse by the reins for another hundred metres and only then mounted and trotted sedately towards the house of the woman he loved, for whom he'd compromised all and for whom he now wished to abandon all else. His heart beat furiously in his breast, but he was sure Ann would go with him. That wasn't what distressed him, but the feeling that he'd reached the island as its governor, in the midday sun and in full view, and would leave like an outlaw, hidden from sight, as if he really had committed treachery.

He reached the corner of the wall to David's house, dismounted and tied his horse to a tree away from the road. He stroked it on the rump and whispered in its ear, 'Shush, wait for me quietly. I'll be back soon!' He slipped along the wall towards the main entrance leading into the garden. He looked out for lights in the house: David wasn't there, but a servant or Ann might be still awake. But he saw no lights at all. He halted by the entrance and listened keenly in case he could hear a noise coming from the house. None at all, and fortunately they didn't have dogs. He intended to vault over the wall, but turned the door handle easily as it was just on the latch. He went into the garden and pulled the door shut behind him. Took three steps inside, stopped in the dark, and pricked up his ears. Everything was silent and apparently sleeping. He walked towards the veranda outside Ann and David's bedroom, remembering the day he'd made love to Ann on the ground floor, standing against that wall, listening to David's footsteps upstairs as he got dressed for dinner. He experienced another attack of horrible remorse for taking what wasn't his but somebody else's, a friend's. It was too late for remorse. Others had forced the game and cast the dice – not he. He was only reacting, trying to win the only way he knew how. If he didn't, if he were too cowardly to go and tell her it was time to board the last boat, he'd never forgive himself, and she would certainly never forgive him.

The branches of a tree reached over the veranda on the first floor. Luís Bernardo started to climb, testing the strength of each branch, as he hoisted himself up to a point from where he could clamber on to the veranda. When he was only half a metre adrift, he stretched a hand out and, gripping the balustrade firmly, lifted one leg over, then the other, and dropped noiselessly on to the veranda floor, steadied himself and listened. Initially, he heard nothing and imagined she must be asleep. Then he thought he heard a muffled sound coming from the bedroom a few metres away. When his eyes got used to the dark, he noticed a feeble light coming from inside, probably from a single lighted candle. He also saw the tassels of a white silk curtain wave now and then in the French windows to the veranda. Another muffled sound from the room made him prick up his ears. The next sound seemed like a moan – a woman's, Ann's.

Luís Bernardo estimated he was some ten metres from the windows. He took three silent steps before he heard another moan. It was Ann; there was no mistake. But his heart was pounding. Ann's moans were now joined by loud, muffled male noises. Ann was making love! She was doing what she did with him, and he'd thought, or liked to imagine, she only gave herself up to him that way. But not so: David had evidently returned from his night fishing trip early, and had gone straight to bed, where she'd welcomed him and surrendered herself. And there was Luís Bernardo, a real idiot, breaking and entering like a cat-burglar, an ingenuous, good-hearted thief who'd come to help the lady of the house free herself from her husband and take flight with him to eternal happiness!

He now understood why she wasn't able to decide: she'd lost her way in that game of words: 'I can leave him, but can't abandon him.' Now he understood why David was always so calm and self-assured against all expectation: he knew that in the end he would win. That, however passionately and romantically his wife swooned elsewhere, he only had to come back early from his fishing, enter her room, flop down still reeking of salt and shark's blood, wake her up and she'd be moaning in his arms. How often must that have happened in the past, when he'd imagined her suffering in his absence, the nights dragging in painful conversation with her husband, she resisting his sexual advances tactfully but firmly. How often must she have gone straight from his body to David's.

He leaned against the wall, his legs unsteady. It had all come to an absurd, shameful end: he'd caught her swooning in her husband's arms and tomorrow they'd both be arrested on charges of adultery. What a miserable finale! His mission was a senseless, humiliating failure! Who would listen to the story of what had really happened? Who would believe him? Who would hear him and not die of laughter? He suddenly longed to flee, to go back to

359

his house alone, down to the beach to swim in the dark, swim to cleanse himself of all that filth and deceit. He started to retrace his steps, when he heard her cry distinctly, the voice that had been his ruination, that had made him mistake flesh for feeling, desire for passion: 'Yes, yes, come!'

It was too much for him. Jealousy is irrational: it feeds on its own suffering, as if it were only satiated and quiescent when the worst imaginings became real, patent and visible. The more blatant the evidence, the more genuine was the reality of betrayal, the happier the spirit of jealousy, consummated at last and almost worthy of respect. That was why he moved quickly towards the French windows in order to see through the curtains into the bedroom. He stealthily approached his nemesis.

Ann was on her back in bed, naked, her dishevelled hair spread over the pillow, her face slightly flushed, her eyes shut, her bosom firm and her nipples erect. Her legs were splayed, one hanging over the edge of the bed. She moaned gently as her body moved to the rhythm of the man penetrating her. He sat on top, his legs tucked under hers, his torso straight, his back glistening with sweat, thrusting furiously. But his back wasn't white and his hair wasn't fair. The man making love to Ann never came from Scotland and was never her husband. He was a black labourer from Angola, went by the name of Gabriel, and Luís Bernardo and David had rescued him from certain death on the Island of Príncipe.

Luís Bernardo moved more swiftly than his mind could cope with. He jumped off the veranda to the tree but missed his footing and fell from the top branch to the one underneath, breaking his fall before he abruptly hit the ground, twisting his ankle. Even so he ran limping to the entrance, opened the door and only breathed when he'd made it to the outside. He bent over to catch his breath, and tottered painfully along to where he recalled tethering his horse. He hoisted himself into the saddle, turned his horse to face him homewards, and then let the reins go, let his steed lead him through the fog into which he'd sunk.

All of a sudden he heard a noise to his left, and a black shape emerged from the darkness. A hold-up, he thought, and felt so indifferent to the prospect of being assaulted he didn't even look at the shape. But the latter approached him and gathered the loose reins. He turned round and even in the darkness distinguished Sebastião's face.

'What are you doing here, Sebastião?' His own voice seemed distant, so distant it was as if someone else asked the question.

'I've been following you, Boss. From the moment you left home this afternoon after the Public Prosecutor's visit. I followed you to the beach, back home and then here.'

'Why did you bother, Sebastião?'

'Forgive me, Boss. But something really evil is about. I smell something rotten in the air.'

'Sebastião. I'm Doctor, not Boss.'

'Yes, Doctor.'

'Nothing in the way of evil, Sebastião. I just had a few doubts. Doubts that are now a thing of the past. It all died a death in that house.'

'That woman, the Englishwoman, will make you unhappy, Boss. I've always felt that.'

Luís Bernardo turned round, intrigued.

'Why do you say that? Why do you say you always felt that?'

'From the first time I saw her enter the house. I'd never ever seen such a beautiful woman.'

'So what?'

'A beautiful woman always heralds sadness on earth.'

'What's that – some sort of proverb?'

'A lesson I have learned from life, Boss.'

They continued in silence. He was like a dead weight on his horse's back; Sebastião walked at his side, holding the reins.

When home came into view, Luís Bernardo broke the silence.

'No need to worry any more about this business, Sebastião. Whatever evil the woman could cause, the deed is done.'

'And does Boss feel any better?'

'Do I feel better? Yes, I swear I feel much better. I feel at peace. Don't worry. I want you to go to bed now, do you hear? I have to write some letters I want to send on the steamer tomorrow, but you must get some sleep because it will be all very intense tomorrow, do you hear me?'

'Yes, Boss.'

'Say: I promise, Doctor.'

'I promise.'

Luís Bernardo ran upstairs to his bedroom. There was one lighted candle on the chest of drawers in the passage and another unlit on his bedside table. He pulled off his ripped, dirty shirt and slipped on a white linen shirt he took from a drawer. He lit the candle and went to the bathroom, where he washed his face, injury and hands. He wiped his wound with a cotton cloth, washed his hands again, then left, blowing out the candle.

The lighted candle was no longer on the drawers in the passage: it was in the hands of Doroteia, who was leaning against the wall. Her white cotton dress was almost entirely open revealing her small, firm adolescent breasts and taut nipples. Her perfect face and prominent cheeks shone smooth as satin in the dark, her full mouth half open, the white of her teeth and eyes gleaming in the flickering candlelight. She halted in the middle of the passage like a vestal virgin illuminating the path of her master. Luís Bernardo paused opposite her and gazed at her. He said nothing and didn't look away: stared into her eyes, as if he wanted to draw them into his own. Luís Bernardo felt an infinite tenderness, a tenderness turned desire to meet what was emanating from her. He drew closer and cupped her face in his large hands. He passed a finger along her parted lips, slipped his hands down her long neck and gently over her shoulders and bosom that he felt heave and tense. She didn't move, didn't say anything. A drop of wax dripped from the candlestick in her trembling hand and burnt Luís Bernardo's wrist.

He bent over and kissed her lightly on her mouth. Then straightened.

'Oh Doroteia, you're too young to understand how the fate of some men is never to love those they ought to love!'

He took the candlestick from her hands and walked down the passage to the receptions rooms and shut himself in his study once again. Sebastião or Doroteia had closed the window after he'd left to keep out the mosquitoes. He flung the window open and stood looking out to the sea.

He sat behind his desk, picked up a sheet of the Governor of São Tomé and Príncipe's headed notepaper, checked the point of his pen and blue ink and wrote. He knew what he wanted to say and the text flowed with no need to draft or scratch out.

To His Majesty King Dom Carlos

From the Governor of São Tomé and Príncipe and São João Baptista de Ajudá

Your Majesty,

It is with the sorrow of someone who knows he is not bringing you good news that I write you this my first and last letter.

I arrived here in March 1906, appointed Governor of these Islands by Your Majesty (if I correctly understood and recall what you explained in Vila Viçosa) to show the world that the shame of slave labour doesn't exist here or in other Portuguese colonies.

As you know, I didn't seek, desire or feel any great satisfaction at accepting this responsibility; but I did so in order to serve my King and Country. I believed that you and your government would appreciate from afar the difficulty of a mission that depended on persuading local growers, entrenched in their ways, that other forms of production, that weren't slave labour, ought to be put in place, so that Britain and the Consul she appointed might be left in no doubt of the improved labour practices on the plantations. During the almost two years of my tour of duty, I strove to impress this view on the growers, while striving equally to make the British Consul believe that things were changing, slowly but surely, towards achieving our goal. Whether here, in Lisbon or in London, we always knew the final test would come now, when – in the terms of Your Majesty's January 1903 decree – five-year contracts with the labourers on the plantations terminated and those who so wished would be free to demand their repatriation to their own lands.

I ordered this repatriation to start in the course of this month and the results received to date and future projections confirm that nothing essential has changed in the organisation of production on the plantations of São Tomé and Príncipe. Similarly, the arguments deployed by the landowners from the islands in the meeting held in Lisbon last November with the representatives of the most important British companies importing cocoa from São Tomé eloquently demonstrate that there exists no serious wish on the landowners' part to change anything whatsoever. They merely repeat ancient legal rhetoric, which now convinces nobody. It is the same will, or lack of will, that I have always found in my contact with Your Majesty's government, which considers its priority to be the continuing commercial prosperity of São Tomé but without an end to the abuses that exist. Their political blindness was such they refused to see that their prosperity depended on the British import market and that they could only continue trading with São Tomé if the abuses stopped.

In other words, I failed the mission with which Your Majesty charged me: whether in relation to the British Consul, whom I didn't convince of the seriousness of our intention to change the status quo, or in relation to the growers, whom I was never able to convince of the need to make those changes.

This and this alone is the reason now leading me to write to you, and present my resignation from this post with immediate effect. I know other voices will reach Your Majesty and suggest there are other reasons for my resignation and my mission's failure. To such an end, they will not hesitate to slander my name and the names of others, recounting insults and lies, adding things that never influenced me or the decisions that I took.

Nevertheless, Your Majesty will receive other news about me, even before this letter reaches your hands. However, at this point in time you will understand it is quite illegitimate for any man to doubt the truth of what I say here to you, at the precise moment when I write this letter.

I am resigning because I failed in my mission to end slave labour on São Tomé and Príncipe – a regime I had always spoken against publicly, and consequently I deserved the honour of being appointed by Your Majesty to assume the mission of ending such a vile practice.

My Dear Dom Carlos, The conditions in which the Angolan labourers, transported to São Tomé and Príncipe against their will, and who we describe as Portuguese citizens for our own diplomatic ends, live and work are unworthy of a civilised nation, unworthy of the name of Portugal and unworthy of the state that you represent. No pseudo-legal arguments can disguise the evidence of the harsh truth I saw with my own eyes and that my conscience dictates I should communicate to you.

I implore Providence that my resignation and attendant circumstances serve to make the nation and particularly its king reflect profoundly. There is much more at stake than the prosperity of a few individuals. What is at stake is a shameful stain besmirching the very name of Portugal that needs to be erased.

By saying this to you thus, I believe I have at least complied with my conscience, if not with the mission Your Majesty entrusted to me.

May God Protect Your Majesty,

Luís Bernardo Valença, Governor

Contrary to the orders he had received from Luís Bernardo, Sebastião did not go to bed. He stayed in the garden sitting next to a tree and watching the lighted candle burn on Luís Bernardo's desk. He wouldn't go to sleep until that light was extinguished. Doroteia also waited sitting on a chair in the passage on the top floor, holding another extinguished candle, but with a box of matches at the ready to light up as soon as she heard Luís Bernardo's footsteps in the passage on his way to bed.

The shot woke up both dozing figures with a start. However, Sebastião was more surprised by the sound of the shot than what the shot implied. He stood up and looked through the study window, where the light was still flickering. Crossed himself, looked at the starless sky and muttered, 'May thy will be done!' Only then did he lumber slowly into the house and head for the study, where Doroteia was already sobbing and embracing Luís Bernardo's inert body. He had shot himself point blank in the heart, while seated on the sofa, and a huge red bloodstain was now spreading across his white shirt. His right hand, which had pulled the trigger, hung down over his legs, the revolver dangling from a single finger. His eyes were still open and staring out of the window.

Sebastião bent over and closed his eyes. He noticed there was a sheet of paper on the ground, where enormous letters exclaimed 'Sebastião. Read this before you do anything else!' He read: there were two letters on the bureau: one was addressed to the Count of Arnoso, Private Secretary to His Majesty the King, and bore the address of the Palace of Necessities: the other was addressed to João in Lisbon, and contained his will, which he took note of immediately. He left João all his furniture and private possessions, left a legacy in favour of Mamoun, Sinhá, Vicente and Tobias and bequeathed the rest of his fortune, in equal parts, to Sebastião and Doroteia, while he nominated João as his executor. Sebastião should take both letters without fail, before any dignitary arrived, and send them to Lisbon on the morning steamer. If anyone asked, he should reply that the Governor had left no letters, no note to explain his lunatic gesture.

Sebastião put the two letters and the sheet of paper in his coat pocket and ordered Doroteia and the other servants who had rushed there to leave well alone. He told Vicente to go to the Public Prosecutor's house and wake him up, and then proclaimed loudly, as if talking to himself, 'So, the vampire has returned to this house!' Then he looked at the clock on the wall: it was 3.25 a.m., 29 January 1908. And added, 'It is their time of day.'

EPILOGUE

O N 1 FEBRUARY 1908, King Dom Carlos and the Royal Prince Dom Luís Filipe had just returned from Vila Viçosa and were riding round the Terreiro do Paço in an open landau when they were ambushed and shot dead by two murderers who were identified as part of a much vaster conspiracy, which for reasons of political convenience was never brought to light. Dom Luís Filipe shot dead Alfredo Costa, his father's murderer, with the revolver he was carrying before he himself was mortally wounded by two bullets from Manuel Buiça, the other gunman. If the royal funerals were impressive, those of the two murderers weren't far behind, a true reflection of the political atmosphere in Portugal at the time. The young surviving Prince, Dom Manuel, slightly wounded in the shoulder during the attack, became King Dom Manuel II that same day and governed for just thirty-two months until the Republic was established.

At the request of the King's widow, Dom Carlos's Private Secretary Bernardo de Pindela, the Count of Arnoso, was kept in post for a few months to put some order into the murdered monarch's papers and correspondence. On one of these mornings, when seated at his office desk in the Palace of Necessities, his secretary, José da Matta, handed him a letter addressed to him, and commented, 'A letter for you from the Governor of São Tomé. He was the one who killed himself, wasn't he?'

'Yes, he killed himself three days before the King and Prince died: it seems he had an inkling . . .'

'But they say he killed himself because of an Englishwoman whose lover he was, the wife of the British Consul . . .'

'Well, lots of things are said about the dead, who are no longer here to defend themselves . . .' Bernardo de Pindela sighed and opened the envelope with a small silver paperknife. There was another sealed envelope inside addressed to 'His Majesty King Dom Carlos', and a short note to himself.

Dear Friend Bernardo de Pindela,

Please don't refuse my request, made posthumously, to deliver this letter directly into the hands of His Majesty, without attempting any mediation.

I would like you to know that often, in the course of these two long-suffering years spent on São Tomé and Príncipe, I have recalled what you said to me in Vila Viçosa, when you saw fit to reinforce the King's request that I should accept the mission he charged me with: 'What greater thing could you take from this life?' The answer is this: I left my life here; what greater thing could I give my King?

It is the truth.

My respects and in friendship as ever,

Luís Bernardo Valença

The Count of Arnoso sighed and opened the letter addressed to Dom Carlos. Began reading, while he walked around the room. When he reached the end, he stopped in front of the window, from where he could see the Tagus and a British frigate moving away beyond the sand bar – it was in fact one of the two vessels belonging to His Majesty the King of Great Britain that had come for the royal funerals. He stood there for a few moments holding the open letter, engrossed in thought.

'So, what does he have to say?' José da Matta was curious. 'Anything that might still be of interest?'

'What can be still of interest now? Everything is over or soon will be. It is the end of an era. What I find upsetting is the thought that I was the person to suggest this man's name to the King. I persuaded him to come to Vila Viçosa and speak to the King. I was the one who insisted he take on the mission to São Tomé. If I hadn't done so, he would still be alive.'

Bernardo de Pindela had seemed even more despondent than ever over the last few days.

'Come now, Count, his mission didn't kill him, love did. And he had sole responsibility for that . . .'

Bernardo de Pindela dismissed him almost contemptuously.

'What do you know, José da Matta? Did you read the letter before me?'

'No.'

'Then, respect the reasons of a man who was led to adopt such a tragic attitude that he ended his own life. Only he and God know the real reasons. The other man who might know part of the truth is dead, and the other, namely myself, who has just heard the truth, will keep the secret to himself.'

He walked over to the open fire and, with a gesture of resignation, threw Luís Bernardo's letter to the King into the flames and watched it burn slowly. And while it burned, he reflected philosophically: All in all, a letter from a man who died after he had written it to someone else who died before he could read it. Considering they died so close together in time, who knows, perhaps they have met on high and are explaining things to each other!

On 22 May 1908, *O Século*, in its section of news from the Colonies, related that David Jameson, the British Consul to São Tomé and Príncipe, had finished his tour of duty and had been posted to the leadership of the Provincial Government of Colombo, in Ceylon. He had embarked, accompanied by his wife, on HMS *Sovereign of the Seas*, which took the route round the Cape.

On 14 March 1909, the British companies Cadbury Bros, of Bournville, J.S. Fry & Co of York and Rowntree & Co of Bristol, in the name of all British importers of cocoa, officially announced their boycott of imports from the Portuguese colony of São Tomé and Príncipe.

ACKNOWLEDGEMENTS

I thank Ana Xavier Cifuentes, who accepted so enthusiastically and generously the invitation to help me in the historical research for this book and who worked tirelessly, from Vila Viçosa to São Tomé and Príncipe, and was always meticulous and stimulating in her enquiries. Without her help, all this would have been infinitely more difficult.

I thank my publishers António Lobato Faria and Gonçalo Bulhosa of the Oficina do Livro, who were publishers in the fullest meaning of the word. First, they convinced and encouraged me to write, then never allowed me to give up during the sixteen months of the project, and then submitted the whole novel to a thorough revision, thus facilitating my own revisions.

I thank Francisco Xavier Mantero, whose longstanding passion for São Tomé and Príncipe made me want to get to know the islands and whose offer, some years ago, of a book on São Tomé, inspired the story. It is proof of the saying that you never give a book to a friend in vain.

I thank my wife Cristina, who always held the hand that wrote this novel, even from a long distance.

I thank the organisations who generously collaborated in the labour of research and tracking down of documentation: The Foundation of the House of Braganza, the São Tomé and Príncipe Historical Archives, the Automobile Club of Portugal, CP and EDP.

SOURCES

ALEXANDRE, Valentim, *Os Sentidos do Império – Questão Nacional e Questão Colonial na Crise do Antigo Regime Português*, Edições Afrontamento, Porto, 1983.

BASTO, António Ferreira Pinto, *Viagens por terra com El-Rei D. Carlos*, Chaves Ferreira, Publicações SA, Lisboa, 1997.

BREYNER, Thomaz de Mello, *Memórias*, Vol. I, II e III, Parceria António Mafia Pereira, Lisboa, 1930 e Oficina Gráfica, Lisboa, 1934.

BREYNER, Thomaz de Mello, *Diário de um Monárquico*, Vol. I, II e III, Edição de Gustavo de Mello Breyner Andresen, Porto, 1993–2003.

CAMPOS, Ezequiel, *Melhoramentos Públicos na Ilha de S. Tomé*, Edição C.M.S. Tomé, Lisboa, 1910.

CÉSAR, Amândio, *Presença do Arquipélago de S. Tomé e Príncipe na Moderna Cultura Portuguesa*, Edição C.M.S. Tomé, 1968.

COMISSÃO DO CENTENÁRIO DE MOUZINHO DE ALBUQUERQUE, *Cartas de Mouzinho de Albuquerque ao Conde de Arnoso*, Lisboa, 1957.

CORPECHOT, Lucien, *Souvenirs de la Reine Amélie de Portugal*, Pierre Lafitte Éditeurs, Paris, 1914.

Dicionário de Geographia Universal, Edição dos Correios e Telégraphos, Lisboa, 1978.

ENNES, António, *A Guerra de Africa em 1895* (edição actualizada). Prefácio, Lisboa, 2002.

FERNANDES, Filipe S., *Fortunas & Negócios – Empresários Portugueses do Século XX*, Oficina do Livro, Lisboa, 2003.

GRAMOPHON, *The Centenary Edition, 1897–1997: Hundred Years of Great Music*, Ed. The Gramophon Company, London, 1998.

LA PIERRE, Dominique e COLLINS, Larry, *Cette nuit la liberté*, Éditions Robert Laffont, Paris, 1975.

LAVRADIO, Sexto Marquês de, *Memórias*, Ática Editores, Lisboa, 1947.

LOUREIRO, João, *Postais Antigos de S. Tomé e Príncipe*, Edição de Autor, Lisboa, 1999.

LOUREIRO, João, *Memórias de Luanda*, Edição de Autor, Lisboa. 2002.

MANTERO, Francisco, *Obras Completas – Vol. I: A mão-de-obra em S. Tomé e Príncipe*, Edição Carlos Mantero, Lisboa, 1954.

MARTINEZ, Pedro Soares, *História Diplomática de Portugal*, Verbo, Lisboa, 1985.

MARTINS, Rocha, *D. Carlos – História do seu reinado*, Edição de Autor, Lisboa, 1926.

MÓNICA, Maria Filomena, *A Queda da Monarquia – Portugal na Viragem do Século*, D. Quixote, Lisboa, 1987.

MÓNICA, Maria Filomena, *Eça de Queirós*, Quetzal, Lisboa, 2001.

NOBRE, Eduardo, *Família Real: Álbum de Fotografias*, Quimera, Lisboa, 2002.

ORNELLAS, Ayres d', *Colectânea das suas principais obras militares e coloniais*, Agência-Geral das Colónias, Lisboa, 1936.

ORNELLAS, Ayres d', *Cartas d'África – Viagem do Príncipe Real*. Ed. Agencia-Geral das Colónias, Lisboa, 1928.

SCHWEINITZ JR., Karl de, *The rise & fall of British India – Imperialism as Inequality*, Routledge, London, New York, 1989.

SILVA, Fernando Emygdio da, *O Regime Tributário das Colónias Portuguesas*, Typographia Universal, Lisboa, 1906.

STRACKEY, Sir John, *India and its Administration and Progress*, London, 1911.

VALENTE, Vasco Pulido, *O Poder e o povo – A revolução de 1910*, D. Quixote, Lisboa, 1974.

VICENTE, Ana e VICENTE, António Pedro, *O Príncipe Real Luís Filipe de Bragança*, Edições Inapa, Lisboa, 1998.

Jornais e Revistas (1904–1908)
Boletim Oficial de S. Tomé e Príncipe
Diário de Notícias
Ilustração Portuguesa
Jornal das Colónias
O Século

A NOTE ON THE TYPE

The text of this book is set in Bembo. This type was first used in 1495 by the Venetian printer Aldus Manutius for Cardinal Bembo's *De Aetna*, and was cut for Manutius by Francesco Griffo. It was one of the types used by Claude Garamond (1480–1561) as a model for his Romain de L'Université, and so it was the forerunner of what became standard European type for the following two centuries. Its modern form follows the original types and was designed for Monotype in 1929.